CLUSTER OF LIES

A JOE HIGHEAGLE NOVEL BOOK 2

In this second thriller in the Joe Higheagle Environmental Sleuth Series, mysterious deaths are taking place in the Rocky Mountain region outside Denver, Colorado. Joe Higheagle—a full-blooded Cheyenne geologist who has recently become an overnight celebrity for bringing down a billionaire corporate polluter—is hired to investigate Dakota Ranch, where four boys have recently died from a rare form of brain cancer, and Silverado Knolls, a glitzy soon-to-be-built development. He quickly finds himself entangled in an environmental cancer cluster investigation as well as a murderous conspiracy in which friend and foe are indistinguishable and a series of seemingly impenetrable roadblocks are thrown in his path.

While the police work to uncover if foul play could have led to the suspicious death of a heavy-equipment company owner, the unconventional Higheagle works in parallel to solve the mystery of what is killing the young boys at Dakota Ranch. His goal is to find out who is ultimately responsible for the cancer cluster and bring them to justice. His search leads him to Hayden Prescott—the suave multimillionaire developer of Dakota Ranch and Silverado Knolls as well as a leading Denver citizen.

Will Higheagle and the police discover the truth behind the cancer cluster and the death of the business owner? Is Hayden Prescott to blame, or could it be one of Higheagle's own clients or even a shadowy third party? Most importantly, will justice at Dakota Ranch and Silverado Knolls be served before more death and treachery comes to the Rockies?

PRAISE FOR *CLUSTER OF LIES*

"In his novels *Blind Thrust* and *Cluster of Lies*, Samuel Marquis vividly combines the excitement of the best modern techno-thrillers, an education in geology, and a clarifying reminder that the choices each of us make have a profound impact on our precious planet."
—Ambassador Marc Grossman, Former U.S. Under Secretary of State

"With *Cluster of Lies*, Marquis continues to keep me awake at night. I enjoy how he blends together science and his knack for storytelling to craft an insightful and entertaining tale. He causes me to stop and think, then jump right back into the action."
—Roy R. Romer, 39th Governor of Colorado

"In *Cluster of Lies*, Samuel Marquis touches all the bases. He starts with a murder and the action doesn't let up until the very last page in this compelling environmental thriller that is often uncomfortably realistic."
—Charles Salzberg, Author of *The Henry Swann Detective Series*

"With *Blind Thrust*, *Cluster of Lies*, and his other works, Samuel Marquis has written true breakout novels that compare favorably with—and even exceed—recent thrillers on the *New York Times* Bestseller List. [He is] constantly tightening plot, character, and upping the stakes and tension to make sure that they are genuinely great stories."
—Pat LoBrutto, Former Editor for Stephen King and Eric Van Lustbader (Bourne Series)

"Marquis is a master of dialogue in this thriller with a social conscience. Deftly taking on the mystery of a cancer cluster at the Dakota Ranch outside Denver, *Cluster of Lies* is an action-packed page-turner. And, "warts and all," geologist Joe Higheagle is a new American hero who won't stop until justice is served."
—Kelly Oliver, Author of *The Jessica James Mysteries*, *Wolf* and *Coyote*.

"In today's environmentally challenged world, Joe Higheagle is the man I want in my corner. Well-written, fast paced, Samuel Marquis' *Cluster of Lies* is a must read thriller."
—Debra H. Goldstein, Author of *Should Have Played Poker*

"*Cluster of Lies* takes you into seamy nether regions, where greed and subterfuge prey on good people's ignorance and government inattention. It takes a potent and imperfect hero to save an imperfect world, and Joe Higheagle's on point. Buckle in for an action-packed enviro-thriller filled with fear and loathing."
—Prof. J.R. Welch, Author/Editor of *Dispatches from the Fort Apache Scout: White Mountain and Cibecue Apache History Through 1881*

PRAISE FOR *THE SLUSH PILE BRIGADE*
#1 *DENVER POST* BESTSELLING NOVEL
AWARD-WINNING FINALIST BEVERLY HILLS BOOK AWARDS

"This high-energy, rollicking misadventure will change the way you look at the publishing industry forever. The plot is unpredictable...twists and turns and counterturns abound. So, too, does the humor...The dialogue is superb...Marquis laid the groundwork as a thriller writer with *The Slush Pile Brigade* and hopefully his following novels build up a James Patterson-esque empire."
—Foreword Reviews – Five-Star Review

"There's a lot going on in Marquis' book, as the author smartly builds off a solid premise...A fresh concept and protagonist that breathe life into a conventional but exciting actioner."
—Kirkus Reviews

"*The Slush Pile Brigade*, by Samuel Marquis, is a hilarious and exciting read filled with one crazy turn after another...The author slams on the accelerator early in the story and doesn't let up, forcing the reader to flip the pages frantically. And once it's over, it's still hard to catch one's breath."
—SP Review - 4.5-Star Review

"Twists, turns and double crosses in literary theft quickly expand to threaten the globe in *The Slush Pile Brigade*, a promising debut from an up-and-coming thriller writer."
—IndieReader Book Review - 4.5-Star Review

"Marquis makes the whole bewildering journey entertaining with his quirky friends who accompany Nick on his mission. The fact that Marquis himself wrote a novel called *Blind Thrust*, bring out the book-within-a-book theme, and the New York City scenes and dialogue feel authentic throughout. Read *The Slush Pile Brigade*...for the enjoyable romp that it is."
—BlueInk Book Review

PRAISE FOR *BLIND THRUST*
#1 *DENVER POST* BESTSELLING NOVEL
WINNER FOREWORD REVIEWS' BOOK OF THE YEAR (HM)
WINNER NEXT GENERATION INDIE BOOK AWARDS
AWARD-WINNING FINALIST USA BEST BOOK AWARDS
AWARD-WINNING FINALIST BEVERLY HILLS BOOK AWARDS

"*Blind Thrust* kept me up until 1 a.m. two nights in a row. I could not put it down. An intriguing mystery that intertwined geology, fracking, and places in Colorado that I know well. Great fun."
—Roy R. Romer, 39th Governor of Colorado

"Mr. Marquis infuses passion and authenticity into every page of the novel, as he is a practicing geologist and paleontology/Western history buff who is an expert on what he writes."
—Pat LoBrutto, Former Editor for Stephen King and Eric Van Lustbader (Bourne Series)

"With believable, intelligent characters, there is a fine thriller on these pages that could shake things up."
—Foreword Reviews – Four-Star Review

"The science of earthquakes is truly fascinating, and Marquis has captured this science and packaged it into a really fine thriller 'against the clock' style for almost anyone to pick up and enjoy, and readers will no doubt want more from Higheagle and his intrepid grandfather once they have devoured this installment."
—SP Review – Four-Star Review

"*Blind Thrust* makes good use of Marquis' background as a professional geologist. It is the novel's characters, however, that really stand out. For suspense fans who enjoy science mixed with their thrills, the novel offers page-turning pleasures."
—BlueInk Review

"A mostly engaging novel by an experienced hydrogeologist who brings a lot of verisimilitude to his tale of earthquake devastation."—Kirkus Reviews

"*Blind Thrust* spins a thrilling tale of what can happen when humans mess with Mother Nature...For those interested in earthquakes or environmental issues, Marquis has created an action-packed novel filled with danger and conflict."
—IndieReader Book Review

PRAISE FOR *BODYGUARD OF DECEPTION* VOLUME 1 OF THE WORLD WAR TWO TRILOGY

"*Bodyguard of Deception* grabbed my attention right from the beginning and never let go. The character development is excellent. Samuel Marquis has a knack for using historic details and events to create captivating and fun to read tales."
—Roy R. Romer, 39th Governor of Colorado

"Readers looking for an unapologetic historical action book should tear through this volume."
—Kirkus Reviews

"A fast-paced, riveting WWII espionage thriller. *Bodyguard of Deception* is as good as the best of Daniel Silva, Ken Follett, Alan Furst, and David Baldacci and brings back fond memories of the classic movie *The Great Escape* and Silva's finest novel, *The Unlikely Spy.*"
—Fred Taylor, President/Co-Founder Northstar Investment Advisors and Espionage Novel Aficionado

"As usual, Marquis's descriptions are vivid, believable, and true to the time period...*Bodyguard of Deception* is an intriguing launch to his new trilogy. Warmly recommended."
—Dr. Wesley Britton, Bookpleasures.com (Crime & Mystery)

"Old-time spy buffs will appreciate the tradecraft and attention to detail, while adventure enthusiasts will enjoy the unique perspective and setting for a WWII story. As Marquis throws in everything but the kitchen sink, he turns this well-told, if byzantine adventure novel into a combination of *The Great Escape*, *Public Enemies*, a genuine old-time Western, and a John Le Carré novel."
—BlueInk Review

"The world hangs in a delicate balance in the heart-pounding World War Two Trilogy opener, *Bodyguard of Deception* by Samuel Marquis. Put together with an intricate plot to follow and a commitment to realistic detail, there's a lot going for the read...a wonderfully nail-biting experience with good characters and solid intrigue."
—SP Review – Four-Star Review

"*Bodyguard of Deception* is a unique and ambitious spy thriller complete with historical figures, exciting action, and a dastardly villain. Fans of prison-break plots will enjoy this story of a loyal German struggling to save his homeland."
—Foreword Reviews

By Samuel Marquis

CLUSTER OF LIES

A JOE HIGHEAGLE NOVEL BOOK 2

SAMUEL MARQUIS

MOUNT SOPRIS PUBLISHING

CLUSTER OF LIES

MOUNT SOPRIS PUBLISHING
Trade paper: ISBN 978-1-943593-16-3
Kindle: ISBN 978-1-943593-17-0
ePub: ISBN 978-1-943593-18-7

First Mount Sopris Publishing premium printing: September 2016
Cover Design: George Foster (www.fostercovers.com)
Formatting: Rik Hall (www.WildSeasFormatting.com)
Printed in the United States of America

To Order Samuel Marquis Books and Contact Samuel:
Visit Samuel Marquis's website, join his mailing list, learn about forthcoming novels and book events, and order his books at www.samuelmarquisbooks.com. Please send all fan mail (including criticism) to samuelmarquisbooks@gmail.com. Thank you for your support!

ATTENTION: ORGANIZATIONS AND CORPORATIONS
Mount Sopris Publishing books may be purchased for educational, business, or sales promotional use. For information, please email the Special Markets Department at samuelmarquisbooks@gmail.com.

Dedication

For the real-world children and families impacted by environmental cancer clusters.

CLUSTER OF LIES
A Joe Higheagle Novel Book 2

It is fair to state that extensive efforts to find causes of community cancer clusters have not been successful. We recommend a multidisciplinary national dialogue on creative, innovative approaches to understanding when and why cancer and other chronic diseases cluster in space and time.

> —Michael Goodman, Joshua S. Naiman, Dina Goodman, and Judy S. LaKind (2012) in *Cancer Clusters in the USA: What do the last twenty years of state and federal investigations tell us?*

I just want the truth. I don't care how long it takes, as long as it's the truth.

> —Lee Brooks (Wilmington, MA, community cancer cluster), whose son Paul died of leukemia at age 23

CHAPTER 1

"GLAD YOU COULD MAKE IT, GUS."

With an ingratiating smile, Hayden Winthrop Prescott III rose from his chair and held out his hand as his guest was ushered into the private corporate luxury box. The smile was a front. In reality, his nerves were tied in knots and he loathed Gus McTavish. Taking an invisible breath, he reminded himself that this evening's dangerous enterprise would go off without a hitch if he maintained his composure and meticulously followed the script. The smile broadened, the two men shook hands, and Prescott motioned Gus to the seat next to him at the back of the suite.

Below on the ice, the first game of the semi-final Stanley Cup series between the Colorado Avalanche and hated Detroit Red Wings was in full swing. The crowd was loud tonight, a good sign, for it meant that he and his companion would be beyond earshot of the fans in the adjacent boxes.

"I don't much like ice hockey," sniffed Gus McTavish. "Let's get this over with."

Who the hell doesn't like the NHL playoffs? thought Prescott, looking over his intended victim with a mixture of disbelief and disdain. The truth was the renowned CEO was uncomfortable mingling with even middle-class people, and though Gus was technically a small-business owner, the guy was but a generation removed from white trash. He wore an outdated Fedora, navy blue polyester pants, and a cheap sports windbreaker—an ensemble which Prescott found not just tasteless, but pathetic.

"Easy now, boy-o," Prescott gently chided him. "It's the Stanley Cup playoffs, we've got my luxury box all to ourselves, and I am going to give you what you want—as long as you speak in a quiet voice." He tilted his head discretely to the fans in the adjacent box. "We don't want to let anyone in on our dirty little secrets now, do we Gus?"

He heard a knock at the door and a waiter appeared to take their drink orders. Prescott felt a pang of last-minute doubt. *Should I go through with it? It's not too late to turn back.* He cast a glance at Gus McTavish, taking in the harsh edges of his stubbly face, the ugly scowl and shabby clothes. He told himself that the greedy bastard deserved everything he had coming to him; and yet, he couldn't help but feel a twinge of guilt at what he was about to do.

"What'll you have, Gus?"

"I'll take a beer and a shot of Jack Black. I don't care what kind of brewski. Just make sure it's not one of those low-calorie thingamajiggers."

Prescott smiled inwardly. *Alcohol and heart medication—now there's a lethal mix.* "And I'll have a Tom Collins," he said to the waiter, who wrote down the orders and headed out the door.

Prescott brushed a virtually invisible fleck of dust from his crisp blue blazer. "How's that pretty niece of yours doing?"

His guest's eyes narrowed. "You stay away from Sally. She doesn't need you messing up her life again."

"Easy, boy-o. I was just asking how she's doing."

"I know what you're up to. The last thing she needs is a gigolo type like you."

"What, I'm no longer good enough for your niece?"

"You just stay away—"

His words were drowned out as the Avalanche scored the game's first goal. The crowd leapt to its feet and roared loud enough to heave the building off its footings.

Prescott thought of Sally.

He had met her two years ago at a Christmas party given by a local law firm. Though the relationship hadn't lasted long—three or four months perhaps—it was serious. The truth was he came to care deeply about her, and that had filled him with panic. He had never fallen for anyone before—especially not a divorced woman saddled with a young boy—and wasn't sure how to deal with his unexpected emotions. Despite his strong feelings for her, he knew he would never be able to offer her any real long-term commitment, so he had, as gracefully as possible, put an end to the romance. He didn't want to hurt her or her son Tommy, who was obviously desperate to have a father figure in his life.

The arena turned quiet again as the teams lined up for the faceoff. There was no way he would ever hurt Sally or Tommy. But he had far different plans for despicable Uncle Gus.

As if on cue, his impending victim flashed an impatient look and snorted, "I'm going to need more than what we talked about."

"Is that so? I hear you've been a naughty boy, Gus, up to your old tricks."

"What the hell are you talking about?"

"You've taken to gambling again and you've been losing big."

"Goddamnit, who told you that?"

"Oh, a little birdie. I told you the last time we went through this to stay away from Central City and Blackhawk. I've already made quite an investment for your silence. And the way I see it, I haven't gotten much in return—except, apparently, another bill to pay."

"This is the last time, I promise. I just need to...to settle things."

"You need more than that. I hear your wife moved out and you have a mountain of debt."

"You bastard. You have people following me?"

"Don't worry. I'm going to give you your money. I've got a good-faith down payment right here." He withdrew a manila envelope from the inside pocket of his jacket and held it out for his victim to see. "But before I give it to you, I want your word that this is the last time."

Gus McTavish's eyes flickered with avarice at the sight of the envelope, his bony fingers creeping across the table like a tarantula.

Prescott quickly stuffed the envelope back in his pocket. "Not so fast, boy-o.

You have to promise me you'll manage your personal finances better. I've already paid you two separate installments above and beyond your normal compensation, and you've squandered them. The key for any blackmailer is to properly manage the money he extorts. Apparently, you haven't learned this most fundamental axiom. Now, I need you to promise me that this is the last time, because there won't be another."

"All right, I promise. Just give it to me, goddamnit."

There was an addict's desperation in his eyes that made Prescott feel pity for the man. *By God, by killing him I'll be doing the poor old sod a favor.* At that moment, the waiter stepped into the box carrying a tray with their drinks, halting the conversation. Suddenly, a hundred different worries stampeded through Prescott's mind as he realized the grave risk he was about to take.

Should I go through with it? What if it doesn't work? What if I get caught? Is Paine in position? Will he come through as planned? Will I really be doing Gus a favor? Am I going to go to hell? What would Father think?

His mouth felt as dry as a cement kiln. Taking a deep breath, he steeled himself as the waiter set the drinks on the table. He withdrew his wallet and paid the young man, giving him a generous tip. The waiter thanked him and stepped out the door.

Gus McTavish tossed back his shot of Jack Daniels and followed with a long pull from his beer, dribbling some down his chin. Prescott glanced to his left and right. To his relief, the fans in the adjacent boxes were not sitting at the tables towards the rear of the suite. Instead, they were seated in the rows up front, which meant that they were unlikely to witness what was about to transpire. He had planned to make his move when Gus went to the restroom to relieve himself, but was gripped with an overwhelming urge to act now. Of course, he didn't want to be too rash and blow the whole thing, but the tug he felt inside was almost unbearable.

And then, he met with a stroke of luck.

An Avalanche player was driven hard into the boards and a brawl ensued in the corner of the Avs zone. Setting down his beer, Gus stepped forward to get a closer look as the crowd roared like a Roman mob at a gladiatorial contest.

This is your chance! You've got to do it now!

Prescott quickly made sure the coast was clear. Then he withdrew a small vial from his pocket, twisted off the cap, and reached for Gus's beer with his right hand, keeping the vial upright and concealed in the palm of his other hand. As he had hoped, his intended victim was still preoccupied with the fight, his fists clenching and face grimacing violently in rhythm with the punches down on the ice. In a fluid motion, Prescott poured the contents of the vial into the beer cup, swished it around, and put the cup back on the table. Then he capped the vial, slipped it back into his pocket, and checked again to see if anyone was watching, breathing a sigh of relief when he saw no one was.

Whew, I've done it. But is it going to work?

He reached for his Tom Collins and tossed back half the cocktail, knowing he would need even steadier nerves for the tricky second phase yet to come. Down on the ice, the referees broke up the melee, assessing a double minor to the Red Wings for boarding and slashing and three matching majors to each team for fighting.

When Gus sat back down, Prescott said innocently, "Boys will be boys."

His victim gave a piglike grunt, picked up the poisoned beer, and took a hefty gulp.

Prescott felt a little knot of guilt, but it was too late to turn back now. He returned his attention to the game. The puck was dropped and the home team, now on the power play, quickly controlled the faceoff, carried the puck into the Red Wings' zone, and passed it around the perimeter. An Avalanche defenseman unleashed a blinding slapshot from the point, and the puck was deflected wide by the masked goaltender.

Four minutes later, nine and a half minutes into the first period, Gus McTavish had finished most of his beer and Prescott saw the expected change. He glanced anxiously to his left and right into the adjacent boxes as he had before. To his relief, everyone was engrossed in the game.

"You don't look so good, Gus. Are you all right?"

"I can't...can't seem to breathe." He tried to open his windbreaker, fumbling with the zipper. "Jesus, some...something's wrong." Already, his face carried a deathly gray pallor.

"What is it?"

"My...my heart." The older man's words came out in a ragged gasp and he clutched his chest. "My God...feels like...being crushed."

"Jesus, what can I do?"

"Pills...need...pills!"

He pulled out a plastic vial and, with shaking fingers, struggled to pull off the cap. An Avs player ripped a blazing snapshot on net. The goaltender threw up his blocker, deflected the puck to the corner, and players from both sides scrambled desperately for possession.

"What can I do, Gus? Talk to me."

"Pill...pill..." His fingers quivered as he grappled to unscrew the cap. "Never...felt...before."

As Prescott reached out to him, the man's eyes rolled back in his head and he collapsed to the floor, spilling the vial of little green capsules. Seeing Gus withering before his very eyes, Prescott felt a frantic rush, as if he had just snorted a massive line of cocaine. He thought of Mumsie, and knew this was the kind of wild, reckless sensation she had thrived on. He looked left and right to see if anyone was watching, but the fans were focused intently on the flurry around the Red Wings net. With bodies flying all over the ice, an Avs player managed to pick up the loose puck and flip it towards the upper right-hand corner, glove side. There was a flicker of movement in the white mesh, the green light flashed, and the crowd jumped to its feet and cheered.

With the whole arena going wild, Prescott quickly stuffed a heart pill into Gus's mouth, grabbed the beer he had been drinking, and poured some of the poisoned fluid down his throat.

There, that ought to do it. Please just die, Gus. Please!

His victim just stared dazedly up at the ceiling, as if in a trance.

Come on! Die goddamnit!

At this massive dosage, Prescott knew that his victim couldn't possibly last more than a minute or two longer, but it was still excruciating to have to wait like this. He had better sound the alarm. He reached into his pocket, grabbed his scrambled untraceable mobile, and called Paine. Then he jumped to his feet and called out to the group of people in the adjacent luxury box.

"My God, I think he's having a heart attack!"

A man and a woman broke from the group and stepped quickly to the partition separating the two luxury boxes.

"A heart attack? Good heavens!" gasped the woman.

"He was trying to get his pills!" He pointed to the little green capsules scattered about the floor. "Please get help! Hurry!"

"We're on it!" the man cried. "Come on, Candice!"

"I'll look after him. Please hurry!"

The man and woman dashed off. Prescott returned his attention to Gus, sprawled on the floor. He had anticipated that there would be bystanders—in fact, he had been counting on there being ample witnesses to vouch for his heroic attempts to save Gus—but he wasn't sure what the response time would be, or who would come to the rescue. Would a medic or doctor be able to tell that Gus had been poisoned based on a cursory examination? He doubted it, but still the thought paralyzed him with fear. And where the hell was Paine?

Now other people from the adjacent luxury boxes were gawking over the partition. Prescott took off his blazer and placed it gently beneath Gus's head, then spoke in a soothing clinical voice for their benefit: "Hang in there, Gus. You're going to be okay. Help is on the way."

Suddenly, a man in a black vest and bow tie materialized in the box. It was Paine.

Finally, you bastard!

"What's the trouble, sir?" he asked in a Texas twang.

"I think he's had a heart attack."

When Paine leaned down next to him, Prescott discretely handed him the plastic beer cup and small vial that had held the poison.

"Don't you die on me, Gus!" he cried, convincingly he hoped. "Hang in there!" Then to Paine. "I'm afraid we're going to lose him! Quick, fetch a doctor!"

"Yes, sir! Right away!" Paine dashed off, cup in hand and vial in his pocket.

Prescott blew out a small sigh of relief as a pair of men climbed over the partition to help him.

And then, he noticed Gus was staring up at him.

There was an accusing look in his eyes, as if he knew the heart attack was no accident. The breath caught in Prescott's throat as he saw the betrayed expression; he knew he had to act fast.

"I've got to try and save him! I'm going to give him CPR!"

For all he knew, one or both of the new Good Samaritans could be a doctor, so before they could intervene, he climbed on top of Gus and pinned him down with the full weight of his body. Then he pinched off his nose, pressed his lips against his mouth, and pretended to blow air in repeated bursts, as if he was giving him mouth-to-mouth resuscitation. He could feel Gus struggling beneath him, grappling to wriggle free, and he could see his eyes, an inch away, bulging with panic.

Don't be a spoiled sport, Gus. Just die, goddamnit. Your life's a mess. All I'm doing is liberating you!

The body quivered beneath him like a mass of jelly and the eyes grew so big Prescott thought they would explode. But the drunken old sod was too weak to offer much resistance and, after a tense moment that seemed an eternity, Prescott felt Gus go slack beneath him. When it was clear that it was over, he faked a sob and shook his head in feigned disbelief.

"Oh my God, look at his face!" one of the men next to him gasped.

Looking down at his victim, Prescott shuddered with horror. Gus McTavish's face had a sickly yellowish-green hue and was twisted into an indelible expression of betrayal—the eyes filled with torment and accusation. With a mixture of horror, revulsion, and fear, Prescott leaned down and closed the eyelids with a brush of his hand.

He felt an overwhelming wave of guilt. *My God, what have I done?*

But at least now it was over. Taking a deep breath to steady his nerves, the sense of triumph returned to him like a hammer blow.

I've done it! I'm going to get away with it! Mumsie would be so proud!

A pair of medics charged into the box, accompanied by three uniformed cops and the man and woman that had scrambled to get help. The medics worked mightily to resuscitate Gus, but their efforts were in vain.

Meanwhile, Zachary Paine was already outside the arena, firing up his Camaro, the plastic cup and empty vial concealed in his pocket.

As Gus McTavish was loaded onto a stretcher, there was one last thing for Hayden Winthrop Prescott III to do. With tears in his eyes and just the right amount of bereavement in his voice, he turned solemnly to the cop standing next to him and declared, "He was my friend—and I couldn't even save him."

CHAPTER 2

"COME ON, GRANDFATHER, you don't have cancer," said Joe Higheagle as he punched the gas pedal of the War Wagon—his rusty, four-wheel drive Ford pickup with the Dead sticker—and headed down Quincy towards Dwight D. Eisenhower Memorial Hospital in Littleton, Colorado.

"How do you know I don't have cancer? I haven't even had the tests done yet. We're on our way to the hospital now."

"I'm just saying we don't know anything yet. Doctor Ekstrom said to—"

"Are you trying to fucking scare me?"

"No, of course not."

"Well, you are. You have that panicky tone in your voice."

"I'm just trying to help, Grandfather, that's all."

The old Cheyenne grinned obstinately. "If the Great Mystery decides my time has come, there isn't a damned thing Dr. Ekstrom or anybody else can do about it."

Is he actually afraid of dying? "Well, you can at least stop eating so much fry bread."

"And if I ate only boiled buffalo, prairie turnips, and gooseberries like our ancestors, I would probably live to be a hundred. But I don't want to live that fucking long."

"Why not? You're as fit as most men half your age. You don't drink and you don't smoke. Well, maybe a little hemp now and again in our sweat lodge, but that shouldn't count."

"I am seventy-five years old. My body is breaking down."

So he is afraid of dying. But who wouldn't be? "You're not falling apart, Grandfather. It's all in your head. The tumor's going to be benign—I just know it."

"No, I'm not talking about that."

"Then what are you talking about?"

"The fact that I can't get a boner anymore. At least not…naturally."

Higheagle burst out in laughter. "You're joking, right?"

"No, I'm dead serious. As painful as it is to admit, I'm a Viagra man. I thought I'd never live to see the horrible day."

"At your age are you even supposed to…you know?"

The old man raised a combative brow. "Is there some law against older people having sex? I'll have you know I got laid twice last week."

"With…with a woman?"

"No, a horse! Who the hell do you think I had sex with? Of course it was a goddamn woman. A very bright, attractive French woman, in fact. She just moved here from Paris."

"A French woman? When were you planning on telling me?"

"I was going to tell you, but with this whole tumor thing I just didn't get around to it."

"So that's where you were the other night. You didn't actually stay over at Cousin Charlie's like you said. You were with this French woman."

The old chief gave a guilty grin. "I didn't want you worrying about me or nosing into my business, not until I knew for sure I could still perform. But now that the cat is out of the bag, I'm telling you the Frenchies sure know how to do it right."

"My God, I can't believe I'm hearing this. You don't sound like my own grandfather—you sound like a teenager sneaking a quickie before his parents come home." Higheagle steered the War Wagon past a sleek Lexus, the steel-belted radial tires letting loose with a squeal. "Okay, how old is she?"

The old man smiled craftily, as if he had just won a poker hand with a royal flush. "Fifty-seven."

"A real whippersnapper."

"It's all a matter of perspective. Let's not forget I am seventy-five."

"Okay, this is getting weird."

"I'll bet you wouldn't be saying that if I was fifty and she was thirty-two. You would be high-fiving me and calling me a regular Casanova."

Would I? Yeah, he's probably right.

"What is it about old people having sex that bothers young people so much?"

"I don't know, Grandfather. Maybe we don't like the idea that you old timers get to have all the fun when right now—in the Year of Our Lord 2009—our generation is saddled with endless debt and the constant threat of new and deadly viruses, and not all of them sexually transmitted."

"You're not miserable. I'm the one who's dying of cancer."

"You're not going to die."

"How do you know? You're not a fucking doctor."

"No, but we come from a long line of medicine men. That makes us experts in shaking rattles, administering useless potions, and giving crappy medical advice."

"Our Cheyenne ancestors were first and foremost warriors. It is our warrior spirit that has always given us our greatest strength."

Higheagle held up a hand. "You don't have to go into your whole spiel about how we're the direct descendants of *Wohkseh-hetaniu*, the Kit Fox Warriors—the fiercest warriors on the Plains along with the Cheyenne Dog Soldiers."

"Do I detect a trace of sarcasm?"

"I'm just not sure this is the time to be talking about this."

"Why not?"

"Because we're on the way to the hospital."

"I thought you said everything was going to be okay?"

"It is. But you still have to remember what Dr. Ekstrom said."

The old chief rolled his eyes. "Be sure to maintain a positive mental attitude," he mimicked sarcastically. "That's what they always say to cancer patients, but it doesn't mean anything. They still end up dead anyway. Oh well, I suppose I've had a good life. And since I know I'm going to die, I might as well smoke hemp again."

Higheagle glanced at him with a mix of amusement, tenderness, and exasperation as they pulled up to the next stoplight. He had to admit his grandfather didn't look like he had cancer. Even at seventy-five, the former tribal lawyer looked strong as an ox from all the hiking he did in the foothills and all the weightlifting and biking he did at the gym. But when it came to cancer, Higheagle knew, looks could be deceiving, especially early on. At this point, all he could do was pray that the tumor was benign. Since his parents' untimely death when he was six years old, his grandfather had always been there for him, and he didn't know what he would do without him. He would especially miss his sense of humor and mischievous nature. His grandfather had always had an air of mischief about him, which Higheagle knew was from his being a Contrary, a Cheyenne holy man who said and did things in opposite to serve an important tribal religious function and as a source of amusement.

"How about some music?" asked the old chief.

"Good idea." Higheagle stuffed an R. Carlos Nakai compact disk into his CD player. The gentle tapping of hand drums floated first from the speakers, followed by the soothing strum of a guitar and ethereal whistle of Nakai's traditional Native American flute. As they drove on, smiles lit up their faces and they began to tap their fingers on the dashboard, keeping in time with the rhythm.

He looked at the old chief. "I love you, Grandfather. I wish you could live forever."

"The Mystery won't allow it, Grandson. But it is nice for you to wish it so."

Six blocks later, they reached the hospital. Higheagle parked the War Wagon, turned off R. Carlos Nakai, and they walked through the automatic doors of the Oncology Wing. The nurse handed his grandfather forms to fill out and they took their seats in the waiting area.

Both unaware that they were about to meet a boy who would change their lives forever.

CHAPTER 3

SALLY MCTAVISH FELT NUMB.

For five minutes, she had been listening to her physician and the radiation oncologist telling her about the cancer growing inside the head of her only child.

On the small video screen in the sterile white hospital room, they had showed her MRIs of her son's brain from multiple angles. They pointed out the bulbous mass growing along the stem of her son Tommy's brain, attached like some kind of giant barnacle. They described how the sheath-like brain-stem connected the main part of the brain, the cerebrum, to the spinal cord and how it was critical to transmitting sensory and motor signals between the brain and body. They told her how the tumor was causing the boy's frequent headaches and drowsiness and how it was invading the healthy cells around it. They muttered cold medical words like thalamus and midbrain, reticular formation and medulla, and she felt only a painful helplessness throughout the entire endeavor.

She knew only that there was something alien infesting the head of her son, something cruel and malignant sapping him of the life she wanted him so much to enjoy.

She rubbed her face with her hands, her numbness giving way to devastation. She tried to choke back the tears, but was unsuccessful. She looked into the blue eyes of her cancer specialist, Dr. Gretchen Ekstrom, then at the troubled face of the stodgy, bespectacled male radiation oncologist whose name she couldn't remember.

She saw nothing reassuring.

My Tommy is dying of cancer, she thought, the wrenching agony distorting what was under normal circumstances a lovely oval face. She sank despondently into the flimsy plastic chair of the hospital room, tears streaming down her face. She felt terribly small, alone. Only once before could she recall being in such despair—when her husband had abandoned her and Tommy for Portland, Oregon, and a younger woman—but the sensations she felt now were far more dreadful. Her life had suddenly turned to one of unspeakable anguish.

"Sally," Dr. Ekstrom said softly, slipping a white-laboratory-jacketed arm over her shoulder. "I know it sounds bad, but you and Tommy can fight this thing. There's a chance..." Her voice trailed off sadly, completely undermining her attempt to instill hope.

Wiping the tears from her eyes, Sally looked at her with a challenging expression. "What kind of chance?"

Dr. Ekstrom glanced at the stubby oncologist. Following the movement, Sally fixed on the cat-green eyes behind the wiry half-frames. She couldn't escape the feeling the oncologist was hiding behind those damned glasses of his.

"What kind of chance does my boy have?" she asked, more stridently this time.

"Around ten percent," the oncologist lied, failing to meet Sally's penetrating stare. The actual chance of survival was less than one percent for this type of cancer, and although the stage was early, the oncologist knew the probability of the boy living to adulthood was virtually non-existent. But he didn't want to present a grim picture. With ten percent, there was hope.

"The good news," said Dr. Ekstrom, "is that the imaging test and biopsy results indicate the cancer is localized and that the cells are sensitive to radiation."

"What does that mean exactly?"

"It means that the tumor is small enough to attack using radiation."

"You mean like x-rays?"

"Actually," interjected the oncologist, "the super voltage linear accelerator that we use to destroy the cancer cells uses either a beam of x-rays or electrons. It's a very sophisticated instrument, capable of penetrating deeply into the affected portions of the brain-stem with far less damage to normal tissues than ordinary radiation."

"Let me get this straight. Are you telling me it kills off healthy cells?"

Dr. Ekstrom walked to the edge of the examination table. "Yes, Sally, there could be some damage to the normal cells in the area surrounding the tumor."

"And because we are dealing with the brain," the oncologist went on, "there are sometimes delayed side effects."

"What kind of...side effects?"

"Sometimes, there's a loss of cognitive abilities and memory. But these are only potential long-term effects and we'll do everything possible to minimize them. There are also some short-term effects."

"Like what?"

"The pressure Tommy is feeling in his head, and the fatigue as well, are likely to increase during the treatment. The pressure is from the tumor, but once the radiation treatment has begun, there will be some swelling of the brain tissue due to water retention. We will give him Decadron, a cortisone medication, to relieve this pressure. He can also continue to use the Tylenol to control his headaches."

"What other side effects are there?"

"There's the possibility of convulsions, but we can give him Dilatin to control them. He may also experience some nausea. We can help him through these episodes with Compazine. But what may bother Tommy most is the least significant side effect from a medical standpoint. After a couple weeks of treatment, Tommy is likely to lose the hair over the treated area. This is commonly distressing to patients because they think they are getting worse."

"A baseball cap or other hat could be used to cover the affected area," Dr. Ekstrom said. "That way he'll feel less self-conscious at school."

"Tommy can go to school?"

"As long as the treatment goes okay and he has his medication with him. Speak to his teachers and let them know what's going on. They should be accommodating. But there's no reason for Tommy to change his lifestyle, except as recommended by us or Tommy himself. You should not try to force him to eat.

Chances are he'll experience a significant loss of appetite. We recommend that he be allowed to nibble throughout the day and not be expected to eat large meals at set times. The main thing for you to remember is Tommy's going to need your complete support. He has to believe he can beat this thing, but at the same time understand it is quite serious."

"If the radiation shows signs of destroying the tumor or at least shrinking it significantly," said the radiation oncologist "then he may not require chemotherapy after the radiation. But if it doesn't have the desired effect, we may need to move forward with chemo."

Sally McTavish shook her head in dismay. It seemed unfathomable that the adorable baby boy she had once rocked to sleep in her arms was stricken with cancer. The little guy that had scuttled across the rug with an ever present smile, whose hand she had held reassuringly his first day of kindergarten, the one she had covered with Band-Aids when he was learning to ride his bike.

My baby boy is dying of cancer.

The horrible thought echoed through her mind as the doctors went on to describe the grim details of the radiation therapy, as well as what to expect should chemotherapy be necessary following the radiation. They described how Tommy's diet would have to be altered, how he would need zinc and other vitamin supplements. They gave her the phone numbers of cancer counseling centers, and a list of books to read to help her through the crisis.

As the doctors droned on, she began to feel a shroud of blackness enveloping her, a miasma of gloom. She wondered whether she and Tommy had any hope of recapturing some semblance of life from the nightmare their life had suddenly become. And when the realization struck her that things would never be the same, she tried to imagine that this wasn't her life, that it was all just a dream. She had to deny it was happening, because she could not lose her Tommy.

For Sally McTavish, a life without her only child was no life at all.

CHAPTER 4

SITTING IN THE WAITING AREA of the Dwight D. Eisenhower Memorial Hospital Oncology Wing, Tommy McTavish had already begun to prepare himself for the bad news his mother would likely be delivering in the next few minutes. She was taking a long time with the doctors and that could mean only one thing: the tumor identified two weeks ago during the CAT scan was most likely the bad kind after all. The MRI and biopsy tests must have come out positive for cancer, which meant, at the very least, that he would have a long, hard fight ahead of him.

Just like his buddy Todd Wilkins, who had died two months ago from the very same type of cancer he probably had.

The funny thing was he didn't feel all that sick. After all, he was still going to school and had played baseball up until last week. The headaches had been coming a lot the past month and he felt drowsy in the afternoon, enough so that he had fallen asleep in class several times recently. But he hadn't keeled over or coughed up blood or anything, which was what he'd expected once he had first learned of the tumor. Most of the time he felt like all he had was a lingering head cold.

Then again, Todd had felt the same way in the beginning. And now he was dead.

Tommy glanced at his Yosemite Sam wristwatch. His mom had been talking with the doctors for over twenty minutes now. *Why is she taking so long?* He touched his palms together and suddenly felt hot and clammy. He took off his dirty-gray cowboy hat and rolled up the shirtsleeves of his turquoise western shirt, exposing scrappy twigs for arms that were sprinkled generously with freckles. His face, too, was covered with freckles along his ski-jump nose, smooth cheeks, and slight cleft chin reminiscent of his mother's.

Growing impatient with worry, he walked over to the magazine rack and rummaged through the magazines, eventually settling on a copy of *National Geographic*. When he returned to his seat, two Native American men, one old and the other young, sat down across from him. The old man began filling out hospital paperwork on a clipboard given to him by the nurse at the front desk.

Tommy smiled at the young man. "You guys are Indians, aren't you?"

The old man looked up from his paperwork, looking a little grumpy. "Last time we checked," he sniffed.

"What tribe are you from?"

"We are Cheyenne."

The young one shook his head. "He's pulling your leg. We're actually professional actors wearing wigs and makeup. We had you fooled too, didn't we,

Kemosabe?"

Tommy giggled. "Nice try, but I'm not that gullible."

"Okay, you got us. We are card-carrying members of the Northern Cheyenne Nation. But we promise not to take your scalp since we're in a public place."

He winked, and already Tommy liked him. "Cheyenne, huh. That's cool. I saw the exhibit on the Dog Soldiers at the Colorado History Museum. It said they were the toughest Cheyenne warriors—the elite. It also said they were outcasts from the other Cheyenne bands because they refused to surrender to the white man and wouldn't sign peace treaties. That's why I think they were cool: they were the last to surrender."

The two Indians looked at one another. "The little pecker appears to know his history," said the old one, reappraising him in a new light.

The young Indian smiled. "What's your white-man name, Little Big Man?"

"Tommy McTavish." He pulled a small red Swiss Army knife from his pocket. "Yours?"

"Joe—Joe Higheagle. And this is my grandfather, Chief John Higheagle."

Tommy nearly jumped up from his chair, having never met a chief before. "Wow, you're really a chief?"

"A retired chief."

"He's just being modest. He's actually one of the ranking chiefs of the Northern Cheyenne tribe."

The old man grinned mischievously, exposing a set of dingy yellow teeth. "And don't you ever forget it, either."

They laughed and Tommy could tell that they were quite fond of one another even if the chief was a little on the grumpy side. Their smiles lingered a moment before the old man returned to filling out his forms. Tommy decided to ask the young one another question.

"I really like Crazy Horse. What do you guys think of him?"

Higheagle smiled with amusement. "The man or the legend?"

As if on cue, the old chief stopped writing and sat up in his chair. "'This is the West, sir!'" he declared in a mock serious voice. "'When the legend becomes fact, print the legend!'"

"*The Man Who Shot Liberty Valance*," said Tommy. "I love that movie."

Again, the two men looked at one another with mild surprise. "So you like Westerns too, do you?" said the chief with a trace of skepticism.

Tommy nodded enthusiastically. "They're my favorite."

"I am beginning to like you, you little pecker." He reached out and ruffled the boy's hair with a big, leathery hand. "Now how do you know so much about Westerns? I thought all kids your age did was tweet one another and play video games."

"I'm just different, I guess. I like Western books too. That's the reason I asked about Crazy Horse. I'm reading a book about him."

"Who is it by?"

"Larry McMurtry."

"A Pulitzer prize winner," said the younger one. "You have good taste, Little Big Man."

"Yeah, you sure do," said the chief. "Are you certain you don't have Indian blood?"

"Not that I know of."

The two men laughed again and Tommy realized he could hang with these two Cheyenne guys all day long. They were fun. He pulled the tweezers from his pocketknife and began fiddling with them. "What are you here for anyway?"

"My grandfather's having some tests done."

"I just had some tests done too. I've been getting these headaches. Sometimes they're really bad. And I get tired a lot. Dr. Ekstrom—that's our doctor—found out I have a tumor near my brain and they ran some more tests. My mom's in there right now talking with Dr. Ekstrom and another doctor about what they found. She's been in there a long time so I know it's not good. My mom wanted to talk to them first. She probably thought I would freak out when I heard the bad news."

"Dr. Ekstrom is your doctor?"

"Yeah. You know her?"

"She's my grandfather's doctor too."

Now the old chief looked grumpy again. "I've got to get this goddamn paperwork in." He rose from his seat and shuffled off towards the admission desk carrying his clipboard.

Tommy wondered what he'd said: he hoped he hadn't upset the chief.

"It's all right. He just hates hospitals."

"That makes two of us. The thing that's weird about my situation is my buddy Todd had the same kind of brain tumor I have. It's really rare. They call it medulla something or other."

"You had a friend who had the same type of tumor?"

"Yeah, he died a couple of months ago. He lived at Dakota Ranch just down the street from me. Dr. Ekstrom was his doctor too."

The Cheyenne looked at him sympathetically.

"But I guess I shouldn't worry until I know for sure what's going on. My tumor may not be the bad kind, even though my friend Todd's was."

"Well, no matter what happens, you've got to keep your chin up. I'm sure Dr. Ekstrom told you that."

"Yeah, she did." He sighed. "I just wish my mom would hurry up. She's been in there a long time."

They fell into an awkward silence. Tommy stared down at the glossy acrylic floor tiles. He didn't want to end on a depressing note like this. He liked talking with this Indian guy and his grandfather the chief too.

"You know what I think, Little Big Man? I think you and my grandfather are going to be just fine. These things have a funny way of working out for the best."

Tommy nodded slowly. Something about the way he said it made him—

"Now it's just a feeling I have, but you know how we Indians are about feelings. We see and feel things. Things beyond this world. Things science can't explain. We don't even try to do it—it just happens naturally."

"You sure you're not just trying to make me feel better."

"No, I've got a real feeling."

"Well, in that case I believe you."

He stuffed his Swiss Army knife back in the pocket of his Wrangler jeans and watched as the silver-haired chief walked back from the front desk. A moment later, he saw his mother step through the door leading to the examination room with Dr. Ekstrom and the other doctor.

"There's my mom and Dr. Ekstrom," he said, as she began walking towards him. He felt himself tense up; he could tell his mother was upset.

"Everything's going to be all right," said Higheagle, his big brown eyes reaching out to the boy reassuringly. "Like I said, I've got a feeling—an Indian kind of feeling."

"I believe you, but I'm still scared."

"It's okay to be scared. But at the same time, you've got to believe in yourself and fight the good fight if the news does happen to be bad. You know what I'm saying?"

"Yeah, I've got to fight, fight, fight. Like a Cheyenne warrior."

"You got it, Little Big Man. You definitely got it."

And he gave him a little wink.

CHAPTER 5

THE NEWS wasn't good, Higheagle could tell. Tommy's mother had obviously been crying, and though she was struggling bravely to present a mask of aplomb, it was apparent that she was deeply distressed.

Which meant that most likely Tommy had cancer after all.

Somehow, even though he didn't really know the kid, it seemed pointedly unfair. He could understand how a sixty-year old chain-smoker would get cancer. But a healthy-looking twelve-year-old boy? Now that was something completely different. But what made it even more perplexing was that Tommy's neighborhood friend Todd had died from the very same type of rare brain tumor. What were the odds of that?

He watched as Tommy's mother said something to Dr. Ekstrom and the other physician. Then the two doctors nodded, turned, and walked back down the corridor towards the examination room, while Tommy's mother started over to where he and Tommy were sitting. He took a moment to study her as she approached, finding her quite attractive despite that she had obviously been crying. She was tall, five-foot-eight he estimated, and her figure could only be described as voluptuous. Her face was well-sculpted, her complexion smooth and healthy-looking, and her strawberry blonde hair fell gently to her shoulders in little curls. She reminded him of a young Ann Margaret in that old John Wayne flick *The Train Robbers* he and his grandfather liked so much.

"Hi, I'm Joseph Higheagle," he said politely, extending his hand as she came walking up.

She appeared unsure of what to make of him. "Nice to meet you. I'm Sally."

"My grandfather and I have been talking to Tommy about cowboys and Indians."

"Have you now? Somehow, that doesn't surprise me."

"He knows so much about the Old West, we think he may have been reincarnated."

Her face lit up and he took pleasure in making her smile. And then, a sudden glimmer of recognition appeared in her eyes, as if she was trying to place him from somewhere.

"Do I know you?" she asked.

"I'm not sure. Do I owe you money?"

She laughed and Higheagle realized that it was even more fun making her laugh than it was making her smile. "Now I remember," she said. "You were all over the news a year ago. You're the earthquake guy. I mean, the geologist who found out about those earthquakes and stopped that madman from pumping toxic waste down those wells. He was causing the earthquakes, right? What was his name?"

"Charles Prometheus Quantrill."

"That's really you? You're the earthquake guy?" exclaimed Tommy, enormously impressed.

"Guilty as charged."

"It appears you're a true celebrity, Mr. Higheagle," said Sally.

"He and his grandfather both." The boy tilted his head towards the old timer. "Mom, meet John Higheagle. He's a Northern Cheyenne chief."

Sally held out her hand. "Nice to meet you." They smiled at one another and then she turned back towards Joseph. "So are you like an earthquake expert?"

"I'm more of an all-around geoscientist. I tend to dabble in a little of everything: quantitative geologic analysis, vertebrate paleontology, soil and groundwater remediation, computer modeling, greenhouse gas emissions, risk assessments, you name it."

"Was that English I just heard or some foreign language because I didn't understand a word you just said?"

"Sorry, sometimes I just go all technospeak."

"Well, you did a great job stopping that toxic waste pumping that was causing those earthquakes. What firm do you work for?"

"I just started my own: Higheagle Environmental."

"It must be exciting starting your own business."

"Actually, it's a hell of a lot of work. But thanks for the moral support."

She glanced at her watch and her expression abruptly changed. "Well, it was good to talk to you, but we have to meet with Dr. Ekstrom now."

"It was a pleasure to meet you two," said John Higheagle.

"Nice to meet you too," said Sally, but Joseph could tell that she was starting to tear up again. His grandfather noticed it, too, and gave her a sympathetic look.

Feeling a stirring of emotion, Higheagle turned away from her and looked down at Tommy. "Hey, Little Big Man. Before you go, there's something I need to tell you. If you're going to be a warrior like your hero Crazy Horse, you've got to have a special battle cry."

The boy's face lit up. "Do you know a good one?"

"Yeah, how about what Crazy Horse said before leading his Lakota warriors and my Cheyenne ancestors against Long Hair Custer at the Little Bighorn?"

"Cool! What did he say?"

The big Cheyenne cleared his throat and, in a robust voice one might use when telling a folk tale, he said the proud words so often repeated to him by Grandfather Higheagle. "*Hokahe!*" he declared, his countenance resolute, a fisted hand held in the air. "It is a good day to fight! It is a good day to die! Strong hearts, brave hearts—to the front!"

"Crazy Horse really said that?"

"Darn right he did," said the old chief. "And I don't think he would mind a young warrior like you using his battle cry. Even a *vehoe*—a white man—like yourself. But you must take my grandson's words to heart. You must fight whatever obstacles lay before you like the Lakota Crazy Horse and our Cheyenne ancestors did on that fateful day of June 25, 1876. You must see with the single eye that is the heart, and never give up the fight."

"I'll do my best."

The old Contrary nodded approvingly. Then he stepped forward and gripped him on the shoulder with his big, leathery mitt. "I do believe you will, Little Big Man. I do believe you will."

CHAPTER 6

HAYDEN WINTHROP PRESCOTT III WAS THINKING OF MURDER.

He sat in the Card Room of the Denver Country Club, *Wall Street Journal* in his lap, a medley of sea scallops, field greens, bacon and red lentil vinaigrette, and orange segments settling quietly in his stomach. He had just finished lunching with an investor in the Member's Grill and was waiting for another man—someone who had important information for him.

Dressed in a beige Hugo Boss suit, he gazed through the French doors overlooking the tennis courts and venerable golf course beyond. Soon a pair of giggling young women in short tennis skirts passed into view, and a pernicious smile lifted the corners of his mouth. *Oh, the things I could do with them at the same time!* Then the women disappeared, the smile evaporated, and his thoughts returned to last night when he had watched Gus McTavish wither before his very eyes.

He felt a deep, penetrating shame at what he had done. But at the same time, Gus had deserved to die. After all, the man was a blackmailer who had threatened Prescott's very existence. Any prominent businessman backed into a similar corner would have done the same thing. Gus McTavish had become a serious threat and it had been imperative to silence him, especially with the cancer cases coming to light.

Prescott thought of the look on Gus's face once he realized he'd been poisoned. The expression was accusatory, betrayed. In that precarious moment, Prescott had realized that he had to quickly silence his victim before he blew the whistle in front of the bystanders. Covering up Gus's face by pretending to give him mouth-to-mouth had been a cunning ploy. Father might not have approved, but Mumsie would have been unabashedly proud. She knew how to take risks, to do whatever it took to triumph over those who threatened her. The faked CPR had been a spur of the moment decision, but it would pay untold dividends in the ongoing police investigation.

He was hardly worried about the investigation. If an autopsy was performed, which, given the suddenness of death, was a distinct possibility, the only substances that would be found would be prescription medication and alcohol. The massive concentration of triflurodigitalis might raise the eyebrow of the Medical Examiner, but the other circumstances of the case would keep the police from suspecting foul play. The drugs found in Gus's stomach and bloodstream had been prescribed by his own doctor and he had the pills on him when he died. He had a history of alcohol abuse, was in poor physical health, and had a miserable personal life that included estrangement from his wife and huge gambling debts. The vial and cup that had held the poison had been destroyed, so there was no incriminating physical evidence. Prescott and Gus were professional acquaintances, and if the cops probed deeply, they would discover nothing more than routine business payments for services rendered. There was also the sworn testimony of the other luxury box bystanders, who had already testified that they had seen him struggling heroically to save Gus's life.

Of course, the police would have to conduct their paltry investigation, but it would lead to nothing. The only loose end was the second waiter who had entered the box once the call for help had been raised. Unfortunately, two bystanders remembered seeing him. No one knew that the mystery waiter was a professional liquidator named Zachary Paine, though, regrettably, one eyewitness had given a somewhat accurate physical description to the police.

When Prescott had plotted the murder, he had no idea killing someone could be so gratifying. It was only when he saw Gus McTavish wane before him that he truly understood the enormous power he held. At that moment, despite the horrible guilt he felt inside, he was gripped with a feeling of ecstasy. He had read books and seen movies of murderers who killed for the macabre pleasure of it, so-called "thrill killers" like Leopold and Loeb who had attempted to pull off the perfect murder in the 1920s. He didn't consider himself such a killer, for he knew that ultimately he was simply a respectable businessman who had been driven to commit a desperate act, a breed apart from the lowly criminals who routinely robbed, raped, and killed. But he could understand how someone might commit murder for pleasure, or to gain a feeling of superiority. There was a certain gratification, an almost sexual titillation, in taking another man's life and getting away with it. Though he hated to admit it, he felt a kind of clandestine supremacy over not only his victim but the police, as if he was a clever spy or master jewel thief.

Not surprisingly, the original decision to kill Gus McTavish hadn't been easy for him. He had wrestled with the terrible dilemma for more than two months, looking for ways to placate his blackmailer without killing him. But, in time, he realized that Gus would just keep popping up like a jack-in-the-box to demand more hush money. The man would, quite simply, never go away. That—and this new thorny childhood cancer issue—had allowed Prescott to justify his actions.

And yet, he still couldn't escape the guilt. Why was that? he wondered. How could it be that despicable Gus, a blackmailer and habitual wife beater, had gone on to a better place and Prescott was now the tormented soul? It seemed grossly unfair. All he had done was to defend himself from a serious threat and ensure his own survival.

But still the guilt gnawed at him. He tried to deny what he felt inside. He tried to tell himself what Father, and even more daring Mumsie, had always told him: that great men always rise to a challenge and put their misgivings aside. But he was unable to turn his feelings on and off like a light switch. Despite his perfectly logical rationalizations, he still felt torn up inside.

Damnit, why the hell do I have to feel this way?

Taking a deep breath, he looked around his impeccable surroundings, hoping that they would ease his guilt, that they would remind him why he was above the lowly world of blackmailing criminals like Gus McTavish. He took in the Card Room's supremely costly, solid-oak paneling and marble fireplace to his right. The same stately oak covered the wall to his left, where framed black-and-white photographs of the Denver Country Club in the jolly old days of Ike peered out at him with regal dignity. He took in the green felt tables bearing neatly arranged packets of playing cards, backgammon boards, and monogrammed DCC score sheets. Each card table was surrounded by four resplendent captain's chairs covered with red-dyed leather tucked in by round-headed brass nails. Finally, Prescott discretely watched the two dapperly dressed gentlemen playing backgammon at one of the tables, their genteel voices mingling with the diners in the adjoining Member's Grill.

Feeling the salving power of his aristocratic surroundings, Prescott began to feel better. He was safe here at the Denver Country Club—safe from the poverty, mediocrity, and broken dreams of the outside world. It was a sanctuary, the perfect refuge and playground for the gilded 1%. Here he interacted only with multi-millionaire venture capitalists, attorneys, oil men, realtors, bankers, politicians, and other developers just like him. There were no ordinary, no desperate, no fallen people at *The Club*—no one from the other hapless 99% was allowed inside the gated bastion, thank heavens. Here he mingled with only the best and brightest, men and women of power, influence, and undeniable good taste. Here he garnered important investors for his enormously successful real estate firm, The Newport Company, and was fawned over by Denver's elite. Yes, here he was not only safe, but venerated.

The Gods had smiled early and often on Hayden Prescott, and in adulthood, nothing had changed. He was the proud owner of a vastly profitable business and had made tens of millions of dollars though he was not yet forty. He was rarely without delectable female companionship when he wanted it; usually glossy, cultured women with B.A. or B.F.A. degrees from places like Smith, Vassar, or Middlebury he met at art auctions and other functions celebrating Denver's A-List. He was also an expert downhill skier, one of the top three tennis players at the Denver Country Club, and reigning champion of the top squash and billiard divisions at the University Club downtown.

But it was his business pedigree that had cemented his reputation in the Mile High City. With swaggering initiative, he had formed the Council for Front Range Competitiveness, a consortium of developers, homebuilders, lawyers, heavy equipment owners, and other executives dedicated to the land development industry. Thanks to Prescott, the group had evolved into a muscular coalition, easily subverting burdensome regulations, co-opting local governments, and generating massive profits for its esteemed members. Because of his success on his own and with the Council, Prescott was regarded as a cutting-edge leader amongst Denver's elite, a man of peerless vision.

He foresaw a great future for the Front Range similar to that of the Orange County-San Diego corridor where he was raised. Extending from Fort Collins to Pueblo, he saw large self-sustaining developments separated by thin aureoles of open space. All the indispensable things people would need would be right there for them: the championship golf courses, the 24-screen movieplexes, and enormous shopping malls. He didn't see his dream as an anathema to the wildlife and panorama of the Front Range as did his opponents. In fact, he couldn't understand why anyone wouldn't support "smart growth"—the catchy buzzword local politicians and developers were chiming in unison, but which all but the most naïve knew really amounted to a plethora of overpriced condos and cloned houses that were hauntingly California-like.

Hayden Winthrop Prescott III had a dream. While many others saw sprawling development along Colorado's Front Range as an ugly nemesis, he saw only a florid vision, a luxurious paradise beneath a sparkling backdrop of mountains. And, like his beloved Mumsie, he was willing to use every means at his disposal to ensure that his dream would become a reality.

Even cold-blooded murder.

CHAPTER 7

SITTING IN THE HOSPITAL WAITING AREA, Higheagle looked up from his magazine as Dr. Ekstrom came walking up.

"I just wanted to let you know your grandfather's fine. We've completed the biopsy and he's now getting his MRI done. He should be out in half an hour."

"That's great." He noticed that she looked a touch anxious, as if she had something more to say.

"While you're waiting, I was hoping we might talk for a minute," she then added, confirming his suspicions.

He looked at her. "Is everything okay?"

"Oh yes. As I said, your grandfather's fine. I wanted to speak with you about something else."

This is a little odd. "Should we talk here?"

"We'll have more privacy in the conference room. Please follow me."

She led him past the receptionist's desk to the small conference room where a few minutes earlier they had gone over the CAT scan results from the preliminary tests conducted last week. She motioned him towards a plush leather chair at a cherrywood conference table, closed the door so that they were alone, and took a seat across the table from him.

"Mr. Higheagle—"

"Please, call me Joe."

"Very well, Joe. What do you know about Dakota Ranch?"

What is going on here? "Not much. Why do you ask?"

"Let's just say I have some concerns about the development."

"What kind of concerns?"

"Concerns about what's causing the cancer out there. You met Sally and Tommy McTavish...I...I saw you talking to Tommy. He and his mother told me you had a nice chat."

He nodded.

"Tommy's a brave little boy. Unfortunately, he has cancer. That's what I wanted to talk to you about."

"You think there's something going on at Dakota Ranch?"

It was her turn to nod. "The question is what's causing it? That's the reason I wanted to talk to you. You are that Joseph Higheagle, right? The environmental crusader?"

"Yep, I wear a cape and tights and fly around saving people from enviro-catastrophes."

She laughed. "I'm sorry, I didn't mean to..."

"It's all right. But just so you know, I'm just a lowly geologist trying to make an honest living and I only occasionally wear tights."

She chuckled. "I read about you in the papers and saw you on the news last year regarding that earthquake business. I didn't recognize you until Tommy told me who you were. What was that billionaire polluter's name again?"

"Charles Prometheus Quantrill."

"Didn't he end up killing himself?"

"Yes, but please don't blame me for that."

"Actually, I thought the whole thing was a nice piece of detective work on your part."

"Thanks, but I'm no Sherlock Holmes." He was anxious to get back to the subject at hand. "So you think there's something going on at Dakota Ranch?"

"Yes, and I wanted to see if you had any ideas. First off, you know about Tommy's friend Todd who died. He was one of my patients."

"Yeah, Tommy told me. I'm sorry."

"But what he didn't tell you—because he doesn't know about it—is that he and Todd aren't the only childhood cancer cases at Dakota Ranch."

"They're not?"

"There have been three other cases."

"How many have died?"

"Four including Todd, all in the last nine months."

"Same type of cancer in all the cases?"

"Medullablastoma. Cancer of the brain stem, an extremely rare and deadly form of brain cancer. By the way, this is all a matter of public record now and that's the reason I'm talking to you about it. I contacted the Colorado Department of Public Health and Environment a month ago, thinking the cases might be related. I haven't heard back from them yet, though."

"So there have been five cases in only the past nine months. That would appear to be statistically significant."

"Actually, there could be more than five. These are just the ones that have been reported at this hospital."

"Strange that there's been no mention of any of this in the news."

"The Health Department hasn't made anything public yet. They've only been working on the case for a few weeks now and are proceeding cautiously."

"How many of the kids have you treated?"

"Just Tommy and Todd. But I've spoken with the doctors handling the other cases. They've all been boys by the way."

"Wait a second. All the victims have been boys?"

"And they're all from Dakota Ranch."

"So what do you think is going on?"

"I don't know. I mean, I have a theory but I don't have much to back it up."

"Can I hear it?"

"Only if you promise to keep it to yourself. And not to laugh at me."

"I'd never do that. After all, I myself wear tights and a cape."

"Very well." She rose from her chair, went to the window, and proceeded in a carefully modulated voice. At first, it seemed like nothing more than another febrile conspiracy theory spawned by the overactive imagination of a quantitative expert who should have known better. But as she pressed on, Higheagle began to hang on every word. Slowly but assuredly, he realized that what he was hearing made a lot of sense from a scientific standpoint. And yet, at the same time, it was so wildly outrageous, so far-reaching and diabolical, he found himself thinking that it couldn't possibly be true.

When she was finished, he gulped hard. They looked at one another for several seconds as an awestruck silence gripped the conference room.

"If you're right about this," he warned, "then Douglas County has a huge problem on its hands."

"I know," she said. "And it scares me to death."

CHAPTER 8

SALLY MCTAVISH felt a dizzy sensation as she hung up the kitchen phone. She turned and looked at Tommy, who had been watching TV in the other room and was now walking into the kitchen, and stared at him in muddled disbelief.

"What is it, mom?"

She hesitated, unable to bring herself to say it.

"Mom, is it something bad?"

"Uncle Gus has passed away."

"What?"

"He died last night."

She took a moment to compose herself. She had never felt any great love for her father's brother—after all, he had been a drunk and a wife beater—but she felt a sense of loss at his passing all the same. He had seemed like such an unhappy man, particularly over the past few months, and it saddened her to think that life could be that painful for anyone.

"That's what Aunt Martha said, honey. He died of a heart attack at last night's Avs game."

"The Avs game? Was Aunt Martha there?"

Sally motioned for them to sit in the caned chairs around the country-style pine kitchen table. "No. She moved out over a month ago. She and Gus have been having problems again."

"I didn't know Uncle Gus liked ice hockey. Who was he with?"

Sally's face turned pensive as she formed a mental image of Hayden Prescott. Had she loved him? A part of her had, she decided. Though their romance had ended two years ago and she had bumped into him only three times since, she still thought of him on occasion. He had been strikingly handsome, polite, ridiculously wealthy, cultured, endearing, quite romantic, and most importantly, kind to Tommy. She recalled the times they had made love, and had to admit she had never had a better lover in her entire life. She bore no animosity towards him even though he had broken things off with her. Unlike most men, he had seemed forthright when he had said he was ending the relationship because he couldn't commit to her and didn't want to lead her on.

"Come on, Mom. Don't space out on me. Who was Uncle Gus with?"

She hesitated, feeling something like guilt, though she didn't know why. "Hayden Prescott."

"Your old boyfriend?"

Sally nodded. *Why do I feel guilty? I haven't done anything wrong.* "Hayden tried to save Gus. That's what Aunt Martha said."

"I didn't know Hayden and Gus even knew each other."

"Gus has done quite a bit of work for Hayden's company over the past few years. They weren't really friends per se, more business acquaintances."

"Does Grandpa know yet?"

Sally felt a surge of dread. "No, and Aunt Martha has so many people to call, I told her I'd call him."

"Were Grandpa and Uncle Gus close?"

"Not really. But Grandpa still loved his older brother. I think he felt badly for Gus and tried to help him with his drinking. But it's hard to help someone who can't help himself."

As soon as the words left her mouth, she regretted saying them. It wasn't proper to disparage the dead. She felt a pang of remorse as she realized how little effort she had made to see Gus and his family over the years, how she had done absolutely nothing to help him or Aunt Martha through their marital troubles. It seemed like the only time she ever saw Gus and his family was when her parents came into town from Phoenix.

"When's the funeral going to be?"

"I don't know. I'll have to talk to Grandpa and Aunt Martha."

"The whole thing seems weird to me. I can't imagine Uncle Gus going to a hockey game. The only sports I ever heard him talk about were football and baseball." His voice turned low and suggestive. "Who knows, maybe he didn't die of a heart attack. Maybe he was...murdered."

"You've been watching too much TV, young man. Why would anybody want to hurt Uncle Gus? And Hayden certainly wouldn't do such a thing."

"I didn't mean him. I was thinking about Aunt Martha."

Sally rolled her eyes. "Are you trying to get a reaction out of me?"

"Okay, suppose it wasn't Aunt Martha, but someone else. Not Hayden, but another guy. Uncle Gus could have known something—some secret—and this other guy arranged for him to die of supposedly natural causes."

"Now why would someone do that to Uncle Gus?"

"To pin the blame on Hayden. I've seen it like that on CSI."

"Oh my, you really have been watching too much television."

"Come on, you know it's possible. You're the one who's always telling me life is stranger than fiction."

She let out a bemused sigh. *You're a nutty kid, but I'm lucky to have you.*

Inevitably, her thoughts turned to the tumor growing inside his head and the grim prospect that he would probably die. She felt a lump take hold in her throat and a wave of tears grappling to break through to the surface. But she had cried so much since Tommy had been diagnosed with cancer, the last thing she wanted to do was cry in front of him again.

"I'd better call Grandpa now," she said, holding back the tears.

She rose from her chair and gave Tommy a kiss on his head. Then she walked to the phone and dialed her father's cell number. A floor manager at a large aerospace facility in Phoenix, Bill McTavish answered on the third ring.

"Dad," she said, "I have some bad news for you..."

CHAPTER 9

IT WAS A START-UP HOUSE that normally would have been occupied by a young, middle-class couple with one or two young children. Single-story. Ranch-style. All wood, with Conestoga wagon wheels and soil-filled barrel planters along the perimeter. A trifecta of sugar maples and an ancient apple tree with a few emerging pink blossoms threw their limbs across the front yard, which was tiny and open to the street. The house had been built back when Bonanza was the rage, when Littleton, Colorado, was little more than a conglomeration of horse farms and suburban Denver was still miles to the north.

To the pleasant tinkling of wind chimes, Higheagle jiggled the front door open and waved his grandfather inside. The old chief was still in a grumpy mood from having to be cooped up inside an MRI chamber for an hour and from having a nub of flesh removed during his biopsy. They stepped inside the house and onto the freshly stained pinewood floor. His grandfather made a beeline for the couch, plopped down, and flipped on the TV with the remote.

Higheagle went into his office, checked his messages, and responded to two business emails. Ten minutes later, he put together a late lunch for the two of them: fry bread bean burritos with grated Monterey Jack cheese, slivers of avocado and tomato, and a handful of sprouts, with a heavy dose of Tapatio hot sauce, a splash of oil and vinegar dressing, and a sprinkle of pepper to round it out and glasses of soy milk to wash it all down.

When they were finished, his grandfather retired to his bedroom for his afternoon nap while Higheagle headed into the living room, padding softly across the handwoven Navaho rug. He popped a Charles Littleleaf flute tape into the CD player, adjusted the volume, and plopped down in the comfortable blue corduroy couch. Turning on the lamp on the antique pine coffee table, he picked up his copy of Sherman Alexie's *Indian Killer* and started reading. He could afford a few minutes of relaxation before he got back to his site investigation report.

But before he had finished his first paragraph, the phone rang.

He set down his book and scrambled into his office, picking up the receiver before the fourth ring.

"Hello."

"Is this Mr. Joseph Higheagle?"

The voice sounded old and ethnic. "Yes," he answered.

"My name is Vincenzo Minesali."

"How can I help you, Mr. Minesali?"

"I would like to meet with you to discuss a business proposal."

Now Higheagle had a better feel for the subtle accent. It sounded Italian-

American, or at least like the voices of the Italian-Americans he was most familiar with, those in mobster movies. He pictured Marlon Brando's Don Corleone on the other end of the line, an unsettling sight.

"Would this business proposal be for environmental services?" he asked, though he knew he shouldn't have to ask that.

The man laughed, a throaty gurgle. "I believe in your business you call them environmental assessments."

Oh good, he just wants an EA. "I'm very interested, Mr. Minesali."

"You have just started your own business, yes?"

How does he know that? "I'm just getting off the ground. But I do have ten years of experience in the industry." He winced, knowing he shouldn't have had to say that either.

"Higheagle Environmental—I like the name. It's a great feeling for a young man when he starts his own business. A great feeling."

He wasn't sure how to respond. Thus far, he had found his new business vastly unprofitable and stressful. "Can you tell me a little bit about the project?"

"Ah, yes. I am a businessman and have the opportunity to invest in a rather large real estate venture. I would simply like to know if there are any environmental issues I should be aware of before committing myself as an investor."

"For marketing reasons, may I ask how you found out about me?"

"I was impressed with the way you took care of that Quantrill affair. When I discovered this new business opportunity, I decided to contact you. I found your advertisement in the phone book."

Higheagle couldn't believe it: someone was actually contacting him through his yellow pages ad! He sat down at his pine desk, grabbed a notepad, and pulled a ballpoint pen from a tin cup.

"What would you provide in a standard environmental assessment?" Minesali asked him.

"The first step would be a public records search: a review of regulatory agency records, aerial photos, previous environmental investigations, that sort of thing. I would interview site personnel, including the property lessee and former employees. Plus I would inspect the subject property and adjacent properties. The specific details would depend on past land use, but I would follow the Phase I environmental site assessment protocols described in ASTM guidance document E-1527."

"ASTM, what is that?"

"The American Society for Testing and Materials."

"You sound very knowledgeable, Mr. Higheagle. I presume you would produce some kind of report at the end of your research?"

"I'd put together a draft report and submit it to you. Once I received your comments, I'd prepare a final report."

"I would like to meet with you and discuss the project in greater detail. I am confident you are the right man for the job, but I would like to meet you in person."

Money in the bank! "When would you like to get together?" he asked, trying hard not to sound overeager.

"How about dinner at my house tomorrow evening?"

That was a little odd. He had never met clients at their homes before, not when he was with HydroGroup and not since he had started his own environmental consulting firm. "What's the address?"

"Four-ninety-seven Polo Club Drive West."

The Polo Club? The guy had to be loaded. "I look forward to seeing you tomorrow night then, Mr. Minesali. What time should I be there?"

"Eight o'clock?"

"Fine. I'll see you then." As he was about to hang up, he realized he had forgotten something. "Wait a second, Mr. Minesali. Can you tell me the name of the property?"

"Oh, I apologize. There are two developments I am interested in. Both are located south of Denver in Douglas County. One is Silverado Knolls, which is about to be built, and the other is Dakota Ranch, which was constructed a few years ago."

Higheagle felt like he had just been dunked in freezing water. The name "Silverado Knolls" meant nothing to him, but the name of the other development rendered him literally speechless. He thought of Sally and Tommy McTavish and Dr. Ekstrom's bizarre theory as the words "Dakota Ranch" rang over and over in his head, like the tolling of a warning bell. Was it a freak coincidence that this Minesali was calling him after what had happened today at the hospital? Or was it perhaps fate?

"I'll see you tomorrow night, Mr. Higheagle."

"I look forward to meeting you, Mr. Minesali," came the automatic reply, but he was already thinking about how this all seemed too easy, how there had to be a catch. There was an element of danger and mystery afoot that he couldn't quite put a finger on. He was reminded once again of Don Corleone and that damned chopped-off horse's head in the bed of that Hollywood big shot who had dared to cross the cosmopolitan mob boss.

"Goodbye, Mr. Higheagle."

"Goodbye." Hanging up the phone, he stared into the wooden darkness of his desk.

Who is this guy? And what the hell did I just get myself into?

CHAPTER 10

THE NEXT EVENING, at precisely five minutes before eight, Joseph Higheagle navigated the War Wagon to the front gate of Vincenzo Minesali's Polo Club mansion. What struck him at first was not its architectural grandeur, but its immensity. It was so big it exceeded his field of vision. He peered through the intricate latticework of the wrought-iron gate, wondering whether it would be fun to live in such an extraordinary home, or whether the sheer vastness and gravity of the place would make it too much like living in a museum.

He leaned out the car window and pressed the buzzer. He expected to hear a butlerish Alfred-from-Batman voice on the other end, but instead was greeted by something a touch more macabre, a Vincent Price inflection. "Yeesss."

"It's uh…Joseph Higheagle. Here to see Mr. Minesali."

"He's been expecting you."

He felt like he was on the movie set of Edgar Allen Poe's *The Pit and the Pendulum*. The guy's voice—actually, make that the whole place—was creepy as hell. For a brief moment, he wondered if he was walking into a trap.

Slowly, the gate began to open. The heavy groaning of the metal hinges prompted an image of a drawbridge lowering across a mote to a monstrous medieval castle. Higheagle tapped his foot lightly on the gas and drove slowly through the opening and across a curved cobblestone driveway, keeping his eyes fixed on the grand structure soaring above him. The style was Tudor, with steep-pitched roofs of dark greenish-gray slate, glazed tapestry brick walls with limestone trim, elaborate dormers and gables, and colossal chimneys with multiple clay pots. At first, he thought the mansion perfect, but then, he began to take in a few deficiencies. Missing slate tiles on the roof, cracked windows, overgrown vines that seemed inconsistent with the grand exterior. He wondered why Vincenzo Minesali, a man of seemingly unlimited wealth, would allow such imperfections, even if they were trivial.

After parking the War Wagon, he walked up the marble steps and stood before a weighty hardwood front door that held a pair of polished brass knockers. He felt underdressed in his simple beige pants, earth-toned Indian belt, cotton shirt, pointy-toed Western boots, and hair plaited in vermilion in the traditional Cheyenne fashion. He was definitely out of his element here.

Slowly, the huge front door started to open.

Higheagle backed up fractionally.

A man appeared at the door. He was tall, middle-aged, and skin-headed, and, to Higheagle's surprise, he wore not the immaculate formal black attire of a butler, but the checkered pants and white jacket of a chef.

"Mr. Higheagle, please follow me," he said with stiff formality.

The Cheyenne stepped tentatively inside, grappling to comprehend, yet again, the strange alchemy that had brought him here tonight. The man closed the door and bolted it shut with a heavy clunk. Higheagle followed him down a black-and-white checkerboard marble hallway, past two ornate Chippendale chests, and up a winding staircase. Reaching the second floor, they walked through a large room that, at least initially, seemed more incredible than any room Higheagle had ever seen.

The walls were adorned with Italian giftwood sconces and large paintings of rolling farmland and ballet dancers that had to be originals by French Impressionists. A giant fireplace of polished marble was built into the imported English pine paneling along the south wall, and a turn-of-the-century Steinway piano rested in the corner. Napoleon chairs, intricate side tables, and soft floral-patterned couches with needlepoint pillows presided over the gigantic Portuguese rug set in the room's center.

Again, however, Higheagle noticed the subtle imperfections, as he had with the exterior of the mansion. The sunlight-faded paint on the walls, the frays in the rug, the peeling finish on a side table, the accumulating dust. As before, the problems were trivial. But the question still lingered: why would someone so apparently wealthy not take care of these things?

They continued walking until they reached a room with a closed door. The bald-headed servant rapped gently and opened the door part way.

"Sir, I present to you Mr. Higheagle."

Holding his breath, Higheagle stepped inside and came to a halt before the gracefully proffered hand of Vincenzo Minesali.

He was shorter than expected, around five foot seven, and his resemblance to Marlon Brando's Don Corleone was far less than Higheagle had imagined. Though he appeared to be in his mid-eighties, his olive-brown face had less crinkles than many of his generation, the miracle of dark pigment. His dove-white hair was gracefully pomenaded, and his black olive eyes flashed with keen intelligence. His nose was classically Roman and his jaw jutted out prominently. Overall, he radiated an aristocratic aura, standing there in his maroon smoking jacket and black-and-white ascot, his comportment graceful and polished.

Most assuredly, here was a gentleman.

"I appreciate your coming, Mr. Higheagle." He looked at his servant. "Thank you, Mr. Forbes."

"I shall return to my dinner preparations then, sir."

"Of course. We shall dine at eight-thirty."

Forbes gave a stiff nod and closed the door.

"Please sit," Minesali said, waving Higheagle towards a leather chair. "Mr. Forbes is quite indispensable, what you might call a factotum. He serves as master chef, butler, head gardener, social coordinator, and of course, confidant. In fact, there's very little around here he doesn't do."

Higheagle set down his satchel and took his seat. His eyes drifted to the dark oil paintings and old black-and-white photographs on the walls, then to the mahogany bookcase filled with leatherbound books and hand-painted porcelain statuettes of Papal Zouaves with baggy red trousers and fixed bayonets. He felt self-conscious even though Minesali seemed friendly enough. Though he had worked for many wealthy industrial clients over the last several years, he had never before stepped into such an opulent setting.

Taking a seat on the leather couch opposite him, Minesali studied him with an appraising eye.

"You have quite a house, Mr. Minesali," Higheagle said nervously.

"Please, call me Vincenzo." His face carried the wistful glow of someone who understood what made the world and the people in it tick. "It was built in the 1920s by a woman whose husband made a fortune in Silverton's Silver Lake Mine. Legend has it she built the perimeter wall nearly ten feet high to spite her snooty neighbors. Apparently, they gossiped incessantly about her promiscuous past in Silverton's infamous red-light district."

"I can only imagine." He could tell that Minesali had a special way about him that made you feel at ease despite his prodigious wealth.

"I saw your speech on the steps of the Capitol during the Quantrill affair. Remarkable."

Higheagle smiled bashfully. He was still not comfortable with his celebrity status, though he had to admit that without it, he might not have been able to start his own business and probably wouldn't be here tonight.

"You are Cheyenne, are you not?"

"Northern Cheyenne."

The old man's eyes lit up with a pining glow. "Heritage, family history, these are important things. My ancestors immigrated to Colorado almost exactly a century ago. They sailed from Naples to New York and took a train straight west. They became coal miners down near Trinidad and eventually settled at a coal camp near Louisville, outside Boulder."

Higheagle looked up at the ancient photographs on the wall. "Are those them?"

Minesali nodded, staring at one black and white in particular. It showed a group of mourners standing around a pair of wood coffins. The coffins were open for about a quarter of their length, enough to see the jacketed shoulders and carefully groomed heads of two deceased men. At the head of one of the coffins was a little boy, his hands folded in prayer.

"My grandfather and uncle are the men in the coffins. That's my grandmother holding onto the railing and, next to her, my father as a young boy."

The photograph obviously meant a great deal to him. "What happened to them?"

"They were killed by the Colorado National Guard during a miner's strike. They were gunned down in their tents without provocation in what became known as the Ludlow Massacre. It happened just prior to World War One."

"I'm sorry."

"The miners were working fourteen-hour days and dying from cave-ins at an alarming rate, but what really drove them to strike was something else entirely. They were tired of having their lives controlled by CF&I. That's the Colorado Fuel and Iron Company, owned by John Rockefeller, Jr. The company forced them to use its own houses and stores, selected the doctors, teachers, and preachers the miners and their families could use, and told them what books they could read. Like Big Brother, CF&I controlled their lives."

Higheagle saw a combination of gentle power and empathy in the old man and found himself taken by him. "What line of work are you in, Mr. Minesali?"

"Please, call me Vincenzo."

"And you can call me Joe."

"I'm in the agricultural supply business, but I also dabble in real estate and other ventures. Minesali, Inc. is my company. Not the most imaginative name, but it is concise. I have around three thousand employees, including my satellite office in Los Angeles. I don't work full-time anymore. I'm in the process of handing over the reins to others."

"Three thousand people. That's a good-sized company."

"I owe all my success to my employees. They're the ones who have built the business."

"What makes them so productive, if you don't mind my asking? The last two decades haven't exactly been pay dirt for the average American worker."

"Oh, I suppose you could say that I get high productivity from my employees because I pay good wages and have a good profit-sharing program. And because of our high health and safety standards. But I think it has to do with something more fundamental."

"What's that?"

"I treat them like family." He tilted his head towards the black-and-white picture on the wall. "To do that, I have only to remind myself of the struggles of my ancestors and, of course, the wrongs of Rockefeller and the other mineral barons of Colorado's past."

There was a subtle edge of command in his whispery voice, and Higheagle found himself wanting to know more about Vincenzo Minesali. Just talking to him these past few minutes, there was no doubt in his mind that he had led a very interesting life.

They talked on a while longer, until a soft rap appeared at the door. Both men looked up as Forbes poked his head in.

"The dinner preparations are complete, sir."

"Very good, Mr. Forbes." Minesali motioned to his guest. "Shall we?"

Higheagle reached down and picked up his satchel. "I take it during dinner we'll talk business."

Minesali rested his hand on his shoulder, and Higheagle felt an electric tingle, as if he was in the presence of greatness.

"Ah, but we have been discussing business, Joseph—the business of life."

CHAPTER 11

THE DINING ROOM was the size of a small gymnasium and as resplendently furnished as a palace. Higheagle took it all in like a kid in a candy store as they sat down at a mahogany table so gargantuan it could have comfortably seated Queen Elizabeth and the entire royal family. Above, moonlight spilled through the colorful stained glass windows, lending the surroundings a magical, almost sublime aura and throwing beautiful twinkles of light on the polished silverware, glassware, and dark wood floor. A Raphaelesque painting of a Madonna clutching a cherubic infant peered down from one of the walls with classical majesty.

Higheagle liked the way each of Minesali's rooms had its own character and decided someone had put a great deal of thought into the decor of each room.

Forbes poured white wine and followed with cups of rich Vichyssoise. The two diners arranged their napkins, raised fat soup spoons, and began eating. Several minutes into the dinner conversation, Higheagle asked Minesali if there was a woman present in the house. The elderly gentleman explained that his wife, Marguerite, had died of pancreatic cancer three years earlier and he was not interested in remarrying. According to Minesali, his wife had lived only a year after being diagnosed, and that year had been the most exhausting and depressing of his life. Higheagle was deeply moved by Minesali's description of how powerless he had felt in trying to care for her and make her last days more comfortable.

Minesali then went on to describe his three sons and two daughters. They were all living outside Colorado and were married with children. He said they usually visited at Christmas and he was very proud of them, though he wished two of his sons would call and write more often.

After they had finished their cold soup, Forbes brought out the main course: seared Atlantic salmon with herbs de Provence, a multicolored medley of thinly cut steamed vegetables, and a small portion of angel hair pasta with fresh roma tomatoes and capers. They talked more about non-business-related subjects as they ate, and eventually Forbes served a small Caesar salad to cleanse their palettes. Once they finished these, Forbes brought *espresso macchiato*. With the pungent aroma of the java swirling towards the eight-inch crowned moldings of the ceiling, Minesali finally turned to the important matter at hand.

"I want to reiterate what I told you last night," he began. "I have a potential investment opportunity at a planned development in Douglas County near Castle Rock. The name of the development is Silverado Knolls. It's being handled by the same developer who put together Dakota Ranch that I also told you about."

As Higheagle listened, he pulled out a pen and notepad from the satchel at his feet.

"The developer's name is Hayden Prescott. His father was a fraternity brother of mine at Stanford many years ago and is currently a major developer in Southern California. We have kept in touch over the years. I want to invest with his son, but I have some concerns. I have recently discovered that the Colorado Department of Public Health and Environment is conducting a childhood cancer study at Dakota Ranch. I do not mean to imply that Hayden Prescott is involved in anything improper. I simply want a little more reassurance about the situation at Dakota Ranch before investing with him in Silverado Knolls. It seems like a good business opportunity, but I want to be certain that I will not be taking on any environmental liability."

"I'm aware of the Health Department's study at Dakota Ranch. They haven't made anything public yet, but I know they're conducting an investigation into the childhood cancer cases."

"How did you find out about it?"

"I was at Eisenhower Memorial yesterday. I spoke with Dr. Ekstrom, my grandfather's oncologist. My grandfather was there to have some tests done."

"Does he have cancer?"

"We don't know yet. That's what the tests will tell us."

"Dr. Ekstrom…isn't she the one who initially reported the four cancer cases?"

"Yes, that's what she told me." He stroked his chin thoughtfully. "If you don't mind my asking, how did you find out about the Health Department's study? I mean, nothing's been made public yet."

"Let's just say it is necessary for a man in my position to keep abreast of things."

"Well, in that case, I think you'll be interested to know that there's now a fifth cancer case."

Minesali raised an eyebrow. "A fifth? Are you sure?"

"I met the boy and his mother."

"Another boy? Is it certain he has the same cancer as the others?"

"It's the same all right. Medullablastoma—cancer of the brain-stem." He thought of Dr. Ekstrom's bizarre theory about what was happening at Dakota Ranch and wondered if he should tell Minesali about it. After a moment's deliberation, he decided not to lest the old man think he was some kind of conspiracy theorist. But the main thing going through his mind was how in the hell Minesali knew so damned much?

"The boy you met at the hospital…what was his name?"

"Tommy McTavish. His mother's name is Sally."

He watched as Minesali wrote the names down in a small, leatherbound planner he pulled from the pocket of his smoking jacket.

Why the hell does he want to know their names?

When finished writing, Minesali took a sip of his *espresso macchiato* and delicately wiped his upper lip with his napkin. Forbes appeared with dessert, silently placing a fine-looking tiramisu in front of each of them and refilling their cups with espresso before shuffling off.

Minesali picked up his silver dessert fork and took a bite of tiramisu, chewing it slowly. "Before I forget, I have some information that may be helpful. Hayden Prescott had a consultant complete an environmental impact study and a site investigation report before Dakota Ranch was developed." He looked at Higheagle quizzically. "Would investigations such as these be routine?"

"It's not uncommon. Developers do this sort of thing to get a clean bill of health from a regulatory agency for a property. They're trying to get the regulator's buy off in case there's subsequent litigation with homeowners or outside parties. It also raises not only the value of a property, but the credibility of a developer. I wouldn't be surprised if the Health Department prepared some kind of sign-off letter based on the reports submitted before Dakota Ranch was developed. These are things worth looking into. As a matter of fact, I've put together an outline on how I would go about my assessment."

He pulled two copies of his proposal from his satchel and handed one to Minesali, keeping a copy for himself. He watched as Minesali glanced over the outline, hoping the old man would be impressed with his organization and professionalism.

"As you can see, the focus of the assessments would be to identify any potential environmental concerns on the properties. To do that, I would perform the tasks presented here. I'd photocopy regulatory agency records from the Health Department and other agencies. They'll have copies of the environmental impact report and the site investigation report. Plus there will be notes from meetings and internal correspondence. I would also gather aerial photographs covering the site over various time periods to see if there was any evidence of surface spills, drums, tanks, excavations, that sort of thing."

Chewing his tiramisu, Minesali asked, "So this would be the initial stage of the assessment?"

Higheagle nodded. "If I found something, then I could try to figure out how it might tie in with the cancer issue."

"I like what you have presented here. Oh, I just remembered something else. Apparently, Prescott's consultant has recently submitted a report to the Health Department on Silverado Knolls too."

"What kind of report?"

"A combined environmental impact and site investigation report, I'm told. My understanding is that Prescott has already made a deal with the county that if the Health Department approves the report, he will be granted an accelerated construction schedule at Silverado Knolls."

Once again, Higheagle couldn't help but wonder how Minesali had come by such information.

"How long would it take you to conduct your assessments and prepare reports for each property?" the old gentleman then asked him.

"I can have them done in three weeks. Will that work for you?"

"Yes, that will be fine."

They were interrupted as Forbes brought a box of cigars.

"No thank you," Higheagle politely declined.

Minesali reached in the box and plucked out a long, slender Spanish cigar. "One of my three vices, along with fine brandy and betting on horseracing," he said with a smile. Forbes produced a silver Zippo lighter and lit the cigar for him with a surprisingly quick snap of his thumb. Minesali took a puff and blew out a bluish cloud of smoke, then gazed at the cigar appreciatively.

When Forbes returned to the kitchen, Minesali asked Higheagle what his costs would be.

"I'd say around ten thousand dollars. That would include completing EAs on both Dakota Ranch and Silverado Knolls and preparing deliverable reports in three weeks."

"I have a better idea. I will pay you twenty thousand."

Higheagle was rendered speechless.

"Ten thousand now and another ten thousand when you have completed the two reports. And for that price, I would expect them to be perfect."

Is this really fucking happening? Suddenly, he felt like he had just asked the most gorgeous woman in the world out on a date, and she had accepted! "I can get to work on the project immediately. But I'd like to have a contract in place."

Minesali picked up the silver bell resting on the table next to him and tinkled it. Forbes walked through the door almost instantly. "Yes, sir."

"Would you please get the information packet we have prepared for Mr. Higheagle?"

"Very well, sir." Forbes walked off again.

Jesus, is this guy serious or what? But what an opportunity! Twenty thousand bucks for three weeks work! Think of my new business!

Minesali interrupted his cerebral celebration. "I have taken the liberty of preparing an agreement. I was hoping we could go over it and sign it here tonight."

Higheagle gave an approving nod.

A minute later Forbes returned with a legal-sized manila envelope, handed it to his master, and stood off to the side, hands crossed. "The agreement's on top," Minesali said. "Mr. Forbes can incorporate any changes you wish to make tonight so that you can get started tomorrow. You will find maps of each development and other pertinent information in the packets."

Higheagle read over the agreement. He quickly realized that Minesali must have been jotting down detailed notes during their phone conversation the night before. The agreement contained much of the same language. He made a few changes, adding a few more details on the agency files to be reviewed. Once finished, he handed the revised agreement to Minesali, who concurred with the changes and handed it to Forbes. The bald-headed servant shuffled off without a word.

Higheagle found it curious how much Forbes seemed to know about what was going on. He seemed unusually well-briefed and protective of the old man for a house servant, even one with such diverse duties. Higheagle had read about multimillionaires who left everything to a butler, chauffeur, or maid rather than sycophantic family members and wondered if Forbes was set to receive millions from Minesali when the old man passed on.

Soon Forbes returned with two copies of the agreement. Higheagle read over both and signed them. He then tucked his copy into the manila envelope in front of him and put the folder in his satchel, while Minesali made out a check for ten thousand dollars.

"I am truly grateful to you, Joseph, for performing this service for me. I should remind you though, anything you find is strictly confidential. Any correspondence, including your final reports, should have the legal wording shown on the second page in your packet."

Higheagle pulled out the page Minesali was referring to and read it over: "CONFIDENTIAL—ATTORNEY/CLIENT PRIVILEGE AND WORK PRODUCT PROTECTED DOCUMENT-Prepared according to the attorney/client, work product and critical self-analysis privileges, in anticipation of litigation and subject to limited distribution."

It was the standard legal disclaimer, but still Higheagle was surprised. "Are you expecting this to go into litigation?"

"One always has to be prepared for such an eventuality."

"In that case, I'll make sure the wording is on every written document," Higheagle said, but in his head he heard a different warning. *You'd better not fuck this up! This guy has endless resources at his disposal and expects serious results!*

Minesali rose from his chair, which Higheagle took as a signal the meeting was finished.

"Thank you very much for dinner, Mr. Minesali. And thank you, Mr. Forbes, for your hospitality."

The servant nodded blandly.

"It was our pleasure," said Minesali, and he took him by the arm and led him towards the red-carpeted staircase. "Now why don't you give me a status report in a few days. Just to keep me in the loop, of course."

"I will. And don't hesitate to contact me for any reason."

They shook hands and Forbes led him down the sweeping staircase. At the bottom of the stairs, Higheagle glanced back at the imperturbable Minesali, looming above him like an Italian nobleman sending off an armada into uncharted waters. Higheagle knew he was the seaman who was supposed to weather the tempests and murky unknown ahead. But he didn't anticipate such melodrama.

His biggest worry was that he would be unable to fulfill the expectations of his new gold-plated client that had just dropped twenty thousand dollars into his lap.

CHAPTER 12

VIC SHARD brought his Jeep Grand Cherokee to a halt in the parking lot of the Denver Country Club and groaned as he pulled his creaky-kneed body from the seat. Hitting the automatic door lock, he ambled towards the entrance of the expansive dark gray, white-trimmed clubhouse. The mingled aromas of blue spruce and pine rose up to greet him as his pointy-toed Justin boots tapped against the concrete walkway.

A doorman bedecked in maroon coattails, black striped pants, and a bellman's hat recognized him and moved quickly to open the door for him. Tipping his white straw cowboy hat to the doorman, Shard shuffled inside and tromped up an elegantly appointed staircase that led to an exquisitely decorated foyer. From here, he veered right down a hallway lined with pictures of mounted English aristocrats loping after foxes, shuttling about in carriages, and firing guns at colorfully-plumed waterfowl. He shuffled past a series of intricately carved wood benches and walls gleaming with golf plaques, eventually arriving at the darkly wooded entrance to the Member's Grill. Taking a sharp left, he walked into the Card Room, his gunmetal-gray eyes coming to rest on Hayden Prescott, who had just set down a copy of the *Wall Street Journal*.

Vic Shard didn't look much like a private investigator. In fact, his somewhat careless and rugged appearance invoked more the impression of a participant in the National Western Rodeo than one of the most highly coveted sleuths in the Mile High City. Stocky, bow-legged, goateed, and sun-burnished like a wrangler, Shard was known to pack a thick wad of Copenhagen longcut chewing tobacco into his lip from time to time and was said to love nothing else in the world, next to his wife and three children, more than dry fly trout fishing. The only outward evidence of his exalted passion were the Royal Wulff and Hare's Ear Soft Hackle flies hooked into the rattlesnake band of the cowboy hat that rarely departed his head. He had logged nearly twenty years with the Denver Police Department before launching his own private investigation firm in the mid-nineties, and was reported to enjoy wearing disguises as part of his tradecraft.

Prescott rose to his feet, summoning Shard forward. They shook hands. Prescott glanced at two men playing backgammon nearby and silently motioned Shard towards the closed French doors.

Stepping outside onto the veranda, they took seats in a pair of cushioned wooden chairs overlooking a row of towering elms and a pair of tennis courts. In the distance loomed the first tee box of the venerable golf course, one of the Front Range's oldest and finest. The sounds of tennis rackets swatting fuzzy projectiles and two-hundred-dollar sneakers screeching across the hard courts drifted up from below. Shard pulled out a small notebook, set it on his lap, and took a moment to study his client, who was staring off, with a pernicious glint in his eye, at a comely young woman in a white tennis skirt bending over to pick up a ball.

After a moment, Prescott tore his gaze from the young hotty and glanced over the railing of the veranda to make sure no one was within earshot. Then he leaned back in his chair, smoothing a hand across his crisply pleated pant leg.

"Talk to me, Vic."

The private detective withdrew two sheets of paper from his notebook, handed one to Prescott, and took a moment to look his sheet over. "Been talking to my little bird inside the Colorado Department of Public Health and Environment. He says the notification came from a Dr. Ekstrom at Eisenhower Memorial. The Health Department's been investigating for a month now. Four kids have died, all in the last nine months. They're calling it a 'potential cancer excess event.' They're still in what's called Stage One, initial contact and response. They've compiled basic information on the cases: name, sex, age, race, diagnosis, date of death, address, length of time in residence, physician con—"

"There's no new reported cases?"

"Not unless something's happened since last Friday."

"That seems unlikely. Go on."

Shard read further down the page. "Let's see. Two of the families have moved. The Haskells and Johnsons. Jamie Haskell was the first to get sick. He died nine months ago. He was thirteen. There's a picture of him in the file, along with the other boys. The parents moved back to Boston three months ago. The father's from back there."

"What about the other family that moved?"

"That would be the Johnsons. Their son was Alex, age eleven, only child. He died about six months ago. The parents moved to the Western Slope...Montrose. They've been interviewed by the Health Department and I have a copy of what they said."

"What about the two families still living at Dakota Ranch?"

"Well, first there's John and Mary Wilkins. Their son Todd was eleven when he died just two months ago. They have two other kids. Live on Ute City Road."

"And the other family?"

"The Parsons. Parents are divorced. The father, Jack, lives alone on Ash Street. The son's name is Cody, age nine. Died a month and a half ago."

Shard watched as Prescott ran his fingers anxiously across his smooth silk tie. "Did the families live close to one another?"

"All within a half mile before they moved."

"These kids...did they all have the same type of cancer?"

"Medullablastoma, cancer of the brain stem. About as rare a cancer as there is."

Shard stopped right there as the sound of shuffling feet and laughter sliced through the air. Prescott peered over the edge of the railing at the pair of caddies snapping dirty DCC towels at one another in front of the metal golf-bag rack. The developer looked a little jumpy; Shard couldn't blame him, given the clandestine nature of their conversation.

"This thing sounds like an epidemic. Are you sure there aren't any more cases?"

"Like I said, I checked with the Health Department and all the area hospitals on Friday. There were no new reported cases then. I suppose there—"

"Just check again at the end of next week." Prescott stared over the railing again, and Shard noticed the worry lines on his face. "I can't believe this is happening right when I'm getting Silverado off the ground. Summer will be here soon and I need to start construction."

"My little bird seems to think the environmental impact and site investigation report will be approved by the end of the month."

"That's some consolation, I suppose," Prescott said without much conviction.

Shard pulled out his tin of Copenhagen and wadded up a chew of longcut, packing it into his upper lip with his tongue. On the far court, a tennis-ball machine began firing like a mortar in the direction of a pot-bellied man with ridiculously skinny white legs. Shard thought how fun it would be to grab the ball machine and rip off a few rounds at the Mercedes, Beamers, and Volvos racing down Speer Boulevard.

Prescott leaned forward again, eyes leveling on Shard. "What has the Health Department come up with so far on the cancer?"

"They're still trying to confirm if this thing is a true statistical excess. Apparently, they've come under a lot of fire from the EPA recently, so they're moving cautiously, trying to keep the investigation under wraps. They don't want the feds looking over their shoulder or taking over the study. They're still sore at the EPA for overstepping its authority on the Petroco Refinery and other enforcement actions. The Health Department, it seems, is a little less enthusiastic about collecting fines for haz waste violations than its federal counterpart."

"So they're being cautious. That's why they've been moving so slowly. Who's in charge of the investigation?"

"Guy named Markworth."

"Dan Markworth?"

"You know him?"

"I'm working with him on Silverado Knolls. But he's not an epidemiologist. He's the director of the Haz Mat-Waste Management Division. I'm surprised he's heading up the investigation. I would have expected it to be handled by their Epidemiology Group."

Shard rifled through his notepad, nodding his head when he found the right page. "He's a toxicologist by training and high up in the hierarchy over there."

"It's not that I have a problem with Markworth. He was happy with the site investigation work we did out at Dakota. I'm just surprised he's handling this cancer thing."

"As of now, the Health Department doesn't have a clue as to the cause. But they do have a passel of people working on it."

"Including your man inside. So what are you saying?"

"That there's more than a fifty-fifty chance these folks could come up with something that could prove non-beneficial to your interests."

Prescott stared off thoughtfully, mulling over his options. "I appreciate your candor, Vic. What do you think the next step should be?"

Shard pulled at his bushy goatee, generously flecked with silver. "I think you should give old Bishop a ring, find out if he's really worth that five hundred an hour you pay him. And while you're at it, call those friends of yours in the state legislature. They control the purse strings of the Health Department."

"Where's this coming from, PI instinct?"

"All I know is if you factor in public sentiment and the power of the Internet, there's a chance this thing could turn into something as ugly as a scrapyard dog."

"Scrapyard dog you say?"

"Yes, Hayden. I'm talking about the kind of mangy canine that sneaks up and bites off half your ass before you know what hit you."

CHAPTER 13

"JUST SIT BACK AND RELAX, HONEY," Sally McTavish said encouragingly. "This is going to make you better."

"I know it will, Mom," replied Tommy, though inside he wasn't so sure.

He searched the face of the gaunt radiation therapy technician standing next to the treatment table, looking for some sign one way or the other, but there was nothing. Wordlessly, the technician leaned over the radiation treatment table and nudged him an inch to the right.

"I think you can wait outside now, Mrs. McTavish. We'll be finished in just a few minutes."

Tommy looked at his mom. He could tell she didn't want to leave. To make her feel better, he reached out and took her hand. "You go on. I'll be okay."

She clutched his hand tightly.

"It's okay, Mom. Really." He could see the tears gathering force behind her eyelids and wished she wouldn't cry. She had been crying so much the past few days it made him sad. "Don't worry—everything's going to be okay."

She kissed him on the forehead, turned hesitantly away, walked to the door. When she reached it, she turned around. He didn't really want her to leave, but he wanted to appear strong so he gave a thumbs-up sign.

"Go on. I'll be fine."

She responded with a thumbs-up of her own, but he knew that as soon as she left the room she would break down and cry.

The door closed and there was a crushing silence.

Feeling an overwhelming emptiness, he told himself not to cry.

"You want some music like the last time?" the technician asked him.

"What?"

"Music. Do you want some?"

"Sure," he said half-heartedly.

"What do you want to hear?"

"Anything but the Jonas Brothers."

The technician smiled. "I can do that."

He adjusted Tommy's position a final time then stepped away from the treatment table to the CD player in the adjacent room. Searching for something light and innocuous, the technician quickly settled on Jackson Browne. He pulled out the CD, placed it in the machine, adjusted the volume to a low setting, and returned to the radiation treatment room as the opening melody of *Take It Easy* came through the ceiling speakers above the treatment couch.

"This is your first session so let me go through the procedure with you. First off, I want you to breathe normally and try not to move during the treatment. The x-ray beam will be passing through those narrow little treatment areas we marked on your head—the portals—so it's important that you remain still. Each pass will take about three minutes. I'll direct the beam from the back first, then to the side. It'll take about a minute and a half for each. You'll be getting about a hundred eighty radiation units this session, so you'll be hot to trot. Are you ready?"

Tommy could feel his stomach twisting in knots, but he wasn't about to let the technician know how terrified he was. "Yep, I'm ready," he said, as bravely as he could manage.

"All right then." The man pushed his glasses up his sharp nose and walked into the next room.

Tommy heard a mechanical clicking sound and closed his eyes in surrender as the focused beam of x-rays passed imperceptibly through the lower portion of his head. He kept perfectly still and tried to imagine that he was cranking down bumps at Breckenridge instead of being bombarded with x-rays from a linear accelerator machine. He hated being here—hated the paper thin hospital gown, the synthetic smell of plastic and cleaning fluids, the white blandness of it all. He was old enough to know what dehumanizing meant, and this was definitely it. He felt weak and sick and powerless to control his own destiny; and he couldn't help but wonder if he had any real chance of surviving this horrible thing that was growing inside his head.

Am I really going to die? he wondered. *Am I really going to die like this?*

CHAPTER 14

HIGHEAGLE fiddled with his pen as he sat waiting in a conference room at the Colorado Department of Public Health and Environment. The room was a testament to the brutal efficiency of government cutbacks: aseptic white walls, bland office furnishings that had to have been around since the Reagan era, frayed and heavily stained carpets, cardboard boxes piled six deep in the corner. The smell of cheap disinfectant and recycled air permeated the room, lending it the stagnancy of a Louisiana swamp.

Higheagle had called Dan Markworth yesterday to schedule an appointment to review the Dakota Ranch files and was waiting expectantly for the director of the Hazardous Materials and Waste Management Division to join him.

Three minutes later, Markworth walked in, leather-bound daytimer in hand. They had worked together on several soil and groundwater remediation projects during the last six years, and had gone out for dinner and beers a few times during local haz mat conferences. As Higheagle rose from his seat, they shook hands. The transplanted Ohioan stood at least a half a head shorter than the Cheyenne and was alabaster-skinned, four-eyed, mustached, and, judging by his ponderous paunch, losing badly in the war against middle age.

Greetings exchanged, they settled into cheap plastic chairs set about the wood grain laminate conference table. Higheagle reiterated what he had told Markworth over the phone, how he was performing environmental assessments at Dakota Ranch and the pending Silverado Knolls development for a potential investor. When he was finished, he was surprised to see Markworth's eyes narrowing on him.

"Thanks for the overview, Joe. Now before I let you take a look at those files"—he pointed a stubby finger at the cardboard boxes on the table—"you're going to have to agree to a few ground rules."

"Ground rules?"

"Regarding how you and I exchange information. Until I've determined whether we have a real statistical excess on our hands, we're going by my playbook."

"Your playbook?"

"That's right. One in three Americans gets cancer in their lifetime. That's a regrettable but indisputable fact of life. But to the uninformed citizens out there, and the overzealous media that feeds their paranoia, every incidence is due to chemical exposure. That's the reality I have to deal with. And I know from that Quantrill business how quickly you can rally the media to your side."

Higheagle held up his hands. "Hold on a second here, Dan. This isn't—"

"I've also got the EPA to consider," Markworth cut him off, undeterred. "They've been ripping our Enforcement Branch. They think we've been too slow in collecting fines from our esteemed local Fortune 500 polluters, and they're probably right, though you didn't hear it from me. I'm not about to give them a reason to look over our shoulder, publically bash us, or steal the job from us. These cancer projects are sensitive enough as it is. That's why you and I need some basic ground rules. And by the way, they're non-negotiable."

This was definitely not CDPHE standard operating procedure. *I'm not going to say it to your face, Dan, but the word that comes to mind is 'paranoid.'* "All right, tell me how you want to handle it," he said diplomatically, knowing he would get nothing if he didn't cooperate.

"I want you, off the record and unofficially, to keep me informed of what you find out about Dakota Ranch and Silverado Knolls."

"I don't know if I can do that. I signed a confidentiality agreement."

"You don't have to tell me who your client is. But you have to keep me posted on everything you find out and talk to no one but me. Or you don't get access to the files or what I keep stored up here." He pointed to his oversized Charlie Brown head. "Do we have a deal?"

"Do I have a choice?"

"Unfortunately for you, no. So are we clear on the ground rules?"

"Yeah. But I've got to be honest, you're sounding a little cloak-and-dagger."

"I'm afraid that's the way it's got to be." He sat back in his chair. "So what do you want to know?"

"Why don't we start with what you've heard about Hayden Prescott?"

"Besides that he's Mr. All-American Denver Businessman and lives in Cherry Hills next door to Elway? Well, I can tell you that he's not popular with the environmentalists, but what developer is? He's been very proactive on Dakota Ranch. He performed a detailed environmental impact report and a site investigation report before developing the property. He was only required by our office to do the impact report. He did the SI on his own a couple years ago, right after the impact report came out."

Higheagle began jotting down notes. "So, from your standpoint, it was a thorough study?"

"Best report to come across my desk until this new report on Silverado. Prescott's consultant sampled all of the drinking water wells four times and analyzed for every Appendix Nine chemical under the sun: VOCs, SVOCs, TPH, metals, pesticides, herbicides, dioxins, PCBs, you name it. Collected a hell of a lot of soil samples, too, using a stats-based random sampling program. The only things found were low levels of motor oil and, of course, background metals."

"Who handled the investigation?"

Markworth flicked up the pointy tip of his mustache with his forefinger, a nervous habit most people, including Higheagle, found irritating. "I can't remember the name of the consultant that actually did the fieldwork, but Doug Hwong's outfit designed the sampling program and ran the analytical."

"Doug Hwong, the owner of Arapaho Technologies?"

"Yeah."

"That's interesting." In Higheagle's view, Hwong's involvement brought a certain analytical rigor and credibility to the study. He was, quite simply, renowned the world over for statistical sampling, analytical methods, quality assurance/quality control, and chemical fingerprinting, and he had served as a scientific expert witness on a large number of high-profile environmental court cases.

"Hwong's sampling program was state-of-the-art. He set up a fancy polygonal grid and used a random number generator to pick the sample locations. He collected over a hundred samples at predetermined cells within the grid, had them analyzed, and calculated ninety-five percent upper confidence limits on every detected analyte. Even if it had been a Superfund site, the EPA wouldn't have required more sampling than what was done. Place looked like Swiss cheese."

"What about air samples?"

"Prescott's consultant took some random samples of ambient air and found nothing."

"Arapaho handled all of the analyses?"

"As I recall."

"So there were no chemicals detected in the groundwater or air samples?"

"Nothing except for background levels of metals in the groundwater."

"Hmm."

"Hmm, that's all you have to say? Why, Joe, if I didn't know you better, I'd say you sound like a dyed-in-the-wool skeptic."

"No, I'm just surprised nothing was detected is all."

"Way out on the prairie? I don't think it's surprising at all. In fact, it seems to me like your client's getting all worked up over nothing."

"Why, Dan, if I didn't know better, I'd say you sound like the PR director for The Newport Company. Have you been taking night classes at DU Law?"

"I'm just telling you, there wasn't a single chemical detected in the air, soil, or groundwater at Dakota at a level that would pose even a ten to the minus nine cancer risk. That's less than one in a billion. Dakota Ranch was clean as a whistle. We had to give Prescott a clean bill of health. The guy always goes above and beyond what any of the other developers are doing. At Dakota, he insisted on not beginning surveying, grading, or construction until we approved the reports, aside from some minor staging-area grading work and road-building."

"So you gave him approval to do light grading and roadwork?"

"Yeah. What, you've got a problem with that?"

"No," he responded, though he thought it important enough to write down. "What can you tell me about this planned Silverado Knolls development?"

"We're in the process of reviewing the environmental impact and investigation report. Hwong's group did the bulk of the work, all of the sampling-related stuff. They subbed out to an ecological consultant for the environmental impact part of the report, just like Dakota. It's a collaborative effort, but Hwong's the lead."

"Is there a copy of the report in the files here?"

"No. The report is still under review."

"Can I have it copied along with these records?"

Markworth glanced at the files on the table. "I don't see why not. I have an extra set in my office."

"Is it true Prescott will be approved for an accelerated construction schedule at Silverado from Douglas County once your office signs off on the reports?"

The blood seemed to drain from Markworth's face. "I don't know anything about that." He licked his livery lips and shifted in his seat, obviously uncomfortable with the direction the conversation was taking. "Joe, I've got to be honest with you. The way you're talking here sounds like a Spanish Inquisition, not a standard run-of-the-mill EA. Why are you doing this?"

"I'm just being thorough." He decided to switch gears again. "You know, I met this kid the other day. He's the newest Dakota cancer case."

Markworth's jaw dropped. "But...but they're all dead."

"Not this kid. He's the fifth reported case and he's very much alive. Don't tell me the hospital hasn't contacted you?"

Shaking his head, Markworth wrote furiously in his daytimer. "When did you see him?"

"Couple days ago."

"That must be why we haven't been notified yet. The hospitals don't contact us until the results are hard copied. Sometimes it takes weeks. What's the kid's name?"

"McTavish—Tommy McTavish. I met him and his mom at the hospital." He wondered whether to tell him about Dr. Ekstrom's bizarre theory. He decided to keep it to himself for the time being; Markworth appeared to be in no mood to entertain wild theories.

"This is all news to me, Joe. And I'm the Dakota Ranch program director and community relations contact." He glanced irritably at his wristwatch and frowned. "I've got a meeting in a few minutes. Are you going to look over the files or just have them all copied?"

"I'll look through them first, in case I need some special color or oversize xeroxing done."

Higheagle watched as Markworth pulled two business cards from his pocket and handed them to him. "All right, you know the drill. Here are the two bonded copier services we use. They'll take about a day to copy the files. I'll have my assistant bring over the Silverado report so you can have it copied too." He snapped his daytimer shut and rose from his chair.

Higheagle stood up. "Thanks for giving me some background on this thing."

"Don't forget our deal. You tell me everything you learn about Dakota and Silverado, and in return, I give you access to our files and keep you posted on the Dakota cancer study."

"Seems a bit one-sided, don't you think? I give you confidential information and, in return, you give me stuff that any person off the street can get his hands on."

"Everyone's gonna be looking over our shoulders on this one, Joe. It's got to be one-sided—at least until I know what the hell we're dealing with out there."

CHAPTER 15

HAYDEN WINTHROP PRESCOTT III stepped up to the window of his lavishly furnished office at the Denver Tech Center. He had just explained to the two men seated in front of his desk about the cancer situation at Dakota Ranch and that the Health Department was conducting a study into its cause. He was waiting for their reaction to the news, mulling over the possibilities with his characteristic focused intensity.

"It's easy to disprove any relationship between cancer and a specific exposure," said Doug Hwong, PhD, with a scientifically authoritative air.

Armani-clad attorney Gregory Bishop was quick to counter him. "But in a trial setting, where emotions run high and scientific data is reduced to the lowest possible denominator, it might not be so difficult to demonstrate a connection."

Prescott turned away from the window and looked at the world-renowned geochemist and Director of Arapaho Technologies. "But I thought there were no proven causes of childhood cancer."

"There aren't really," answered Hwong. "But some studies have shown that, among children and parents of children with specific types of cancer, certain exposure events occur more frequently than among normal populations. Epidemiologists call these 'probable risk factors' because if an exposure has occurred, the child may be at greater risk for cancer."

"So these are like events that scientists think may contribute to a kid developing cancer, but they're not absolutely certain."

"Precisely." Hwong's thin lips curved into a self-complimentary smile. "For childhood brain cancers, there are a lot of probable risk factors. You've got exposure to chemicals and paints, sidestream cigarette smoke, parental use of diuretics and heavy make-up, consumption of cured meats, prenatal radiation, infections during pregnancy, among others. That's a lot of factors in addition to those in the children themselves. That is, factors resulting from diet, lifestyle, natural genetic mutation, and hormones."

Prescott looked at Bishop. Brilliantine-haired, middle-aged, and paunchy, he was a senior partner at Anderson, Milton, which had presided over downtown Denver since the turbulent silver boom days and was supposedly of equal caliber to the most expensive law firms in New York, Washington, and Los Angeles. Clearing some scale from his bulbous throat, the attorney then ventured, "The question is which of these factors could have played a role at Dakota Ranch?"

"No," countered Prescott, "the real question is which of these factors is the Health Department going to consider?"

"They're certainly going to investigate chemical exposure," said Hwong.

"But I thought the only cancer events definitively linked to specific chemicals involved plant workers."

"That's true. And the reason is in occupational settings the dosages are so high. Like leukemia among workers exposed to benzene, and lung cancer among those working with asbestos on a regular basis. Non-occupational, on the other hand, is a totally different ball game. There have been virtually no community cancer clusters where a proven chemical cause has been discovered. Between the Kennedy and Bush Two administrations, the Centers for Disease Control and Prevention studied over two hundred cancer clusters from every state and several foreign countries. And you know what they found? Not one case where it was one-hundred-percent conclusive that chemicals were the primary cause of the cancer. Not one."

"But case studies have come out in the last few years showing long-term or chronic exposure to low doses are suspect causes," Bishop pointed out. He then turned to his client in a didactic pose. "These are exposures that have not been scientifically validated, but preliminary evidence suggests exposure to certain chemicals may contribute to the cancer."

Prescott considered: *This is the part that scares the shit out of me. Could this have happened at Dakota? And if so, can it be proved in a court of law?*

"It's unlikely the kids could have contracted cancer from dermal contact," said Hwong. "Plus there are no contaminated water supply wells on the property, so water ingestion is out. That leaves soil ingestion and inhalation. They're high risk pathways, but I still can't imagine how these kids could be exposed above a ten to the minus six carcinogenic risk. Unless you've got high occupational levels, or prolonged exposure to low levels, the probability is extremely low."

Prescott wasn't completely convinced by Hwong's argument, even though it seemed plausible. He looked at Bishop. "Tell me about these case studies."

"Well, first you've got the drinking water cases: Toms River, New Jersey. Woburn, Mass. Winona, Texas. Port St. Lucie, Florida. There's a consensus that carcinogenic VOCs in drinking water contributed to the childhood cancer clusters in these cases. Then you've got the smoking-related cluster events. Like West Contra Costa County, California, where there was a high incidence of lung cancer. There are also the high renal cancer cases among certain ethnic groups in Minnesota that eat a lot of meat and smoked food, and the elevated breast cancer rates on Long Island."

"What about the ones involving kids?"

"There's a bunch. Rochester, New York. Christian County, Illinois. McFarland, California—"

"Don't forget Rosamond," Hwong said.

"Yeah, and Rosamond. That's in So Cal too. But Doug's right. In most of these cases, a specific chemical cause has never been proven, even though there's a high incidence of cancer."

Prescott looked at Hwong. "Could chemical exposure be what's happening at Dakota?"

"It's possible, but as I said before, there are so many factors that increase cancer risk. The childhood brain cancer rate at Rosamond was six times the national average. I don't know that the incidence of cancer at Dakota is any higher than the national average. And there are always statistical anomalies, outliers of data that can't be resolved. After more than twenty-five years of study, the DTSC still hasn't found an environmental cause for Rosamond. The media, general public, and personal injury lawyers are the only ones that don't understand cancer clusters are more likely to result from chance alone than chemicals in the environment. It's a fucking myth that pollution is the leading cause of cancer clusters."

"Yeah, but unfortunately perception is reality." Prescott turned to his attorney. "How would you go about defending this case, if you had to, Greg?"

"The main goal in situations like these is not to attack the credibility of the opposition's experts, but to go after the sampling protocols, analytical methods, and the reproducibility of the results. Try to plant a seed of doubt in the judge or jury's mind that the correct procedures weren't followed."

"Doug?"

"Refute any statistical and epidemiological relationships the opposition tries to establish between the cancer and chemicals. And shatter any doubt that one could reasonably be expected to know of the carcinogenicity of the chemicals in question."

"If the opposition can prove both of those things," said Bishop, "then it can prove wrongful death based on a preponderance of evidence. Assuming it's a civil case."

Prescott took a doleful breath, letting it out slowly. "And murder beyond a reasonable doubt if it's criminal."

"But the chances of that happening are less than one in a million. There's really only one thing certain about these cancer cluster cases, chemically-induced or not."

"Yeah, what's that?"

"Once the cluster is identified, the cancer itself generally stops pretty quickly. Maybe it's because polluters get more cautious, or because the chemicals causing the cancer are biodegrading or attenuating by other natural means in the environment. The bottom line is that a lot of these so-called *cancer clusters* are chance phenomena, which run their course by the time scientists have determined their presence and the concentrations of the chemicals involved."

"So what does that mean in this case?"

The lawyer gave a crooked smile. "Hopefully, that no more kids get cancer. That way the Health Department won't have a large enough sample population to prove a goddamned thing."

CHAPTER 16

VINCENZO MINESALI snored deeply from the couch in his study, an open three-ring binder resting on his lap.

Even in a somnolent state, the old gentleman looked positively dapper. Silver cuff links gleamed at the wrists of his monogrammed shirt. A sleek tie bearing a Cubist design reminiscent of several Picasso works snuck down his gently expanding chest. Gray, cuffed suit pants hung comfortably over sparkling burnt-sienna dress shoes, which, like the apparel enveloping Minesali's slender frame and the jacket resting on the couch next to him, were custom-designed in Turin, Italy.

The sun was fading beyond the massive Front Range to the west, throwing thin streaks of light past the airy silk curtains at the window. Minesali had returned from the office an hour earlier and was, at the moment, unaware of Forbes tiptoeing towards him. The multifarious house servant carefully pried the binder loose from Minesali's hands, closed it, and set it on the side table. Shaking his head disapprovingly, he then edged quietly towards the door.

Minesali raised a fluttering eyelid. "Is that you, Forbes?"

The Welshman halted and spoke in a whisper. "Yes, sir. I didn't want to wake you."

Minesali rubbed the sleep from his ancient, baggy eyes. Then he glanced around as if he had lost something. It took him a moment to locate the binder on the side table next to a pair of porcelain snuffboxes. Curiously, the binder didn't contain anything relating to Minesali's work, but rather clippings from the *Denver Post* and various scientific articles. Breathing a sigh of relief, Minesali set the binder on the couch next to him.

"If you don't mind me saying so, sir, I think it's time you move on with...things."

Minesali shifted on the black leather couch. "You believe I've become consumed?"

Forbes stepped forward into the dappled sunlight sneaking through the window. White rays danced off his slick bald head, flickering like distant stars. "The mind has a way, sir, of not letting go of its grip—even when it is most advisable to do so."

"What if I don't want to let go?"

"But you must. Day after day you are like this. There must be some resolution."

"There will be."

"With Mr. Higheagle, I suppose." He said the words as if purging a nasty taste from his mouth, flicking his employer a look of mild exasperation. "You seem to carry an unnecessary burden, sir. It's not healthy. At your age, you should be enjoying yourself, not brooding needlessly."

"Why you sound like a doting wife. Are you truly worried for me?"

"If I may speak frankly, sir?"

"You always do."

"To be perfectly candid, sir, I think it's time for the man of the house to seek a companion."

Minesali resisted the urge to roll his eyes. *Forbes does look after me so. A new wife? Such nonsense. He truly has outdone himself this time. I don't know what I'd do without him. It's almost as if I never lost Marguerite—*

"It's the right course of action, sir."

"So you believe a woman is the cure for what ails me. How about if I bring home a twenty-two year old vixen? Would that satisfy you?"

"You know that's not what I mean, sir. I was thinking of a longer-term companion...someone with a bit more...refinement. Perhaps Mrs. Landau or Mrs. Xavier."

"Ah, yes, the widows." Minesali chuckled to himself. "Somehow, it sounds a bit ridiculous for a man my age to be on the prowl for a wife."

"Many men do it, sir."

"What you hope for is a replacement for Mrs. Minesali. Tough shoes to fill, I must say."

"All widowers say these things, sir. But when they make the effort to meet someone new, they often find fulfillment. And you know that men who remarry after losing a wife in their later years live on average at least two years longer."

"So to extend my time here on earth, I should find a new bride. I suppose that prospect would be more rewarding than a life-support system."

"I am not referring to just any woman, sir. What I had in mind is a patron of the arts like yourself, a woman of substance and culture. A woman who can, at a mere glance, distinguish Monet from Manet and is intimately familiar with Classical literature and the varied flora of your beloved greenhouse. I am certain it is the only way for you to put this sad business behind you. You seem to have a great deal of faith in this...Higheagle." He wrinkled his nose as if he had just caught a whiff of something malodorous. "Let him perform his service while you engage yourself in more, shall we say, lighthearted and amorous pursuits."

"With you around to coddle me, Forbes, I should think I hardly need a new bride. But I will take your advice, and try to refrain from, as you say, brooding needlessly."

"Very good, sir." He turned on the faded but costly Oriental rug and started for the door.

"Uh, Forbes."

"Yes, sir." He turned around.

"You needn't look upon our plait-haired friend with such a dubious air."

"He did seem a bit uncertain, sir, regarding the possible outcome of the enterprise."

"It was calculated. He knows how difficult matters of this nature are to resolve."

Forbes appeared unconvinced. "As long as you have faith in him, sir. But to be quite honest, when I first saw the big red fellow, I could not help but imagine him as a wild savage gallivanting about the high plains buck naked save for a breechcloth, a few streaks of war paint, and a bow and quiver of arrows strapped across his back."

"That's quite an image, Forbes," observed Minesali, amused with his factotum's jaded perspective of the Cheyenne.

"I just hope he's not out spending your retainer by swigging shooters at the Campus Lounge, Cherry Cricket, or some other such establishment of depravity."

Minesali chuckled. "You obviously don't have a good feel for him, do you?"

"Feel for him, sir?"

"If you had seen him speak in front of the Capitol last year, you would not so easily underestimate our Cheyenne friend. No, our recently baptized entrepreneur is cut from a different cloth: that of a man who rises each and every day with something to prove."

"And what on earth would that be?"

"His heritage means everything to him. You must remember that, in his eyes, his actions do not merely reflect upon himself, but upon his people, his tribe. And not just those living today, but his ancestors going back all the way to the time of Lewis and Clark when the Cheyenne first became a nomadic horse people."

"So you trust that, when the time comes, he'll do the right thing?"

"Yes I do, my good man. Yes I do, indeed."

CHAPTER 17

HIGHEAGLE sat at his antique pine desk in his home office, finishing sorting through a set of low-altitude aerial photographs. Simply yet tastefully furnished, the room served a triple function as work place, library, and quiet refuge.

One of the bookcases was packed with arcane scientific journals like *Ground Water Monitoring & Remediation*, *Journal of Hydrology*, and *Soil & Groundwater Cleanup*, as well as more than fifty textbooks with titles like *Applied Numerical Modeling*, *Dinosaur Paleoecology*, *Greenhouse Gas Policy*, and *Subsurface Fate and Transport Processes*. The other smaller bookcase next to his desk provided an escape from the quantitative: works by Vine Deloria, Peter Mathieson, Russell Means, N. Scott Momaday, Dee Brown, Sherman Alexie, and Thomas Berger were well represented, reflecting Higheagle's proclivity for books about Native Americans and the West.

Hanging from the wall was a panel of four colored drawings from the late 1860s rendered by his great-great grandfather High Eagle, a respected Cheyenne Kit Fox warrior and, in his later years, statesman. The panel, entitled "Fighting the Wolf Men," depicted a running battle between High Eagle and several other resplendently painted Cheyenne warriors and their hated enemies the Pawnees, culminating in the daring rescue of the Dog Soldier Chief Red Wolf with arrows and bullets zipping overhead. Rarely a day went by where Higheagle didn't sit and gaze at the remarkable drawings, pondering the many coups and battles won by his venerable ancestors.

He finished sorting the aerials. There were about eighty stereoscopic pairs of photographs, all glossy black-and-whites depicting both Dakota Ranch and Silverado Knolls. He had chosen a representative suite from the Denver Aerial Map Gallery so he could reconstruct land use at both properties. For each property, he picked two aerials from each decade from 1930 to 1990 and every aerial from 1990 to the most recent flight in March 2009. He also had in front of him a pair of USGS topographic quadrangle maps, upon which he'd hand drawn the boundaries of the two developments. He began studying the photographs, starting with Dakota.

He set each pair of aerials side by side and mounted the stereoscope on top of them. Each of the paired photographs had been taken from the plane performing the survey at slightly different angles; when they were viewed simultaneously through the stereoscope, the images entered the eyes separately and produced an enlarged, three-dimensional image. Peering through the device, what he saw was the pre- and post-development Dakota Ranch in all her geomorphic glory. Small drainages, hillocks, and houses stood out prominently and were easily distinguished by his well-trained eyes.

For a half hour, he studied the twelve pre-development aerials of Dakota Ranch. The land had been used for cattle grazing from August 1935, the date of the oldest aerial, through at least May 2005, the date of the last aerial before substantial roads had been built in the area. In the photographs covering the seventy-year period, he was able to identify a small ranch house, a pair of barns, several feed lots, and a single unpaved road leading to the house.

There were two major drainages visible through the three-dimensional stereoscope. The bigger of the two was along the property's west fence line. The surface of the drainage was black with a white glossy sheen in places, indicating an active stream filled with surface water. The other, smaller drainage navigated through the center of what later became the Dakota Ranch development and was a lighter shade than the surrounding terrain. In some photographs, there were a few dark patches, hints of collected surface water, but in most the drainage appeared dry.

A coulee.

He turned his eyes to the aerials showing the property during and after the construction of Dakota Ranch. The development had expanded in stages after the initial spec houses had been built. Some neighborhoods had gone up before others, but they eventually coalesced to form a single large development. He noted that by March 2007 there were only scattered pockets of open space along the perimeter of the development where homes had yet to be constructed.

He focused his attention on the aerials from immediately before and during the earliest stages of development. He located the shallow coulee in the 2004 through 2006 aerials and compared its location to the houses that popped up around it in subsequent photographs.

It was then he saw something that didn't make sense.

The relief of the ephemeral drainage changed between March 2005 and May 2006. Near its headwall and extending perhaps a quarter mile downstream, the drainage was shallowing. Over a period of a little over a year, the feature appeared to have transformed from a shallow coulee to a partially backfilled depression to a flat and featureless dirt lot. The backfilling of the drainage coincided with the first grading of the site beyond the roads.

Intrigued, he scanned the aerials spanning the time period from May 2006 through March 2009, the last date for which an aerial was available. He discovered that the backfilled drainage had remained a vacant lot for over two and a half years. Sometime in the winter of 2008-2009, a large building had been constructed over part of the soil-filled lot. Pulling out the blueprint Minesali had given him, he saw that the building was a recreation center.

Why had The Newport Company spent the considerable time and money to fill in such a huge channel? Why not just build and landscape around it, as was done at most developments?

Puzzled, he stroked his chin and stared at the January 2009 aerial. Then the more important question struck him.

What kind of material was used as backfill?

CHAPTER 18

"COME RIGHT IN, Detective Marshak. Good to see you again."

Prescott stood up from his chair and smiled at the plainclothed detective from the Denver Police Department. The face was a mask, however, as he preferred not to speak to the cops under any circumstances. In this case, the appearance of cooperation demanded it. With an athletic gait, he rounded his desk and shook hands with Marshak, then tipped his head at his comely personal secretary, whom he had bent over his desk on several prior occasions when working late.

"Thank you, Sophie. That will be all."

She gave a coquettish smile, wiggled her perfectly honed ass, and closed the door.

Prescott gestured towards the corpulent man rising from one of the two black leather chairs in front of his desk. "This is my attorney, Greg Bishop."

Marshak stepped forward dutifully to shake the attorney's hand. The detective was a squatty man, built like a bulldog, and his face was, somewhat amusingly, compressed just like a bulldog's. He wore a drab tweed jacket, a striped polyester dress shirt, and brown cotton slacks Prescott felt certain must have been purchased at Wal-Mart.

What an insipid and humorless little man. Mumsie and Father would despise him.

With the introductions complete, they took seats around a glass and chrome table. Prescott and Bishop sat in the chairs on one side of the table, forcing the detective to sit on the black couch against the wall. Not only would they have the home court advantage—having declined Marshak's invitation to interview at the police station—but they would also have the advantage of two against one. The couch was also set lower than the chairs, giving them a further psychological edge since they would be looking down upon Marshak.

"I have just a few questions, Mr. Prescott. This is not an interrogation, but an interview. Same as the other night when we talked."

Bishop smiled superciliously. "My client is happy to assist the DPD, with the understanding that the investigation is not being handled as a homicide and he is considered nothing but a material witness."

"Why would you think the case is being handled as a homicide?"

"I don't, but you *are* a homicide detective."

"Former homicide detective. Now I'm special investigations."

"Which means you handle only the most important cases, those involving celebrities, corporate big shots, or high-ranking government officials. Correct?"

Prescott thought about how the police liked to play good cop-bad cop during interrogations. He decided to take a page from their playbook. "I know you're only doing your job, Greg, but I don't think we need to be adversarial. I'll be glad to answer the detective's questions."

"Thank you, Mr. Prescott. Now to be up front, you are one of several witnesses and are not a suspect. The case is not being considered a homicide, but as an accidental death brought on by an overdose of the victim's medication. Of course, that situation could change based on additional evidence or testimony. Why don't we start with you describing the events of the night in question?"

It took Prescott a full five minutes. Marshak listened patiently and jotted down copious notes. When Prescott was finished, the detective stared off at the wall for several seconds before speaking, as if marshalling his thoughts.

"You know one thing still puzzles me."

Prescott held his breath.

"You made no mention of the second waiter."

He played dumb. "The second waiter?"

"Yeah, there were two waiters. The second one didn't come into the box until McTavish experienced heart failure. Three eyewitnesses confirmed he was in the box, but only for a moment."

"I remember only one waiter, Detective. But I was busy trying to save Gus. I suppose there could have been another waiter, but—"

"The eyewitnesses could also be mistaken," interjected Bishop. "There may not have been a second waiter."

"We're reasonably certain there was. And the thing about him is no one knows who he is, how he got there, or what happened to him. He left without a trace."

"Are you telling us you haven't identified this man, even though he's a Pepsi Center employee?"

"That's the thing. The subject doesn't appear to have been an employee. We're also fairly certain that once he entered the box, he announced that he was going to get help and then disappeared without actually getting any. Given these unusual circumstances, we cannot rule out the possibility Gus McTavish was murdered."

"Are you saying this is a case of homicide after you said it wasn't?"

"No, what I'm saying is there are unusual circumstances surrounding the death, circumstances that need to be explained before I can finalize my report."

Prescott scrutinized Marshak, sizing him up. There was something intriguing—and dangerous—about the detective. Despite his bland, blue-collar-cop personae, the man seemed far cleverer than he was letting on.

"From the descriptions of various witnesses, we've put together this composite," Marshak said, pulling out a police artist's sketch and pushing it towards Prescott. "Are you sure you didn't see this man in the box Saturday night?"

Prescott studied the sketch closely. He was curious as to how accurately the police artist had captured his partner-in-crime, Zachary Paine. The nose was drawn a little too sharp, the eyes too close together, and the ears were all wrong, but overall it was not a bad alikeness. Still, there were thousands of men in the Denver metro area who could be the man in the picture. Prescott looked up from the sketch, directly into Marshak's eyes, and made a big show of shaking his head.

"Definitely didn't see that man at the game. In fact, I'm positive I've never seen him before in my life. I would have remembered him. He looks...dangerous."

Bishop took a gander at the photo. "Are you saying this man's a murder suspect, Detective?"

"At this point, he's being sought for questioning."

"If you want any more help from my client, you'd better give a better reason as to why you suspect this guy. The last thing a prominent figure like Mr. Prescott can afford is to be dragged into an ongoing murder investigation. What did the autopsy results from the Coroner's Office tell you?"

Marshak hesitated. Prescott could tell that he wasn't used to being interrogated and was accustomed to performing the questioning.

He decided to try to gain Marshak's sympathy. "It seems I have a right to know what's going on, Detective. If foul play's suspected, how do you know that someone—this second waiter perhaps—wasn't trying to kill me? In my line of work, one always has enemies. Angry environmentalists, homebuilders, well drillers, ranchers, county commissioners, competing developers. How do you know I wasn't the target?"

"Okay, I suppose you have a right to know. The results from the autopsy indicate McTavish had high levels of triflurodigitalis in his system. A drug for his heart condition."

"And was this triflurowhatever the same medication as the pills he was taking? I told you that Gus pulled pills from his pocket and I gave him one when he asked me to."

"It was the same medication."

"So what's the problem, Detective?" demanded Bishop. "It looks like the heart attack was brought about by an existing heart condition exacerbated by poor physical health, alcohol, and an overdose of prescription medication."

"The concentrations in his bloodstream were so high that he would have had to have taken four or five pills in less than an hour. But only one pill was found in his stomach and it wasn't fully digested. Must have been the pill you gave him, Mr. Prescott. The way I figure it, there should have been one or two more if he had taken that many in such a short time period. Plus, why would he take four or five pills before coming to the game? Why would a guy take that many if he was having heart troubles? Seems to me he would just call 911."

"I still fail to see what any of this has to do with Mr. Prescott."

Marshak ignored him and looked at the developer. "You worked with Gus. Do you know anyone that might have wanted him dead?"

"No, but I didn't know him that well. As I told you before, he was a business acquaintance. I didn't know about his personal life and have no idea if someone had reason to kill him."

"But you knew he was a heavy drinker and that he had a heart condition."

Bishop held up a hand. "Hold on here, Detective. If you persist in this line of questioning, this interview, as you call it, is finished."

Marshak's face read like a blank sheet of paper. There was no evidence of emotion, or weakness either, and in that illuminating instant Prescott realized he was witnessing a shrewd adversary in action.

"I'm just trying to establish the facts of the case," the detective said with what appeared to be contrived innocence.

"Like hell you are," sniffed Bishop.

"It's all right, Greg. I can answer Detective Marshak's question. I've got nothing to hide. Yes, I knew Gus liked to drink and that he was taking heart medication. I'd seen him taking his pills before at job sites. But I had no idea how bad his condition was. When I saw him taking his medication, it seemed no different to me than someone taking vitamins, to tell you the truth."

"And you're sure you've never seen the waiter before?"

"No, Detective, I'm afraid not."

"Is it possible it was someone from Gus McTavish's company, A&M Grading? Someone who would stand to benefit from his passing on?"

"I have no idea. I don't know his employees."

Marshak scrutinized him closely and paused to jot down a note. Prescott felt his heart rate click up a notch. *Did my face or body language give something away?*

Bishop, who had been closely monitoring the exchange, frowned. "I think you've taken up enough of my client's time."

Marshak rose to his feet. "You've been very helpful, Mr. Prescott. I hope I haven't inconvenienced you."

"Not at all." He felt a little shaken, but managed to put forward a mask of professional civility. "I'm always willing to help out the police. But do you really think this so-called second waiter could have committed murder?"

"I don't know," replied Marshak. "But that's a question I'm definitely going to find an answer to. Good day, Mr. Prescott."

CHAPTER 19

HIGHEAGLE SPENT ALL MORNING and the better part of the afternoon in his office studying the Health Department's files on Dakota Ranch. He pored over work plans, meeting minutes, internal correspondence, and full reports with compiled lab results. He examined photographs and medical histories of the four boys in addition to Tommy McTavish who had contracted cancer. By the end of his exhaustive review, he had found one curious item he believed might be significant. He decided to make a call to follow up.

He dialed the number on one of the photocopied pages before him. It was written on company letterhead and taken from the site investigation work plan.

A voice came from the other end after two rings. "Jack Obermeyer, Consulting Hydrogeologist."

"Hi, Jack, this is Joe Higheagle. I'm with Higheagle Environmental in Denver. I was hoping I might be able to talk to you a minute about your field investigation at Dakota Ranch in June 2006?"

"May I ask who you're representing?"

"I'm working with the Colorado Department of Public Health and Environment. We're putting together a chronology on the work conducted out there."

He kept his fingers crossed as he listened to the silence on the other end of the line. It was only a partial lie, since he really was reporting what he found out to Markworth, but he still felt guilty. All the same, he knew that a professed association to an accredited regulatory agency might be the only way to get Obermeyer to open up without being suspicious.

"I remember that job well," Obermeyer said finally, apparently concluding Higheagle was nothing more than a scrupulous consultant trying to track down legitimate information. "It was my first big one right after I went on my own. A few months after I passed the California Registered Geologist exam. I was just happy to have the work."

Higheagle sensed an opportunity to establish something in common between them. "Tell me about it. I just started my own company three months ago. It's been brutal."

"I don't envy you at all. That first year is a bitch. But you'll pull through. Just build up your client base. And remember, established clients will be ninety percent of your business, so you've got to bend over backwards to keep them happy."

"Good advice. I'll keep that in mind, Jack." He felt another stab of guilt for manipulating the situation to his advantage, but what was he supposed to do? "Getting back to Dakota, I noticed you prepared the work plan for the investigation."

"I conducted the field work too. But I didn't write the report. That was handled by Arapaho Technologies in Denver."

Higheagle started taking notes. "Isn't that Doug Hwong's outfit?" he asked, feigning innocence.

"Yeah. I was supposed to prepare the report initially, but Hwong ended up doing it instead. I didn't care at the time because I was still paid for the report, even though I didn't do it."

Higheagle jotted this down and underlined it. How strange, he thought, for a client to pay for a report, but have someone else actually complete it. "Your client was The Newport Company, right? Isn't that Hayden Prescott's company?"

"Yeah. He's a friend of my family's from Newport Beach where I grew up. He threw me a little work my way when I was just starting out. You know, to help me out."

So that's the connection. Higheagle made another note. "I saw in the report that a stats-based random technique was used for the soil sampling."

"Yeah, it was all done prior to the development of the property. I mean the site was for the most part open prairie. There were a few roads and some open spots for equipment staging that looked like they'd been cleared, grubbed, and lightly graded. Hwong set up the grid over the site, which as I recall was several hundred acres. He picked the soil sampling locations using a random number generator. I ran the field investigation. I collected, I don't know, something like a hundred soil samples and had them analyzed for VOCs, SVOCs, metals—the full Appendix Nine list."

"It says in the report that you took a hundred and eleven soil samples."

"Is that what it was? I knew it was around a hundred."

Now it was time to cut to the chase, to raise the issue that had been vexing him most. "In the work plan, it also said you were going to take seven split samples," he said, referring to soil samples collected from the same field location as the primary samples, but analyzed by a different lab to verify analytical precision and accuracy. "But there's no mention of those results in the report Hwong prepared."

As he had expected, the line went silent.

"I take it you weren't aware of that," he said, driving home the point.

"No, I wasn't. All I know is that I sent the splits to another lab and had them analyzed."

Careful, don't lose him now. "Do you remember the name of the lab?"

"It was Redhill Laboratories in Irvine. But I don't understand why the split results weren't included in Hwong's report. Redhill was supposed to forward them to him."

"Probably just an oversight." But he suspected different. "Do you have a phone number for Redhill?" He looked at his wristwatch. *Ten after four—I can reach them today.*

"Just a second," Obermeyer said.

While Higheagle waited, he stared out the open window at his grandfather, who was busy watering plants on the front porch. The old chief wore a Colorado Outlaws Lacrosse cap backwards and was humming a traditional Cheyenne braveheart song. In the summer, Higheagle played professional outdoor lacrosse for the Denver Outlaws as a midfielder, and his grandfather was his biggest fan. The old Contrary watched his grandson play at every home game at Mile High Stadium and was often heard proudly shouting in the stands, "That's my grandson!" after Joseph scored a goal or made a head-turning assist. In contrast to overpaid professional football, baseball, and basketball players, professional outdoor and indoor lacrosse players like Higheagle didn't earn enough money to support themselves from the sport, so they worked at day jobs throughout the year and played professional lacrosse for the love of the game and thrill of competing against the best in the world rather than the paycheck.

Obermeyer's voice returned: "Here's the number: 714-253-1668."

Higheagle jotted down the number. "Oh, before I forget, did you use the same sample numbering system for the splits that you sent to Redhill?"

"I'm pretty sure I did."

"And you had the same analyses run as Arapaho?"

"No, I only analyzed for the chemicals of concern: VOCs, pesticides, and metals. The detection limits were the same though."

Higheagle decided to wrap things up. He wanted to end on a positive note, so Obermeyer wouldn't even consider calling the Health Department, Hwong, or Prescott to check up on his story. "You've been very helpful, Jack."

"Glad I could help out. Good luck with that new business of yours."

"Thanks man." He hung up and immediately dialed Redhill Laboratories in Irvine. He managed to get the lab director on line after being put on hold for a minute. He explained to her that he was working for The Newport Company and requested the results for the seven split soil samples, making up a story about how the hard copy of the analytical results had been misplaced during an office move. At her request, he gave her all the information he had on the project: the site name, date the soil samples were collected, and analyses run on the samples.

But then the lab director surprised him. "Who did you say you were working for again?"

Higheagle pictured her skeptical face on the other end. "Uh, The Newport Company."

The phone remained silent a long moment. He felt a sinking feeling in the pit of his stomach. Finally, the voice on the other end came back, notable this time for its businesslike bluntness.

"I'm sorry, Mr. Higheagle, but I'm afraid we can't give out that information without written authorization from The Newport Company."

CHAPTER 20

PRESCOTT STARED with carefully concealed irritation into the bejowled face of Dan Markworth. The senior-level environmental regulator was seated in a leather couch across from him describing the Colorado Department of Public Health and Environment's preliminary findings on the cancer study. After a moment, Prescott discretely shifted his gaze to State Senate Majority Leader John Dahlquist, R-Dakota Ranch, who was seated in the sleek leather chair next to him. *Now there's a man in full,* he thought, taking in the determined grayish-green eyes, aquiline nose, and lengthy physique filling the pinstriped Brooks Brothers suit. He then turned his attention to his other influential ally, State House Representative Cynthia Chavez of Castle Rock, a conservative Democrat in the Salazar mode. She sat on the black couch next to Markworth. She didn't wield the power of Dahlquist, but she was still a pit bull, concealing her toughness behind a mask of nouveau riche diplomacy.

"We've just completed Stage One—initial contact and response—and are now entering into our Stage Two assessment," Markworth was saying. "We've gathered basic data on the cases, the geographic area, and time period of concern. There's been four deaths so far, all boys between nine and thirteen years of age. We've obtained copies of the pathology reports from the affected families' physicians. The diagnosis was the same for all of the boys. A rare form of brain-stem cancer called medullablastoma. The residence time at Dakota Ranch was over eight years in all cases, suggesting a potential common origin. We've also done preliminary calculations to determine whether a statistical cancer excess has occurred. The results suggest we're dealing with a true excess event. Therefore, further investigation is definitely warranted."

What Markworth purposely left out was that a fifth boy, Tommy McTavish, had recently been diagnosed with the disease. He thought it best not to disclose this information, not yet anyway, since he'd heard about it only unofficially from Higheagle and hadn't yet verified the diagnosis.

"True excess event. What does that mean exactly?" asked Representative Chavez, her charcoal-gray business suit clinging snugly to her buxom figure.

"It means there's a statistically higher-than-expected number of brain-stem cancer cases for boys in the nine- to thirteen-year-old age bracket."

"How much higher?" asked Prescott.

"From six to twenty-two times the expected norm depending on the reference population."

The room went silent.

"Forgive me if I sound stunned, Dan. But are you telling me I've got a cancer cluster on my hands?"

"That's what the preliminary data suggests."

"Cancer cluster—now there's a loaded term," Dahlquist said with a dyspeptic expression on his lean, hawk-like face. "It's just the kind of sensationalized word the liberal media uses to throw the public into a panic. It's my understanding these so-called cancer clusters usually happen by chance. Even when a cause is identified, the real culprit is usually a person's lifestyle. A poor diet, too much booze, too many cigarettes."

"In many cases, that's true. But I still have to contend with the public health ramifications. The truth is the perception of a cluster in a community may be as important as, or more important than, an actual cluster. That's why the next step is to verify the preliminary findings."

Prescott didn't like the direction the discussion was taking, but with the help of his two allies from the state legislature and Bishop, he had already laid out a strategy to deal with just such an eventuality. "You said before your results varied depending on the reference population. What populations did you use?"

"Once we mapped out the cases, we compared the observed brain-stem cancer rate to expected rates for other geographic areas over the same time period. We first looked at age- and sex-adjusted mortality/morbidity ratios for this type of cancer and ran chi-square statistical tests of observed versus expected frequencies. We used a Poisson distribution since it's low frequency data. The data show a definitive excess.

"Then we looked at the Dakota rates in relation to the number of kids enrolled in the nine- to thirteen-year age bracket at the two neighborhood elementary schools. Again, we found an excess. The four boys that died are from the same census tract in Douglas County, so we also compared the cancer rates to those for outlying census tracts and for every county outside Douglas County. What we found is that we have an above-expected occurrence of medullablastoma no matter how the data is analyzed. The bottom line is we have spatial and temporal clustering."

"But what's causing it?"

"We're a long way from determining that. Even though we've found an excess, the likelihood of establishing a definitive cause-and-effect relationship between the cancer and a specific exposure is low. Rare diseases like medullablastoma can cluster in ways that are statistically significant, but these events may still be statistical phenomena unrelated to exposure."

That's the best news so far, thought Prescott. "What's the next step?"

"We're proceeding with an in-depth occurrence evaluation to verify the excess and describe the characteristics of the cluster. We would then move on to an epidemiological feasibility study and etiologic investigation to establish whether there's a link between the cancer and a specific exposure. In other words, we would look into the risk factors the children have in common. Similarities in health, diet, lifestyle, possible chemical exposure, that sort of thing. We feel that if there's a common basis for the cancer, there might be a causal mechanism they all shared."

Prescott winced inside at the sobering situation, but now at least he knew what he was up against. Markworth would have to be reined in, of course, but today was not the day to do it. For this meeting, he had three objectives. First, to determine the status of the cancer study; second, to convince Markworth to keep the study out of the public forum, at least for the time being; and third, to get him to expedite the review of the Silverado Knolls report. Something would have to be done to bring Markworth and his Health Department task force under tighter control, but that something would be reserved for another time. And before it could be arranged, Prescott knew he would have to do some serious strategic planning with Bishop, Dahlquist, and Chavez.

He decided he had heard enough technical details. It was time now to fulfill his second objective. "What's been the community's involvement in all this, Dan?"

"There hasn't been much, so far. The medical records were released to us by the parents, but other than that there hasn't been any community involvement. The original notification came from Dr. Ekstrom at Eisenhower Memorial, not the community or a concerned environmental group, which is usually how we find out about these things. We have a program in place for responding to public concerns, but we haven't had reason to implement it until now."

"Now?"

"Now that we've run the cancer numbers."

The room went silent again. After a moment Dahlquist stirred. "We understand the public has a right to know what's happened to these boys. But we also have to weigh the public's concerns against the damage unsubstantiated accusations could cause. If the community locks onto this thing, then the damned media will get involved, and we all know where that will lead us. They'll hand out indictments before the facts are in and make a circus out of this situation before any of us even know what we're dealing with. That has to be avoided at all costs."

"That's why we feel a low-profile investigation would be in the best interest of all parties," said Chavez, echoing the State Senate Majority Leader's sentiments but with a lighter touch.

Markworth nodded, as if he concurred with the basic logic. "My department doesn't want this thing blown out of proportion either. But now that we've discovered the excess, if the public wants answers, we have to give them to them. We're a public agency."

"But you said you still need to verify whether the cluster is real or not," pointed out Prescott.

"Yes, that's true."

"Then can't you hold off on notifying the community and media until you've verified it?"

Markworth hesitated.

Dahlquist jumped into the opening quickly. "You said yourself the risk perceived by a community in these situations typically exceeds the actual scientific risk. If that's the case, I would think you would want to keep this under the radar until you're damned certain of what you've got."

Prescott could see Markworth weighing the risks. *He's wavering. You need to press him.* "We all know how the media works, Dan. They want an easy target to blame, and they'll do anything to generate controversy. If the community and media jump into this situation prematurely, everyone loses—including you."

"What are you asking me to do?"

Again, Dahlquist quickly pressed the advantage. "Continue your little study, but do so quietly and cautiously. Why get the public all stirred up at this early stage? If concerned citizens contact you, that's one thing. But it would be premature, perhaps even harmful, to bring them in the loop before you have something definitive."

Markworth looked mildly perturbed at being treated like a child, but it appeared he would go along with it. "Okay, sounds reasonable."

Prescott breathed a sigh of relief. "Good. That settles it then." Now he could move on to his third pressing action item. "Let's shift gears. Where do we stand on Silverado Knolls?"

"We're in the final stages of reviewing the environmental impact and site investigation report."

"We were hoping you could expedite the approval process," Chavez said with an ingratiating smile, smoothing her hand across her gray business suit.

"What did you have in mind?"

Dahlquist spoke up bluntly. "We'd like you to issue a formal approval letter to Mr. Prescott by the end of the month. The letter should make explicit reference to the integrity of the site and should approve commencement of heavy construction activities. It should be straightforward. There have been no impacts to any of the animal species out there and there's been enough test holes and wells drilled to prove beyond a shadow of a doubt the property's clean."

A flicker of irritation passed across Markworth's face. He didn't like being strong-armed, but at the same time he recognized that he was powerless to stop it. "I suppose I could have my people speed up the review."

"And we don't want any NODs," Dahlquist said, referring to Notice of Deficiencies.

Markworth started to protest, but then thought better of it. "I'll take care of it, Senator."

Prescott decided to appeal to his common sense so the meeting would not end on a negative note. "You and I have worked together well over the years, Dan. It's important for you to understand what we're trying to accomplish here. I've spent hundreds of thousands of dollars making sure my properties are environmentally safe and geologically stable in terms of swelling clays. And I've made a voluntary effort to relocate more than a thousand prairie dogs. Like you, I'm an environmentalist. But, at the same time, I'm a businessman. That's why I need to get the ball rolling at Silverado. It means jobs and smart growth for the Front Range. And as far as Dakota goes, I can't allow the media and green activists to make up stories or engage in hyperbole about what's going on out there. Kids have died of cancer. That's unfortunate and I sympathize with them. But I can't afford to have uninformed people indulging in wild speculation, like they're doing back east on Long Island with the breast cancer situation. I spent a fortune proving Dakota Ranch was clean and safe, and I'm doing the same at Silverado Knolls."

"I agree you have gone above the call of duty when it comes to environmental compliance. I understand your position and I'm going to work with you on this."

Chavez quickly added, "We'd like to have an open line of communication directly with you. To keep on top of any new developments."

"I can do that. If there's nothing else then, I should be going."

Prescott didn't bother to look at his pinch hitters to see if they had any unresolved issues. He had accomplished everything he wanted. All the same, he decided to issue his closing remarks in a cautionary tone.

"I know we need to find out about what's happened to those poor boys at Dakota. But it's important that we do it in a careful, responsible way. The last thing we want to do is cause a panic. That, I'm afraid, would pose a huge problem for everyone—especially you, Dan."

CHAPTER 21

THE BURIAL SERVICE that laid Gus McTavish to rest drew less than thirty people. It was held in Lakewood not far from Green Mountain, on a rolling cemetery shaded by leafy box elders and sprinkled with spring flowers. Sally felt the crisp breeze cuffing her face as she looked up at the sun, a muted yellow orb that failed to lift her spirits.

She was standing with Tommy at the graveside with friends and family members, including her father and mother who had flown in from Phoenix. The guests wore wool and cashmere sweaters, long overcoats, and parkas. The priest was making the usual uplifting remarks about how kind and generous Gus had been in life. Sally knew it was all a lie. Though she was saddened by her uncle's unexpected death, she didn't feel any deep remorse for him. Though he had for the most part treated her well, he could be gruff and intimidating when he was drinking. However, he had reserved his harshest cruelty for Aunt Martha, whom, it was well known, he had physically abused over the years.

Gazing at the faces, Sally was hard-pressed to find anyone who looked genuinely grief-stricken over her uncle's death, except her father. He stood next to her mother Gail with tears spilling down his cheeks. She realized that, in his eyes, Gus wasn't a wife beater or a drunk but the older brother he had worshiped as a child. Together they had forged alliances against mom and dad, shot off firecrackers, hunted and fished, cheered on the Buffs and Broncos, and gotten into trouble during, arguably, the best years of their lives. Her father had always loved Gus despite his failings and had spent a considerable portion of his adult life trying to navigate his brother through difficult times.

When the priest finished his sermon, the shiny wood coffin was lowered into the hole. People began passing the casket to pay their final respects. Some threw a handful of dirt onto it; others tossed in a few white or red roses. One woman pitched in a whole bouquet of flowers. Now Sally could see the tears streaming down Aunt Martha's cheeks through her black veil. The emotion struck her as so palpably human. Here her aunt was shedding tears for the very man who had tormented her all these years.

As the service came to a close, the marble headstone was brought up on a rickety old pickup truck. It was time for her uncle to be covered up forever and the marker he probably didn't deserve to be driven into the ground. The people began to move off, and as Sally looked around to see where her father had gone, she saw a man standing by himself next to a towering cottonwood. Recognizing him instantly, she realized that he had remained in the background during the entire service. At first, she thought it peculiar, but then she realized he had probably done it out of etiquette, allowing the family and close friends to attend the ceremony in private. She quickly delivered Tommy to her mother and father, who were consoling her Aunt Martha, and walked towards the man.

He had the same handsome bad-boy features she remembered so well, but at the moment he looked sober and respectful. He was dressed in a blue suit with a gold tie. Sally couldn't help but think back to the many times they had made love. He had been a wonderful, unselfish lover and she couldn't help but remember how he had made her writhe with pleasure. That was two years ago, yet she could almost feel the sensation right now, as though he was inside her. Then she remembered how friendly he had been with Tommy, how rich, cultured, and charming he was, and the funeral began to seem like a long-vanished memory.

He smiled softly as she approached and she wondered: *How could I have let a catch like Hayden Prescott get away?*

ψψψ

As he gently sandwiched Sally's hand between his own in a gesture of condolence, Prescott felt a pang of guilt. After all, here he was standing before his former lover at the funeral of her uncle, a man he had murdered a mere four nights ago. But with an effort, he was able to push aside his guilt and maintain a carefully composed mask of gravity.

What he had done had been harsh but necessary. It had been a business decision, a difficult one that had proved costly to Gus, but a business decision nonetheless. Father had always told him that a good businessman never questioned his decisions, and Mumsie had taught him that sometimes the little people simply got in the way, like insects. Gus McTavish had been one of those insects, a meddlesome cockroach that he had been forced to terminate with a carefully administered dose of pesticide.

"I am so sorry, Sally," he said, keeping just the right amount of bereavement in his voice.

"Thanks, Hayden. I'm sure Gus would appreciate your being here."

A little twitch of guilt passed across his face at the irony, but to his relief he saw that Sally had missed it. She smiled a perfect smile and her blue eyes twinkled like exquisitely cut sapphires. Suddenly, what had attracted him to her originally came back in a small rush. It wasn't so much her beauty, though she was most assuredly a head-turner, but that she was so genuine, wholesome, caring, and devoted to being good.

The exact opposite of Mumsie in every respect, he thought.

"What are you doing standing way over here, Hayden?"

"What...oh, I just thought you and your family should be left in peace," he said with beguiling innocence. "And to tell you the truth, I feel a little guilty about all this. If only I had given him mouth-to-mouth a few seconds earlier, maybe I could have saved him." He was certain Sally had read about his courageous attempt to save Gus; it was all over the news.

"You did all you could. You can be proud of that." She shook her head sadly and shivered in the cold air. In that vulnerable moment, he realized he would never have forgiven himself if he had hurt her in their relationship. "My uncle wasn't a good man by any stretch of the imagination. He was abusive towards his wife, wasn't much of a father, and drank way too much. But what you did was a brave thing. You tried to save his life."

Another guilt alarm sounded in Prescott's head. "I didn't know Gus that well. Our relationship was purely professional, but I had heard talk about his personal problems. That's one of the reasons I had agreed to meet with him. I was hoping to increase his involvement at my new development, Silverado Knolls."

"So that's why he was at the hockey game with you. To talk business."

"He must have gotten a little excited. You know, with the game and the prospect of new work coming in the door." He gave a contemplative sigh, looking to the heavens. "I only wish I could have come through for him."

"You shouldn't hold yourself responsible. You did all you could."

Why do I find it so hard to lie to this woman? I feel like I'm throwing stones at Mother Teresa for Christ's sake! He decided to change the subject. "So, besides this, how have you been, Sally?"

"You know the story, Hayden. Single mom blues."

"Are you still mad at me?"

"I was never *mad* at you. At least you were honest." She bit her lip, as if suppressing a devilish smile. "Besides, I knew I wasn't your type. I'm old enough to vote."

He acknowledged her playful sarcasm with the same roguish smile that drove most women crazy with desire. "Are you pulling my chain, Sally McTavish?"

"Let's just say I heard a rumor you have a thing for nubile young women with lots of disposable income and an appreciation for fine art."

His smile widened, showing off perfectly stacked teeth the color of ivory. "And do you believe these...rumors?"

"Do you deny they're true?"

He laughed, but not loud enough to be heard by the people still lingering at the graveside. "Touché," he said, suddenly feeling a little swell of desire in his loins, a flicker of euphoria, standing here at a funeral talking to his former lover when he had just killed her uncle. Perhaps it was the threat of danger, the possibility that his dark secret might be revealed that brought it on. He didn't know for certain, but he did know that Sally looked positively ravishing and he was intensely aroused.

"As much as I hate to admit it, it's good to see you, Hayden."

"It's nice to see you too," he said with genuine feeling.

"You and I would have never made it together, though. You've got a devilish streak in you that all the young girls go wild over. But I need stability. I need a rock. You may be a lot of things, Hayden, but you'll never be a rock."

Prescott did his best not to look hurt, but he was. He had always thought she had been completely enamored with him during their courtship. "Thanks for the vote of confidence," he said.

"I'm sorry. I didn't mean it like that."

"I know you didn't," he said, still trying to conceal his hurt.

The two looked up as Sally's parents, Bill and Gail McTavish, walked over with Tommy. Prescott instantly recognized the family resemblance between the older man and Gus. Once again, he was filled with shame. He tried to tell himself that Gus McTavish was an evil man who had deserved to die, but he couldn't shake the feeling of guilt. Coming face to face with Sally was one thing, but seeing a man who was the spitting image of Gus a half-decade ago was agonizing.

Sally made the introductions. "Dad, Mom, this is Hayden Prescott."

Bill McTavish stepped forward, hand extended. He wasn't about to let the solemnity of the event preclude him from showing courtesy. "The hero who tried to save my brother's life. God bless you, son."

Prescott gulped hard, working mightily to give the most bereft expression he had in his bag of tricks. He quickly decided to use the same tactic he had used on Sally. "My heartfelt condolences to the entire McTavish family. I only wish I could have done more."

Gail McTavish stepped forward and gently touched his arm, like a kindly grandmother. "The Lord knows you did all you could."

He felt like snickering at the sappy remark, but instead held his tongue and nodded thanks. He looked at Tommy, who had grown quite a bit since the last time he had seen him. "Hi there, Tommy."

"Hey, Hayden. What are you doing standing way over here?"

Am I mistaken or does he seem suspicious? He suppressed a nervous laugh. "I didn't want to interrupt your family. It just didn't seem to be my place."

Bill McTavish touched him on the shoulder. "I understand, son, but you can't blame yourself. My brother was on his last legs. He was in poor health and it was bound to happen sooner or later."

This was almost too much for Prescott to take. It was infuriating! These fucking Norman Rockwell cutouts thought he had tried to save Gus when he had murdered the blackmailing son of a bitch in cold blood! His mind flashed back to the look on Gus's face when he realized he had been poisoned. During the past few days, Prescott had relived the experience over and over in his mind, like a macabre instant replay. Old Gus had been on the precipice of death, but for a few terrifying seconds, it had seemed as though he would blow the whistle. In desperation, Prescott had acted quickly, pressing his lips to those of the dying man, pretending to offer him breath but instead silencing him forever.

"We should be going to the reception now, dear," Gail McTavish said to her husband.

He looked off at the long black Lincoln parked at the curb. "Yes, we'd better be going."

"Your being here, Hayden, does this mean you're going to be dating my mom again?"

"Tommy!" Sally's mother gasped.

Sally laughed. "It's all right, Mom. I'd like to hear what he has to say."

Prescott knew she wasn't really painting him in a corner. She was simply teasing him and he realized that was one of the other things he had enjoyed about her during their brief romance. She had a wonderful sense of humor.

He smiled at her parents, who were looking at him expectantly. "I'm afraid, Mr. and Mrs. McTavish, I'll have to leave that up to Sally. After all, I *am* a gentleman."

CHAPTER 22

VIC SHARD WAS SURPRISED.

Standing next to a family plot from the 1880s shadowed by hardy box elders, some three hundred feet uphill from Prescott and his companions, he looked like the Vietnam vet he actually was in his clever disguise. He wore black-and-green camo fatigues and a hunter-green jacket emblazoned with combat decorations he had earned at Tet and the Mekong Delta; impervious Ray-Ban sunglasses; a green Special Forces beret set at a rakish angle atop a wig of shoulder-length brown hair; and spit-polished Panama-soled "Jungle boots."

His disguise was critical to today's enterprise, which was to snoop on his client without being discovered.

He lowered his high-powered Leupold 5x binoculars and reached for the tin of Copenhagen in his back pocket, thinking through what he had just seen. Pulling off the aluminum top, he took a hefty pinch and stuffed it into his upper lip. He pushed the moist tobacco upward with his tongue, as if ramrodding a howitzer, and spit a thin stream of amber chew juice onto the grass. Slipping the can back into his pocket, he pressed the binoculars to his eyes again, focusing on his client and the four people with him in his group as they made their way to the vehicles parked curbside.

What surprised him was Hayden Prescott's body language. It seemed to suggest he had once been intimate with Gus McTavish's niece.

Shard had seen Sally McTavish once before, three months earlier when he had dug into Gus's life, and he never forgot a pretty face. The main question in his mind now was what had gone on between her and Prescott, and did it connect in any way to McTavish's death?

Working his chew with his tongue, Shard took a moment to piece together the current facts of the case, as the group lingered by the shiny black Town Car parked along the curb. First, Prescott had hired McTavish to do land grading work in the past, as well as leased heavy equipment from him. That seemed to be the principal connection between the two men. Second, Prescott had invited McTavish to the Avs game, where the man had promptly died of a heart attack in his arms. The main question was whether McTavish's death was accidental or not, especially given the suspicious presence of a second waiter during the heart attack, a mystery man not yet found according to Shard's contacts at the DPD. Third, somehow Prescott knew McTavish's niece, and by the familiar and seemingly flirtatious way they had been interacting with one another, Shard suspected they had once been lovers. Fourth, Shard had been hired by Prescott to look into McTavish, and there must have been an important reason for that. Invariably, his job was to dig up dirt on people, and more often than not, whatever he dug up was used against whomever he was investigating, sometimes in very cruel ways.

Why should this case be any different?

But that was just it: this case was different. Hugely different. After all, people were dying. So far Gus McTavish and four young boys. And yet, what was the connection? Or was there one?

He felt a sudden surge of wind whip past his ears, a frightening howl. He pulled his jacket tightly around himself. It was creepy out here in the world of the dead, with the stark gravestones sticking up all around, the branches of the trees swaying in the slashing gusts of wind, the desolation of the cemetery serving as a grim reminder of his own mortality.

Peering down again on Prescott and the others, he felt a stab of guilt for prying into his client's affairs. His job was to conduct surveillance and dig up information on people who posed a threat, real or imagined, to his clients. If, in the process, he uncovered distasteful information on those clients, he was supposed to look the other way. The men who hired him expected complete secrecy and unconditional loyalty, and thus far in his career he had never violated anyone's trust.

He had earned his reputation as one of the leading sleuths in the Rocky Mountain region not merely because of his expertise, but his discretion. He had built up his client base from trust, but now he was violating that trust. He told himself it was because this case was different, that the normal rules didn't apply. But there were other reasons as well, ones that at this point he could only dimly comprehend.

He returned to the established facts of the case, facts which when considered together were beginning to reveal a disturbing picture.

Prescott had hired Shard to run a background check on Gus McTavish, whose outfit had been the prime contractor at Dakota Ranch. Three months later McTavish had showed up in Prescott's box at the Avs game and died of a sudden heart attack. The man who died was the uncle of a woman Prescott knew fairly well, perhaps even intimately. And four kids who had lived within a short distance of one another at a property recently developed by Prescott had died of a rare brain cancer, all in the last nine months. In his mind, the odds of these suspicious circumstances not being interrelated seemed improbably low.

With these vexing thoughts on his mind, he watched Prescott drive off in his shiny Range Rover, followed, moments later, by the full funeral procession. When everyone was gone, he stuffed his binoculars in his handbag, slung the bag over his shoulder, headed to his Jeep Cherokee, and fired the engine.

Then he drove back to his office, mulling over the dangerous possibilities.

CHAPTER 23

HIGHEAGLE REJOICED ALOUD as the cover sheet from Redhill Laboratories spit out from his fax machine. The lab director had put up stout resistance, but he had finally convinced her to comply with his request after faxing over the old chain-of-custody form and laboratory sample identification numbers he'd managed to coax from Jack Obermeyer.

This could prove to be the break he was looking for!

As he reached for the first glossy fax sheet, his grandfather stepped into the room. "What's all this ruckus about?"

"I just got an important fax."

"You have been working non-stop these past two days. What has this Minesali fellow gotten you into?"

"He hasn't *gotten* me into anything. What makes you say that?"

"Like hell he hasn't. I googled him. He's one of those eccentric multimillionaires that are always up to funny business. I don't trust him."

"You're talking about my client, Grandfather. The man who is paying my bills—and paying them handsomely, I might add. The real person you should be worried about is Hayden Prescott."

"That name sounds familiar. Who the hell is he again?"

"A big developer. He built Dakota Ranch."

"That place down south where that boy Tommy and his mother live?"

"That's the one."

"The same place where those four boys died?"

Higheagle nodded.

"Hmm, you think Dr. Ekstrom's right about what's happening down there?"

"I don't know. But I definitely have questions."

"Hayden Prescott...where have I heard that name before? Was he in the paper recently?"

"Probably. He's in the Society and Business pages a lot." He grabbed a handful of the glossy sheets coming off the fax machine. "I'm sorry, but I really have to look at this stuff."

"All right, I'll leave you alone. I'm going to cook up some fry bread. You want any?"

"Maybe later."

The old chief left him to his work, closing the door behind him. Two minutes later, Higheagle had received the analytical results for all seven of the Dakota Ranch split soil samples, as well as the COC documenting where, when, and how the samples were collected. Sitting at his desk, he compared the data presented in the site investigation report prepared by Hwong at Arapaho Technologies to the faxed results from Redhill. Matching the soil boring numbers and depths of the samples analyzed by each lab, he compared the concentrations of each of the detected analytes.

There were no volatile organic compound or pesticide detections in the Redhill samples, but he found that two of the splits, collected from soil borings SB-67 and SB-68, showed elevated metals concentrations. Collected five feet below ground surface, the samples contained arsenic, lead, cadmium, nickel, and hexavalent chromium—the most hazardous form of chromium—in addition to a dozen other metals. Pristine soils generally contain low levels of naturally-occurring metals from the minerals in the matrix, but the concentrations he saw were uncommonly high and inconsistent with Hwong's results, which fell within the expected range of background values for Western soils. The concentrations in the two Redhill samples were in the tens to hundreds of thousands of milligrams per kilogram range, well above the low levels detected in the samples analyzed by Arapaho.

Why the tremendous discrepancy between the two data sets?

Leaning back in his chair, he pondered the possibilities. Though split sample results from a secondary lab never matched the original data from the primary lab exactly—the variation was sometimes as much as 50%—the three- to four-order-of-magnitude differences observed here were far too large to have resulted from sample heterogeneity, statistical variability, or differences in analytical protocols alone. It appeared as if the Redhill data set was completely different from Hwong's, even though the samples were supposed to have been collected from the same location and depth, as well as sampled and analyzed following the same procedures.

Oddly, the samples collected from only six inches below ground surface in SB-67 and SB-68 contained only low concentrations of metals for both labs. Assuming the Redhill results were valid, this suggested the contamination did not originate at ground surface, as might happen from tipping over a drum and allowing the chemicals to seep into the ground. The profile seemed most consistent with material dumped in an open area, then covered with a layer of imported, non-contaminated backfill, so-called "clean" soil.

On the table, Higheagle spread out the Dakota Ranch base map Minesali had given him. The base map showed all of the streets, houses, and buildings on the property. He followed by pulling out the soil sample location map from Hwong's report and a 2006 aerial photograph. He spent a few minutes sketching in the backfilled coulee shown in the aerial. Then he drew in the two soil sample locations that showed high concentrations of heavy metals. He made a small table next to each showing the concentrations and drew an arrow to the two soil borings. Next, he wrote down Hwong's low and non-detected results beside the anomalously high Redhill results. As he had expected, the two elevated concentrations occurred within the backfilled coulee.

When he was finished, he reviewed what he had discovered thus far. He knew that soil, or soil-like material, had been used to backfill the ephemeral drainage channel in the center of the site. The backfilling had occurred around the same time significant dirt roads were laid out on the property, but before any houses or other buildings had been constructed. If the split results were truly representative of actual site conditions, then the material used to backfill the open drainage contained high concentrations of potentially hazardous metals.

At first he was excited, but as he pondered the limited nature of the evidence, he tempered his assessment. He did not know with absolute certainty that the material used to backfill the drainage was toxic waste, at least according to regulatory definitions of such materials. And even if actual toxic materials had been dumped, Prescott and Hwong were not necessarily implicated. The metals could have originated with a sleazy backfill supplier, or been dumped there by an unknown party. Furthermore, field sample handling and laboratory testing procedures themselves were often fraught with problems. Contamination could be introduced not only in the field during sampling and shipping, but from the containers used to store the samples and the laboratory testing equipment itself. He also had to consider that his assessment hinged on only two soil samples. The results from only two samples would hardly serve as the basis for any significant conclusion.

He had to admit, though, that his preliminary findings did raise serious questions. More importantly, Dr. Ekstrom's seemingly far-fetched theory now didn't seem so far-fetched after all.

With that in mind, he decided to pay someone a visit.

CHAPTER 24

A HALF HOUR LATER, he found himself sitting in the reception area of Arapaho Technologies, watching Douglas Hwong, PhD, striding briskly towards him. His pulse quickened. He had told a few white lies the past two days to get information, but now he would have to do it in person, mano a mano. He took a deep breath to steady his nerves. It seemed unthinkable he was about to question one of the top scientists in the environmental arena, a revered geochemist who had served as an expert witness on some of the biggest legal cases in the world, published more than a hundred professional papers, and given a staggering number of technical presentations before the world's scientific elite.

What in the hell are you thinking? This is a lousy idea.

The short, lean geochemist walked up to him, hand extended and body bowed with cordial grace.

He took the proffered hand. "I appreciate your taking the time to meet with me under such short notice, Dr. Hwong. I've seen you speak many times before. We actually met at the NGWA conference in Houston a couple years ago, but you probably don't remember me."

Hwong studied him a moment. "No, but I read a great deal about you in the newspapers regarding that Quantrill incident. That was a good piece of detective work. Perhaps you are in the wrong profession, Mr. Higheagle." His thin, bloodless lips curled into a faintly arrogant smile.

Higheagle noted something that he hadn't noticed over the phone: Hwong's English had improved markedly since the last time Higheagle had seen the celebrated Taiwanese scientist speak. He must have taken special voice lessons or something because his pronunciation was flawless.

"Please, why don't we go to my office?"

They walked through the door, down a hallway, past several glass-enclosed laboratories, and into Hwong's office. A plethora of framed diplomas and awards peered down from the vanity wall to the right. The other walls were lined with six-foot-tall bookcases crammed with books and white three-ring binders, all carefully labeled. Hwong closed the door behind them and offered him a seat in front of his glossy teakwood desk, which held a huge computer screen and a neat pile of scientific articles.

"So you're with the Health Department now."

Higheagle felt a stab of anxiety. He hated lying, but it seemed the only way to obtain the information he sought. "Actually, I'm working with the Health Department as a consultant." He pulled out a business card and handed it across the desk.

Hwong looked over the card for a moment. "I do some consulting work for the CDPHE from time to time...on special projects."

"My project's not that special. I just wanted to ask a few questions about the Dakota Ranch investigation conducted a few years back. I'm putting together a chronology of the project and I came across something. A fax received from a lab in California—Redhill Laboratories."

A flicker of surprise passed across Hwong's face, swiftly suppressed. "What is the date of the fax?"

"I don't know. All I have is a copy of the original lab results. Do you want to see them?"

Hwong nodded guardedly. Higheagle reached for the stapled fax in his satchel. Retrieving the faxed pages, he rose from his chair, set the pages down on the desk, and began flipping through them. He had already removed the cover page so Hwong wouldn't know Redhill had sent the fax to him directly. He had also trimmed the edges so the fax header wasn't on any of the sheets. He stopped when he came to the results from the two soil borings in question.

Hwong leaned across the desk to have a look.

"As you can see, there were high metals concentrations detected in the soil samples collected from SB-67 and SB-68," Higheagle said, pointing to the map. "But when you look at the results from your lab, there were only low levels. Typical of what you'd expect for background."

A look of recognition and something else—was it irritation or guilt?—came over Hwong's face. "I have seen these before," he said, looking over the pages. "This lab is unqualified. It was stripped of its certification by Cal-EPA several years ago, so we could not use these results."

"But how do you explain the large discrepancy?"

Hwong spat out his reply as if he were purging a nasty taste from his mouth. "The Redhill results are invalid. That laboratory has no business analyzing samples. I routinely perform audits for the EPA and state regulatory agencies on laboratories around the country. And Redhill has had violations on more than one occasion."

Hwong sat back down, a satisfied expression on his face, as if that settled the matter.

"I didn't know that," Higheagle said, and he, too, returned to his chair.

"You can call them yourself if you'd like. Or better yet, call Cal-EPA."

"I should have figured it was something like this." But in his mind, he wasn't so sure. *Is Hwong lying? I can check on the lab's EPA violations easily enough to find out.*

"Real estate developers are touchy about the integrity of their analytical data. They want it perfect because they are exposed to so much litigation. These results were available when we prepared the report, but the lab's reputation was suspect so we didn't include them. We didn't need them anyway. All QA/QC parameters were within established control limits."

I can check up on that too. "So you think these high levels are lab artifacts?"

Higheagle knew it was possible, but unlikely, for such high concentrations to be introduced in the laboratory. Lab contamination generally resulted from either faulty or improperly maintained analytical equipment. Standard lab chemicals used to clean equipment or extract the constituents being analyzed, like methylene chloride or acetone, were often the culprits. But in this case, the metals detected by Redhill Laboratories were not the types of chemicals introduced as laboratory artifacts and the concentrations were far too high. That narrowed it down to problems with the analytical testing equipment itself. But the equipment blanks— the samples that had been analyzed by the instrument that performed the tests— were uncontaminated.

Hwong looked as though he was carefully considering the alternatives. Studying him, Higheagle had the sneaky suspicion that the world-renowned geochemist was actually a fucking fraud. But how did he fit into the puzzle of Dakota Ranch?

"There are various possibilities," Hwong said finally. "But none of them are worth pursuing because of the lab's questionable QA/QC protocols. In any court of law, this data would be thrown out."

"But the equipment blanks came up negative. Which rules out the possibility of instrument error."

Now Hwong raised his voice. "All I know is the data are unreliable." Realizing that he sounded testy and defensive, he gave an overcompensating smile. "Look, Redhill has failed to meet both state and federal standards. They shouldn't be in business. Beyond that, I cannot make a judgment."

Higheagle shrugged innocently. "Looks like that's it then." He rose from his chair. "I'd like to thank you for your time, Dr. Hwong. I didn't mean to sound like I was questioning your lab results."

"Yes, well the Health Department always likes its contractors to be thorough. You're working with Bob Markworth on this, right?"

Oh, shit. What do I say? "No, I'm not working with Bob. But I know him. Good man."

Panic stormed through his nervous system as Hwong's eyes locked onto him like twin laser beams. Suddenly, the roles were reversed and he was the one on the defensive. To his mortification, Hwong seemed to pick up on his flustered body language.

"You're not working with Bob Markworth? But he's the community relations contact for the Dakota Ranch project."

"I guess he might know about it. I just meant that I'm not dealing with him directly."

"Who are you working with then? Perhaps I know him."

"Actually it's a she—Mary Casserly," he said, blurting out the most obscure name he could recall at the agency.

"I haven't heard of her. Oh well, I'm sorry you won't have anything to report."

"Oh, but I do have something."

Hwong gave him a look of surprise.

"Sometimes finding nothing means you have found something." He placed the fax back into his business satchel and held out his hand. "Thanks again, Dr. Hwong, for your time."

The celebrated Taiwanese scientist looked a tad paler than when the meeting began. "I suspect we'll be seeing you around. Now that you're working with the Health Department."

"I look forward to it," replied Higheagle pleasantly, and Hwong escorted him to the front door.

ψψψ

When the good Dr. Hwong returned to his office, he immediately dialed a number. His hands were trembling, his face filled with panic. The phone rang once, twice, three times.

Pick up, damnit! Pick up!

But no one did. Then he dialed a cell number and a home phone number. Still nothing.

When he heard the voice from the home answering machine, he slammed the phone down hard without leaving a message.

This was one call Douglas Hwong, PhD, had to make in person.

CHAPTER 25

SALLY MCTAVISH FOLDED the last article of clean laundry and set it on top of a neatly arranged pile on the dryer. Grabbing the three pairs of socks lying next to the clothes, she hoisted the entire bundle, pressing the top with her chin to keep the clothes in place. She carried the pile up the staircase to Tommy's room and set it down in front of his baseball-sticker-covered dresser.

A smile crossed her face when she saw the toy cavalry soldiers and Indians arranged in a battle scene in the corner. There were about fifty of the little figures, all colorfully painted. It appeared the Indians were about to vanquish the cavalry, or at least inflict heavy casualties. She pushed away a few strands of the strawberry-blonde hair dangling before her eyes and began placing Tommy's socks and little white jockey briefs in the top drawer.

Her parents had returned to Phoenix this morning, and Tommy was playing down the street at Tim Edson's house. As usual, her thoughts were with her son. The doctors had said how important it was to allow Tommy to follow his normal routine even though he was sick, but she still couldn't help but worry about him. She became anxious when he was out of her sight. She knew complications could arise suddenly in brain cancer cases because of the sensitivity and complexity of the brain itself.

I called Jane ahead of time. She knows to call me if he isn't feeling well. Nothing's going to happen, right?

She opened the second and third drawers and refolded Tommy's T-shirts and pants. He had carelessly stuffed the clothes back in the drawers after hastily rummaging through them, no doubt to find his favorite X-Men T-shirt. Sometimes she wondered why she even bothered to fold his clothes when he would just mess everything up again. Though she always reprimanded him for it, he couldn't manage to keep the drawers tidy for more than a day or two before returning to his old ways.

She could feel her anxiety mounting as she folded the last T-shirt. *I wonder if I should give Jane a call? Suppose Tommy gets one of his headaches. I could remind her again to keep an eye on him. No, I don't want to seem paranoid.*

She placed the final pair of faded jeans in the third drawer and closed the dresser. As she was about to turn to leave, her eye caught the colored photograph on the dresser. She and Tommy stood proudly on top of Mount Quandary, the first fourteener they had climbed together two summers ago. Since then they had conquered a dozen more, but Quandary had been first so it was special. Their orange ponchos flapped in the wind and their faces appeared rosy, ignited with pride at their accomplishment. They looked as though there would be many more triumphs ahead. Sally picked up the photograph and studied it closely, feeling a tide of joy wash over her.

Her musing was interrupted by the sound of the doorbell. She set the picture down and headed downstairs. Peering through the window, she saw a pony-tailed man dressed in a cowboy hat, faded jeans, and a western shirt. Though she recognized him, she wondered what he was doing here. Guardedly, she opened the door part way.

"Hello, Sally. I'm Joe Higheagle. We met the other day at the hospital."

She smiled politely, but wondered what he wanted.

He produced a business card. "I'm working on an environmental project out here at Dakota Ranch and was wondering if I could ask you a few questions."

"I don't know that I'll be of much help, but I can try." She wasn't sure what to say next, so she took the card from him and looked it over.

When she looked back at him, his gaze was fixed on the small robin's nest in the corner above the door. Two little brown heads with dark beaks peered out nervously, heads twitching.

"The latest addition to our family," she said.

"Mom must be out worm-hunting."

"She'll be back soon. She never leaves them alone for very long."

When he smiled, his brown eyes lit up and she saw how handsome he was. Tall, dark, and Indian was an interesting combination. But what she liked most was how carefree and down-to-earth he seemed. She could tell that he got along easily with people, even complete strangers.

She opened the door all the way. "Please come in. I apologize for my house being a mess."

"Don't worry, there's no way it could be as messy as mine."

They laughed nervously. As he stepped inside, she caught her reflection in the mirror and felt suddenly self-conscious about her appearance. She didn't have on any makeup, not even a dash.

Too late now.

"I was in the neighborhood and thought it might be good to talk to you," he said.

She suspected he hadn't just been in the neighborhood, but had come specifically to speak to her. The thought excited her just a little, though she tried not to let it show on her face.

"Let's talk in the other room." She led him from the wood-floored foyer through the short hallway and into the kitchen. "Can I get you something to drink?" she asked as they came to a halt before a knotty pine kitchen table.

"No thanks," he replied, placing his hands on one of the caned chairs around the table. "Sorry I didn't call beforehand. I know your hands are full."

"These last few days have been a little rough." As she motioned for him to sit, they were interrupted by barking noises.

"That's our dog Max," she said, and they turned to look out the sliding glass door at a big black Lab running alongside the fence, barking at a squirrel skittering across the top.

"I'll bet Tommy has a good time with him."

"A boy's best friend."

They sat down. An uncomfortable moment of silence passed between them, as neither seemed to know what to say next.

"How's Tommy doing?" he asked finally.

"He seems to be handling things as well as could be expected. No major side effects since the first few days of radiation treatment. He was nauseous and had these terrible headaches, but the medication's helping. He gets tired easily, especially right after treatment. And he doesn't have much of an appetite. But other than that he's doing okay. The doctors said they were fortunate to catch the cancer early."

"So you're staying home with him?"

"Actually, he's been well enough to go to school in the morning. I pick him up in the afternoon and take him to therapy. The law firm I work for is letting me work just three days a week and still retain full benefits until things settle down a bit."

"What's the name of your firm?"

"Davis, Ramsey. It's downtown."

"That's funny. I wouldn't have pegged you for a lawyer."

"I'm not one actually. I'm a paralegal."

"Lucky you, you're not on the receiving end of bad lawyer jokes."

"Yeah, but I'm paid like an airline attendant."

"That makes two of us," he said, smiling in that carefree way again. He glanced up at one of Tommy's drawings on the refrigerator. The colored sketch showed mounted Indian warriors battling dismounted cavalrymen in a skirmish line. When he looked back at her, his expression had turned serious. "Mrs. McTavish—"

"Please, call me Sally."

"And you can call me Joe."

"I've always liked that name." She watched his eyebrows dance a little and his face brighten, and she felt a little connection between them.

"Thanks," he said, but his tone quickly turned business-like again. "Sally, the investigation I'm working on...well, I think we can help each other." He quickly told her about his environmental assessment at Dakota Ranch, providing few specifics.

When finished, he asked, "Has the Health Department contacted you?"

"A man named Dan Markworth came by and spoke to me yesterday. He told me about the study they're doing and asked if I would release Tommy's medical records. I told him I would. Are you working with him?"

"Not exactly. The Health Department is conducting an epidemiologic study on the cancer cases. I'm performing an environmental assessment. But I have a hunch the two might be related."

"I'd like to help out any way I can."

"I need to find out more about the vacant lot where the rec center was built."

"Well, I can tell you that Tommy and a lot of the neighborhood kids used to play there. They'd ride their bikes and build jumps and things. The sixteenth hole of the golf course was supposed to run through there, but the development group ended up putting the rec center there instead. I don't know why they did that.

Everybody was upset the rec center took so long to finish. They kept telling us it was going to be done, but the homeowners association, bank, and developer couldn't agree on what facilities it would have."

"How long was it a dirt lot?"

"Until a few months ago."

"I'd like to take a look over there. Do you think you could show me the lot sometime? It might give me some idea of what it looked like when the kids used to play there."

"I'd be glad to," Sally said, though she was unsure of how that might help him.

They were interrupted by a sound at the front door. "Mom, I'm home."

"I'm in the kitchen, honey." Leaning across the table, she then said in a low voice, "If you want, we could give you a tour right now."

"That would be great."

"I should warn you though. Knowing Tommy, he's going to want to be Mr. Watson to your Sherlock Holmes."

"That's even better," he said with a smile.

CHAPTER 26

TOMMY STARED AT THE REC CENTER.

What had been a dirt lot last Christmas was now covered by a series of grassy playing fields and a large brick building. The rec center proper stretched three-quarters of a football field and was flanked on the right by six tennis courts and an in-line roller hockey rink. On the left stood an enclosed play area for younger children and the playing fields. Taking his bearings, Tommy tried to visualize what the dirt lot had looked like before the rec center was built.

"It seems so much different than before," said Sally, befuddled. "I couldn't even begin to tell you where the kids played."

I remember, thought Tommy. "Follow me."

"I told you," his mother said to Higheagle, giving him a look of bemusement.

The three of them walked through the asphalt parking lot, past the children's play area, and across a grass field until they were parallel with the row of houses north of the rec center.

"This is where the dirt lot was. Most of the time we rode our bikes right around here," Tommy said.

"In line with those houses?" asked Higheagle.

"That's how I remember it. There was a bike path that ran even with the homes. Some of the older kids used to bring shovels and we'd dig dirt and make jumps. Big ones."

Higheagle opened a three-ring binder and began taking notes. "When you dug around did you churn up dust?"

"Yeah. On weekends, when there were a lot of kids and the wind kicked up, it was like a dust storm."

"Any other places where you and the other kids played?"

"There were a few other trails that came off the main one. Four or five of them. I don't remember where they were though. I just know the main trail was even with the houses."

Tommy watched as Higheagle started sketching a map in his notebook. It reminded him of a detective drawing a crime scene on TV. "Did you play any other games where you kicked up dust or dug up soil?"

"We used to play kick-the-can and capture the flag, and we'd toss a football or baseball around once in a while. Mostly we rode bikes. A couple of kids had minibikes too."

He felt his mom come up behind him and put her hands on his shoulders. "Tommy was good friends with Todd Wilkins, one of the boys who died."

"Tommy told me at the hospital. I'm sorry."

The boy felt a twinge of sadness, knowing he would never see his buddy again. He wondered if Todd had gone to heaven. He hoped so. "The bikes and minibikes turned up a lot of dust, but we never thought twice about it. We dug way down in places and loosened the dirt, you know, to make our jumps and stuff. We didn't know the dirt could hurt us. Or the dust."

"I don't know for sure that it did. At this point, all I can say is skin contact with the soil and breathing airborne dust are potential ways the kids may have been exposed. I don't want to jump to any conclusions until all the facts are in."

"Sounds like a reasonable approach," said Sally.

Tommy thought of something. "When we were digging in the dirt, we used to come across this white stuff."

"White stuff? Was it liquid or solid?"

"It was like these powdery crystals, like salt. There were thin layers and little pockets of the stuff. We thought it was part of the dirt, you know, like the white crust you see on mudcracks when a puddle dries up. Gypsum or whatever it's called."

"This white stuff, do you think it's hazardous?" Sally asked Higheagle.

"I don't know." He looked back at Tommy. "Did you or the others kids ever get headaches or skin rashes when you played in the soil?"

"You did get that rash on your arm, honey. Last summer."

"Jeez, that's right. I got it last fall too. And two summers ago. I remember, because it was right before the Fourth of July and I had a rash on my arm when I was lighting off firecrackers."

"I thought it was poison oak or something," Sally said, looking a little guilty.

"What about headaches or other symptoms?"

"Sometimes I got headaches. I would just take aspirin when I got home. But Todd had trouble seeing one time. His vision got all blurry. And he got those skin rashes too. They usually went away after a day or two, so I didn't think it was a big deal."

"Did you only get the rashes after digging in the soil?"

"I can't remember for sure. We only dug in the dirt when we were making our jumps and stuff. Plus sometimes I wore gloves. Like when Todd brought his minibike out."

Higheagle stopped writing and began flipping through the pages of his binder, apparently searching for something. Tommy thought: *Joe sure is smart. He's like a private eye or something, the way he asks all these questions.* Higheagle stopped when he came to a color Xerox photograph, grainy but high-quality.

"Hey, that's Todd," Tommy said with surprise when he recognized the picture. "Where'd you get that?"

"From the Health Department. Would you mind if I showed you the pictures of the other boys who got sick? I'd like to verify whether they all played here. If they did, it would at least establish that they could have been exposed."

"Sure," said Tommy, and the three of them huddled closer together to examine the picture of Todd Wilkins.

"You said you and Todd played out here a lot, right?"

"All the time. Even in the winter, when the weather was nice."

"Can you give me a more precise estimate...one day a week, two?"

"Oh, no, it was more than that. I would say it was at least four days a week."

"But you probably played here mostly in the summer, right?"

He nodded. "I'd say on average Todd and I played here four or five times a week in the summer and three or so in the fall and spring. And in the winter, maybe a couple times a week depending on the snow. I mean this was our hangout in all seasons."

Higheagle took a moment to write this down. Then he flipped to a picture of a blond-haired kid in a Champ Bailey jersey, Number 24. "What about this boy? Do you remember seeing him here?"

Tommy recognized the face instantly. "That's Alex Johnson."

"That's right. He was about your age."

"He went to private school at Colorado Academy so I didn't know him that well. He lived over there," Tommy said, pointing to the neighborhood south of the rec center. "But he was here a lot. I didn't know he had cancer."

Next Higheagle showed him a tough looking kid with a buzz cut. "What about this boy?"

"I don't remember his name, but he played here a lot with the bigger kids. He was kind of a bully. He had a minibike like Todd. But he was older and we stayed away from him."

"His name was Jamie Haskell. His family moved to Boston." Higheagle flipped to one last picture, Cody Parsons, age nine, and Tommy confirmed that he knew the boy and had played with him around the dirt lot.

Putting away the pictures, Higheagle asked, "Would you say these other kids were out here as often as you. Four or five days a week when the weather was nice?"

He thought about it a moment. "Sounds about right."

"Did girls play out here too? Or was it mostly boys?"

"There were some girls, but they didn't do the jumps and stuff, or ride around in the dust. They played other games, over there." He pointed to the rec center. "And they didn't play here as much."

"Is it important that only boys have been affected?" asked Sally.

"Could be," Higheagle replied. "If the dust and physical contact with the soil were exposure routes, and only boys played in the high-risk areas, it would make sense for only boys to be affected. But I have a lot more work to do before I'll know for sure." He closed his binder and looked at Tommy. "You and your mom have helped me out a lot. Thanks."

Tommy felt the same positive vibe he had felt at the hospital. He realized, with sudden clarity, that Joe was exactly what he had wanted his father to be. He was smart and nice, yet he was also tough. That was the thing that had disappointed Tommy most about his dad: the guy was a wuss. He was clumsy at sports and he didn't like outdoorsy stuff like hiking, camping, or rafting and he was always fussing over himself in the mirror and everything had to be neat and tidy or he got pissed off.

"I'm glad you're letting us help you out, Joe. And I hope my mom and I will get to see you again."

As soon as the words left his mouth, he could see that his mom was embarrassed. But luckily Joe jumped in quickly.

"Oh, I'll be seeing you around, Little Big Man. You can bet on that. It's going to take all three of us to figure out what's gone on out here." His easy manner dropped and he spoke in a more serious voice. "But I'm going to have to ask both of you to keep what I've told you to yourselves. At least for the time being."

"I can keep a secret."

His mom rolled her eyes. "I'll make sure both of our lips are sealed."

"We want to help you find out what's going on here at Dakota Ranch, Joe. Not just for me, but for Todd and the other kids. Even that bully, Jamie Haskell."

Higheagle pulled a business card from his pocket and handed it to his mom. "If you or Tommy think of anything else—anything at all—you be sure to call me."

"We'll do that," Sally said.

"Thanks, Joe," said Tommy. "Thanks for being here for us."

Higheagle patted him on the shoulder. "I can't tell you yet what's happened out here, Little Big Man. But I can guarantee one thing."

"What's that?"

"I'm not going to quit until I've figured it out."

CHAPTER 27

OPENING THE GREENHOUSE DOOR, Vincenzo Minesali was greeted by a wave of warm, moist air that seemed to instantly relieve the stiffness in his creaky joints. Bedecked in a short-sleeved khaki shirt, loose-fitting khaki pants, and a Panama straw hat, he looked like a 19th century aristocrat on safari as he stepped inside and closed the door behind him. He used a walking cane to support himself; it was a handsome thing, nearly four feet long, fashioned out of knotty birch, with a silver dog's head at the top of the staff, a hearty Cornish Labrador with a curled tongue.

He let his eyes take in the lush greenery all around him while inhaling the pleasant perfume. The greenhouse projected from his vast Tudor mansion like a small cottage and was floored with herringbone brick damp with mist. A free-flowing artistic design permeated the room, courtesy of his late wife Marguerite, whose refined taste in art, music, and decor was superseded only by her exquisite cultivation of flora.

Minesali walked slowly down one of the meandering walkways, clicking and clacking with his walking cane. Flowering plants spilled out from tiered wrought-iron benches and unfolded in vibrant color from earthen pots and huge urns. Clusters of palms, ferns, and ivy twisted towards the glass roof, mimicking a miniature tropical rainforest.

He came to a halt before a potted star orchid, Marguerite's favorite. Leaning over, he caressed the flower gently, as if it was the back of a young lover. The sun's late afternoon rays shone through the glass and reflected off the five petals, providing a brilliant contrast between the flower's yellowish-green background and maroon speckles.

"How I miss you, my dear," he said in a soft voice, his mind reaching back to another era, back when he was young, strapping Corporal Minesali chugging through the French tableland with Patton's Third Army following the Normandy Invasion in June 1944. It was at this pivotal crossroads in history that he had met the lovely farm girl from Melun with brown eyes the size of ripe plums. For three days when he was on leave following a week's worth of savage fighting at the Falaise Pocket, they sat dreamily along the banks of the mighty Seine, sipping wine, holding each other close, finding themselves falling completely in love though they spoke only with head nods and soft kisses.

Even at the time, the romance seemed like an illusion, and it became even more unbelievable when, after the war, Minesali wrote Marguerite Bagnold asking her to sail to America so they could be wedded. A smile creased his lips as he recalled his outrageous proposal and how everything had worked out. They were locked in each other's arms for only a few days; yet six months after the war, and another two after receiving his offer of marriage, she had sailed across the Atlantic to New York and took a train to Denver—the dusty old cowtown was no host to global summits, national political conventions, or world champion sports teams in those days—to marry a man with nothing more than GI Bill benefits to his name.

Feeling a powerful wave of nostalgia, he stared out at the flowering plants she had treasured so dearly. Since her death, he had maintained the greenhouse and outdoor gardens exactly the way she had kept them. He wanted a constant reminder of how much he loved her, how devoted to one another they had been. With a wrinkled hand, he reached out and stroked the star orchid again.

Sometimes I feel as though I did not lose you, Marguerite. When I am among the flowers, I can feel your presence. In spirit, we are still together.

He continued through the misty greenhouse, touching a flower here and there, taking in the heady fragrance. With painful remembrance, he thought back to his wife's long-drawn-out death from pancreatic cancer. That had been the worst time of his life—even worse than the hand-to-hand fighting at Bastogne—watching his beautiful French flower wilt before his eyes. He did everything possible to ease her suffering: nursing her at all hours of the night, hiring the best cancer specialists to treat her, constantly striving to keep her spirits up. But throughout it all, deep down, he had felt powerless to help her, and when she finally died, he had felt utterly defeated.

He recalled something his father had once told him. When a woman loses a husband to death, Dominico Minesali had said, she picks her chin up and moves on. But when a man loses a woman, half of him dies right along with her. Minesali knew he had died by at least half when he had lost his beloved Marguerite to cancer.

Feeling his eyes begin to water, he pulled a monogrammed handkerchief from the top pocket of his khaki shirt. As he wiped away the tears, his mind turned to his children.

His three sons and two daughters were all grown up and living elsewhere, raising families of their own. He missed them immensely and looked forward to seeing them during the Christmas holidays, the only time they usually visited. He yearned for their companionship, just as he did his late wife, but they were rarely there for him. They had all moved on to their own lives, their own families, leaving him only fragmentary memories of them growing up.

Putting away his handkerchief, Minesali picked up a pair of pruning shears. He began snipping back a pair of pink roses, reflecting, as he so often did at this stage of his life, on the long road he had traveled in this world. First as a headstrong boy outside Louisville, Colorado, not far from the old coal mining camps of his grandfather and great-grandfather; then as a footsoldier in Patton's Third Army, a source of immeasurable pride to him; then as a loving husband, father, and eminently successful entrepreneur.

He had much for which to be grateful.

He had risen from humble origins and lived a rich and vigorous life. He had set foot on every continent except Antarctica. He had watched his small manufacturing business grow to one of the largest of its kind in the west, and he had loved a woman, the same woman, passionately for fifty years. He had donated millions to charity and the arts. And today, he had a loyal friend and confidant in Forbes, as well as his wondrous gardens, a constant reminder of his enduring love for Marguerite. His life had been filled with triumph, triumph earned by scrupulous business decisions and hard toil, triumph of his own making.

Yet, curiously, for all his achievements and patronage to those less fortunate, he often felt inadequate and terribly alone. The cause of his unrest was not that he had lost his wife to cancer and his children to adulthood; rather, it stemmed from the one great error of his life, one that haunted him and tarnished what would otherwise be a life without flaw, a life packed only with stellar achievement and altruism.

A single grievous error.

He longed to be able to look back on a life not merely filled with outstanding accomplishment, but one without imperfection. He had made only one great mistake in his life and he didn't want to die without having reconciled it. He was an old man now, well into his twilight years. He wanted more than anything else to look back upon his life through a lens of untarnished purity.

Vincenzo Minesali could not allow himself to pass to the next world until he had smoothed and polished that single jagged stone of imperfection that chafed against him every day, gnawing his soul. He had to do it for himself, for his coal-mining ancestors, for Marguerite and the children, indeed for everyone that had ever believed in him.

But most of all, he had to do it for five young boys he had never met.

CHAPTER 28

WHEN HIGHEAGLE stepped into the greenhouse, he felt the dense, warm air spread over him like steam from a sweat lodge.

"Do you know anything about flowers, Joseph?"

"Wildflowers. Don't know much about the domesticated kind."

"Come, I will show you."

The elderly entrepreneur spoke like a kindly king, and Higheagle felt himself once again taken in by Vincenzo Minesali's charismatic Old World charm. They walked down some short steps to the click of Minesali's cane, and passed row upon row of green plants and flowers in earthen pots, huge urns, and wrought iron benches. They came to a halt before some delicate yellowish-green flowers with maroon speckles.

"Flowers are like people, Joseph. Some are more temperamental than others." He held out a hand and touched the flower. "These are my favorite."

"What kind is it?"

"Star orchid. All of the flowers in this part of the greenhouse are orchids. Like many flowers, the orchid attracts only certain insects. The tools of its trade are its fragrance and the artistry of its blossoms."

"What critter would be seduced by these?" Higheagle pointed to a yellow flower with dark brown streaks.

"I'll give you a hint. Its stinger is one-tenth of an inch long and the other nine-tenths is pure imagination."

"A bee."

"Correct you are. This particular variety of orchid not only masquerades as a bee, it gives off the scent of one. That is how it attracts the little devils." They continued along the walkway. "The interesting thing about the relationship between the orchid and the bee is that it is symbiotic. The bee carries pollen from one flower to the next and helps give rise to seedlings." He stopped and looked him directly in the eye. "The bee does not merely dump its waste and leave. It does not bring any harm to the plant, nor does it bring about death. It contributes to the process of life."

Higheagle felt certain the old man was trying to tell him something.

"Now before we talk business, Joseph, I thought we might take a relaxing stroll through my outdoor gardens as well. I get so few opportunities to show them off. I hope you don't mind."

"Not at all."

They stepped outside and started through the grounds. Soon they came upon a maze of exquisitely trimmed hedges and gardens filled with blossoming flowers, colored bright yellow, salmon pink, and slatey blue. Like the greenhouse, Minesali's outdoor gardens were impressive: the arrangements and flower color schemes had an artistic elegance that rivaled the Denver Botanic Gardens.

"As you will note, the grounds have a distinctive French touch. My late wife's influence."

"It reminds me of pictures I've seen of Versailles."

"An astute observation. Have you been to France, Joseph?"

"Nope, but I've been to Lame Deer, Montana." He grinned and Minesali answered with a smile of his own.

"You see, Joseph, the gardens of the French are extremely orderly and symmetrical. They are different from those of the English, which have more of a pastoral charm. Everywhere in the world are different gardeners. The Japanese, for instance, have an economy of style unmatched elsewhere in my opinion. You might say they are the Hemingway of flora. Come, let me show you."

And with that, Minesali led him through each and every garden, instructively pointing out the various flowers, describing their history and giving Latin names and their translations where he saw fit.

"It's great that you love this so much," Higheagle said as they retired to a sandstone bench set against an eight-foot high hedge. "I've never been much of a green thumb myself. My favorite hobbies have always involved purging male aggression. That's why I play lacrosse for the Denver Outlaws."

"Indeed, I have seen you play on TV. You are quite the goal-scoring midfielder. But your competitive nature is also why you conduct unorthodox environmental assessments, is it not?"

Higheagle smiled. "Let's just say I like a good challenge."

"Indeed." Minesali winked as he sat down on the bench. "Now that we have had a peaceful walk through my gardens, Joseph, please tell me what you have found out in your investigation thus far. I am most anxious to hear what you have to say."

ψψψ

Minesali listened attentively as Higheagle told him about the backfilled drainage and the anomalously high metals concentrations in soil. He was impressed with how much progress the geologist had made and was pleased with having selected someone so well suited for the job. He was also touched by how sympathetically Higheagle spoke of Sally and Tommy McTavish, from whom he had obviously learned a great deal. It seemed as if part of the reason he was doing this was for them, which was just fine with Minesali.

His foremost priority was results.

"So you found nothing unusual about the air or water samples?"

"Nothing irregular. The chain-of-custody forms were all in order and the results were all non-detect, except for low levels of metals in the groundwater samples. The concentrations were well below secondary drinking water action levels."

"So it is the soil then that is of concern?"

"Based on what I've found so far."

My Cheyenne friend is being cautious. You must lead him in the right direction. "What do you think the next step should be?"

"I'm not sure."

"Well, don't you think you should look further into this white material in the soil? It can't be just metals, can it?"

"No, I don't think so."

"Isn't there some way you could take samples and determine what it is?"

"I suppose. But we are talking about trespassing onto private property."

"Sometimes the cat burglar works best when he is dressed as the electrician." He tried to make it sound like an offhand remark, not wanting to overplay his hand.

"In broad daylight? Now that would be interesting."

There was a glimmer in Higheagle's eye and Minesali knew he was more than up to the task. *He wants to do it. The sense of danger appeals to him. Remember, that's why you chose him in the first place.*

Minesali opened the palms of both hands towards the sky. "A workman performing some necessary activity, a groundskeeper or maintenance man perhaps?"

"The area I'd have to sample is all grass. I would need to collect probably twenty samples and map in the coordinates. It would take the better part of a day."

"But it could be done."

"Yes." The thoughtful expression disappeared and his expression turned quizzical. "I don't want to sound like I'm prying, but if you have concerns about what Prescott's done at Dakota, why don't you just back out of investing with him on Silverado? Why go through all this effort?"

It was the million dollar question, and Minesali knew he would look suspicious if he didn't answer it. The bottom line was, he had to have a good explanation as to why he was willing to go to this extreme, so there would be no doubt of his motives. Fortunately, Forbes and he had worked out an answer to this very question more than a month ago, long before Higheagle had been contracted to perform the environmental assessment.

"Obviously, Joseph, your work is more than a scientific exercise to me. When we first spoke, my main objective was due diligence with regard to Hayden Prescott's environmental record. I needed to have a good handle on my potential liability should I choose to invest with him. The truth is there have been rumors over the years, rumors that he's not as environmentally responsible as advertised. I had no idea whether the rumors were true or not, and that is why I wanted you to investigate. I didn't want to bias you one way or another, or alarm you unnecessarily. Now however, it appears there's some heft to the rumors and I can no longer entertain the idea of investing in Silverado Knolls. My priority now is to find out what's happened to these boys at Dakota Ranch."

He paused a moment, to let the sincerity of his expression and solemnity of his words have the desired effect.

"As you know, my wife died from pancreatic cancer. Not a day goes by that I don't grieve over what she went through. That is why I'd like to see your investigation through to the end even though I am no longer considering investing. I want to know how these young boys may have gotten cancer. I want to know if they could have died from exposure to this white material in the soil. It is for them that we must find out what has happened at Dakota Ranch. And it is for other children, as yet unknown to us, that we must closely examine Silverado Knolls."

In the reflective silence that followed, Minesali tried to gauge Higheagle's reaction. He could tell he had struck a chord with the geologist, but would it be enough? He thought back to how much he had admired Higheagle when he had first seen him on television during the Quantrill affair. Even back then, he had known that one day his destiny might be linked to this young man.

"Listen to me, Joseph. A lawn and garden consultant would take samples of grass or soil, would he not? Well then, who better to pose as a lawn expert than an earth scientist. I can give you some gardening supplies to add to your, shall we say, professional appearance."

Slowly but assuredly, a mischievous Huck Finn smile spread across Higheagle's face. "I can't think of a good reason not to do it—except that I might get thrown in jail."

"You won't have to worry about that. Before jumping into the fire, you shall have full legal protection."

"Great, a get-out-of-jail-free card. Can you throw in Kevlar body armor too?"

"Perhaps that could be arranged."

They laughed.

"All right, I know damn well I shouldn't be doing this. But tell me, Vincenzo, what exactly do you have in mind?"

CHAPTER 29

COPPERSKINNED AND RECHARGED after a weekend of downhill skiing punctuated with prodigious wild sex with his favorite brunette from the Denver art circuit, Prescott felt as virile as ever as he punched the elevator button for the ninth floor and then two more buttons for three other passengers. When the doors clicked shut, he discretely studied his reflection in the shiny metallic wall of the elevator. A dashing bachelor in a colorful Armani tie and sleek brown suit gazed back at him through matching chestnut eyes that carried a trace of devilishness.

Here, most assuredly, was a card-carrying member of the elite 1%.

Satisfied with his appearance, he smiled inwardly and thought of the many tasks he had to complete today. The most important was a ten o'clock appointment with a group of Douglas County commissioners, who he hoped, after the meeting, would be more than happy to do his bidding. Two stops later, the doors opened and he stepped from the elevator.

To his surprise, his new receptionist, hired only three weeks earlier, was motioning frantically from her teakwood desk.

"Thank God you're here, Mr. Prescott! Mr. Hwong and Mr. Bishop are here to see you!"

Though taken by surprise, he wasn't about to let his fine day start off in panic mode. He gave her a charming smile as he pulled up in front of her station. "Well, good morning to you too, Cynthia."

"I'm sorry, Mr. Prescott. Good morning."

"Now that wasn't so bad, was it? Where can I find them?"

"They're in your office. Chip offered to look after them." It seemed as though she wanted to say something more, but Prescott decided not to press her for more detail. He thanked her and walked down the hallway at a relaxed gait, covering his nervousness with an air of unconcern. What could be so damned important that Bishop and Hwong were waiting for him in his office?

When he opened his door, his young eager-beaver assistant was on his feet instantly. "Good morning, Mr. Prescott."

"Morning, Chip." His easy expression dropped as he took in the two stony-faced men seated in front of his desk. Bishop, as always, was clad in a conservative business suit, this one a navy-blue Armani pinstripe. Hwong was outfitted in tan cotton slacks, a white short-sleeved shirt, and a green tie.

"Good morning, gentlemen." He walked over to his desk and set down his briefcase. "Thanks, Chip, for looking after my associates. I'll call you if I need anything."

The young man gave an obedient nod and walked out the room. Prescott waited until the door closed before speaking. "I thought we weren't supposed to meet until two." He held out his watch. "Mine says eight-fifteen."

"There's been a new development," Bishop said worriedly. "We've got a fucking boy scout on the loose."

"His name's Joseph Higheagle," Hwong said. "You'll find a message on all your voice mails if you bothered to check them."

Prescott's eyes narrowed. "You know I don't take calls when I'm away for the weekend. I value my free time. And furthermore, I instructed you that in the event of an emergency to always contact my secretary—and she'd put you in touch with me." He looked at Bishop. "This Higheagle, you don't mean that geologist who found out about that deep-well-injection-earthquake thing?"

"That's the one. The environmental boy scout."

Prescott was more than a little peeved that someone was digging into his business affairs. "What the hell is he up to?"

Hwong jumped in before Bishop could respond, his face twisted with displeasure. "He came to my office on Friday. Somehow, he got his hands on some split sample results from the Dakota investigation. Remember, the soil samples sent to Redhill Labs by your consultant friend."

"Jack Obermeyer. But how?"

"Higheagle said he was working for the Health Department and got the results from them."

Bishop looked at Hwong. "What's the name of the woman he said he was working with?"

"Mary Casserly. At least that's what he told me."

"Refresh my memory," Prescott said, trying to conceal his vexation. "I thought those results were sent to us and that was the end of it."

"The lab still has the records. And they're notorious for giving away the results to any Joe Blow who calls up and gives them project information."

"Why wasn't this taken care of back then?"

"Because you didn't hire me to begin with. You had that damned Obermeyer do the field work and look where it's gotten us."

Prescott ignored Hwong's impertinence and looked at Bishop, feeling his anger growing. "I'm paying you fucking five hundred an hour, Greg. Start talking."

"We need to call the Health Department and find out if Higheagle's really working for them. That's the first step."

"All right, let's call Markworth right now." He reached for the phone and in less than thirty seconds had the Haz Mat director on the line. "Dan, this is Hayden Prescott. I'm here with Doug Hwong and we were wondering how things were coming along with the Silverado report." He didn't bother to introduce Bishop, not wanting Markworth to know the attorney was in on the conference call.

"We should be finished with our review by the end of the week and get an approval letter to you soon thereafter."

"That's great. Any issues that need to be addressed?"

"Nothing that will hold up your schedule. We have a few comments on surface water, but they can be addressed in a follow-up addendum. The graphics look sensational, Doug."

Hwong tilted his head towards the speakerphone. "Glad to hear it."

"We look forward to receiving your approval letter," said Prescott. "Obviously, we're anxious to begin grading and construction soon."

"As I said, we should have it to you by the end of the week."

"That's great." Prescott paused to marshal his thoughts; it was time to get to the real purpose of the call. "Oh, I almost forgot. There's a guy Doug's seen at the hazmat conferences over the years who I understand is doing some contract work for your office. His name is Joseph Higheagle."

The line went silent; clearly Markworth hadn't expected this. "Uh, I know Joe. He's not working for us, not that I know of anyway."

"That's odd. He said he was working with a woman from your office named Mary Casserly."

This time the hesitation was even more pronounced. "Did you speak to Joe recently?"

"Yeah, he came by and asked a few questions," said Hwong. "I thought he was working with your group, so of course I helped him out."

The phone went silent. Prescott cursed under his breath. He didn't know the exact nature of Higheagle's game, but it was definitely not good. Not only had he misled people to get information, but he and Markworth had at least a professional relationship, one which Markworth appeared reluctant to disclose.

"I can look into it and get back to you," Markworth said.

You're hiding something, you lying bastard! But he knew he was playing a risky game and realized he had no choice except to end the call. His pretense of innocent inquiry was wearing dangerously thin. Besides, he had found out what he needed and was unlikely to get anything more out of Markworth.

"It's no big deal, Dan. We just wanted to make sure this guy was on the level. The main reason we called was to check up on the Silverado report. Don't hesitate to give us a call if we can answer any questions for you."

"I won't. Goodbye, gentlemen."

ψψψ

Hanging up, Prescott gave a nettled look that said, "Well?"

"There's no doubt we've got a fox in the henhouse," said Bishop. "And I think Markworth's known about it from the beginning. Still, I don't think he or anyone else in the Health Department will pose a problem. Just set up another meeting with Dahlquist. He'll make sure old Danny Boy understands the role that's been scripted for him."

Hwong's reptilian eyes narrowed. "What if Higheagle gets to him first?"

"He probably already has," said Prescott. "In any case, Dahlquist will take care of him and his lackeys. The only problem is the senator's out of town and won't be back until later this week."

Bishop said, "I think we can assume Higheagle got the lab data from Redhill and not from the Health Department. The question is can we make the lab's copy go away?"

Hwong shook his head. "It's on their network hard drive and backup disks.

They probably purge their analytical reports every five years or so, but until then there's little we can do. However, you should know that Redhill has had QA/QC violations. Nothing in the last few years, but we can discredit the lab if it ever comes to that. Its certification was revoked temporarily about a year before the sampling."

Prescott thought: *I'll threaten them with a lawsuit for releasing confidential client information without my approval. Then they'll pull the goddamned records!*

"I wonder how Higheagle knew to call the lab," Bishop said.

"He must have reviewed the work plan and seen that split samples were proposed," surmised Hwong. "When he couldn't find any results in the report, he must have called Obermeyer."

Prescott took a deep breath and smoothed back his glistening black hair. Years ago, it had seemed like a good idea to have a third party consultant from out of state collect the soil samples. Jack Obermeyer was a family friend, he was just getting his business started, he was naive, and he had no ties to Hwong's lab—which at the time had made him the perfect consultant for the sampling. However, now with the split sample results floating around, hiring Obermeyer appeared to have been a costly mistake.

"My guess is Obermeyer didn't tell Higheagle anything else of importance," Bishop said. "Probably just that the splits were collected and sent to Redhill. He never actually saw the sample results. And you paid him for completing the report even though he didn't, so he shouldn't have reason to be angry with you."

"He seemed perfectly happy with the arrangement. I don't see why he would have given any information to Higheagle. That's a flagrant violation of client confidentiality."

"That's about as important to a consultant as campaign finance reform is to a politician."

"I'll bet Higheagle told Obermeyer the same lie he told me, that he's working for the Health Department."

Prescott rose from his chair and began pacing in front of the window. "How the fuck did this happen?"

"One slip-up in the paper trail is all it ever takes," said Bishop.

"So what do we do?"

"I can think of four things. First, call Obermeyer and find out what he said to Higheagle. Tell him not to talk to anyone further and to contact you if our boy scout calls again. Second, set up a meeting with Markworth and have Dahlquist put him in his place. Third, set up a meeting with Higheagle to find out where he's headed with this thing. I should be there to—"

"No, I want to dance with Higheagle on my own."

"I don't think that's a good idea."

"Tough shit. What's the fourth piece of...legal advice?"

"Get Shard on our boy scout right fucking now."

CHAPTER 30

WITH THE SUN directly overhead, Higheagle began staking soil sampling locations in the grassy field next to the rec center. Masquerading as a kind of hybrid soil scientist/lawn technician, he wore a visor cap, faded jeans, a khaki shirt, and black high-top Red Wing boots. His field garb and soil sampling and gardening tools made him look reasonably official. Still, he wasn't sure he should be performing this clandestine operation his octogenarian client had talked him into, though it was too late to back out now.

Around noon, he began collecting soil samples. He had designed an equally spaced grid over the backfilled area and selected random soil sampling locations before his arrival so that he could make an unbiased stochastic assessment of the extent of the potential soil impacts. He collected samples at the random locations within the established grid and at the two locations where elevated metals concentrations were detected, vectoring in the GPS coordinates for each sample location using his hand-held Trimble global positioning system plugger unit.

To drill down, he used a four-foot-long, steel hand auger, which worked like a corkscrew, twisting through the ground and packing soil into the auger's column. At each location, he pounded a steel drive-sampler loaded with brass tubes to collect the samples. He covered each end of the soil-filled tubes with a Teflon strip, plastic end-cap, and duct tape then labeled the samples with a depth and ID number. He wrote down the necessary sampling information and analytical methods on the chain-of-custody form that would accompany the samples to the laboratory. He followed EPA protocols rigorously, thoroughly scrubbing and rinsing all of the sampling equipment between each sample point.

As he was digging, he noticed a striking color contrast between the soil extending approximately one-foot below ground surface and the deeper soil. Above the one-foot depth, the soil was dark yellowish brown, and below this depth the soil turned to a brownish gray with lenses and pockets of the white crystalline salt-like material Tommy had described. He had no idea what the white stuff was, but he was having the samples analyzed for every chemical known to man so he would know soon enough. Judging by the sharp contact, the overlying dark yellowish-brown soil appeared to be "clean" fill brought in to cap the impacted soil. In each boring, he collected samples in the deeper zone bearing the white material, using the three-foot depth for consistency.

It took him the full afternoon to complete the sampling. He didn't notice anyone watching him, nor did anyone stop to ask him what he was doing. But that didn't assuage his anxiety. After all, he was trespassing and he could get caught.

After placing the final soil sample in his ice-chest, he gathered his field supplies, put them in the wheelbarrow, and headed towards the War Wagon. When he reached the edge of the pavement, he saw a man in a beige uniform walking purposefully towards him. He felt a sudden stab of panic. Though he had already invented a plausible cover story to justify his being here, he was taken off guard.

"Can I help you with something?"

Higheagle smiled politely at the man. "I don't believe so, but thanks," he said, ignoring what the man was really trying to say and continuing to back his wheelbarrow down the concrete curb.

"I'm Bob Watkins, Head of Maintenance and Groundskeeping."

Higheagle felt his heart flutter in his chest, but forced himself to appear relaxed as he brought the wheelbarrow to a halt and extended a gloved hand. "John Quintero, soil scientist. I'm all finished here now."

The man's face was a study in skepticism as they shook hands. "What are you doing exactly?"

He knew he had to show no hesitation and present an air of authority. "Collecting soil samples. We're having them analyzed for moisture content, pH, alkalinity, nitrogen, phosphorous, and other nutrient levels. You mean The Newport Company didn't contact you?"

"No, and I'm the one who has to approve all outside contractors. I'm the Head of Maintenance and Groundskeeping," he said with greater emphasis this time.

"All I know is I was hired to collect samples and have them analyzed to make sure you have the right soil here. Apparently, it's deficient in general minerals and the root systems aren't holding quite as well as they should."

He hoped like hell this Watkins guy was buying his technobabble, but to his dismay, the man's face was still shrouded with distrust.

But then he said, "I'm going to need a copy of the results."

It took great effort for Higheagle not to smile. Here he thought the guy was going to call the cops and impound his samples and all he wanted was a copy of the lab data! "Sure, I can do that. Why don't you give me your business card and I'll send you a copy."

The man pulled one from his wallet and handed it to him. Higheagle looked the card over, pretending to be impressed. "Okay, Bob. I'll take care of it." He glanced at his watch, faking surprise. "Oh man, it's after four. Two of the analyses have to be performed within six hours of sample collection. Sorry, I've got to run or my boss will have me drawn and quartered."

The man took measure of him again, as if not fully convinced he was on the level. Higheagle started to pull away with his wheelbarrow.

"Hold on—one last thing."

Higheagle came to a halt, his heart palpitating wildly.

"We're not going to have to resod, are we? I mean, the grass looks fine to me."

The Cheyenne breathed a sigh of relief. "I don't think so, Bob, but I'm just the field technician. I don't make the big decisions. That's The Newport Company's job." He looked at his watch again, as if responsibility beckoned, and gave a courteous smile. "I'll make sure you get those results."

Then he pushed the wheelbarrow to the War Wagon, loaded up, and drove away.

CHAPTER 31

FOR THE FOURTH TIME the past week, Sally carried Tommy to his bed directly from the car after his afternoon radiation therapy session. He usually fell asleep on the way home, physically exhausted from the x-ray barrage. She quietly pulled off his shoes, covered him with the quilt at the foot of his bed, and took a seat in the chair next to the bed so she could watch him sleep. It took less than two minutes for the tears to begin to flow; this, too, was becoming part of the ritual.

She had been religiously reading the literature on how to maintain a positive attitude during a family cancer crisis, but it did little to ease her sadness. She tried to remain cheerful around Tommy, and was generally successful, but it was merely a mask, a front on his behalf. In reality, with each passing day she was losing hope and withdrawing from the world.

Since Tommy had been diagnosed with cancer, she had been blaming herself for not just his illness, but for all the misfortune in her life. She was the one who had failed in her marriage. She wasn't smart enough, sexually adventurous enough, interesting enough. Their stillborn second child was her fault. She was the reason why her husband had slept around, packed up and left, and quietly filed for divorce from distant Portland, Oregon. She was to blame for his being routinely late with the child support payments. She was the reason he had no interest in seeing Tommy; the boy was an extension of her.

She inexplicably found a way to fix the blame for her son's cancer and her ex-husband's failings on herself, and had no idea how to begin to patch together her life, or at least make the most out of what she had. The truth was she drew her strength from Tommy. He made her life worth living and gave her a singular maternal purpose. If she lost her only child, her life would have virtually no meaning.

The doorbell rang, pulling her from her saturnine thoughts. She considered not answering, but eventually dragged herself from the chair and walked downstairs.

Looking through the window, she saw a familiar face. Before opening the door, she turned away to wipe the tears from her face so she would look presentable.

"Hello, Joseph."

"This is the second time I've dropped in on you unannounced, but this time I really was in the area." He held out a hardcover book. "I thought Tommy might like this."

"How thoughtful of you." She took the book from him and glanced at the cover: *Crazy Horse: Strange Man of the Oglalas* by Mari Sandoz. "What a wonderful present. Do you want to come inside for a minute?"

"Just for a minute. I have to get to the lab."

She opened the door and he stepped inside. "I'm sorry you won't be able to give this to Tommy yourself. He's asleep and I don't want to wake him. We just got back a few minutes ago from his treatment session." She closed the door. "Let's talk out back."

They walked through the hallway to the kitchen. Sally set the book on the kitchen table and opened the sliding glass door. As they stepped outside, Max reared up on his stout hind legs and lunged at her guest.

"Down, Max."

Higheagle laughed playfully. "Feel like dancing, boy." He took the big black Lab by the front legs and performed a jig on the lawn.

"He likes you," said Sally.

"Most dogs do. Which is ironic given Cheyenne history."

"Oh really, why is that?"

"Back in the old days we used to eat dogs. They were considered a delicacy. Old Max here obviously doesn't know that historical tidbit or he wouldn't be so friendly."

"Well then, I suppose ignorance is bliss."

He let go of Max's legs and the dog dropped to all fours and ran off across the yard, flush with excitement. Sally sat down on the edge of the wood deck and Higheagle followed suit.

"The reason I came by, Sally...I wanted to tell you I took soil samples from the field you and Tommy showed me."

"You're having them analyzed?"

"It will take a few days to get the results back, but I'm pretty sure they'll be hot. You could see the chemical discoloration in the soil. The soil was brown on top and dirty gray and white a foot down, as if clean fill had been placed on top of the waste."

"Waste?"

"There's no other name for it. It was dumped there, Sally. And it was covered up so no one would find it. I just don't know what it is yet. But I will soon enough."

Sally gave an approving nod, but she wondered how any of this would help Tommy. She was pleased that Joseph was progressing with his investigation and that she had gained an important ally, but she failed to see any tangible benefit. After all, what he was doing wasn't going to save Tommy or bring the other boys back to life.

"How's Tommy doing, by the way?"

"About the same. We won't know for certain if the treatment's working until they run the next CAT scan."

"He's a good kid."

She detected a trace of emotion in his voice and realized that he had probably come here as much to see Tommy as her. They sat there in reflective silence, watching Max racing around the yard.

"Well, I'd better be going. I need to get the samples to the lab."

She wished he didn't have to go so soon.

"I'll keep you posted on the results. And please let Tommy know that I stopped by and am plugging away on this thing."

"I will. Let us know if we can help in any way."

"I'll do that." They headed back inside, leaving Max to run around the yard. When they reached the front door, Higheagle turned and said, "I'll see you later then, Sally."

"Thanks for the book. I know Tommy's going to love it."

He gave a parting nod and she watched helplessly as he started down the steps. She wanted to ask him if they could maybe get together sometime, but she was terrified of coming across as desperate or appearing as though she was asking him on a date.

He continued down the steps, his long raven-black hair tumbling wildly down his broad shoulders, and she felt opportunity slipping away. She had felt the same helpless sensation so often these past few years and she always hated herself for it. But this time, she resolved herself to do something.

"Wait," she said, the firmness of her voice surprising even herself.

He turned before taking the last step and looked at her expectantly.

"I was wondering if you might want to come back when you're finished and have dinner with us."

"Sure, but I don't want to put you out."

"Oh, it's no trouble at all."

He grinned and she thought to herself, *I could get used to a smile like that.*

"What time?" he asked.

"Seven?" she said, fidgeting with her hands. "Or is that too late?"

"It'll give me time to drop the samples off at the lab and shower up."

Sally's face took on a luminous quality. "Great. Any special requests or dietary restrictions I should know about?"

"I'm partial mostly to buffalo tongue, pemmican, and prairie turnips. You've got all that stuff handy, right?"

"I'm not sure I—" She stopped right there as she realized he was joking. "You had me there."

"I'll see you at seven," he said with a wink.

She waved goodbye and closed the door. As she turned around, she caught her reflection in the mirror in the foyer. There was a sparkle in her eyes like sunlight on water, and her face looked smooth as silk.

She smiled.

In that instant, as a sense of rapture bubbled through her like a fresh spring, all the misery and frustration of the past few weeks disappeared, and she felt happy to be alive.

CHAPTER 32

TO VIC SHARD, Hayden Prescott's gigantic mansion in conservative Cherry Hills stood out like a bright red cherry on a plain white cake. The soaring, sharp-angled mass of glass and steel was built in an uncompromisingly modernistic style, with a disregard for convention that must have been true to the vision of its slightly deranged architect. Shard found it ironic that Prescott built only prefab modules for the suburban patsies of Douglas County, when his true passion seemed to be flamboyant modern architecture that bordered on downright subversive.

The PI killed the Jeep's engine and walked to the front door. Before ringing the doorbell, he peeked inside and saw Prescott sitting in the den wearing a monogrammed bathrobe and leather slippers, reading a copy of the *Wall Street Journal* with his feet propped up on a leather ottoman, an expensive cigar dangling carelessly from his mouth. Shard was reminded of Hugh Hefner lounging about his Playboy mansion. All that was missing was a sign above the doorway that read POVERTY SUCKS!

The interior was gorgeously refined. A steel staircase spiraled down from the second floor like a corkscrew, and a hand-blown glass chandelier dangled from the ceiling. The handsome white-oak floor supported an hourglass-shaped coffee table and an elegant sofa. Carved into the shiny stucco walls was a white glass fireplace and shelves bearing tableau arrangements of bowls and glassware. Two early Jackson Pollack paintings exploded from the wall behind Prescott in splatters of vibrant color, though Shard wasn't particularly impressed by his client's taste in art.

He pushed the doorbell button. A moment later, the renowned developer appeared and the door was enthusiastically flung open.

"Ah, if it isn't the great Phil Marlowe. Thanks for meeting me at home, Vic. Come right in."

The PI was surprised to see Prescott in such a festive mood. Given the current scrutiny by the Health Department and Higheagle, he had expected his client to be on edge. Maybe he had closed a big deal today and that was why he was so happy.

They shook hands and Shard stepped inside. Prescott closed the door, locked it, and led the private detective to his palatial home office, waving a hand towards a fancy leather sofa. "Have a seat. What can I get you to drink?"

"Bourbon straight up."

"Happens to be a specialty of the house." He went to the sideboard, pulled out a bottle of Old Yellowstone, and poured four fingers into a glass. Then he grabbed an Amstel Light from the small refrigerator for himself and walked to where Shard was sitting.

Shard took the bourbon from him. "Thanks."

Prescott sat down in the chair across from him and looked at him expectantly. But Shard was in no hurry. He took a big swig and held it in his mouth a moment, allowing the fiery liquor to linger a moment and burn away his exhaustion. Sighing with satisfaction as the whiskey made its way down his gullet, he tilted up the curved rim of his white straw cowboy hat and took a brief gander at his surroundings. The Andy Warhol silk-screen prints on the walls caught his eye, one showing a strutting Mick Jagger, the other recurring images of Marilyn Monroe. He frowned at the puffy-lipped Jagger, but found the voluptuous Marilyn to his infinite liking.

Now there's a woman in full.

"What did you find out, Vic?"

Shard tossed back the rest of his bourbon and set the glass down on the table. "Let's see here," he said, pulling out a small notepad and flipping to the first page. "Your boy was born and raised on the Northern Cheyenne Reservation up in Lame Deer, Montana. Date of birth 1977, which makes him thirty-two. Born to Russell and Melissa Higheagle. Both full-blooded Northern Cheyenne, or as full blooded as a marauding Plains Indian can be, I suppose. He was raised by his grandfather mostly. Parents were killed along with his grandmother when he was six."

"How did his parents die?"

"They were murdered."

"Murdered?"

"Right in front of the boy's eyes. The police called it a simple armed robbery, but the case was never solved."

"Must have been hard on the young lad, losing his parents and grandmother like that."

Shard was surprised by the note of sensitivity in his client's voice; usually Prescott was all blood and thunder. "I expect it was," he said.

"What about the father?"

"Marine Corps, fought in Viet Nam. He was on a three-week stateside leave from overseas duty when the murder happened. He was a winner of the Distinguished Service Cross. Semper fi."

"So he was a war hero. That's about what I would have expected. And what about this grandfather that raised Higheagle?"

"War hero too...Korea. The son of a bitch won two different combat decorations as well as a Purple Heart at Pork Chop Hill in '53."

"Impressive. Tell me more about him."

"Name's John Higheagle. He was a tribal lawyer and acting tribal chief, but he's now retired. He serves as an informal senior advisor in councils and provides some litigation support on water and mineral rights issues up on the rez. Higheagle started living with him when he was six years old after his parents and grandmother were killed. They lived on the old chief's ranch along the South Platte until Higheagle went off to college."

"Where did he go?"

"Dartmouth."

"Our boy scout's an Ivy Leaguer? That's just my luck. And I suppose you're going to tell me he graduated sigma cum laude."

"Actually, he almost didn't make it. He was on academic probation his freshman year. Damned near flunked out."

"And after his freshman year?"

"He was a B-student his sophomore year and got straight As his last three years. He was a double major in geology and paleontology with a minor in American history, which is why he took five years to graduate."

"Again impressive. Play any sports in college?"

Shard had figured Prescott would want to know about that. After all, his three great passions were sports, business, and women. "He played lacrosse."

"Dartmouth's Division 1. Kudos again. Was he any good?"

"He was team captain and first team All-American his junior and senior years. He's also been playing professional lacrosse the past four seasons for the Denver Outlaws. Their season runs from May through July."

"Shit, he's a professional lax player too? I may have to get to an Outlaws game. This guy just keeps getting more interesting by the minute. Now what about his geological career?"

"His first eight years in the business, he worked for a firm called HydroGroup here in Denver. They do environmental consulting, water resources, that sort of thing. He moved up rapidly. He was a senior hydrogeologist making ninety-five grand a year when he left the firm to form his own company. He makes another twenty thousand per year playing for the Outlaws in the summer."

"Did he leave and start his own environmental firm because of the Quantrill business?"

"That seems to have been the reason."

"And this new firm of his, what's it called?"

"Higheagle Environmental. Started around six months ago."

"Who are his clients?"

"Gates Rubber and ConocoPhillips are the only two I know of so far."

"So you still don't know yet who he's working for on this Dakota thing?"

Shard detected a note of challenge in his client's voice. "Well, we know it's not the Health Department. And he couldn't possibly be handling this alone. Someone's got to be paying him."

Prescott sat thoughtfully mute for a moment; Shard just watched him. *What are you up to, Hayden? What the hell have you gotten me into?*

"The top priority is to find out who he's working for," said Prescott at length. "I'm counting on you, Vic. You need to get me a name." He maintained an admonishing expression for several seconds, underscoring his authority, before leaning forward in his chair and holding his beer between his palms. "Now tell me about the Quantrill business."

"You know the story from the papers. Quantrill was making a fortune pumping toxic wastewater down some deep injection wells in an area that was supposed to not have any faults or be capable of seismic activity. Then one day his operation started causing earthquakes. You remember, there were a bunch of them, all east of Castle Rock. The worst was a 7.9. Over a thousand people were killed in that one. Your boy found out about it. Held a big press conference on the steps of the capitol and exposed Quantrill and his top lieutenants. Man ended up killing himself. End of story."

"So Higheagle worked for him?"

"At the time, he was with HydroGroup and Quantrill was his client. But he quit the company before the announcement."

"So he turns in his own client and the man ends up killing himself."

"Hell of a way to go. But there's another thing about your boy. He could have reaped a ton of money in TV, magazine, movie, and book deals, but he didn't want to have anything to do with it. I mean, this was the biggest crime in state history and he wanted no part of fame or fortune. He gave a single press conference and that was it."

Prescott scratched his chin thoughtfully. "Interesting fellow, this Higheagle."

"When are you meeting with him?"

"Hopefully tomorrow. I left a message, but I haven't heard back yet."

"Do you want my opinion?"

"Of course."

"He strikes me as a fellow who's not going to go away very easily."

"That's looking more and more apparent. And just how would you recommend reining him in?"

Did you kill Gus McTavish? That's what I really want to know, you slippery bastard! "Depends on how far you're willing to go to solve the problem."

"A little file purging might be in order. I presume Higheagle's assembled a fairly extensive database for his little pet project. Of course, it must be handled discretely."

Shard frowned. "Not the kind of service I normally provide."

"There's ten thousand dollars in it if you change your policy. I have other associates who can do it for a lot cheaper, but they lack a certain...discretion."

If you're talking about Mr. Paine and Mr. Morelli, that's not the only thing they lack. He pulled out his tin of Copenhagen, took a pinch of tangy longcut tobacco, and stuffed it in his upper lip, working it with his tongue. If he broke into Higheagle's house and stole records, Shard reasoned, he would be an accomplice to whatever Prescott was involved in. That was not something he wanted at all. But at the same time, he would also have the opportunity to learn what Higheagle knew and stay on top of the case, as well as directly influence its outcome. He could make copies of whatever he took just to be safe. After a moment's deliberation, he decided the pros outweighed the cons—assuming, of course, that he wouldn't get caught.

"All right, I'll take care of it."

Prescott rose and went to the window. "Maybe I should have his house and phone bugged."

"I wouldn't do that if I were you. That's a federal rap."

"So how do you propose keeping tabs on him?"

"I'll keep him under surveillance. He'll lead me to his client soon enough. You said yourself that's the top priority."

"Is that a guarantee?"

"Nope, but it's the next best thing."

"Make it happen, Vic. I have enough to worry about without a renegade Indian creeping around behind my back. Now let me see you out."

ψψψ

Two minutes later, Prescott returned to his den, picked up his *Wall Street Journal*, propped his feet back on the ottoman, and relit his smooth, creamy Montecristo #2 cigar when his cell phone rang. Setting down his paper, he took the call.

"Prescott."

"Hello? This is Joe Higheagle."

So that's what our boy-o sounds like. "Ah, yes. Thanks for returning my call."

"You left a message about wanting to meet."

The tone was direct with a whiff of derision behind it. Prescott remained silent for a moment, feeling a mixture of emotions. On the one hand, it perturbed him that Higheagle was meddling in his affairs; on the other, he was curious to know more about his adversary, specifically how much he knew and just how far he was willing to go in this dangerous little game of his. But this had to be handled delicately, very delicately.

"I'd like to talk with you about the project you're working on with the Colorado Department of Public Health and Environment. It seems there's been some kind of mix-up on the analytical results at Dakota Ranch. I was hoping you might be able to clear things up for me." He kept his tone cordial, having decided that the best approach was to play the role of a concerned businessman who had been misled by his scientific consultants. "But first, I'd like to explain how all this got started."

"All right, go ahead."

"I received a call today from my previous environmental consultant, Jack Obermeyer, who said you called him about some split soil samples collected at Dakota. He said you were working with the Health Department and he gave you the number for Redhill Labs in California, the lab that analyzed the samples. I contacted Redhill and received a copy of the results myself. I showed the results to my current consultant, Doug Hwong. He mentioned you came by to see him last week. What concerns me is the elevated concentrations of heavy metals in these split samples. Is it simply lab contamination, instrument error, that sort of thing, or are there really contaminants in the soil that I should be worried about?"

"I'd say that's a reasonable concern."

"Unfortunately, I wasn't made aware of these results before," he said, as if Obermeyer and Hwong were the ones at fault. "I was hoping to meet with you...get kind of a second opinion. I spent a lot of money proving the property was clean before I developed it. From what it sounds like, my consultants, or one of these labs, may have messed up. I'd appreciate your input and may be interested in retaining your services. You have quite the reputation."

"I suppose I could meet with you."

I suppose? Who the fuck do you think you are? "Good," Prescott said cheerfully. "How about lunch tomorrow?"

"That's going to be tough. I'm really busy right now."

Busy meddling in my affairs, you mean. He blew out a nebula of cigar smoke, trying to maintain his composure. "I understand. When could you meet?"

"Wednesday."

"How about the University Club? Corner of Seventeenth and Sherman. Let's say noon?"

"I'll be there."

"I look forward to meeting you, Joe."

"Likewise."

And then he heard a click and the Cheyenne was gone. Hanging up, Prescott looked at his burning Cuban appreciatively. Though angered by Higheagle's intrusion into his affairs and impertinent manner, he nonetheless had accomplished what he wanted. He had set up a meeting, which was a necessary first step to determining the strengths and weaknesses of his opponent. He had presented himself as polite and accommodating, giving the impression that he was a reasonable man. And he had planted a seed of doubt in Higheagle's mind about who was ultimately responsible for the detected metals by pointing the finger at Obermeyer, Hwong, and the labs.

He took another puff from his Montecristo #2, sticking out his chin to produce a predatory profile.

"We'll find out soon enough what you're made of, Indian Joe," he said with hauteur. "But mice or man, I'm still probably going to have to fucking destroy you."

CHAPTER 33

WHEN THE DOORBELL RANG, Sally glanced one last time at the dinner table and was pleased with what she saw. The table was decorated with a salmon-pink damask, a pair of polished silver candlesticks, and a tall glass vase filled with yellow daffodils. For each of the three place settings, she had set out the family heirloom silver, hand blown glass goblets, and French porcelain plates, with folded napkins arranged in a decorative manner on top of each. The table furnishings were the best in her possession, all rarely used wedding gifts.

Tommy beat her to the door and swung it open enthusiastically. "Hey, Joe."

"Hey, Little Big Man. What do you know?"

"Oh, not much. Glad you could make it for dinner."

Sally stepped to the front door, Max trotting alongside her. "It appears you have three groupies at your beck and call. You must feel like a rock star."

She offered her hand and he took it. She liked the earthy color of his face, his long raven-black hair, the hint of wildness about him. Under his arm, he casually toted a six-pack of Red Dog Ale.

Tommy closed the door and locked it. They walked into the family room, Max wagging his tail. Sally angled through the kitchen, opened the sliding glass door overlooking the back yard, and coaxed Max outside, closing the door behind the exuberant canine.

"Everything go okay at the lab?"

"Yep. I should have the results by Wednesday. Would you like a Red Dog Ale?"

"Thanks, but I'll stick to my Chianti." She flicked him a sassy grin, picked up her wine glass, took a sip, and stepped to the counter to finish preparing the Greek salad.

Higheagle looked around the room. "Your house looks great."

"That's because I did the vacuuming," Tommy said. "By the way, thanks for the book, Joe."

"You're welcome, Little Big Man. I'm glad you like it." He turned to Sally. "Hey, can I lend a hand in here?"

"I've got it covered. But thanks."

"There must be something I can do."

Sally recalled how her ex-husband had rarely helped out in the kitchen. He used to come home expecting her to make dinner, even though she had worked a full day herself, and he almost never did any dishes. "How about taking the pasta and bread from the oven? You can handle that, right?"

"I don't know. That could be a stretch."

They laughed. She handed him a hot pad. As he stepped past her to open the oven, they brushed up against one another accidentally and he reached out, as if to steady her. She could feel the warmth of his hand on her arm and his touch was light, his palm dry. She found the sensation pleasant and gave a little shudder.

Tommy smiled. "You two like each other. I saw that coming."

Sally felt her face blush.

Higheagle broke into a guilty grin. "Nope, Little Big Man, your mom and I are just friends."

"Yeah, that's what they all say. And then nine months later a baby pops out."

"Tommy!"

"I was just joking, Mom!"

Higheagle chuckled. "Ouch, the kid knows how to lower the boom. He sounds like my grandfather."

"Yeah, but the difference is, your grandfather's a chief. He can get away with saying stuff like that."

They laughed again. Higheagle carefully removed the large white casserole dish from the oven, which he then set on the stove. Steam rose from the concoction of corkscrew fusilli and fresh vegetables. "Smells great. What kind of spices are in here?" he asked as he bent down and pulled out the French bread and set it next to the pasta dish.

"Oh, the usual suspects." She grabbed a bottle of Newman's oil and vinegar salad dressing from the refrigerator and set it on the counter. "Fresh parsley, garlic, oregano, and basil."

"Not exactly a typical dinner at my house. All I practically ever eat is fry bread and Mexican take-out. I've got a thing for gorditas, chalupas, and green corn tamales."

"That's why we're having you over for dinner," said Tommy. "You looked like you weren't eating very well and we felt sorry for you."

They laughed again and sat down at the table to eat.

ψψψ

After dinner, they moved into the family room, plopped down on the couch, and talked. Just before ten, Tommy went to bed and Sally and Higheagle moved outside onto the deck. They spoke a few minutes about what he had found out thus far regarding Dakota Ranch before Sally dropped her bombshell that she had once had a relationship with Hayden Prescott.

"Wait a second. You're telling me you used to go out with this guy? You've got to be kidding me."

"I guess I should have told you."

"You guess?"

She felt her entire body coil up on the defensive. "I'm sorry. I just didn't see the connection."

"Here I am digging holes all over the property of a guy you used to go out with, but you didn't see a connection?"

"Somehow it just never clicked that Hayden could be responsible for what might be going on out here."

"Whatever happened between you two is none of my business. I'm just concerned for you. If Prescott has dumped waste at Dakota Ranch, don't you think he might go to great lengths to keep it a secret?"

"Are you saying he might be dangerous?"

"I don't know, but I don't think we should wait around to find out."

"Come on, you don't know for certain he's part of this. And just because he wants to meet with you doesn't mean he's done these terrible things."

"For now, I'll give you and him both the benefit of the doubt. But I suspect you might feel differently once I get the analytical results back from the lab. How close were you two anyway?"

"I thought you said our relationship was none of your business."

"Maybe I changed my mind."

He seemed a touch jealous so she decided to downplay the whole thing. "It wasn't a big deal. We only dated for a few months. In all that time, he never seemed capable of something illegal. He was a little self-possessed, like a lot of young hot-shot businessmen, but he didn't seem malicious or anything."

"By the way you're playing it down I'd say that you were in love with the guy."

"No, I wasn't," she retorted briskly, though deep down she was less certain. A part of her must have loved him, she realized. Another part of her didn't want to admit that he could be involved in something illegal. It would mean admitting that she had been a bad judge of character, that her affections had been gravely misplaced.

She decided to turn the tables on him. "If I'm not mistaken, you sound like you're jealous."

"I don't think so."

"You sure?"

"Okay, maybe a little."

She grinned. "Good. I wouldn't have it any other way."

ψψψ

They talked for a few more minutes longer, joking around and flirting, cheerfully exposing a little more of themselves, before the subject reverted back to Tommy. Sally admitted that she was worried about him. He was undergoing his second week of radiation treatment, and that's when the nausea and exhaustion typically took their toll. The doctors had warned her that it would be far more difficult than anything Tommy had experienced thus far and that she needed to prepare herself for the worst.

"But being tired and rundown is just a side effect from the radiation, right?" said Higheagle. "It doesn't mean the cancer's getting worse."

"It's hard for people to accept though, especially a child. His hair will be falling out too. How can I make him understand it's all right, that it's only a side effect?"

"I don't know. Tell him straight out, I guess."

"Luckily, the hair loss will be just around the portal, where the x-ray beam goes. But it's still going to put a tremendous strain on him. These side effects...I'm just afraid they'll make Tommy feel as though he's getting worse."

"But the doctors have prepared you both for what to expect, right?"

"They have, but it's still hard." She could feel the tears forming and looked away, fixing her gaze on the watercolor on the wall that Tommy had drawn. It showed a serene blue lake surrounded by gently swaying trees.

He held out a hand to console her. "It's all right. Go ahead and cry."

She gave a determined look. "No, not this time. I've been doing it too much lately."

"Just let it out. Hell, I'd cry along with you but I'm Cheyenne and we have a long tradition of masking our true emotions."

"I'm Scottish and so did we until I came along."

Together, they joined in a cathartic laugh and soon she began to feel better. What was it about Joseph that made her feel as if everything was going to be all right? Even though she barely knew him, she felt as if she were in the presence of a guardian angel. An Indian guardian angel.

"You're a genuinely good guy, aren't you? It's not an act."

"I don't know. Ask me again after I've kissed you." He leaned forward on the couch and gave her a little caress on the lips.

She nodded with satisfaction. "You're a good guy all right. Anybody who kisses like that has got to be."

He grinned mischievously. "That's what they said about Butch Cassidy and John Dillinger."

"Well then, those two desperate outlaws must not have been that bad after all."

And with that, she leaned forward and they kissed again.

CHAPTER 34

"YOU AND I have had an excellent working relationship, Dan. But what concerns me, and my respected colleagues, is this unscrupulous geologist who's running around pretending to be someone he's not. You know who I'm talking about: this Joseph Higheagle character who claims to be working on behalf of your department."

Prescott stopped right there to let the reprimand resonate. Markworth shifted uncomfortably in his seat, and Prescott couldn't help but feel a little sorry for him. He looked so pathetic and helplessly bureaucratic. They were sitting in Prescott's plush office along with State Senate Majority Leader John Dahlquist and House Rep Cynthia Chavez, both of whom looked like Dobermans ready to pounce at the order of their master.

"As I told you over the phone, I know nothing about it. Joseph Higheagle's not working for us. I spoke with Mary Casserly, as you asked me to do, and she has no idea what's going on either."

"So let me understand. You're saying you and your staff know nothing about this?"

"That's exactly what I'm telling you."

Dahlquist leaned forward, his body assuming a bellicose tilt. "But you do know this Higheagle, correct?"

"Everyone knows him. He solved that earthquake case last—"

"Yes, yes, we know all about that. But we don't care about what he did in the past. We care about what he's doing right now. And what this man's engaged in is an act of fraud and he's going to be punished to the full extent of the law. But first we need to know why he's doing it."

Prescott couldn't help but smile inwardly. The senator was a piece of work—worth every penny of the hefty campaign contribution Prescott had given him before the last election.

"What we'd like to know specifically is who Mr. Higheagle is representing," Chavez said, her brown eyes penetrating despite the polite tone. "Do you know who that might be?"

"I couldn't begin to guess who he's working for. All I know is he just started his own environmental consulting firm a few months ago. To the best of my knowledge, his only client is Gates Rubber."

"We've learned that he came to your office last week to review the Dakota Ranch files," pointed out Dahlquist accusingly. "And that you personally met with him to discuss the contents of the files. We're going to need to know specifically what the two of you talked about."

Prescott saw a flash of guilty surprise cross Markworth's face. *Sorry, boy-o, but we've got you by the short hairs.*

"Who told you this?" he demanded, looking first at Dahlquist then Chavez.

"Come now, you know very well Representative Chavez and I have eyes and ears all over this town."

"You have no right. Where are you getting this information? From someone on my staff?"

"You needn't concern yourself with that. What you should be worried about is managing the cancer study in a way satisfactory to us."

Prescott watched Markworth take a moment to regroup; he was clearly not used to being manipulated like a kindergartner. "Okay, Joe came in to review the records. It happened before our meeting here last week. What was I supposed to do, turn him away? We're a public agency. And besides, I didn't think it was a big deal. Just a common citizen exercising his right to public review."

"Mr. Higheagle is hardly a common citizen," Chavez pointed out, flicking her spindly black bangs away from her eyes. "He is a trained professional and environmental activist. We all remember the Quantrill affair. If the pendulum swings the wrong way, he can make things very messy for all of us, especially you."

Prescott decided it was an opportune moment to play up his good-cop role. "I know you were only doing your job, Dan. But we would have appreciated it if you had contacted us. In our last meeting, we all agreed we have a very sensitive situation on our hands. You said you would keep us informed if there were any new developments. None of us wants the environmental lobby, media, or EPA to start sticking their fingers into this thing. And since we don't know for certain whether Higheagle is acting as a lone wolf or working on behalf of some third party, we have to be careful who we talk to."

Markworth nodded thoughtfully, as if he agreed with the fundamental logic. *Good boy, Danny, now you're thinking clearly.*

"What can you tell us of this Mary Casserly?" Chavez asked. "Is it possible she's working in collusion with Mr. Higheagle and she's kept you out of the loop?"

"No, that's not possible."

"But how do you know?"

"She's not even on this project. She's in USTs."

"What's that?"

"Underground storage tanks."

Now it was Dahlquist's turn: "Did Higheagle give you anything, reports or other information?"

Markworth shook his head. "He was just there to review the files."

"Did he review or copy any material related to the cancer study?"

"No. Those files are confidential. The work's still ongoing."

The room went silent. Markworth's eyes had been moving between all three of his inquisitors for the past few minutes, like a spectator at a tennis match. Now he just stared at the floor, looking out of place in the filigreed corporate stronghold. His pallid, bejowled face and cheap business suit served to heighten the contrast between the besieged environmental bureaucrat and the three dapper power brokers sitting across from him. Looking at the man, Prescott couldn't help but feel sorry for him.

"Dan, I think it's pretty clear what's in the best interest of all of us. You need to cut off contact with Higheagle. It puts you—and us—in a potentially compromising position. I would also ask that you notify Senator Dahlquist and me if Higheagle, or anyone else, contacts you again. We can't afford any surprises, and neither can you. I know you can appreciate the delicacy of the situation and we look forward to your cooperation in this matter. Now, having said that, I'd now like to move on to where you stand with the cancer study."

Frazzled, Markworth took a moment to regroup. "As I told you last week, we've established that a statistical excess has occurred. We're trying to determine now if it represents a true cluster event. If it does, we would look into the risk factors the children have in common. Similarities in health, diet, lifestyle, possible chemical exposure, that sort of thing. We feel that if there's a common basis for the cancer, then there should be a causal mechanism they all shared."

Again, Dahlquist took over the line of questioning. "Are you suggesting that chemicals in the environment may have caused the cancer?"

"I'm saying chemical exposure is one possibility. We're starting to investigate all relevant cancer-causing mechanisms, chemical exposure being just one of them."

"What kind of cancer-causing mechanisms are we talking about?"

"Smoking, dietary imbalances, chronic infections leading to inflammation, and hormones are the major ones."

"But you said chemical exposure would also be considered."

"It's one of the things we'll have to look at. At this point, we can't discount that the kids may have been exposed to chemicals of some kind."

"Have you found anything that might suggest this?" asked Chavez, her tone more diplomatic than her senatorial cohort.

Markworth shook his head and folded his hands demurely in his lap. "We're still compiling interviews and collecting background info."

Dahlquist leaned forward aggressively in his chair. "Do you know how much sampling Mr. Prescott has performed at Dakota Ranch? Why he's drilled enough test holes that the place is pockmarked like the surface of the moon. And nothing's ever been found, except one spot of motor oil, which was hauled off and properly disposed of. I don't think I need to remind you that the environmental impact and site investigation reports were signed off by you. How can you come in here after all the exhaustive field work done out there and tell us chemicals may be killing these kids?"

An uncomfortable silence hung over the room.

"We understand the public has a right to know what's happening," Chavez said, her tone and manner blandly logical. "But we also have to weigh the public's concerns against the damage that unsubstantiated accusations could cause. We certainly can't have people like Mr. Higheagle poking his nose where it doesn't belong until you've found out what's going on."

"We're not saying you have to terminate the study, not yet anyway," snorted

Dahlquist. "But we are telling you to make sure this thing doesn't become a matter of public record until you've completed your study. And you had better be one-hundred-percent certain of what has caused the cancer before you make any conclusions." He wagged his finger crossly. "My colleagues on the hill will not tolerate unfounded accusations and pseudoscience."

"But there's no such thing as one-hundred-percent certainty in cases like these."

"All we're asking is that you go about your work discretely and make sure you don't make any outlandish claims about chemicals in the environment," Chavez said to mollify him. "The public, media, and environmental groups aren't savvy enough to understand the large uncertainties in these cases. They think toxic chemicals are everywhere and respond to what the media tells them. You mention cancer and chemicals in the same sentence and they go nuts, without the slightest understanding of the science involved."

It was time for Prescott to put his own stamp on the proceedings. "The investigation at Dakota, Dan, showed the property has not been impacted, with the exception of a smattering of motor oil. Hundreds of soil and groundwater samples say it's clean. That's why you need to tread softly. If people were more informed and capable of making scrupulous decisions about these things, we wouldn't even be talking with you. But unfortunately, that's not the case."

"And, let's not forget, your agency would bear most of the responsibility if someone were to make accusations about toxic chemicals," Dahlquist said gruffly. "You signed off on the reports. If lawsuits were to emerge from this, I can guarantee the Health Department will be named in the—"

"I think he gets the point, Senator," Prescott cut him off, pretending to be sympathetic. He looked the beleaguered regulator in the eye. "Can we count on you to handle this in a proper manner, Dan?"

Several seconds passed before Markworth responded. "Yes, I'll take care of it."

"Wise decision," said Dahlquist. "I'm sure there's a simple explanation for why those kids got sick. They've probably been sneaking cigarettes and eating junk food. Or maybe they have bad genes. Whatever, nothing good can come out of making arm-waving accusations. Glad you're with us now on this. You are with us, aren't you, Dan?"

"Yeah, I'm with you."

The senator gave a crocodilian smile. "In that case, you have nothing to worry about."

CHAPTER 35

STEPPING INSIDE the historic, tan-bricked University Club building on Sherman Street at precisely 11:43 a.m., Higheagle stopped at the reception desk and was greeted by a rosy-cheeked woman with an English accent. He informed her that he was here to meet Hayden Prescott for lunch at noon. Smiling punctiliously, she told him to head to the right to the College Room. Thanking her, he walked down a narrow hallway until he came upon a huge Elizabethan dining room with resplendent stained glass windows projecting radiant shafts of light.

A waiter in a red vest walked up to him. "Welcome, sir. You dining alone today?"

"I'm supposed to meet someone for lunch in the College Room."

"You've come to the right place, sir."

"The person I'm having lunch with isn't here yet. I'll just look around for a minute if that's all right."

"Very good, sir. Let me know if you need anything."

Higheagle looked up again at the impressive stained glass windows. After a moment, he located the college seal for his alma mater, Dartmouth College. The seal showed a ray of light shining down from the sky on a pair of Indians. They had feathers in their hair and were walking towards one of Dartmouth's hallowed buildings. The shaft of light held an open book, symbolizing the great reward of knowledge that higher education brings. Higheagle was amazed at how accurately it depicted his ascension in the white world. He was a perfect example of the civilized, integrated Indian the original social engineers who had founded Dartmouth College had hoped to manufacture. He had received an excellent education for free, but in the process he had given up part of what made him Cheyenne.

And that bothered him.

He turned his attention to the other features of the room. It had a stately yet droll elegance. The walls were covered with handsome English oak paneling. Baronial brass chandeliers hung down from the ceiling like a giant latticework of ice crystals. Perched next to the staircase was a balcony for theatrical performances with ornately carved wooden Shakespearian caricatures. Off to his right, he saw a spectacular limestone fireplace and mantelpiece, a grand piano, and several potted ferns. The tables were decorated with white linen tablecloths, floral centerpieces of tiny magenta carnations and white daisies, and full place settings.

Everything about the room was collegiate, manly, fraternal. The room spoke of the bibulous fellowship of the rich and powerful and preserved perfectly the monied grandeur of early twentieth century Colorado. He recalled the words of

Balzac: *Behind every great fortune there is a crime.* Thousands of great fortunes had undoubtedly been built up by members of this club, and behind most of them, there was probably something unethical, if not outright illegal. He saw his surroundings as a kind of falsely chivalrous underworld, a place where white-collar multimillionaire crooks hammered out shady deals and plotted the downfall of their enemies while dining on lobster thermidor and filet mignon and hoisting glasses of champagne.

He was suddenly gripped with the same awe he had felt upon visiting Minesali's mansion in the Polo Club. He felt like an outsider. He thought of all the whispered secrets that must have been overheard by these walls over the years. He glanced up at the magnificent stained glass windows and again picked out his Dartmouth insignia. He was a graduate of one of the finest universities in the nation, yet he didn't feel like he belonged here at the University Club.

It was men like Hayden Prescott who belonged here.

His thoughts were interrupted by a voice behind him.

"Joseph Higheagle, your reputation precedes you."

He turned to see a sumptuously well-appointed man, late thirties, right hand extended cordially.

"Hayden Prescott at your service. So pleased you could make it."

Higheagle took the hand and gripped it firmly. "Nice club."

"It serves its purpose. Follow me, my table is right over here."

ψψψ

After directing his guest to a chair, Prescott took his customary seat directly across from him that bore his personal-engraved, silver nameplate on the back. They spent the next few minutes looking over their menus and making small talk, while he committed Higheagle's face to memory and sized him up. So this was his adversary: a tall, broad-chested Cheyenne Indian with intelligent brown eyes and an athletic physical presence undoubtedly passed onto him by fierce warrior ancestors. But it was the look of determination just beneath the easygoing outward facade that intrigued Prescott most. All in all an able foe, he decided, a man who would not capitulate easily.

Soon a waiter appeared and took their order. Prescott opted for the grilled salmon in lemon butter with a medley of steamed vegetables, Higheagle the rainbow trout smothered in almonds with wild rice and julienne carrots. Both ordered iced tea to drink. The waiter shuffled off.

Prescott leaned forward in his chair, tired of chit-chat. It was time to find out how much his opponent knew. His first tactic would be to ingratiate himself by reaffirming his innocence. He quickly recapped what he had said over the phone, how he had been contacted by Obermeyer, called Redhill Labs and obtained the data, and later spoke with Hwong. He would continue to play the role of innocent layperson given confusing and contradictory reports from his technical specialists. It was all a fabrication, of course, but it was critical to plant in Higheagle's mind the idea that Obermeyer had originally set things in motion.

When he had finished laying out the concocted sequence of events, he said,

123

"Doug Hwong told me about your visit."

"He said the metals detections must have resulted from lab error, but I don't see how that's possible."

"So you believe the soil has been contaminated. Any idea what the source might be?"

"Illegal dumping's the most likely possibility."

Prescott tried not to let his consternation show on his face. "How can you be certain? I thought metals occur naturally in soils."

"They do."

"Then how do you know this isn't some natural process?"

"The concentrations are too high."

"It appears I should have hired you to begin with, Joe. Obviously, one of my consultants has bungled badly. I'm sure you can appreciate my displeasure. I've spent a fortune proving the property was clean to begin with and now I'm going to have to spend even more."

Higheagle said nothing. Prescott couldn't tell if his adversary was buying his charade or not, but he had the feeling he wasn't. He silently cursed himself for involving a family friend like Obermeyer in the first place. If only he had hired Hwong do the work to begin with, he wouldn't be in this mess. Somehow, he had to get Higheagle talking about what he knew. As luck would have it, the Cheyenne obliged him without prompting.

"The interesting thing is if there was dumping on the property, it had to have happened just before the development was built. That's what the aerial photographs show anyway."

Prescott felt a little catch in his throat. "You examined aerial photographs of Dakota Ranch?"

"You could see that the coulee was backfilled at the same time the area was being cleared and grubbed."

Prescott feigned a look of outrage. "I can't believe someone would do this."

Higheagle didn't respond. The developer continued to study the Cheyenne closely, trying to size him up, but found his face inscrutable. The guy was hard to read, but even if he was buying into the charade, it was a forgone conclusion he would leave no stone unturned.

"Joe, I hope you're not implying I had anything to do with this."

Higheagle said nothing, just continued to look at him.

"Dr. Hwong came highly recommended to me by the Health Department. He's supposed to be one of the leading experts in the world. I hired the best because I wanted to ensure the integrity of the property before I put up a single house. I've gone out of my way to comply with the regulations. Yet you seem to be accusing me."

"I'm not saying you did it. But the waste is still on your property, and by Colorado law that makes you responsible for cleaning it up."

Prescott frowned. It was clear Higheagle knew too much and posed an unacceptable risk. Hell, the guy was already convinced of his guilt! He decided to turn the tables and put him on the defensive.

"I spoke with Dan Markworth today. He told me something quite shocking. He said you're not actually working for the Health Department. Please tell me that's not true."

Higheagle stiffened noticeably.

Now that's more like it. "I don't get it. Why would you say you're working for the Health Department if you're not? Were you trying to get information?"

Though Higheagle said nothing, the tension at the table was palpable.

"I don't want to meddle in your business, Joe. But seeing as you're meddling in mine, I believe I have a right to know what's going on. So I'm going to have to ask you, if you're not working for the Health Department, who are you working for?"

"Maybe I'm not working for anyone. Maybe I'm working for myself."

"I highly doubt that." Prescott decided not to press him further. He had learned enough and didn't want to overplay his hand. Not only did he have a better understanding of what Higheagle knew and what his intentions were, he was gaining a sense of the man. However, he was by no means reassured by what he had learned thus far. Though Higheagle seemed somewhat impetuous, he also appeared clever and determined. All and all, there was much to fear from this man. Perhaps he would have to be dealt with like Gus after all.

Lunch was served. Burrowing the sterling silver tines of his fork into his tender grilled salmon, Prescott said, "I'm in the dark just like you, Joe. I have no idea who's responsible for these metals or whether it has anything to do with these kids who are getting cancer. What I do know is I had a consultant collect soil and groundwater samples all over Dakota Ranch to verify that it was clean before I built on the property. And nothing was found."

This was his standard pitch, the same one given Shard and Markworth to satisfy their suspicions. People always wanted to hear it from the horse's mouth, his father had told him in his early years in the business, and the key was to lie convincingly. He continued on, keeping his face appropriately serious, modulating his voice to portray a man misled by those around him. In time, he would take more aggressive action and put the screws to Higheagle.

But not yet.

He finished his oration with a compelling flourish: "I certainly don't want waste being dumped out at Dakota, and I damn well don't want kids dying. That's why I'm going to make it my number one priority to find out what's going on. Because frankly, Joe, I don't know who the hell to believe anymore."

CHAPTER 36

THE FOLLOWING MORNING, Higheagle found himself sitting on a stiff black sofa in the reception area of the Colorado Department of Public Health and Environment. He wore a collarless Western shirt, tan cotton pants, and worn elkskin moccasins. He was waiting for Dan Markworth, idly watching the overhead light dance off the computer screen on the receptionist's desk.

Spotting an issue of *Chemical Engineering* on the table in front of him, he picked it up and thumbed through it absently. A minute later, Markworth appeared wearing an expression that was distinctly unfriendly.

"Let's talk in my office," he said brusquely, without extending his hand.

Without uttering a syllable, the Cheyenne obediently rose from his seat and followed him down the hallway. They walked past several cramped cubicles and offices filled with stacked boxes of reports. Markworth waved him into his office and shut the door hard.

"Sit," he commanded, wagging a finger towards one of the battered chairs in front of his desk, upholstered with a cheap synthetic fabric.

Higheagle set down his satchel on the floor and took his assigned seat as Markworth brought his portly frame around his wooden desk, which bore ample scrapes, coffee mug rings, and piles of project files.

"I've heard you've been busy, Joe."

"That's why I'm here, to tell you all about it. That was our deal, right?"

"Yeah, but I don't recall authorizing you to drag our name through the mud."

"I didn't drag—"

"You shouldn't have said you were working for us. I thought I laid down the ground rules before the first inning began."

So that's why he's pissed: Prescott complained. "I didn't say I was working for you. I said I was working with you, which is true."

"I don't subscribe to the Jack Abramoff-Bernie Madoff school of ethics. There are limits to what a person should do to obtain information."

"I wouldn't have said I was working with your group if there was any other way. So who called you, Prescott or Hwong?"

"Both. Hwong said you told him you were working with Mary Casserly. My God, couldn't you come up with someone better? She's not even in the Haz Mat group anymore. She's in USTs."

Higheagle remained silent. What could he possibly say?

"I had to tell them the truth that you weren't working for us. I had no choice. I'm not going to be party to this cloak-and-dagger crap. I have a responsibility to the public."

"And I have one to the truth."

"Oh, cut the sanctimony. We're talking about breaking laws here. You're like a renegade cop who plants evidence so he can catch some asshole he only suspects is guilty."

Higheagle knew he was in a winless situation and decided that a swift apology was his best option. "I'm sorry, Dan. I went too far. I'll make sure it doesn't happen again."

Markworth weighed the apology. "Okay, that's a start, but I'm still angry at you. Got it? Now tell me what you've found out about Dakota. I know it has to be something big."

"Two of the seven split soil samples collected during the original field investigation came up hot with metals."

"How hot?"

"Over a hundred thousand milligrams per kilogram, depending on the metal."

"So I suppose you're going to tell me how these were overlooked by us?"

"You didn't overlook anything. Hwong fudged the analytical and the split results were kept out of the report."

"And Santa Claus is Satan. Look, Joe, you're a helluva geologist, but you're accusing one of the top scientists in the industry. Hwong's outfit is one of our contracted labs, and he's served as an expert witness on dozens of big-time cases, including two for us. These are strong allegations."

"The splits were submitted to an outside lab by the previous consultant. The consultant was from California, a family friend of Prescott's. He sent the samples to Redhill Laboratories, one of the labs he used out there. I talked to this guy and got the results from him. He collected the splits at the exact same spot as two of the samples analyzed by Arapaho Technologies. The only difference was, Hwong's detects were at background levels."

Markworth pulled off his thick-framed glasses and rubbed his eyes with his pudgy right hand. "Where are the two hot samples from?"

"I'll show you." Higheagle took a moment to pull his maps, aerial photos, analytical data sheets, and stereoscope from his satchel. He set three of the aerials and the stereoscope on the table next to the desk, and the two of them gathered over the evidence. "When you look through these, you can clearly see the dry drainage was backfilled with something. A combination of solids and liquids, which must have been odorless." Markworth looked at the top photograph through the stereoscope, then the two others, while Higheagle summarized the analytical results and explained how the backfilling had occurred in stages. It was amazing how closely his interpretation fit the wild theory put forward by Dr. Ekstrom; he privately wondered if she was clairvoyant or just plain lucky.

"Hard to miss it in 3-D," Markworth agreed when he was finished looking.

Higheagle was glad he seemed to be on his side again. He slid across a manila packet containing a copy of the lab data and a map showing the sampling locations and results. "I'm giving you a copy. The two hot splits came from that backfilled area where the kids played before the rec center was built. I grabbed confirmatory samples from there yesterday and sent them in for analysis."

Markworth's jaw dropped. "You what?"

"You heard me. I went out there and took samples."

"You just walked out there in broad daylight? Don't tell me you said you were working for us?"

"Not this time. I'll have results by Thursday or Friday."

"Trespass and fraud. Perhaps you haven't heard, those activities are illegal."

That's not the issue here. You guys fucked up and didn't even know about the split results!

"You are one audacious son of a...you really have no idea how big this is, do you? I had an enlightening conversation yesterday with two members of our state legislature. They want to know every single detail about our cancer study and have stated, in no uncertain terms, that we're not to disclose any findings to the press or public until the study is complete. As a matter of fact, they have serious doubts as to whether an investigation is even warranted. Can you imagine what was going through my mind at that meeting? I was thinking about you, Joe. I was thinking about you and your damned EA. Except I had no idea you'd be masquerading as a CDPHE official and trespassing on private property."

"Come on, Dan, kids may be dying from this."

"You paid a visit to that McTavish woman, didn't you?"

"She has a right to know what's happened out there."

"I should have known this was your handiwork. She's called a public meeting and is insisting that a representative from our office attend."

"A meeting? When?"

"Thursday night at William F. Cody High."

Higheagle couldn't believe what he was hearing. Sally had planned a public meeting! What in the hell had possessed her to do such a thing? Didn't she know that a public meeting could jeopardize his entire investigation? Someone must have put her up to it. But who?

"I don't know what you told this lady, but you'd better make sure she keeps a lid on it. We could both get into serious trouble if the media gets involved. As for my role at the meeting, I'm not going to be able to say much of anything. Only that we're looking into the cancer cases."

"People are going to want to hear more than that and you know it."

"That's not my problem. Prescott has two high-ranking state legislators on his payroll that can run my investigation any way they see fit and take away my job if they want. And they can make your life miserable as well."

"I'll keep that in mind."

"You just get those results to me as soon as they come in and we'll talk again. But you and I can't meet here anymore." He snatched a pen and a post-it from his desk drawer, wrote down his cell phone number, and handed the post-it to him. "If you need to get in touch with me, call me on my cell." He pointed to the packet. "Also, I can't let anyone know I got this stuff from you. I'll need to contact Redhill on my own and get them to send me what they've got."

"You're a pain in the ass, Dan. But together we're going to figure this little mystery out."

"Sure, if we're not thrown in the slammer or put six feet under first. You just keep that McTavish woman under control, you hear?"

CHAPTER 37

TOMMY MCTAVISH trudged down the hallway of the Radiation Oncology Wing of Eisenhower Memorial, keeping his eyes focused on the shiny white floor in front of him. He felt sleepy and foggy-headed, having just been bombarded with his daily dose of x-rays.

When he walked through the swinging door with his mom, he was surprised to see Joe reading a magazine in the waiting area. He walked up to him.

"Hey, Joe."

The Cheyenne looked up from his magazine and his face brightened. "Little Big Man, just the dude I want to see. How you feeling?"

"I've felt better. But as long as the x-rays are doing their job, I can't complain."

"I hear you." He set down his magazine and stood up. "Hello, Sally."

"Joseph. I'm surprised to see you here."

"Yeah, me too," said Tommy, picking up the magazine he had just set down. "*Parenting Magazine*? You planning on having kids anytime soon?"

"I wonder who the lucky lady is," Sally chimed in, a frolicsome grin on her face.

"How do you know it's not you?" he said, and he kissed her on the cheek.

"Wow, can you guys do that again in super slo-mo?"

They looked embarrassed, but they obliged him. This time Sally kissed Joe on the cheek.

"Mom's a better kisser than you."

"That's the way it is, kid," she said. "Women are better at most things than men. They just don't feel the need to boast about it."

"Ouch," said Higheagle, and they all laughed.

Tommy said, "So seriously, Joe, how'd you know we'd be here?"

"Your mom told me. Monday through Friday at three fifteen."

"Very sweet of you, Joseph," Sally said softly.

"Actually, I had an ulterior motive. I was hoping you might let me take Tommy to the four-hour director's cut of *Dances With Wolves* on Saturday night. It's playing at the Mayan on South Broadway."

The boy wheeled excitedly. "The four hour director's cut? Awesome. Can I go, Mom? Can I?"

"I don't know. Grandma and Grandpa will be here then."

"But I'll see them all weekend. Come on, Mom, please?"

"Well, I guess it would be all right." She turned towards Higheagle. "Very thoughtful of you, Joseph. I suppose I was being overprotective."

"Did you tell Joe about the meeting, Mom?"

Higheagle's expression stiffened and Tommy realized he had said something. "Yes, I heard about that. Tommy, I need to talk with your mom alone for a minute."

The boy crossed his arms defiantly. "I'm not going anywhere. My mom and I are in this together. And don't blame her for calling the meeting. It was my idea."

"Your idea?"

"I just thought the people in our neighborhood should know what's going on, that's all."

He watched as the big Cheyenne wheeled on his mom. "So Tommy talked you into this?"

"He didn't talk me into anything. I thought it was a good idea."

"Okay, so when were you going to tell me about it?"

"I left you a message on your voice mail. Look, I only called Dan Markworth this morning. I didn't want to give him a chance to duck out of it so I scheduled it for this Thursday at Cody High. I don't see what the big deal is. It's just a neighborhood meeting."

"Unfortunately, it's not that simple."

"I don't know why not."

"I know you and Tommy are going through a tough situation and want to take action. I'm just afraid you might say something inappropriate at the meeting or have unreasonable expectations. Is Hayden Prescott going to be there?"

"I was going to contact him."

"When?"

"A couple of hours before the meeting. I'm not going to allow him to derail the whole thing."

"I met with Dan Markworth this morning after you spoke to him. The Health Department hasn't made any progress on its end and he's not going to be able to tell you very much at this stage. Dan's definitely not going to talk about chemicals in the environment or anything like that, if that's what you're thinking."

Why not? Tommy wondered. *If there's bad stuff in the dirt, why can't the Health Department just figure out who put it there and go after them?*

"Look, Tommy and I just want something to be done about this and to keep people informed. I'm not going to say anything about your investigation if that's what you're worried about."

"You're still going to have to be careful. Look, from what I've told you, I know it sounds like I think Prescott's broken the law. But the truth is I don't know whether he's involved or not. The same goes for Hwong."

"So let me get this straight, they're innocent?"

"No, I didn't say that either. But do you really want to accuse these guys in a public forum without one-hundred-percent certainty? And what about the work I'm doing? I'm sworn to confidentiality, not only to my client, but to the Health Department. And let's not forget that I trespassed to collect the soil samples. I could get in a lot of trouble, maybe even go to jail."

Tommy realized that he and his mom hadn't thought through what might happen to Joe if they went ahead with the meeting. He didn't want to get him into trouble and he definitely didn't want to ruin their chances of finding out what was going on at Dakota Ranch. But he and his mom had to do something. The people in their neighborhood deserved to know that kids were dying and to find out what was causing it.

"If you go through with this, Sally, you've got to make sure to keep the media and police out of it. And you can't whisper a word about my work. I'm telling you, they could ruin the whole thing and people could get hurt. And whether Prescott's involved or not, the waste is on his property, so he's going to have to bear a substantial portion of the cleanup cost regardless. I met with him for lunch and I can tell you he's not happy about that. At the very least, he has the resources to make your lives miserable, as well as mine. And so does the state legislature, who apparently Prescott has in his pocket. The bottom line is I don't really know what's going on or who's involved. That's why you need to tread carefully."

"We will. But we still have to find out who's responsible. And if it's Hayden Prescott, then he has to pay. It's as simple as that."

"You're going to have to limit yourself to the cancer. And you can't make any mention of what I'm doing or let Prescott know I've been in contact with you."

"Why is that?

"Because we don't want to tip our hand. This guy is rich and powerful and can make our lives a living hell. I don't care if he's your old boyfriend or not."

"Is that what this is really about? You're actually jealous?"

"No, but I do care about you both and don't want anything to happen to you."

"We know you care, Joe. But my mom and I, we've got to do this."

"You're taking a big risk."

"You're probably right. But it's still the right thing to do."

CHAPTER 38

A HALF HOUR LATER, Higheagle pulled into his driveway, parked the War Wagon, stepped from the truck, and looked up to see his grandfather opening the screen door and stepping out onto the back porch.

"So the prodigal grandson returns."

"Hello, Grandfather. Did you have a good nap today?"

"What the hell kind of question is that? Do you think I'm a goddamn invalid or something?"

"No, I just wasn't sure what to expect. You know how you are when you haven't had your afternoon nap."

"Okay, so I'm a grouch. You would be too if you were a hundred twenty years old."

The old Contrary grinned mischievously. Higheagle had the funny feeling he was up to one of his usual tricks and was only pretending to be grumpy. "But you're only seventy-five, Grandfather."

"But I usually feel like I'm a hundred twenty. Just not today." He gave a little wink and Higheagle knew he had been right to be suspicious.

"All right, what is it?"

"For some reason, I feel much younger today."

Higheagle had no idea what he was talking about—and then it suddenly hit him. "You heard from the doctors, didn't you? You're okay!"

The old chief broke into a grin. "Dr. Ekstrom called me a few minutes ago."

"You don't have cancer! That's great news, Grandfather!" He took him in a bear hug. "I'm so happy for you! You're going to be okay!"

"I knew it all along."

"Yeah, like hell you did, you old fart."

They pulled apart, beamed at one another, and bear hugged once again. "I still have to get this damned lump beneath my arm removed. But you know what this means, don't you?"

"No, what?"

"I get to smoke hemp again."

They laughed. "You're crazy, Grandfather—totally fucking crazy. But this definitely calls for a celebration."

"To kick it off, I'm going for a walk to our special place. Want to come?"

"You bet. And afterwards we'll have a good sweat, smoke a little hemp, and I'll take you out to dinner. How about The Fort?"

"As long as you're buying."

They struck west on foot for a mile until they came to a small bluff of crumbly sandstone that looked out onto a small grassy park and beyond the towering Rockies—historically called the Shining Mountains by the Cheyenne. The sky overhead was pinkish-hued and the few clouds present looked like ripple marks on a sandy ocean bed. The sun's fading rays touched the tops of the mountains to the west, which stood gray and jagged against the dusky sky. Higheagle could hear birds chirping over the sound of the wind whistling gently through the cottonwoods along the small creek in the foreground.

This was their special place.

Standing here next to his grandfather, Higheagle felt a swell of sentiment as he gazed out at the hallowed ground upon which his Cheyenne ancestors had lived and died. Before the mining camp of Denver City had sprouted up in 1859, the Cheyenne and Arapaho had erected their great villages for more than three generations at the confluence of Buffalo Tallow River—called the South Platte by *vehoes*—and Cherry Creek, the latter named by the indigenous tribes for the profusion of wild berries that grew along her banks. Standing upon the sacred hunting and camping grounds of his ancestors, fully immersed in a world of solitude, Higheagle was proud to be a *Tsistsistas*, proud to be a Cheyenne. But most of all, he was relieved and ecstatic that his grandfather didn't have cancer. The Great Mystery, the Wise One Above, had come through for the crafty old chieftain after all.

They continued walking along the edge of the bluff, picking up the occasional loose pebble and tossing it over the edge. When the sun set, they headed back to the house, stripped down to their boxer shorts, went into the backyard, and prepared for their sweat bath. In accordance with tradition, the sweat lodge faced east and consisted of a dome of arched willow branches covered with animal hides and canvas and a thick floor mat of sage. They heated big blocks of basalt on the propane grill, carried them into the sweat lodge with a shovel, and placed the heated rocks in the pit in the center. The inside was lit with a pair of candles. Once they had enough hot stones, they closed the canvas flap to keep in the heat and slid into the willow and canvas backrests around the pit.

Higheagle picked up the hollowed buffalo-horn spoon on the ground and dipped it into the water bucket. He flicked water repeatedly over the stones, producing hissing sounds and puffs of steam, while his grandfather busily packed hemp into a hatchet pipe with his thumb. The feathered cantlandite pipe had originally belonged to their great ancestor High Eagle, a famous Cheyenne warrior and statesman.

When the old chief finished packing the bowl, he raised the pipe and paid tribute to *Heammawihio* and the Four Sacred Directions—North, South, East, and West. Then he lit the pipe and puffed on it. Higheagle always felt a sense of joy watching his grandfather smoke the pipe in the old way. For as long as he could remember, the ritual had been performed in precisely this fashion.

"So what's new with your study?" the old chief asked him after they had passed the pipe for a few minutes.

"It's getting more complicated, that's for sure." He quickly brought him up to date about his tense visits with Markworth and Sally and Tommy.

"Hmm, that does make things trickier. You sure you're not in over your head?"

"Thanks for the vote of confidence, Grandfather."

"This Hayden Prescott is rich and powerful. You can bet he has an army of attorneys, enforcers, and private investigators working for him this very minute. And you already told me that Sally suspects there may have been foul play in her uncle's death."

"Are you trying to scare me? Is that it?"

"No, but you do need to ask yourself a question. What makes you so sure this man will not harm you? If he has done the things you suggest, he has every reason to make sure you don't talk."

Higheagle took a draw from the pipe and exhaled a cloud of bluish smoke. The mingled aromas of the burning hemp and sweet sage on the sweat lodge floor were pleasantly overpowering. "Message understood. What do you think I should do?"

"I would keep that scattergun under your bed loaded at all times. It'll probably come in handy—and so will my Winchester."

"That's what you said the last time."

"And I was right, wasn't I? The bad guys came gunning for us."

"Okay, I promise we'll be locked and loaded for bear. But I don't think we're the ones we should be worried about. It's Sally. She should never have called that damned public meeting."

"Are you worried that she might bring your study out in the open?"

"I'm more worried how Prescott will respond. I can't quite read him. But there's another twist: Sally and Prescott used to be involved."

"So that's what you meant by complicated. What about you? Don't tell me you're falling for this woman?"

Higheagle said nothing, but knew his face said it all. Feeling self-conscious, he took the pipe from the old man and puffed on it, handing it back when he was finished. Then he picked up the buffalo-horn spoon, dipped it in the water bucket, and tossed some water on the hot basalt rocks in the fire pit. The water hissed and turned to a cloud of steam that warmed his face.

"I thought I told you never to mess with white women."

"You're the one with the white girlfriend."

"Yeah, but she's French and our relationship is purely sexual. You did see *Last Tango in Paris*, didn't you, so you know where I'm coming from?"

"You're crazy, Grandfather, and with Viagra and a French woman in the mix, I would say you're also dangerous. What's the world coming to?"

"I would think you would be happy for me. After all, I'm still coupling with the young babes in my twilight years."

"Coupling? Has anyone used that word since Wounded Knee? And besides, I wouldn't call sixty-year-olds babes."

"Maybe you wouldn't, but I do." He grinned salaciously. "Seriously, you should find a nice young Indian girl and get married. Just make sure she's not Crow or Blackfoot. Those bastards will always be our enemies. Who knows, you might be able to find a sweet Cheyenne girl that fits the bill right on the Internet. I've heard that's how it's done these days."

"Hell, why don't I just get a mail order bride like in the Old West? Come on, Grandfather, nothing's happened between me and Sally."

"That's how it always is. Nothing happens and then nine months later a baby pops out."

"That's exactly what Tommy said."

"It is? Fucking-A, that little pecker really is a good kid."

"It's true I have feelings for her, and I like Tommy, but it's not what you think."

"Then what is it?"

"I don't know. The truth is I still feel a little awkward around them. Maybe I'm afraid to get involved with a divorced mother and her son. Or maybe I'm just afraid to confront the fact that Tommy may die of cancer. I don't know what it is exactly. I feel badly for them and want to help, yet at the same time I find myself wanting to keep my distance. And recently, I've found myself wondering whether I would make a good father."

"Have you been thinking of your own father?"

"I wish I had gotten the chance to know him better. I was so young when he was killed. I only have a few memories. And with each passing year, even the few memories I do have seem to fade. I know what you've told me about him, how he was a good father and Marine and how he won the war medal."

"Maybe you are serving as something of a father to this McTavish boy."

"He's a good kid. I guess I feel like he's being cheated from the kind of childhood every kid deserves. I want to be like a father to him, but Sally and I aren't really together. I find myself calling and visiting them and bringing the boy presents, but I'm not even sure why I'm doing it. I know I want to help. But a part of me doesn't want to get too attached to them because Tommy probably won't live through the summer."

"I felt the same way when I was in Korea. I was afraid of becoming friends with the guys in my platoon because, at any moment, they might get killed. I thought it would be easier to deal with death if I didn't get too close to anyone."

"That's the same way it is with me. It's like I want to prove to myself I'd make a good husband and father, but I don't want to get too close."

John Higheagle tapped the bowl of the pipe against one of the rocks in the fire pit. "It sounds to me like you're not just falling for this woman—you're falling for her *and* her son."

"I think you might be right."

"Maybe you need to pull back. You could be getting too emotionally involved with these people."

"You think it's clouding my judgment?"

"Only you can answer that question. But sometimes it's best to go about one's business with emotional detachment. You were hired to perform a job and cannot afford to let your feelings for these people affect your decisions. Your foremost priority must be to complete your investigation. But in the process, you must be careful."

"Nothing's going to happen to me, Grandfather."

"I sure as hell hope not. You're the only family this old man has got left in this crazy fucking world."

CHAPTER 39

PRESCOTT SAT at his desk imagining storm waves lashing furiously against the rocky cliffs of Corona del Mar, not far from the Newport Beach estate where he grew up. The tide was coming in and the surf was roiling with foam. Even with the slashing wind and rain, there was a regularity and beautiful symmetry to the monstrous waves as they pounded the blocky coast. He was transfixed by the awesome power of nature, its indisputability.

The voice of his attorney rose over the roar of the waves, snapping him from his reverie. "What did Shard find at Higheagle's last night?"

Bishop and Hwong were sitting in the black leather chairs in front of his desk. Outside the office, The Newport Company was in full gear, the cubes and offices humming with industry.

"He didn't find anything. Whatever Higheagle had, he took it with him when he and his grandfather went out to dinner. His laptop, hard copy files, the works."

Bishop ran a fat hand through his brilliantine hair. "So he suspects you might make a move to destroy his evidence. Smart fellow."

"You're going to have to take stronger measures at some point," said Hwong. "Why not have him muscled around a little? Let him know you mean business."

Prescott's brown eyes locked onto him like a smart bomb. "I'm surprised at you, Doug. Here I thought you were a nerdy academic, but you're actually Bugsy Fucking Siegel."

"He's going to have to be dealt with eventually."

"For holding two master's and a doctorate, you show too much of the lion and not enough of the fox. Haven't you heard of the law of unintended consequences?"

Hwong snapped silent, a dour expression on his ferret face.

"I'll play hardball with our Indian friend when the time comes. But that will be between me and my...other associates. For now, I need you to focus on other matters. We need to be prepared if this thing ever gets to court."

"What did you have in mind?" asked Bishop, flicking away a piece of lint from his three-piece Armani.

Prescott looked at Hwong. "You said the lab that analyzed the soil samples had several EPA violations, right?" He now spoke in his teamwork tone, hoping to put their disagreement behind them. "I want you to discredit the results. Get the complete background on the lab, anything and everything dirty. It should have the reliability of the FBI crime lab when you get finished with it."

"I'll find out every conceivable way the sample results could be tainted: holding times, trip blanks, method and equipment blanks, matrix spikes, instrument calibration problems, the works."

"Good—have at it. As for you, Greg, I want you to pull together everything you can on every cancer cluster case handled in state and federal court. Make a copy for Doug here. I want you both to go through it thoroughly and we'll talk next week. I want to know of any opinion or precedent that will leave me hanging with my neck in a noose. I have to know what I'm up against. Also, I need you two to find out who the top guns are on these cancer clusters. We need the best defense experts on our team. We need to make sure the other side doesn't have a leg to stand on if this goes to settlement or court."

The phone rang, surprising them.

Prescott checked the caller ID. It was the front desk.

He pressed the intercom button. "Yes, what is it, Cynthia?"

"Detective Marshak is here to see you."

Prescott gave an involuntary start and looked at Bishop.

The attorney motioned towards the phone. "Mute," he whispered.

"Just a second, Cynthia." Prescott hit the mute button and looked again at his attorney.

"We can't turn him away. He'll be suspicious," said Bishop.

"Who the fuck is Detective Marshak?" Hwong demanded, looking none too pleased for having been kept in the dark.

"Don't worry, he's nobody," replied Prescott irritably. To Bishop: "Why not say I'm in a meeting and can't be disturbed?"

"He'll just come back. And the next time I might not be here."

Hwong was nonplussed. "What the hell is going on? What does this Marshak want?"

"Shut up, Doug," growled Prescott.

"We have to get him out of here," Bishop said, tipping his head towards Hwong.

"Why the fuck are you two talking as if I'm not even here?"

"I thought I told you to shut up, Doug." Prescott waved his hand to silence the world-renowned geochemist then hit the mute button again and spoke directly into the speakerphone. "Cynthia, would you be a good girl and call Sophie. Have her come down and escort Detective Marshak to my office."

"Yes, Mr. Prescott."

That would buy him some time. He punched off the intercom button and looked at Hwong. "You have to get the hell out of here."

"What the fuck is going on? Is this about McTavish? Is that why this police detective is here?"

Prescott looked warily at Bishop.

Hwong shook his head in disbelief. "So it wasn't an accident. You killed him, didn't you?"

"I didn't kill anyone. He died of a fucking heart attack." Prescott rose from his chair and moved like a panther, smoothly yet aggressively, towards Hwong.

"No, you did it. I can tell. Jesus Christ, I can't believe you got me into—"

"Shut up and get the fuck out of here. Now!"

And with that, he grabbed Hwong by the collar and shoved him out the door.

CHAPTER 40

PRESCOTT MOTIONED Marshak to one of the chairs around his conference table. As the detective sat down, he glanced at Bishop disapprovingly. Clearly, he hadn't counted on the cagey legal eagle being here.

"So what can we do for you today, Detective?" asked Prescott pleasantly.

"I just wanted to check up on a couple of things. Routine really."

Bishop frowned. "As I told you last time, Detective, my client is more than happy to answer your questions. Provided, of course, the investigation is not being handled as a homicide and he is considered nothing but a material witness. That is the case, isn't it?"

"That's correct. Mr. Prescott is not a suspect and the case is not being considered a homicide. I just have a few things that don't quite add up, and we owe it to Mr. McTavish's family to get the events of the evening in question properly sorted out."

You're lying just like last time, Prescott felt like saying, but he held his tongue. "Fire away, Detective. Hopefully, I can help you out."

"Thanks, Mr. Prescott. Now the problem I still have is the second waiter. What happened to him? No one knows. Who was he? Again, no one knows. He definitely wasn't a Pepsi Center employee. Then where did he get the waiters' uniform, correct down to the last detail? Again, we don't know. Don't you think it's a little odd that this mystery guy comes into the box, announces that he's going to get help, and then disappears without actually getting anyone?"

"I have no idea who the waiter was or why he chose not to get help, Detective. As I told you before, I was busy trying to save Gus's life."

"There you have it," Bishop said, as if no further explanation was required.

"I'm not rushing to conclusions here. All I'm trying to point out is the strange circumstances surrounding the death, circumstances that need to be explained before I can complete my report."

"Are you suggesting there was foul play, Detective?" asked Prescott.

"It remains a possibility."

"What evidence do you have that would point in that direction besides this heart medication you told us about last time? As I recall, you said it was a massive dose and that's what made you suspicious."

Marshak didn't respond, as if his sense of procedural propriety compelled him to withhold this particular information.

"Looks like we're back at square one then," Bishop said with asperity. "What we've got here is obviously a simple heart attack brought about by poor physical health, alcohol, and too much heart medication. So why do you persist in trying to make it more than that, taking up the valuable time of my client in the process?"

Again, Marshak said nothing, his face reading like a blank slate. "I have just a couple more questions. You said during the second interview that you knew Gus was taking heart medication regularly. Why didn't you tell me about that when we first spoke at the Pepsi Center?"

"I suppose I didn't think of it. I had just been through a traumatic experience."

"And you and Gus had the whole luxury box to yourselves that night? Is that correct?"

"I own the box."

"There must be enough seats for a dozen people at least. All that room, big playoff game and all, and it was just you and old Gus?"

"Is there something wrong with that, Detective?" demanded Bishop.

"No, I guess not. I just think it's a little odd." He pulled out a computerized police artist composite and pushed it across the glass table. "And you're sure you don't know this man?"

Prescott looked down at the crude likeness of Zachary Paine. "I've already told you, Detective. I've never seen him before in my life."

There was a little flicker in Marshak's eyes, and Prescott realized that somehow his face must have betrayed him. The detective took the picture back and scribbled some notes in his notebook. Prescott cursed himself for his mental lapse.

"As we all know, there were two waiters that night," Marshak continued. "The first one to show up at the box was legitimate, the second was an imposter. The first waiter, Fred Cavendor, said he took one and only one drink order from you, a few minutes into the game. He said you and Gus each ordered one round of drinks. Is that correct?"

"I don't remember, Detective. I guess so."

"And as far as the second waiter goes, he said he was going to get help but never did. The two people who actually did go get help were James and Candice Griffin, from the adjoining box. They managed to wave down two policemen, one of whom went and got the paramedics. But no one else tried to get help. Don't you think that's odd?"

"My client's opinion is hardly—"

"Why didn't you give Gus mouth to mouth immediately? Why did you hesitate?"

"This has gone too far. You're deliberately badgering my client."

"Just answer the question please."

To his dismay, Prescott felt his face go flush with guilt. In his defense, all he could think to do was to look at his watch and pretend to be alarmed about the lateness of the hour. "I'm afraid I'm going to have to cut this short. I have an important meeting," he said lamely.

"Just answer the question and I'll be on my way."

Bishop rose from his seat, signaling that the interview was over. "This has gone quite far enough, Detective."

"Settle down, Counselor. It's just a simple question."

"No, we're done here. My client has bent over backwards to cooperate with your investigation and yet you persist in giving him the third degree. We're fucking done."

Marshak's jaw clenched in a stubborn pose. But slowly, his expression changed from indignation to frustration as he realized he'd been outmaneuvered and had no real authority to pursue his inquiries any further without an actual indictment.

Prescott felt a surge of triumph. How dare this lowly police detective burst into his world of power and influence and grill him with endless questions. And yet, Marshak had gotten to him, he couldn't deny it. The man was irritatingly clever and persistent. Not wanting the detective to know he was ruffled, he served up his most gracious smile.

"Well, since you have no further questions, Detective, I bid you adieu. But before you go, I'd like to offer you one small piece of advice."

The detective squinted like a bulldog.

"You really must learn to show better manners. After all, I am a reputable businessman who carries some weight in this dusty old cowtown."

CHAPTER 41

MINESALI TOOK the anisette from Forbes and thanked him. Pressing his lips gently to the glass, he took a sip and allowed the liquor to sit in his mouth, letting its warmth tingle his palette. As it drained slowly down his throat, he sighed with satisfaction. Setting the glass on an ornate side table, he settled comfortably into his armchair with his leather bound copy of *The Old Man and the Sea*.

He had always enjoyed quietly reposing with a digestif and good book in this room, the Reading Room, with his late wife Marguerite near him and a warm fire popping softly in the limestone hearth. He found it the most peaceful room in the house, even more so than his Library or Private Study. Here he read to relax and drift to another place, a world more mellow and distant.

He watched out of the corner of his eye as Forbes poured himself a scotch and sat down with the latest edition of the *Wall Street Journal* in Marguerite's favorite chair, a salmon pink Queen Ann. He smiled to himself. He had lost a wife, one he had loved unrequitedly, and yet he had, in a sense, acquired another. He wasn't sure what he would do without his long-time friend, devoted servant, and confidante—the fastidious factotum of the Minesali mansion.

"I should think Mr. Hemingway a little quaint for your tastes, sir," sniffed Forbes, looking up from his paper. "I myself have always found him vastly overrated."

Minesali stopped reading and looked at him. "You surprise me, Forbes. One can always learn a great deal from Papa Hemingway."

"I have always loathed that appellation attached to the late novelist. It seems a bit too endearing for someone of such barbaric and chauvinistic sensibilities."

"Don't spoil it for me. I'm enjoying this book very much. This is the third time I've read it."

"I don't suppose this time the old man fails to catch the bloody swordfish."

"If Santiago didn't catch the fish, there would be no story. He has to catch the fish so that he may redeem his honor."

"Hemingway. Bravado heaped upon bravado."

"Where you see bravado, I see the impeccable craft of a true master. The story of Santiago is the story of all great men. He refuses to accept defeat as an option. His relentless courage leads to his redemption."

"But it's all a bit melodramatic, don't you think?"

"The book is purer than life itself. Santiago will not give in until he has caught the big fish, even though he knows the creature may end up killing him. The story is about the invincibility of the human spirit, and surely there is nothing nobler than that."

The Welshman's response came laced with peat-moss sarcasm. "I suppose our friend, Mr. Higheagle, has the same relentless spirit as your beloved protagonist."

"He does remind me of the old man. Perhaps that was why I dusted off this book to read these last few days. Your powers of perception are remarkable, Forbes. I must commend you." He picked up his glass of anisette and took a delicate sip.

"Let's just hope that Mr. Higheagle's relentless spirit is not too relentless. Otherwise, he might not seem such an able protagonist. He is, after all, on a fact-finding mission in which you play a central role."

"Whatever Mr. Higheagle comes up with I shall have to live with."

"Even should his big fish prove to be you?"

"I believe him a man of honor. I am confident he will do the right thing when the time comes."

Forbes rolled his eyes from the Queen Ann. "You've always been a hopeless romantic, sir."

"Thank you for reminding me. I'm not sure how I'd survive without you. I've grown very fond of our niggling. As you well know, Mrs. Minesali and I rarely indulged in such endeavors. In fact, I'm not sure we ever had an argument over anything. "

"She was a wonderful woman: charming, beautiful, scrupulously refined. All in all, a brilliant ray of light in this hopelessly uncultured town, where the most prominent historical figure was a buckskin-clad egomaniac who shot ten thousand buffalo and scalped heathen savages for pleasure."

"Ah yes, Buffalo Bill, another hopeless romantic like myself."

"Forget about that gaudy showman and buffalo hunter. The point I was making was about your lovely departed. She was the most charming and cultured woman I ever had the pleasure to know."

"And I must say you've done a wonderful job filling her shoes." He smoothed the satin collar of his smoking jacket. "I don't know what I'd do without you, my old friend."

"And I don't know what I'd do without you, sir. You do make things…rather interesting."

CHAPTER 42

STANDING AT THE PODIUM, Sally studied the crowd in the plainly furnished auditorium at William F. Cody High School. She could feel the gnawing tension in the room as the audience fidgeted uncomfortably in their seats, waiting impatiently for her to begin her presentation. She was disappointed that there weren't more people in the audience, having hoped for a better turnout than the thirty or so in attendance. But then again, she had put together the meeting at the last minute.

Gazing at the crowd, she saw the familiar faces of John and Mary Wilkins, the parents of Tommy's friend Todd. She didn't know them very well, but she had spoken to Mary several times since Tommy had been diagnosed with cancer. The Wilkins's were sitting in the front row, a few seats from Tommy. In the third row sat John Parsons, the father of the boy Cody who had died. She had spoken with Parsons for the first time yesterday.

Looking to her right, she saw her old flame Hayden Prescott. Though she hated to admit it, he looked strikingly handsome in his beige business suit. He was sitting with another man who had to be his lawyer. Prescott looked at her with a somber, almost betrayed, look on his face, and she felt a wave of guilt. She had deliberately contacted his office only two hours before the meeting, to make sure he couldn't come up with some clever ploy to cancel the event. Deep down, she hoped he wasn't involved in all this, but from what Joseph had told her, that seemed unlikely. Still, looking at him now, it was hard to believe he might be responsible for the deaths of four boys and Tommy's current illness.

Bob Markworth sat in the front row off to her far left. She had spoken to him over the phone and they had talked briefly a few minutes before she had taken the podium. Her eyes drifted to the rear of the auditorium, where she saw Joseph leaning against the wall in the shadows, looking incognito. He obviously wanted to keep a low profile here tonight.

She tapped the microphone gently and cleared her throat before speaking. "I appreciate you all coming under such short notice. I only wish it could have been under less painful circumstances." She paused to glance at the top page of her neatly typed notes. "My name is Sally McTavish and I have lived at Dakota Ranch for four years now. I have called this meeting to tell you about what's happening to the children of our community. Thus far, there have been five known cases of a disease known as medullablastoma. It is a rare form of cancer that affects the brain stem. All of the cases have been reported in the last nine months and have involved children who lived near the rec center on Avocet Lane.

"The goal of tonight's meeting is to make you all aware of what's going on and to tell you what action is being taken by the Colorado Department of Public Health and Environment. But for me, this whole thing is deeply personal as well. My son Tommy was recently diagnosed with the disease and is being treated at Eisenhower Memorial. We both know we have a tough fight ahead, but we are ever hopeful."

She paused to smile at her son in the first row before continuing.

"So far four children have died from the disease. The unfortunate victims include Jamie Haskell, age thirteen, Alex Johnson, age eleven, Todd Wilkins, age eleven, and Cody Parsons, age nine. All of the victims to date have been boys and all lived within a short distance of the rec center, as I stated a moment ago. Todd's father and mother, John and Mary, are here with us tonight, and so is Cody's father, John. I'm afraid the other parents have moved away.

"The Colorado Department of Public Health and Environment is conducting a study into the cancer. Dan Markworth and his staff at the CDPHE have determined, at least preliminarily, that we do have an above-normal cancer rate here. What he calls a statistical excess event. But the origin of the cancer remains unknown and the CDPHE doesn't know for certain whether the cases represent an actual cancer cluster.

"In situations like these, it's common to look into environmental impacts— such as hazardous waste—as potential causes or contributing factors. Dan will be speaking to you in a moment and he has assured me that they will be looking closely into such factors. He's here tonight to answer questions and to help us focus attention on the problem. But I believe it is up to us—everyone in our community and especially those present here tonight—to decide when no further work is required. We are the ones suffering. We are the ones who want some answers. We are the ones who must have the truth."

In response to her opening remarks, she saw Hayden Prescott and the man with him frown at her, but that only doubled her resolve. She was taking charge of the situation, and nothing could stop her now.

"The people of this community have a right to know what steps are being taken, now and in the longer term. As I understand it, it is customary in cases like these for the CDPHE to distribute fact sheets to the impacted communities. We have not yet received any, but look forward to receiving them on a regular basis in the future.

"I have questions, you have questions, and, at some point, the media will have questions. I have spoken with Bob Markworth, and at this early stage, he believes it would be most prudent to keep the media out of it, if possible. He believes it can only hamper the Health Department's investigation and unnecessarily alarm the community before all the facts are in. Personally, I think this is something we should discuss here tonight. There are many other issues that must be addressed, especially what the community's involvement will be in the future. And now, everyone, I'd like to turn the meeting over to Bob Markworth of the CDPHE. Thank you all for listening."

At the cue, Markworth hoisted his ponderous frame from his front row seat and lumbered up the stairs to the podium. It looked like there were a thousand places he'd rather be, and Sally felt a sinking feeling in her stomach. She looked to her right and saw Hayden Prescott. Again, his eyes narrowed on her. Was he angry or warning her to back off?

After handing off to Markworth, she stepped quietly from the stage and took her seat in the front row next to Tommy.

"Thank you, Sally. And thank you all for coming here tonight," Markworth began. "As you're now aware, the CDPHE is conducting an investigation into the causes of the five childhood cancer cases. This investigation was launched approximately one month ago. I have brought fact sheets and will distribute copies after the meeting. Thus far, our investigation has not identified a specific, common mechanism for the cancer cases. In fact, we are still in the process of verifying whether the statistical excursion we have identified is, in fact, a cluster event. Therefore, it is premature to even suggest that there might be hazardous constituents out at Dakota Ranch. Because, at the present time, there is no evidence to suggest anything like that has taken place."

A hushed silence fell over the room. Sally felt like Markworth was undermining her, making her out to be nothing more than a paranoid mother. It made her feel embarrassed and angry. For a fleeting instant, she allowed herself the fantasy that Markworth was in cahoots with Hayden Prescott.

Markworth continued his presentation. Sally listened to him ramble on about all the problems encountered in investigations of cancer clusters, how difficult it was to establish a link between a cancer event and a specific exposure. It was the same uninspired, overly cautious scientific drivel she had hoped she wouldn't have to hear tonight. As he spoke, she felt frustration building inside her and wished she could tell the audience about Joseph's investigation and how soon, very soon, she was going to unleash the power of the media.

"At this time, we're speaking with the victims' families and building a database on the cases. We're reviewing documents and piecing together background information. It's important for us to gather all the facts before we reach any conclusions. We don't want to be premature in our assessment because these cases are quite complex. It's going to take some time, so we're all going to have to be patient..."

As Markworth droned on, Sally felt the situation slipping further and further from her control. The meeting was turning out to be a disaster. She was no closer to exposing those responsible, enlightening her neighbors, or laying down a foundation for meaningful action than she had been the day before, a week before, a month before. She had a sudden urge to jump up from her seat and tell everyone what was really going on.

She glanced around the room at the audience. They looked uncertain, confused, as if they couldn't quite fathom what was happening.

Damn Markworth! He was just confusing them with all his scientific caveats and technobabble.

She looked at Tommy. He, too, looked uncertain, confused. Suddenly, unable to push away the emotions raging inside her, she leapt to her feet, clasping Tommy's hand.

Markworth stopped speaking and the room went abruptly silent. Every eye in the auditorium was upon her.

Sally froze. The instant before, she had known exactly what she was going to say, but now, with everyone staring at her, she couldn't bring herself to utter a single word.

She stood there, stunned, like a deer trapped in headlights.

The moment seemed suspended in time. Then Tommy coughed, and the sound, while not loud, reverberated through the hollow auditorium. It was no ordinary cough, but rather a weak, sickly rattle—and it served as a grim reminder that he was dying of cancer. She felt a sense of desperation. Ignoring the gaping-mouthed audience, she turned towards Hayden Prescott and pointed an accusing finger at him, her eyes flashing with fulminous anger.

"You did this, you bastard! You did this to us! And I'm telling you right now, in front of all these people, you'll never get away with it! Never!"

CHAPTER 43

SNAKEBIT CHARLEY'S was a juke joint on South Broadway with a perpetual smell of craft brew, sweaty body odor, and cannabis that made the air heavy as molasses. It was the perfect place to go if you wanted to get snot-slinging drunk and listen to some gritty, foot-stomping, old-fashioned blues—and right now that's all Higheagle wanted to do.

They played every kind of blues at Snakebit Charley's, and seldom much else. The walls were packed with National steel-bodied guitars, acoustic 12-strings, 1950s Strats, and hollow-bodied Gibsons, as well as a multitude of black and white photographs of venerable blues masters like Robert Johnson, Muddy Waters, Howlin' Wolf, Willie Dixon, Jimmy Reed, Lightnin' Hopkins, Elmore James, Little Walter, John Lee Hooker, and B.B. King. The owner, "Snakebit Charley" Reynolds, didn't fancy any other kind of music and never thought much of keeping up with fashionable trends. Yet, surprisingly, the house was packed every night of the week except Sundays.

Higheagle sat alone at the back of the packed bar, working on his fifth microbrew. On stage was the Texas blues band Anson and the Rockets. They had just finished covering Freddie King's *Hideaway*, a fast-paced instrumental, and were now hunkering down with a slow blues, T-Bone Walker's *Stormy Monday*. The band was loud, but Anson's soaring Strat brought sweetness to the music that seemed to offset the decibel level. With his short-cropped blond hair, wiry frame, and clean-shaven face, he looked more like a squeaky-clean 1950's high school kid than the leader of a wayfaring, new-millennium blues band.

Watching with satisfaction as the bluesman ripped into his solo, Higheagle thought of Sally. He had never seen a more hateful look in his life than when she stood up at the meeting and accused Prescott. The developer and his attorney were so unnerved by her outburst that they quickly fled the auditorium, as if the audience would swiftly transform into a lynch mob. At that point, Higheagle too tried to slip inconspicuously from the room, but Sally called out to him and demanded that he come forward to address the assembled group. Of course, he refused. Later, after the meeting, he tried to talk to her outside the auditorium as she and Tommy were heading to their car, but she was so upset she simply pushed him away.

The waitress reappeared and asked if he would like another beer. He grinned drunkenly at her, ordered another Fat Tire, and turned his attention back to the stage as Anson and the Rockets launched into a Hendrix-tinged version of *Come On (Baby Let the Good Times Roll)*. The dance floor quickly filled up with enthusiasts. Higheagle took a final swig from his Fat Tire and set it down. The bottle wobbled, and by the time it came to rest, a heavyset man in a white straw cowboy hat was standing over him.

ψψψ

Vic Shard saw Higheagle looking up at him through beer-soaked eyes.

"Mind if I join you," he asked over the din of music. His goatee was gone; he had cut it off now that he had Higheagle under routine surveillance, which would give him more flexibility with his various disguises. "Looks like you've got a bit of room." He glanced at the three unoccupied chairs around the table.

"Sure, have a seat," offered the Cheyenne.

The private detective set down his bottle of Bud and took the chair next to him. "Shard's the name," he said loud enough for Higheagle to hear him. "Vic Shard."

They shook hands, and the PI saw something he liked in the cut of the Indian.

"You like blues, Mr. Shard."

He didn't know B.B. King from Freddie or Albert King, but he smiled and said, "Surely do."

Higheagle nodded, as if it had been a test and Shard had passed. He returned his eyes to the stage where Anson began unleashing a furious solo on his Strat. A minute into it, they were interrupted by the waitress, who delivered Higheagle's frosty beverage. As she walked away, he turned to Shard and said, "Old Anson can play with the best of 'em."

Shard smiled. *If he knew all I ever listen to are Hank Williams, Jerry Jeff Walker, and Tim McGraw, that would be the end of this here conversation.*

The two watched the band in silence and knocked back their beers for a few minutes. When the song wound down, Snakebit Charley shambled up to the stage and announced there would be a short break.

Taking advantage of the lull, Shard leaned in close and shook things up with a simple pronouncement: "I saw you earlier tonight at Cody High."

As expected, the words struck Higheagle like a slap on the face. "Who the hell are you?"

"Private investigator. Work for Hayden Prescott."

"Why the fuck would I want to talk to you?"

Shard ignored the caustic tone. "Because I might be able to help you. Down the road, that is."

"Is that so? And what if I told you to fuck off?"

"Look, I'm here to find out one thing and one thing only—and it doesn't have anything to do with my client. It's something I want to know...for personal reasons."

"I thought guys like you would give your left nut before you compromised your client's interests."

"Like I said, my particular problem ain't business. It's personal."

He looked Shard over appraisingly, as if trying to determine his motives. After a moment, his face softened, but just a little. "All right, say your fucking piece. I'll give you until I finish my beer."

Shard glanced at the tall amber beer bottle and saw that a little over half remained. He got right to the point. "I've got a feeling what Sally McTavish said at the meeting isn't as far off the mark as Dan Markworth led everyone to believe. What I want to know is if there was illegal dumping at Dakota, could it have caused the deaths of those boys? Somehow, that wouldn't sit right in my craw."

"Oh, so you're a private dick with a conscience. Now isn't that quaint."

"The question still stands."

"And the answer is a matter of scientific probability."

"How about beyond a reasonable doubt?"

"I'd be guessing. Bottom line is I don't know. Not yet anyway."

"I know about the Redhill splits and the aerials." The Cheyenne's face flashed anger, but he said nothing, so Shard pressed on. "Is that all the evidence you've got? Because if it is, it seems to me you need more."

"Do you actually believe I would answer that question? You must think I'm really dumb."

"No, I know you're a smart fellow. That's why old Charles Quantrill jumped to his death at the top of Pikes Peak...on account of you being so smart."

"You can't be much of a private dick if you're getting your information from your client and old Internet articles."

"In both our lines of work, sometimes we learn a thing or two from our clients. Who you working for anyway?"

"Nice try, but I'm not that drunk."

"How about answering my first question then?"

"All right, that I can do. There's no doubt in my mind that Prescott, or someone close to him, dumped waste at Dakota. But proving in a court of law that the waste caused, or even contributed to, the cancer is another thing altogether."

"Fair enough. Now supposing my client did dump some nasty stuff out there. In your professional judgment, do you think it could have led to the deaths of those boys?"

Higheagle took a long pull from his beer. Only about a quarter remained, and Shard knew he had to hurry. "Like I told you, I'd be guessing."

"That doesn't help me much."

"Look, I don't know why I'm even talking to you. If you want to play for the bad guys, that's your decision. But don't follow me around like a bloodhound and pester me with questions and expect sympathy or cooperation. Unless you can help me, you don't mean shit to me. The way I look at it, you're either for me or against me. And from where I sit, it looks like the latter."

"Things are never that simple, son. I reckon you know that or you wouldn't be talking to me."

Higheagle slammed the bottle on the table, eliciting stares from the adjacent table. "When I look at you, you know what I see: a whore who sells himself to the highest bidder." He stared at Shard long and hard. "In the old days, there were Indian scouts who hunted down their own people for the Army. They were whores just like you. All they got in return for selling their souls was an extra wool blanket, a grain-fed horse, and a shiny new rifle. You, Mr. Private Dickhead, are the same as them. Except you whore yourself out to millionaire scumbags like Prescott instead of the U.S. Cavalry."

Shard held his breath a moment to control his temper. Despite his comfortable six-figure salary, he didn't think of himself as anything like the greedy multimillionaires he worked for. *Don't let him get to you. You've got to make him understand you're on his side.*

"I'd be inclined to call that a questionable analogy. I was thinking more along the lines of an environmental consultant working on behalf of Fortune 500 polluters, writing his reports to fit their agendas. Sound familiar?"

Higheagle smiled grudgingly. "You're a cocksure son of a bitch, coming in here like this."

"Someone said it takes a rounder to know one."

Higheagle grabbed his beer and poured the last drops down his throat. When he was finished, he slapped the bottle down on the table, more a declaration of finality than anger. "My beer's finished, and so is this fucking conversation."

"I'll be in touch."

"Don't tell me, your real name's Maxwell Smart and you'll contact me with a shoe phone?"

Shard stood up from his chair with surprising fluidity for an older man, his face a study in carefully controlled anger. "You might want to be a little more respectful towards me, Joe. After all, next to Sally McTavish and that boy of hers, I may be the only friend you've got on this case."

CHAPTER 44

THE NEXT MORNING, Higheagle met with Minesali. As Forbes led him into the Library, he caught the old gentleman in a private moment of thought. He was quietly sipping an espresso and staring pensively up at the framed black-and-white photo on the wall of the two dead men in the coffins. Higheagle remembered that the men were Minesali's grandfather and uncle, gunned down by the Colorado National Guard during the 1914 Ludlow Massacre. Following Minesali's gaze, he looked up and studied the expression of the young boy standing above one of the coffins, bundled up against the cold. It was Minesali's father, praying over his own father, and though he looked crestfallen, he projected quiet strength.

Forbes cleared his throat to get Minesali's attention. "Sir, Mr. Higheagle is here to see you."

Minesali turned away abruptly from the photo, like a child caught daydreaming. Higheagle knew that the picture meant a great deal to him, but it went beyond that. Somehow, Minesali's world was inextricably linked to what had happened to his ancestors nearly one hundred years earlier.

"Ah, Joseph. Thank you for coming. Would you like something to drink?"

"A glass of water would be great."

Forbes nodded solemnly and stepped from the room as Minesali motioned his guest towards the ornate chair opposite him. Higheagle sat down and removed a sheet of paper from his satchel, then placed the satchel at his feet.

Putting down his espresso, Minesali said without preamble, "So you've received the laboratory results. Tell me what you've found."

"I'm not sure where to begin, except to say that a strong case could be made to put Dakota Ranch on the Superfund list. There's a lot more than metals out there."

"What exactly?"

"Dioxins."

"Dioxins? At what levels?"

"More than a hundred thousand milligrams per kilogram. The three compounds detected at the highest concentrations were 2,4-D, 2,4,5-T, and TCDD." He looked down at his sheet of paper. "That's 2,4-Dichlorophenoxy-acetic acid, 2,4,5-Trichlorophenoxy-acetic acid, and 2,3,7,8-Tetrachlorodibenzo-p-dioxin. All impurities in herbicides and pesticides. But there's a whole suite of other chlorinated dioxin isomers, toxic ones, in the low hundreds to thousands of milligrams per kilogram range. When you throw in the heavy metals—hexavalent chromium, lead, and arsenic—you've got quite a lethal brew cooking out there."

They looked up as the door opened. Forbes walked into the room, handed Higheagle a glass of ice and a Perrier, and left.

"How many of the soil samples were contaminated?" asked Minesali.

"All but three."

"It would seem, then, that you have concrete proof of what's gone on out there."

"Yeah, but I still don't know who is responsible for it, how many people are involved, or how the operation was handled. Prescott's role may not be what you'd expect. Maybe he just looked the other way. He could even be innocent and Hwong or someone else may be the guilty party, working in collusion with generators I don't know about. I'm just not sure yet."

"I presume these chemicals you have found cause cancer?"

"Many of them fall into Group A, Known Human Carcinogens. Others are Group B, Probable, or Group C, Possible. A few fall into Group D, Not Classifiable, which means there isn't adequate human or animal evidence of carcinogenicity. Between all of them, you've got chemicals that at high dosages can cause death, chromosome damage, miscarriages, birth defects, and fetotoxicity. Some of the chemicals have occupational exposure limits of less than one part per billion."

"So all of these chemicals acting together could have killed the children?"

"I don't know if it can be proven in a court of law, but I believe the answer is yes. All five of the cancer victims had the opportunity to be exposed to the chemicals. They played in the soil on a regular basis before the rec center was built. Three to five days per week, except during the winter. They came into physical contact with the waste and also stirred up a lot of dust. So there was a dual exposure pathway through dermal adsorption and inhalation. Many of the chemicals in the soil are known or probable human carcinogens, and they affect a variety of target organs, including the brain. The concentrations were in the thousands of milligrams per kilogram range and up, high enough to pose a significant health risk. So the quantity of chemicals they were exposed to, as well as the frequency and duration of the exposure, would have been enough to do the damage. All in all, I think the chemicals had to have played a crucial role in the boys getting cancer."

"My God, you've convinced me. Why can't it be proved in court?"

"Because even though I've established a likely exposure scenario, cancer clusters are still open to serious questions. Cumulative risks from chemical exposure can be antagonistic, additive, or synergistic. In other words, the total health risk associated with several chemicals may be less than, equal to, or greater than the risk you get from adding together the risks of each compound. And whether chemicals are promoters or initiators is open to question. Whether they can simply cause cell turnover or whether they actually cause chromosome damage. The whole field is undergoing a revolution. The newest thinking is that you get more exposure from what you eat and drink every day, as well as from natural cell mutation and hormonal changes. Environmental risks simply aren't that high, unless you're exposed to extremely high levels, or to moderate levels for a long time. That's called chronic exposure."

"But before you said there was a chance you could prove it?"

"Yeah, but I warned you it wouldn't be easy. The only way to do it would be to collect fat samples from the victims and have them analyzed. The problem is the concentrations would be in the parts per trillion range or lower, beyond the detection limit of most laboratory testing equipment. Plus a lot of contaminants occur naturally at background levels in the human body, including dioxins, so it could be argued the concentrations are just background. But the biggest problem is a lack of a good control group. Tommy's the only living child with the cancer, so any lab studies of fat or blood samples would be based on a single control point. Data from Tommy alone wouldn't prove anything conclusive."

He paused to let the reality sink in. Minesali let out a rueful sigh. He was clearly distressed by the hard truth and Higheagle felt sympathy for him. But at the same time, he couldn't help but wonder: *Could the old man somehow be involved in all this?*

"You have to realize, the first step is to establish who's responsible for the waste, and I haven't even done that. Personally, I believe the chemicals are major contributing factors to the cancer. But it's going to be difficult to prove. You know how the American justice system works. It's heavily slanted towards wealthy people and corporations. Prescott—or whoever's ultimately responsible for this mess—will have twenty experts on child and brain oncology, geology, toxicology, epidemiology, you name it. He'll be able to spend millions on a defense, while none of the field data I've collected so far will be admissible because I trespassed to collect it. I need to convince the Health Department or EPA to go out to the rec center and collect its own samples."

"So what you're telling me is that you don't have one-hundred-percent proof the waste caused the cancer?"

Higheagle nodded. "But I haven't done a risk assessment."

"A risk assessment?"

"Yeah. I could calculate the cancer risks of the nastiest chemicals and present a conceptual model of the exposure scenario I just laid out for you. For what you're paying me, I could throw that in at no extra charge. In fact, I'd like to do it just to see where the risk numbers come out. Of course, I still won't be able to prove conclusively that the chemicals caused the cancer. But I do believe I can make a convincing case that the chemicals found onsite contributed to the cancer. And that should be enough to spark a major resampling effort by the Health Department or EPA."

Minesali reached for his espresso, his face brightening. "I would very much like for you to complete this risk assessment. And I shall pay you a bonus for it." He took a sip and set the tiny espresso cup back down. "You have done a fine job, Joseph. I congratulate you on your efforts."

"Thanks." Higheagle followed the old man's eyes as they laddered up to the black-and-white picture on the wall. "That old photograph means a lot to you, doesn't it?"

Minesali nodded without taking his eyes off the picture. "It's always amazed me how my grandfather and the other coal miners were willing to risk their lives for a wage increase of a few pennies and the promise of better working conditions."

"I suppose even canaries would have been too much for Rockefeller's bottom line."

"For me, it hits close to home because my ancestors were part of it all, part of the ignominious history of the Ludlow Massacre. I vowed long ago never to treat my employees as my grandfather and uncle were treated. All these years, I have kept this one simple promise to myself."

Higheagle looked up again at Minesali's father as a young boy, solemnly praying behind the coffin. As before, the boy seemed sad, but in a strong way. It was the same quiet strength Higheagle had seen on Tommy's face the other night when the boy had showed him his poster of Sitting Bull.

Higheagle looked back at Minesali. The old man appeared choked with emotion; there were actual tears in his eyes. *Jesus, does that picture have a grip on him or what?*

"I'd better be going now," Higheagle said, wanting to give the old man some privacy.

Minesali wiped the tears from his eyes. "No, please stay Joseph. We still have to talk about Silverado Knolls. Why don't we take a walk through my gardens. I think I just need some fresh air."

ψψψ

They took in the heady fragrance of the daffodils, tulips, crocuses, and hyacinths as they strolled through the outdoor gardens. Higheagle noticed that hundreds of flowers had been planted since his last visit; many of the empty plots were now burgeoning with color. The hedges were exquisitely trimmed and ran in labyrinths throughout the grounds.

As they walked along, Minesali instructively pointed out the Latin names of the various flower species and their salient characteristics. There seemed to be a special, almost romantic, bond between the old man and his flora. Higheagle recalled him saying something about how his wife Marguerite had been an avid green thumb. Perhaps this was his way of keeping her memory alive.

Soon they began talking about what to do about Silverado Knolls. After going back and forth for several minutes, Higheagle agreed to take a look at the site tomorrow.

"What about sampling?" asked Minesali. "What happened at Dakota Ranch may very well be taking place at Silverado Knolls too. And the only way to find out for certain is to sample, correct?"

"Yes, but I'm not sure the best way to go about it. A lawn expert on the open prairie would look pretty ridiculous. I'd have to sample at night."

Minesali chuckled. "A commando geologist. If I were a few years younger, I would be quite tempted to join you. After all, I swept across France with Patton's Third Army. A glorious time, simply glorious."

Higheagle suspected that marching, fighting, killing, and freezing one's ass off under Old Blood and Guts had not been glorious at all, but rather, with the passing years, that was how Minesali remembered it. It reminded him of the old Cheyenne warriors, boasting about how they had fought under Tall Bull, Dull Knife, and Lame White Man. Long after the arrows and bullets stopped flying, a charismatic war leader was an endless source of pride for the ordinary warriors or soldiers who had followed him into battle.

They talked on. Higheagle agreed that if he observed anything suspicious or out of the ordinary in either of the coulees running through the Silverado Knolls property, he would collect soil samples.

"I take it the legal agreement we have drawn up is satisfactory," Minesali then said.

"The agreement's fine," replied Higheagle.

Minesali smiled disarmingly, like a kindly emperor. Higheagle found something maddeningly cunning about the man, but he was still taken in by his personal magnetism. He couldn't quite put a finger on it. It was as if part of him wasn't doing all this for Sally, Tommy, and the other boys who had died, or for the money, but to gain the old man's approval.

"So, you're all set," Minesali said to wrap up. "I shall have Forbes prepare another check to cover your expenses then."

"That'll be fine." As the words left his mouth, he looked up to see the stoic house servant staring down at them from the wrought-iron balcony on the second floor. Damn if the guy wasn't creepy. More importantly, he had to be a hell of a lot more than just a house servant. And what about Minesali? Was it possible that he was part of all this? But if that was the case, why would the old man have contracted him in the first place? If Minesali was involved, it didn't make any sense for him to hire someone to gather evidence of wrongdoing that could be used against him. And why were there high concentrations of heavy metals in the soil? Metals weren't part of the herbicide production process and that's what Minesali's Denver operation was—a herbicide and pesticide processing plant—though the specific organic constituents generated on-site remained proprietary.

It was all so very puzzling.

He looked at Minesali. At some point, he was going to have to confront the old man to get answers to his questions. But it would probably be best if he waited until he had spoken with his grandfather. The wily tribal lawyer knew the best ways to get information from people without tipping them off to one's true motives.

"I'd better be going," said Higheagle. "I have another meeting in a few minutes."

Minesali gave a look of mild surprise. "Oh, who are you meeting with?"

"Hayden Prescott."

"Good heavens! Really?"

"Yes, and it should be interesting. Don't you think?"

CHAPTER 45

THE SECOND MEETING, TOO, WAS HELD AT THE ESTEEMED
UNIVERSITY CLUB.

Higheagle knew he'd taken a wrong turn somewhere because he found himself
in a reading room filled with fancy couches, pastoral oil paintings, and humorless
old white men in conservative business suits. A few glanced up from their *Wall
Street Journals* to stare condescendingly at him as he passed through the room. He
wore a short-sleeved Western shirt beneath a tweed jacket, faded Wrangler jeans,
and scratched-up cowboy boots. Together with his ponytail, his attire must have
served as a public declaration that he wasn't U Club material.

He turned left into an open hallway containing a table with six neat rows of
magazines: *Forbes, Cigar Aficionado, Money Review, Civilization, The New
Yorker, Fortune, US News, Market Watch,* and *Nation's Business.* Looking over
the titles, he realized, to his infinite relief, that he had never read any of these
magazines except *The New Yorker* and *US News.*

He walked into the Pool Room where he was to meet Prescott. Four long
billiards tables spread sportily before him, illuminated by suspended lights.
Handcrafted wooden side tables and sitting chairs lined the masculine room. Hand
painted crests depicting various aristocratic professions and arts were emblazoned
on the dark wood paneling along the walls. He quickly spotted Prescott, jacketless
with a white shirt, red suspenders, and pin-striped suit pants. He stood next to a
pool table, a ghost of a smile on his lips and pool cue in his right hand.

Higheagle walked up to him.

"So, we meet again, Joe."

The tone of voice was friendly enough, yet as they shook hands, Higheagle felt
a frisson of tension between them. He tried to keep his face neutral, but the
chilliness between them was so palpable, he couldn't help a little frown.

"Have you ever played Three-Hundred?"

Higheagle looked over the billiards table. It was around ten feet long, a couple
of feet longer than the battered barroom pool tables he was used to playing on. The
pockets were tight and didn't flare out at the edges like a conventional pool table,
and there were fifteen red balls instead of fifteen numbered balls of various colors.
This was a game for country club gentlemen.

"Can't say I have."

"Each of the six pockets is worth a certain number of points." Prescott walked
around the table, pointing out the pockets and reading off their value. "One, two,
three, five, ten, and twenty. Whoever gets to three-hundred points first wins. Oh,
and you can take your jacket off. We're not that formal here in the Pool Room."

A waiter appeared and they ordered drinks and lunch: a pair of iced teas along with bowls of creamy New England clam chowder and entrees of pan-grilled Maryland crab cakes.

"What are the stakes?" Higheagle asked when the waiter walked off.

"What did you have in mind?"

"If I win, you come clean to the EPA about your secret waste operation. If you win, I drop my investigation."

Prescott laughed, exposing two rows of perfectly aligned white teeth. "You have a fanciful imagination, Joe. Behind every door there's a vast conspiracy, is that it?"

"Are you refusing my friendly wager?"

"Remember, boy-o, you're on my turf. This is the U Club, not the Cheyenne Social Club. I'm the top handicap at the club and I don't take candy from babies." He pointed his monogrammed, custom-designed billiards cue, shiny as silver, towards the rack on the west wall. "You'd better choose your weapon. The bet is one dollar. I think you can afford that."

Higheagle ignored the barb, calmly removed his tweed jacket with the elbow patches, set it down on one of the wood chairs lining the room, then walked over and pulled down a cue from the rack.

When he returned to the table, the waiter delivered their iced teas.

Prescott said, "They say all players here are creatures of habit in that they seldom sign in and frequently drink to excess." He twirled his stick like a pro. "For now, let's just play the game. We can talk business at lunch. You break, and may the best man win."

Higheagle chalked his tip and lined up his shot, using his right thumb and forefinger for a bridge. He drove the cue ball into the triangle of red balls, putting one in the corner pocket.

"Congratulations. That's ten points. Now fire away until you miss. Then score it up on the string." Prescott tapped his pool cue against the string of wooden beads running beneath the ceiling.

Higheagle lined up the next shot, a three-pointer on one of the center pockets. He missed.

Prescott took the ball out and set it back on the table on the circle where the balls had originally been racked. "You have to put the balls back on the table after a run," he said before proceeding to knock in seven balls for a total of forty-nine points.

Higheagle noted that his form was perfect.

After his adversary's impressive run, Higheagle dropped two more balls, then it was Prescott's turn again. Five times in a row a red ball tumbled into a pocket. When he was finished with his run, he flicked over twenty-eight more of the wooden beads on the overhead string. As they played on Higheagle could feel the tension rising, the undercurrent of animosity between them growing with every shot. He wondered how Sally could have ever gone out with him. Beneath the cultured exterior seemed to lurk a very real danger.

Ten minutes later the carnage was over and the soup was served. The string read 300 for Prescott, 106 for Higheagle.

"Aren't you glad I didn't take that bet?" Prescott declared haughtily, taking the one-dollar bill from him. "Or were you planning on being an Indian giver from the get-go?"

"The only Indian givers I've ever known were white."

Prescott's eyes gleamed with competitive fire; clearly he relished the confrontation. "'The only good Indians I ever saw were dead.' Phillip Henry Sheridan."

"You remind me of him: a short little man with a Napoleon complex and a Waterloo just around the corner. Only Sheridan's Waterloo was a battle he planned out but failed to make it to: the Little Bighorn."

Prescott smiled wolfishly, showing grudging respect for his foe. "You're feisty, Joe. I admire that in a man. But now that we know how big each other's dicks are, why don't we sit down, eat some fucking chowder, and try to resolve our differences."

CHAPTER 46

THEY TOOK SEATS in the wooden chairs against the east wall. The chairs were fitted with attached serving trays and were separated by side tables containing two sets of silverware wrapped in green linen napkins. Placing his napkin in his lap, Prescott parted through the glittering sheen of butter on top of his clam chowder and spooned out a portion. He was having fun despite the gravity of the situation. He liked taking on the best and usually crushed them, whether it was business or one of the many sports in which he excelled—tennis, racquetball, downhill skiing, and billiards. He had never really known defeat; his skill and timing had always been impeccable.

Just like Father.

Still, it was time to broker a deal—without admitting to any wrongdoing, of course. In fact, he wanted to pass off his tough-guy demeanor as that of a falsely accused man defending himself from an unwanted intrusion into his personal affairs. If Higheagle refused the deal…well, in that case, more draconian measures would have to be—

"So tell me, Joe, why are you doing this?"

"I don't know. I guess I like to dig up stuff and see what I find."

"I suspect you could dig up a lot of skeletons on half the members of this club. But why would you want to do something like that? Unless, of course, you were being paid handsomely for it?"

"I know you've heard of client confidentiality. That's why you know I can't tell you about that."

"There's a big difference between making accusations and winning a legal battle. I'm not convinced you know the difference."

"Who says I need to go to court?"

"Oh, that's right. The last time you got involved in one of these little escapades a man killed himself. Am I to suffer the same fate as poor Charles Prometheus Quantrill?"

"That depends."

Prescott loaded his spoon with potatoes and clams, delicately devoured them, and gently daubed the skein of buttery cream from his mouth with his green linen napkin. His gaze drifted to the hand-painted medieval crests mounted on the wall. He felt a certain privilege in his surroundings, and couldn't help but think his adversary looked out of place.

"You're clever, my Indian friend, I'll give you that. Posing as a contractor to the Health Department to get information. Really, Joe. There's an F word for that, but it has five letters instead of four. You could go to jail, you know. Fraud is a serious crime."

"Nice little speech. Only problem with it is you don't want the police involved in this thing any more than I do. They might start digging around just like me."

Prescott hated to admit it, but he was right. *I've got to take him down. Make him crack. But what's his weakness?* "Look here, boy-o. The score on that table over there was three hundred to one hundred six. This game you're playing now won't even be that close when I'm finished with you. I'm innocent in all this, of course. But in this brave new world of Facebook and Twitter, innocent people's reputations can be tarnished at the tap of a computer keyboard. I can't let that happen."

The waiter arrived with lunch: for each, a pair of golden-brown Maryland blue crab cakes served with remoulade sauce, corn and bell pepper risotto, and a colorful medley of fresh grilled vegetables. After the waiter refilled their glasses and moved off, Prescott squeezed some lemon juice on his crab cake, cut through it with his knife, and took a bite. *Delicious!* he thought, as he heard the crackle of a billiards ball driven hard by one of the men at the table near the bar.

"So Joe, you're something of a hero with the press as I recall."

"I figure your life story—you know the silver spoon waste-dumper angle—would be right up their alley."

"Yes, but I believe you're forgetting that there are four ways to make people go away, just as there are fifty ways to leave your lover."

"Oh really, why don't you enlighten me?"

"It would be my pleasure. First, you can buy them. That works maybe half the time, but you sometimes get stuck with these guys who want more and more money. They're like Jack Russell terriers and just can't let go. The second way is to make their life miserable, by destroying their credit, work, life, or by threatening someone close to him. You know, like a dear old grandfather. Then there's the third way. That's when you don't care what they say or do because you know you'll have your day in court. And the fourth approach, well that's the best of all—"

"Don't tell me. The Jimmy Hoffa scenario?"

Prescott cupped his hands together and then opened them up, simulating a magician making something disappear. "Poof." He gave a macabre smile.

"If I had to guess, I'd say you're threatening me."

"No, I'm giving you four options so you can make the right decision. Should I run through them one more time for you?"

"Just the first one," Higheagle replied, forking a carrot from the medley of fresh grilled vegetables. "What kind of financial incentives package did you have in mind?"

"But I figured such a noble savage as you could never be bought off."

"Depends on the offer. The cold wind blows harder when you're on your own."

"You could have spared us both a lot of wasted time if you'd told me this earlier." He scrutinized his opponent closely, wondering if he really would take a bribe. "If I paid, it wouldn't be an admission of wrongdoing."

"You sound like a PR officer for a multinational corporation."

"Like them, I don't like bad publicity."

"And like them, you haven't done anything wrong even though you're willing to pay. So what's your offer?"

"Fifty K kind of has a ring to it."

"Not even close. I would need at least a quarter million."

Prescott's mouth fell open. "A quarter million? Who in the hell do you think you are?"

"Come on, a quarter mil's no skin off your back. You're worth more than a hundred times that amount."

Prescott chewed on it for a minute, watching the pool players at the table near the bar. It wasn't easy, but he finally convinced himself he could live with paying the proposed amount. "All right, two hundred fifty K and you walk away. You don't talk to anyone. Not the Health Department, not the EPA, not the DOJ. You also have to disclose the name of your employer and hand over all electronic and hard copy files on the project."

"No. The deal is a quarter million in cash. And for that, I become Mr. Zipper Lip until I'm sleeping permanently in a pine box. Take it or leave it."

How dare you talk to me that way? I could wipe you off the face of the earth without a fucking trace!

"The moment you show me the money, I'll hang it up. But not before."

Prescott stared at his adversary long and hard, trying to determine whether he could be trusted. "All right, you've got a deal. It's going to take me a few days to get the money together though."

"I'll be working on the case until then, so I wouldn't take too long."

Prescott looked over at the pool table near the bar, making sure no one was eavesdropping. "You know what will happen to you if you go back on this?"

"I'm not convinced you'd do a damned thing. You seem like the kind of excessively coddled blueblood who hides behind an army of attorneys." He wiped his mouth with his napkin. "Actually, I take it all back. You can forget about trying to buy me off. I couldn't possibly accept money from a weasel like you. I just wanted to see how far you were willing to go."

Prescott felt his whole body shudder with rage. He wagged his forefinger at Higheagle's face like a saber.

"You do realize that you're turning purple," said the Cheyenne, deliberately trying to provoke him. "Didn't they teach you in social etiquette school how to control your own temper?"

"You watch your tongue, you bastard. I'm a businessman, no different from millions of others, except for one thing."

"Yeah, what's that?"

"To protect my interests, I'm not afraid to cross a line that most people are afraid to cross."

"Really?"

"Yes, really." Prescott threw his napkin onto his plate and spoke in a snakelike hiss. "This lunch is finished, and if you persist in this little game of yours, so the fuck are you."

CHAPTER 47

SALLY MCTAVISH shuddered when she saw the back of Tommy's head. He and Joseph had enjoyed themselves at *Dances With Wolves*, but the boy had fallen asleep on the way home and she had put him straight to bed. Looking at him now with his baseball cap off and head resting on the pillow, she couldn't help but cringe. The back of his head looked like a clear-cut forest. All week, his hair had been changing color and becoming thinner from the radiation treatment, but now the whole process seemed to be speeding up.

The doctors had warned her that this would happen. They told her not to worry and that it didn't mean Tommy was getting worse, but how could he be getting better when his hair was falling out and he appeared gaunt and haggard and had dark circles under his eyes that made him look much older than his age. To her dismay, she felt as though she was staring at a ghost of her son, a shadow of what had been.

Why is this happening to him? What did he do to deserve this?

Feeling the usual wave of sadness, she forced herself to fight back the tears and went downstairs. Her mother was in the kitchen drying the last of the dishes, while her father sat on the couch in the family room, haphazardly channel surfing. Gail and Bill McTavish had flown in again just this morning from Phoenix to help out.

As she stepped into the kitchen, she glanced at the refrigerator at a picture of her and Tommy on a whitewater rafting trip. It had been taken on the Arkansas River last summer. They looked so happy together paddling through the Class 4 rapids, laughing with the foamy spray flying up at them. The whole scene seemed light years away from what was going on now in their lives. She hoped with all her heart Tommy would survive his terrible disease, that somehow they would be able to recapture brilliant moments like the one in the photograph.

Her musing was interrupted by the doorbell.

"Expecting someone?" her mother asked.

"Not that I know of." She set down her wash towel, walked out of the kitchen, and went to the front door. When she looked through the window, she was at first stunned before experiencing a surge of anger. She jerked on the door handle and threw open the front door.

"What are you doing here?"

"I need to talk to you."

"I don't think that's a good idea."

Hayden Prescott licked his lips nervously, and she realized that she had never seen him as anxious as he appeared right now. He held a large bouquet of flowers and another present of some kind and in no way looked threatening. She was torn between a morbid curiosity to hear what he had to say and a powerful urge to slap him in the face and call the police.

"Look Sally, I know you think I've done some terrible things, but you've only heard one side of the story. I would never do anything to hurt you or Tommy. I have my own consultants looking into this cancer thing because...because I want to figure out what's going on just like you."

She wanted to slam the door in his face, but something inside, a faded memory of their brief but sweet relationship together, made her give him a chance. "Why should I believe you?"

"Because you know me, Sally. You know the kind of person I am."

"I'm not sure I ever really knew you, Hayden."

"You know I'm a man of my word. When I broke up with you, it was because I didn't want to lead you on and pretend to be something I'm not. I can't believe those things you said about me. How can you think I'm responsible for what's happening to Tommy?"

I need to act tougher. I have to push him and flush out the truth. She glared at him coldly. "It doesn't matter what I think. The facts speak for themselves."

"Sally, you've got to believe me. I have no idea what's going on here. There's this guy...a geologist named Joseph Higheagle...he's out to get me. He's been going around saying he's working for the Health Department, but he's not. I think he's working for some radical environmental group or one of my competitors. He's out to crucify me, Sally."

"Joseph's not out to crucify you. He's just trying to—" She stopped right there and covered her mouth with her hand, suddenly realizing her folly.

"I don't believe this. You know him?"

"Of course not...I was just..."

"My God, you do know him. Why the hell is he doing this to me?"

She was unable to speak. A part of her, she realized, longed to believe her old boyfriend was telling the truth. She remembered how he had lavished her with flowers and gifts, how he had played baseball with Tommy in the backyard, how unselfishly he had made love to her.

Could he really be capable of these things? It just doesn't seem possible.

"You should have told me about Tommy. You know how much I care about him," he said, and she felt a wave of guilt.

"Oh, Hayden," she murmured helplessly, unaware of the footsteps coming up behind her. "I just don't know what to believe."

"Now where did I put my Barry Eisler book," Bill McTavish mumbled as he sidled up to the table in the foyer. Glancing towards the open door, his face tightened into a grimace. "You!" he snarled accusingly, stepping forward aggressively. "What are you doing here?"

For a moment, Prescott stared at the older man with bewilderment. Then he set down the wrapped gift and flowers he had brought and took a step backwards.

"Dad, what are you doing?"

Her father pushed her aside and started through the door with clenched fists. "You get out of here right now, or I'll call the police! You murdering bastard, I know what you've done!"

Prescott retreated to the second step. "I don't know what you're talking about."

Sally grabbed her father from behind, but he was big and strong and pulled her along with him. "Dad, stop it! He didn't come here to hurt anybody!"

"You killed my brother, you son of a bitch! Gus was onto you and you killed him for it!"

"That's a lie. I tried to save his life. There were a dozen witnesses."

"Yeah, I know all about your cozy little alibi. I talked to Detective Marshak. He called me and asked a lot of questions about you. Did I know you? Did I know anything about your business relationship with Gus? Had you two ever disagreed about money? He wouldn't give me the details because it's an open case, but I can tell he's on to you, pal. Gus had something on you and you killed him for it. I'm here to tell you right now you'll never get away with it! Never!"

Sally looked at her old lover, wondering if it was possible.

"Don't listen to him, Sally. He just wants someone to blame."

"You murdering bastard! If you're not off this property in the next five seconds, I'm going to break your goddamned neck!"

It took all of Sally's strength to hold her father back as he lunged forward, arms outstretched. The neighbors across the street were looking out their windows.

"It's not true, Sally! You can't believe this!" Prescott turned and bolted for his Range Rover parked out front. When he reached it, he looked back, his eyes pleading for her to believe him. She had never seen a look on his face like that before. He seemed to be surrendering himself before her, and she felt in her heart that Joseph and her father had to be mistaken. They were unfairly trying to pin the blame on him, to find a scapegoat as she had the other night at the meeting.

"My God, what's going on here?"

Sally turned to see her mother in the doorway. Ignoring her, she grabbed her father by the arm. "That's enough, Dad. Get inside."

Prescott opened his car door. "You've got the wrong man! It's Higheagle you should be worried about! I've done nothing wrong!"

"Like hell! You're a goddamned monster! You killed my brother!"

Feeling embarrassed, confused, and angry, Sally herded her father back inside the house before he made a further scene in front of the neighbors. He was breathing heavily, his shirt damp with sweat. Sally closed the door and locked it.

Her mother was shaking her head in disbelief. "Good heavens, what's gotten into the two of you? You've worked yourselves into a frenzy."

"We're not leaving tomorrow," Bill McTavish said with stern finality. "I'm going to call Jim Fisher and request a leave of absence. They'll have to find someone else to manage the floor on an interim basis."

"No, Dad, you two are leaving tomorrow as planned. Look at what you just did. You're just making things worse."

Her mother reached out to touch her. "Honey, you can't mean that. Your father's only trying to protect you."

Sally pushed her hand away. "I can take care of myself."

"But that terrible man."

"You don't know a damned thing about him, Mother!" And with that, she tromped up the stairs and locked herself in her room.

CHAPTER 48

HIGHEAGLE was half-asleep when he heard the sound.

It wasn't particularly loud, no more obtrusive than a clicking water pipe or a faint susurrus of wind, but it was enough to awaken him. He listened for a moment half-consciously, hoping the noise would stop so he could roll over and go back to sleep. Then he heard the floorboards creak. He remained silent and motionless, casting an ear towards the sound again.

Again, he heard a creak.

Someone was in the house!

He slid quietly from the bed, slipped on the pair of jeans hanging from the chair, and reached under the bed for his Ithaca 12-gauge slide-action shotgun. He moved stealthily to the wall next to the open doorway, gripping the loaded shotgun tightly with both hands.

There he listened for what seemed like an eternity. Finally, he stepped through the doorway, clasping the shotgun in his left hand. Carefully, he slid his right hand along the bumpy wall, feeling for the light switch.

He flicked on the switch, but there was no sign of anyone. He tiptoed down the hallway to the kitchen, turning on the light and peering inside.

Again nothing.

He checked the living room and his office.

Still nothing.

Then he peaked into his grandfather's room, but the old chief was fast asleep, snoring loudly.

Blowing out a sigh of relief, he returned to his bedroom, stuffed his shotgun beneath his bed, climbed under the covers, closed his eyes, and tried to go back to sleep.

It was then that they struck. In that terrifying instant, he realized they had been in his room all along. *In my goddamned room! Watching me!*

He tried to reach for his shotgun, but felt his hand smashed with a hard object—the butt of a pistol?—at the same time he was grabbed by someone else from the other side of the bed. He fought hard to wrestle free, as his senses were assaulted by the pungent smell of aftershave, but his adversaries had the advantage of surprise and numbers, quickly overpowering him. While a pair of strong arms pinned him down, a clammy hand slipped over his mouth, preventing him from crying out, and something cool and sharp pressed against his neck. A knife? Still struggling to break free, he heard a whisper in a blue-collar, unmistakable New York voice.

"Stop moving and keep quiet—or we'll cut you from ear to ear!"

Higheagle stopped resisting, but remained tense. A thin ray of buttery moonlight filtered through the blinds, but he was unable to make out the faces of his assailants with his eyes still adjusting to the dark.

Another voice came from his right, this one rural West Texas from the sound of it. "We're only here to do a little talking, son. But we'll give you a Rocky Mountain necktie right here and now if you make any sound we don't much care for." He pressed the knife further into Higheagle's neck. "Nod if you understand, Cochise."

Higheagle relaxed his muscles and moved his head slightly. He felt the man to his left, the one with the potent aftershave, release his grip. Then he felt another cool piece of metal press up against his left temple. His pupils were beginning to adjust to the light. Out of the corner of his eye, he could just make out the barrel of the handgun and outline of the intruders. The man on his left with the gun, the New Yorker, was bulky; the man on his right, the Texan, tall and stringy. *What an odd pair,* he thought.

He heard a footfall outside the room. His grandfather appeared wearing only a pair of baggy boxer shorts. Behind him, a third interloper materialized like a phantom, pointing a gun at the old man's back.

"You and your grandfather have disappointed me, Joe. It's not supposed to be easy to sneak up on an Indian."

Prescott! Higheagle cringed at the sneering voice. "Leave my grandfather alone. He's not part of this."

The renowned developer and leading Denver citizen shoved the old chieftain in the back and motioned him with the nose of his pistol to stand next to the bed.

"Keep your hands where I can see them, Chief." He turned back towards Higheagle. "You've been causing me some problems, Joe. Now, I'm above all else a gentleman, but I can't have people meddling in my business affairs. As a new business owner yourself, I'm sure you can appreciate the delicacy of my position."

Higheagle felt the man to his right press the knife blade harder against his neck. He was defenseless against two armed men, but still his brain worked feverishly to figure a way out of this, though at this point his main goal was to protect his grandfather.

"I believe you have a few things that belong to me, Joe, or rather, that *don't* belong to you. Pull him up, gentlemen, and follow me. And bring our esteemed chief here too."

The two thugs allowed Higheagle to raise himself up under his own power and escorted him roughly down the hallway along with his grandfather, keeping guns pressed against their backs. When they reached the office, Prescott pulled the shade down. He then turned on a lamp and pointed it at the two captives, blinding them with the 100-watt light, as the two thugs bound him and his grandfather each to a chair with duct tape.

No one saw the man in the disguise peering in through the living room window.

"I apologize for not making the introductions sooner, Joe," Prescott said, and he nodded towards the lanky man. "This here is Mr. Paine, and this is his highly-skilled cohort, Mr. Morelli. Another alias, as I'm sure you can appreciate.

Needless to say, neither of my charming colleagues has appeared alongside me in the *Denver Post* society section."

"Gee, I wonder why?" said Higheagle, eyeing the two brutes.

"Why, Joe, I didn't know you had a sense of humor. Now that you and my humble associates have been properly acquainted, why don't you tell me about you and Sally McTavish? You've been putting a lot of foolish, not to mention dangerous, ideas in her head lately."

Higheagle realized Prescott wasn't here just to threaten him or scare him into backing off from the investigation. The purpose was also interrogation. This left him with three options. He could lie outright, tell the truth, or mix lies with truth. If he lied outright and was caught, he and his grandfather might not make it out of this situation alive. If he told the truth, Sally, Tommy, Minesali, Markworth, and perhaps others could be hurt. He quickly decided on the third option: He would lie only when necessary to protect others—or when he thought he could get away with it.

"I saw Sally for the first time at the public meeting the other night."

"And that's when you told her about your little witch hunt?"

Higheagle looked at his grandfather, who gave a shrug, unsure of how to play it either.

"Don't fuck with me, boy-o."

Prescott tipped his head, summoning the man called Paine. Higheagle watched in silent horror as the man pulled out his knife again, came up behind him, and pressed the cold blade against his throat, this time drawing blood.

"Okay, okay. I met her at the hospital when my grandfather was going in for some tests."

"Go on."

"When I found out that Tommy and four other kids had gotten cancer, I called her and told her to contact the Health Department. I told her that they might have information about the cancer cases. She must have called them when she set up the public meeting. I didn't see her again until just before the meeting. We only talked for a few minutes."

"That's when you told her you were conducting your own investigation?"

With the harsh, bright lights on his face, he felt like Dustin Hoffman in *Marathon Man*. "No, I told her over the phone when she called to tell me that she was organizing a meeting."

"How did you know there were other cases?"

"My doctor at the hospital, Doctor Ekstrom, told us," responded John Higheagle.

Prescott stood still a moment, trying to decipher whether they were telling the truth. "Why, gentlemen, that's almost believable. Almost—but not quite." With a jackal's smile, he tipped his head silently towards his two goons, commanding them into threatening action.

The thickset one called Morelli stepped up to the old Contrary and pointed his pistol at his temple while Higheagle felt the blade of Paine's knife dig deeper into his throat. Feeling desperate, he decided to turn the questioning around.

"Did Sally say anything at the meeting about what I'm doing? No, because she doesn't know anything!"

Prescott weighed this a moment. "Is there something going on between you and Sally?"

"No, of course not. I barely know her."

"That's funny. I saw her earlier tonight, and when I brought your name up, she acted strangely. It was almost like she cares about you or something." He stopped in mid-stride and spun around. "You find her desirable, don't you, Joe? You *want* her."

"You're fucking crazy."

Prescott ignored him and drew closer, so close that Joe could smell roast beef mingled with Scotch on his breath. "Come on, you can tell me. I may be able to give you some tips. I know every inch of that woman."

Higheagle said nothing. What could he possibly say to that?

"Oh, it doesn't matter anyway," Prescott said dismissively, though it was obvious that it mattered to him a great deal.

Higheagle looked at his grandfather. His mind was working frantically, too, on how the hell they were going to get out of this situation.

Prescott ran his black-gloved finger along the keyboard of the laptop on the desk. "Looks like a nice PC, Joe. Too bad you're going to have to part with it and all the records you have here."

"The lab will still have all the analytical. And if anything happens to me, others will pick up the scent. I've seen to that."

"I hope you don't mean your friend Dan Markworth. I'm afraid old Danny Boy's not going to be of much help to you from here on out."

What the fuck does that mean? Has he done something to Markworth?

"I'm growing tired of this little game. Here's my proposition and it's non-negotiable. You are to put an immediate end to this little study of yours. If you do, you'll never see me or my two associates again and your grandfather here—the big chief and hero of Hamburger Hill—gets to spend his golden years in a comfortable rocker dreaming about the good old days. But if you make any further contact with anyone in regards to this matter, or meddle in any of my business, my friends here will pay you and Chiefie another visit. Mr. Paine, you might want to fill in our boy on some of your specialties."

Feeling the knife point burrowing deeper, Higheagle held his head totally still. "It might be a week after we catch you snooping around, Cochise. Or it might be a month. But make no mistake, we'll find you. That's when we'll give you our own little special present: a Rocky Mountain necktie."

The other man, the one called Morelli, stepped forward "They say when a man gets cut from ear to ear he doesn't really die from the wound. He suffocates by drowning in his own blood. You don't want that to happen to you and old Gramps here. Fricking tongue gets all twisted around, blood everywhere. It's a gruesome sight."

Prescott gave a shrug. "What can I say, Joe? As you can see, my associates are quite serious. Like any true professionals, they thoroughly enjoy their work." He took a seat on the desk. "Got a few more questions for you, boy-o. And I'm encouraging you to be as forthcoming as possible. Because if you aren't, I'm going to have to let Mr. Paine and Mr. Morelli here indulge in their unconventional areas of expertise. Now who are you working for?"

Higheagle just looked at him, grappling to figure a way out.

"Come on, answer the man!" snapped Paine.

He drove the blade deeper and Higheagle squirmed in the chair.

"Don't tell him!" cried his grandfather. "If you do, he'll just send these goons after him!"

"Don't fuck with me, Joe. I told you what would happen if—"

The sound of revving engines brought Prescott up short. Paine and Morelli dashed quickly into the living room and went to the window looking out onto the street.

A pair of police cruisers screeched to a halt, dome lights flashing.

"Jesus Christ!" cursed Morelli. "The fucking cops!"

Prescott darted to the window to have a look for himself. "I don't believe this shit!"

Higheagle realized one of his neighbors must have called the police. This was his chance. He waited until he heard a car door open then yelled at the top of his lungs. "HELLLP!"

Prescott turned from the door. "Shut him the fuck up!"

His grandfather yelled for help, too, as four cops started forward, guns drawn. Prescott and his two henchmen scrambled back into the room. Paine slapped his hand over Higheagle's screaming mouth, muffling the sound, and Morelli did the same to the old chief.

"We've got to get the hell out of here!" said Morelli in an urgent whisper.

"Not yet!" commanded Prescott, also keeping his voice low so the police wouldn't hear them. "First we have to get his goddamned computer and his files!" He pointed to the hard drive and stacks of folders on the desk.

"It's too fucking late for that!" whispered Paine.

"Yeah, I'm outta here!" agreed Morelli. He then smacked the butt of his pistol against the old man's head, knocking him out, and bolted from the room on his stubby legs.

At the same time, Higheagle bit Paine's hand, eliciting a howl of agony, and screamed again for help as Prescott dashed to the desk and grabbed a paperweight. In the next grisly instant, Higheagle saw Prescott's arm rise above his head and felt a tremendous force crash down upon his skull.

Then he felt nothing, nothing at all, as blackness consumed him.

CHAPTER 49

VIC SHARD GRINNED as Hayden Prescott and his two unlawful associates vaulted off the back porch, charged across the lawn, and tumbled over the fence leading to the back alley. A moment later, he heard a car engine spurt to life and saw the frantic trio drive off into the night, headlights off.

Shard slipped through the open door, closed and locked it. He could hear the voices of the cops coming from next door. He had called 911 on his two-way radio when he had seen the tall, skinny one threatening Higheagle with the knife. The police had thankfully showed up sooner than Shard had expected—to apprehend the supposed burglar at 347 Mayfair Lane, the house next door. Shard's plan had worked to perfection: Prescott and his two goons had been frightened off and Higheagle would not be subjected to questioning by the nosy police.

Shard walked down the hallway to Higheagle's office. The geologist and his grandfather were both out cold and tied to a chair with duct tape. Shard checked their pulses, untied them, and propped them up in their chairs. For several minutes, he waited for the expected knock on the front door. When it came, he didn't answer and eventually the police left, after searching the area for a few minutes. Once they were gone, he rousted Higheagle by throwing a glass of cold water on him, leaving the old man alone. The big Cheyenne groaned and looked up at him through half-hooded eyes.

"Like your taste in art, Joe."

Shard waved expansively at the four colored pencil drawings on the wall showing a running fight between a group of mounted Cheyenne warriors and their Pawnee enemies.

Higheagle gingerly touched his head, where a welt was growing like a magma chamber. "What the hell happened?"

Shard turned away from the colorful drawings and their eyes met. "I called in the cavalry and broke up your little shindig. Said there was a burglary in progress next door."

Higheagle nodded groggily and looked worriedly at his grandfather.

"He's okay. I already checked him. He's a tough old bird and I don't see any reason to wake him. That way you and I can talk in private."

Higheagle took a moment to verify that the old man was breathing normally and wasn't too badly hurt. "I don't know whether to thank you or punch you," he said to Shard. "You may have helped me out of a scrape, but you're still tailing me, you fuck."

"I've got to make ends meet just like every other working stiff out there. So cut the crap."

"I'm just telling you, working this from both sides is going to get you into trouble."

"You let me worry about that. Now tell me, any new developments in your case against my crooked client?"

Higheagle grimaced as he rubbed his head. Shard could tell he was in serious pain. "I have nothing to say to you. Not after you told Prescott about Sally and me."

"I didn't tell him a damned thing. He figured it out for himself."

"I don't believe you."

"You'd better start. Look, the man ain't stupid. I knew something was up when he told me not to keep an eye on you tonight."

Higheagle's dark eyes flickered with hostility. "He's a criminal and you're working for him, you fucking asshole."

"So was Charles Quantrill and you had no qualms about taking his money, not until he killed himself anyway."

"That was different."

"Bullshit. All you need to remember is that by the end of all this, I will have hurt my client a hell of a lot more than I helped him. Just like you when you worked for Quantrill."

John Higheagle gave a groan and began stirring to life. Not wanting to be seen by the old man, Shard stepped quietly to the door of the office.

"Looks like the chief is coming to. We'll be in touch, Joe."

"I still don't trust you, you asshole."

Shard grinned and tipped his cowboy hat. "Like I told you before, Joe, you might want to treat me with a little more respect."

"Yeah, why's that?"

"Because you're smack dab in the middle of quite a little fracas here—and I reckon I'm the best friend you've got."

CHAPTER 50

WHEN HE REACHED HIS MANSION, Prescott took off all his dark clothing and tossed it in a pile on the plush armoire in his bedroom, then headed for the bathroom to take a shower. As he passed the twinned marble washbasins, he caught his reflection in the mirror and stopped to examine himself.

Standing naked before the mirror, he couldn't help but see his mother. Like her, his body was lean, sinewy, and bronze from the many hours he spent under the watchful gaze of his personal trainer and in the tanning salon of his deluxe health club. Her features stood out prominently: the smooth Mediterranean skin; the full, almost succulent lips; the jet-black hair, eyelashes, and eyebrows that routinely drove members of the opposite sex crazy with desire. Ironically, the attributes women found irresistible were those he had inherited from his mother.

Dearest Mumsie.

She was a piece of work all right. He had always been drawn to her unorthodox and adventurous approach to life, and replicated it in his own. She moved through the world like an overindulged queen, beholden to no one: devilishly tossing out controversial subjects at parties and public places to spark conflict; swimming far out to sea alone during family vacations to Bermuda, the Virgin Islands, and Hawaii; smashing tennis balls down the throats of country club men and laughing uproariously; mischievously driving up prices at art auctions only to bail out at the last second; stealing away to have sex with men nearly half her age; and hosting wildly extravagant parties for the fabulously wealthy of Newport Beach. It was her sheer hedonism, lust for danger, and cavalier disregard for social convention that had always intrigued him, and for many years now he had imitated her example.

Like her, he thrilled at the prospect of danger. Like tonight when he had broken into Higheagle's house. And on all the other occasions in the last month: when he had first schemed to kill Gus McTavish; when he had faked the mouth-to-mouth; when the police had questioned him afterwards; and when that worthless Detective Marshak had tried to bully him into confessing. There was something electrifying about living on the edge, about pushing the envelope—like Mumsie.

She was a part of him.

Yet, he was also quite like Father, he had to admit as he studied his square, manly jawline and pondered his business accomplishments. Clearly, his lust for danger and zealous pursuit of his goals were gifts in large part from Mumsie, but the many similarities between him and his father also extended beyond the merely physical attributes handed down from one generation to the next. Father had always been a closer, a winner, a fierce competitor, and Prescott knew he was like the old man in that way. But there had always been limits to what his father would do to achieve his goals. Mumsie, on the other hand, had always seemed without bounds, the perfect iconoclast.

He remembered back to their first time together on his sixteenth birthday: how her bright red fingernails had dug into the carpet, how her taught buttocks had thrust back and forth almost violently as he plunged inside her from behind, how insanely terrified yet excited he had been. A part of him would always hate her for what she'd made him do. Yet over the years, he had continued to go back for more, for there was no one who could make him feel more wanted and manly than Mumsie.

Despite being emotionally and physically sickened by what had happened, he found his mother was like a drug. He could not live without the feel and smell of her body, the sense of forbidden danger. But their liaisons were always on her terms, when she needed instant gratification and Father was out swatting golf balls or away on business. That was Mumsie's way.

She had cast a curious spell over him from which he had never quite recovered.

It wasn't until his senior year of high school, when he began to track her movements closely, that he realized his gorgeous mother was actually quite promiscuous. He was certain his father must have known about her lascivious ways, but perhaps he was cheating on her too and that's why he didn't care. In any case, she showed little discretion in her lechery. Over the years, the men in her life came and went—tennis pros, personal trainers, bartenders, lawyers—but there was one constant. They were always young, handsome, hard-bodied, and never around very long before a new one stepped in.

He had continued to have intercourse with dear Mumsie until he was twenty-three and had graduated from college. That's when he forced himself to quit her.

Cold turkey—it wasn't easy.

Ironically, almost without exception the women Prescott bedded resembled his mother. They had dark hair and black sassy eyes and their skin was closer to the color of bronze than ivory. He liked cultured bluebloods from back East with liberal art's degrees and hair piled high on their heads and legs that stopped inches from their necks. Women just like Mumsie, a rich girl from Greenwich, Connecticut, who had majored in art history at Smith.

Only Sally had been different from the others. Sally wasn't like Mumsie at all. And in some strange way that he would probably never fully understand, he had loved her.

Prescott turned away from the mirror and turned on the shower. He adjusted the knobs until the water was a comfortable temperature before stepping into the spray.

He thought again of Father.

Hayden Prescott II was a man in full. A remarkable athlete with Ivy League credentials and a roguishly handsome face, he had always worked hard and played hard. By the end of the Reagan years, he had leapfrogged over a dozen senior managers to become second-in-command of the powerful Southern California real estate company Mission Viejo. It was at that time Prescott began interning with him during his summer breaks from college and learned the ropes of being a developer. The old man taught him all the tricks he would need to succeed: how to scuttle cumbersome environmental standards; how to subvert zoning requirements; how to discourage public comment by threatening lawsuits; how to coerce puppet commissioners into doing what he wanted; how to force recalcitrant landowners to sell by getting their property condemned; how to kill growth control initiatives by throwing an army of attorneys at the opposition. From his father, Prescott learned about the power of forceful persuasion, the art of negotiation, when to twist the rules and when to break them. He learned how to be creative in financing and handling money, how to withhold payment to contractors to increase cash flow and boost earnings, how to quietly coerce the opposition into submission.

His father had taught him well.

And yet, he hated the man. Hated him for doing nothing to stop his own wife and son from sinking into a world of oedipal decadence.

But as much as he detested his father for not putting a stop to it all and his mother for holding him captive under her salacious spell, he hated himself far worse. The shame and guilt would never subside, and the questions would always haunt him: Why hadn't he been stronger on that hot summer day when Mumsie had lured him into her bedroom? Why had he continued to have sex with her until he was in his early twenties? How could he have betrayed his own father?

He reached for the bottle of avocado and lemon shampoo and applied a gelatinous blob to his hair. He didn't want to think about the past anymore, so he pushed the troubling thoughts aside and turned his attention to tonight's events.

He wondered who had called the police. It couldn't have been Higheagle or his grandfather because they had been taken by surprise. Moreover, Higheagle's house wasn't equipped with any alarm; Morelli, the expert in such criminal matters, had assured them that that was the case. That left one of the neighbors. Someone must have heard the break-in and called 911.

Regrettably, the endeavor had not been successful. Higheagle still had his computer and all of the aerial photographs and analytical data. They had no doubt put the scare into him, but probably not enough that he would walk away from his investigation. It was still unclear how well he knew Sally and how much she knew about Dakota Ranch. And Higheagle's client was still unknown.

All in all, the night was a miserable failure.

The Cheyenne was proving to be a huge thorn in his side. While Markworth, Marshak, and Sally posed some complications, they could be managed. The far bigger problem was Higheagle. His computer hard drive would have to be seized along with all his records, and Shard would have to watch him like a hawk. If he showed any signs of continuing his meddlesome investigation, he would have to be dealt with like greedy Gus. But with Marshak still running around like a loose cannon, killing the Indian would have to be a last resort.

Still, there was no way he could allow himself to continue to be outwitted by some two-bit geologist. He had to take the gloves off. For wherever the contest would be waged, it would be a bareknuckle brawl until only one man was left standing. And that man, he was convinced, would be himself.

Hayden Winthrop Prescott III.

CHAPTER 51

THE FOLLOWING MORNING, Higheagle and his grandfather, battered and bruised, sat in the kitchen eating soggy cheerios and crispy fry bread.

"How much do you know about this man who hired you?"

Higheagle squinted across the pine breakfast table at the old chief. "You talking about Minesali?"

"There's a reason I brought it up. I forgot to tell you something last night."

"What?"

"I know someone who used to work at his plant in Denver."

Higheagle wondered where this was heading.

"The man's name is Hank Johanson. He was an old flame of your grandmother's."

Why the hell are you telling me this now? "How do you know this guy?"

"Met him a few times. Only son of a bitch I ever liked that Katy used to run around with before she met me."

"What can Johanson tell me?"

The old chief dipped his fry bread into a bowl of Tupelo honey. "I'm not sure. But after last night, I remembered Hank used to work at a plant owned by some Italian guy—a plant that manufactures pesticides and herbicides, among other things. I got to thinking it might be the place owned by your client."

Higheagle thought of the white material in the soil and suddenly he felt incredibly stupid. Minesali manufactured pesticides and herbicides, of course, and while such materials often came in liquid form they also came as solid powders, pellets, and granular mixtures that were later applied to water and other liquids prior to field spraying applications. Could it be that the material buried in the rec center field was solid waste from Minesali's operation? But if Minesali was the actual generator of the waste, why would he hire someone to gather evidence of wrongdoing that could be used against him? That was the part that didn't make any sense. And what about the high concentrations of heavy metals in the soil? The organic compounds detected at Dakota Ranch were active ingredients or byproducts of the herbicide production process. But hexavalent chromium and the other toxic metals weren't used in making herbicides or pesticides.

So what the hell did it all mean?

He looked at his grandfather. "Tell me about this Hank Johanson."

"Old Hank's a character, that's for sure. He knows every damn thing there is to know about Denver...all the old society stuff."

"That's not what I mean. What do you think he knows about Minesali's operation?"

"A lot, I would guess. He was plant foreman for twenty years."

"So you believe that there might be a connection to Dakota Ranch in all this?"

"I don't know. I'm just thinking Hank might know a thing or two that could prove helpful. I must have his number lying around somewhere. Why don't I go ahead and set up a meeting between the two of you?"

"Don't you want to be there?"

"I think you should hear what Hank has to say and decide for yourself if you should tell me. After all, you did sign a client confidentiality agreement. It's one thing for you to tell me something. It's another to have me present at a meeting with a third party. Besides, I have a feeling whatever Hank tells you might change things a bit."

"Change things how?"

"You'll see."

"Mysterious. So when should we call him?"

"After breakfast and my nap. My head is still fucking sore as hell."

"So what's Hank's story besides that he used to date Grandma Kate and worked for Minesali?"

"Like I said, he's quite a character. And he's one big son of a bitch. He goes about six-six and three hundred pounds. Played some pro ball in the late sixties with the Vikings. Left tackle, protecting Joe Kapp's blind side. He always told me he should have married Katy when he had the chance. Maybe that's why I liked the son of a bitch. Because he didn't go through with it and I won your grandmother's heart instead."

"Is Hank Indian?"

"He's half Ute. But you wouldn't know it looking at him."

Higheagle felt his grandfather was holding something back. "You think Minesali's not being straight with me, is that it?"

The old chief stared out the window, his countenance inscrutable. "I don't know. That's what you have to find out."

"I already told you why he's interested in the case. His wife died of pancreatic cancer and it tore him up inside. Plus he has it out for Prescott."

"And why is that?"

"I don't know. But that can't be Minesali's waste out at Dakota or why the hell would he have hired me? That's the last thing he'd do if he was part of this, don't you think?"

"You're right, it doesn't make sense."

"Yet you still don't trust him?"

"I was a trial lawyer for over thirty years. I don't trust anybody, not even you. That's why I'm going with you tonight to collect those samples at Silverado Knolls. To watch your back."

Higheagle shook his head, as if to quickly kill the idea. "Unfortunately, Minesali's legal agreement doesn't cover you."

"Actually, it does. You just have to read the fine print. It says that you and all of your subcontractors, including companies providing sampling and monitoring equipment, laboratory services, and other support services, are covered under the agreement. I'm telling you, your client has thought of everything. That's one of the reasons I think he might be up to funny business."

"I'm sorry, but you can't come with me out to Silverado, Grandfather."

"Why the hell not?"

"Because after last night, it's not safe. And even if Prescott and his goons didn't pose a threat, there's too much risk from a field protocol standpoint. You don't have the proper health and safety training."

"You're forgetting those goons threatened me too. Hell, it's probably more dangerous to leave me at home. Have you thought of that?"

To his chagrin, he saw that his grandfather was right.

"Look at it this way. You get your very own Kit Fox warrior and Contrary. I'll be right there beside you with my trusty Winchester."

"Just what I need, a seventy-five year old AARP member who thinks he's fighting the ghost of George Armstrong Custer. I think that fat bastard Morelli must have scrambled your brains."

"Maybe he did. But that still doesn't change one thing."

"And what would that be?"

"It's a good night for a fight, Grandson. It's a good night for a fight, indeed."

CHAPTER 52

PRESCOTT WAS WATCHING the clash of words with a mixture of surprise and fascination. They were sitting in his office and Senator Dahlquist was battling it out with Markworth. What was shocking was that the Colorado Department of Public Health and Environment director was holding his own. He appeared determined to refuse Dahlquist's demands altogether and to conduct the cancer study as he saw fit—a situation Prescott was not about to tolerate.

"I won't do it. I won't massage data to fit your agenda or anyone else's. There are kids dying out there and I'm going to find out what's behind it. It's not only my job, it's the right thing to do."

Dahlquist sneered. "I'm telling you that you're not going to find anything conclusive."

"That's not part of my job descrip—"

"Your job is to do whatever the hell I tell you! I'm the senate majority leader of the goddamned state legislature!"

Markworth recoiled like a wounded animal. Dahlquist pulled one of his long, ape-like arms from the armrest of his chair and waved a bony finger at him as he continued his diatribe.

"You shouldn't have told that McTavish woman the names of the cancer cases. Hell, you should have said no to the public meeting from the get-go. Give those people out there all the fact sheets you want, but I'm warning you, if that woman or anyone else organizes another meeting, you'd better make sure you're not within twenty miles of it!"

The room snapped silent. Prescott studied Markworth with a mixture of contempt and pity. He could still see defiance, but there was genuine fear now too.

"You're going to devote minimal staff to this project and bring it to a swift conclusion. And your report is going to say nothing—absolutely nothing. Now I don't think I need to remind you that David Hanley, your boss, is a good friend of mine. Nor do I need to tell you that several members of the legislature were not pleased with the way you handled the Summitville Mine project."

"But that wasn't my—"

"We don't care whose fault it was!"

It was time to jump in and pretend to be the neutral referee. "We don't want this to turn into an ugly situation, Dan," Prescott said in a placating voice. "We just want to do what's best for all parties."

Dahlquist nodded belligerently. "A government bureaucrat in his late-forties on the street looking for work during a recession…with a wife and four kids to care for and college bills on the way…now that's not a pretty sight."

"You can't do this. What you're asking me to do goes against—"

"Just who in the hell do you think runs the Health Department?"

"I believe he gets the point, Senator," said Prescott, interjecting again by pretending to be sympathetic. "Now all we're asking, Dan, is that you go about your work quietly. No more public meetings, and put an end to this arm waving about waste dumping and chemical exposure. Now is that asking too much? We all know the public and media can't be trusted. They always twist scientific logic around just to get a good story."

Dahlquist wagged a bony finger. "And don't forget, the Health Department stands to lose the most if there are accusations about toxic chemicals. You yourself signed off on the reports. If lawsuits emerge, I can promise you will be personally named."

At this Markworth blanched, but Prescott still saw a flicker of fight remaining in the man. He looked like a prizefighter that refuses to stay down. *Why doesn't he just throw in the towel? Doesn't he realize he can't win?*

"I don't understand you people. I don't care about your agendas. My job is to protect human health and the environment."

Dahlquist waved his hand dismissively. "This is not the time to act all high and mighty. If you knew the endless options available to destroy you, it would make your head spin. You have no control over any of this and you never did. I can have you removed from your job with a single phone call. I can tell Director Hanley that, unless he gets rid of you, there will be a freeze on senior manager pay increases and he won't get that new office building he's expecting under next year's budget. Or, I can have your division merged with another and you'll be on East Colfax within a week, begging for handouts with a cardboard sign around your neck. It's your goddamned choice!"

Markworth sank back into the couch. His disbelief had turned to rage, and his rage now turned to resignation. "All right," he said finally, his voice scarcely above a whisper. "I suppose I could..."

He broke off right there, unable to bring himself to finish. Instead, Dahlquist did it for him.

"This agreement means, of course, that you are not to speak with anyone—including the media, EPA, or any other regulatory agencies—unless authorized by me. You're also not to talk to this Higheagle, nor are you to participate in any public meetings with the homeowners. You can give vague, equivocal answers to questions from concerned citizens and hand out fact sheets, but they must be approved by me. Violate any of these conditions and you're out of a job. Also, I will personally review the draft cancer study document before it goes out for public comment. You will make all changes to the document that I recommend and will destroy all hard copies and electronic versions of the draft report. Now, if you fulfill your end of the bargain satisfactorily, I am confident you will be looking at a promotion and a pay increase on the order of twenty percent."

A long, uncomfortable silence followed.

"Are you with us, Dan?" asked Prescott, still pretending to be sympathetic. "Do you see now how we're only looking out for what's best for all parties, including you and your family?"

Markworth sat slumped in the couch, a dazed expression on his face. After what seemed a long time, he rose to his feet, slowly, like a woozy boxer. The fight had literally been knocked out of him.

"I'll do what you want," he croaked. "Just leave me and my family alone."

CHAPTER 53

TO THE SOOTHING MELODY of Charles Littleleaf's *Ancient Reflections*, Higheagle guided the War Wagon through the dark of night. There was no traffic along the back roads once he and his grandfather pulled off I-25. Above, the moon shone fitfully through the swiftly moving cloud cover. After a few minutes, they came to a halt before the locked aluminum gate Higheagle had located during his recon on Saturday afternoon. It looked no more conspicuous than the entrance to any Front Range cattle ranch, except for the gigantic billboard posted on the other side of the barbed wire fence.

WELCOME TO SILVERADO KNOLLS
THE BEST IN THE WEST

SPLENDID 4, 5, 6 BEDROOMS   HOMES FROM THE 800s
MASTERS AND CUSTOM SERIES
TWO 18-HOLE CHAMPIONSHIP GOLF COURSES
DELUXE GATED COMMUNITY AVAILABLE THIS SUMMER
THE NEWPORT COMPANY: BRINGING REALiTY TO YOUR DREAMS

His grandfather shook his head. "Just what we fucking need: another deluxe gated community with multimillion dollar homes and championship golf courses."

"It's FUBAR all right—Fucked Up Beyond All Recognition." Higheagle pointed the War Wagon to the south and headed down the road parallel to the property line. It was risky bringing his grandfather out here, but he had made a promise and wasn't about to go back on it. He only hoped someone wasn't following them; he hadn't seen anyone on their tail, but that didn't necessarily mean Shard, or one of Prescott's henchmen, wasn't out there, somewhere, watching. He felt like a cowboy in an old-time Western, looking over his shoulder at every turn to see if he was being pursued.

They came to a stop at a section where the perimeter fence was down. Higheagle got out and pulled back the wire to give them a clear point of entry. Sliding back in the truck, he eased across a shallow drainage ditch and through the opening.

They followed the fence line back to the entrance before turning east. Higheagle set the odometer to zero and drove slowly along a dirt road, which sloped gently uphill. Several minutes passed before they reached the headwall of the first major drainage. He checked the coordinates on his hand-held Trimble global positioning system plugger unit against the USGS map coordinates to make sure he had the right location, then got out and did a quick recon while his grandfather looked on.

The area had been cleared and grubbed recently. There was no vegetation and the yellowish-brown soil looked fresh and compacted, as if the coulee had been backfilled with imported soil. It looked just like the aerials showing the early stages of Dakota Ranch.

Climbing back in the truck, they drove alongside the backfill on a well-used trail rutted with tire tracks. They drove for a quarter mile, until the flat, compacted yellowish-brown soil gave way to an open coulee fifteen feet lower than the surrounding prairie. Higheagle took another GPS bearing, recorded it, and turned the truck around. They drove back to the headwall area and laid out all the sampling equipment: a steel hand auger for digging through the soil; a metal drive sampler; two ice-filled chests to hold the samples; supplies to decontaminate the sampling equipment; and a backpack containing the GPS, health and safety equipment, a field notebook, a flash camera, and chain-of-custody forms.

When everything was set up, they began sampling. They worked efficiently through division of labor, wearing standard Level C protection of full-face respirators and latex gloves. Higheagle vectored in each sampling location with the GPS, augered through the soil, collected and labeled the samples, and documented observations in his notebook. His grandfather took photographs with the autofocus flash camera and decontaminated the sampling equipment. At around the five-foot depth, they came upon a discolored soil layer, with pockets and lenses of oozing sludge and metal-like filings. They collected two soil samples at a depth of six feet from each sample location, deep enough to be in the impacted zone. They moved their way downstream as they sampled, periodically moving the truck.

The air was cool. The scattered clouds overhead scudded south, allowing the moonlight to sneak through every so often. Coyotes howled in the distance, but there was no sign of any other animals.

Two hours into the sampling, after collecting their twenty-second sample at the eleventh boring location, they heard an unexpected noise. They paused from their work and pricked their ears alertly to the west, in the direction of a gentle rise. The sound was unmistakable: the dull roar of massive machinery on wheels.

Higheagle scanned the dark horizon, hoping to catch a flash of something silhouetted against the night sky, but he saw nothing. The rumbling sound, still faint, grew louder. The ground began to vibrate beneath their feet.

"We've got enough samples. Let's put everything away and head to the truck."

Hurriedly, they dumped out the rinse water from the 5-gallon buckets they had used to decontaminate the equipment, kicked some dry dirt over the puddle to cover up the decon operation, and gathered up the supplies, loading them in the nearby truck. When they hopped inside the cab, Higheagle turned off the headlights. They peered through the window breathlessly, but still they saw nothing.

Then, more suddenly than expected, they saw a flicker of light along the skyline.

Higheagle turned the key and hit the gas pedal. He headed south, keeping his eyes peeled on the light, which gradually metamorphosed into a pair of headlights. Soon a line of heavy vehicles materialized, perhaps a half mile off, coming straight for them.

Guided by the moonlight, they drove along the backfilled coulee until they reached the open channel where material had yet to be placed. Higheagle drove the War Wagon down a steep slope and then down the coulee a short distance until they reached a bend. He parked the truck downstream of the bend. The two hopped out and crept up the slope to take a closer look.

When they neared the leading edge of the backfill, they came upon two small outcroppings of sandstone. They tucked themselves behind the one that had a short piñon pine growing beside it. Peering from behind the outcrop, they saw a fleet of heavy equipment trucks lumbering along the road. A moment later, the lead vehicle veered towards them, taking the road along the backfilled drainage.

From this vantage point, what they witnessed over the next hour was an impeccably smooth waste disposal operation in action. Huge transport trucks the size of moving vans worked their way to the leading edge of the backfill, where steel, 55-gallon drums were lowered by hydraulic lifts. A small contingent of workers in Tyvek suits, full-face respirators, and thick Neoprene gloves opened the sealed drums and pumped the liquid contents into the drainage with cart-mounted centrifugal pumps. A large yellow trackhoe toiled below the laborers, moving dry soil into the channel and mixing it with the waste until it was no longer liquid but a wet solid. Smaller backhoes dug along the margins and placed fresh soil in big end-dump trucks. The dump trucks then piled the clean soil until it was applied as a thick cover over the contaminated soil. Finally, a water truck equipped with a fire hose was used to rinse out the drums, and a smooth-roll compactor packed down the soil tightly along the leading edge of the backfill.

The work area was well lit by big floodlights. Higheagle noticed that virtually every one of the workers was Hispanic and he could overhear snippets of conversation in Spanish over the sound of the machinery. He suspected most of the workers were illegals or legitimate short-term laborers from south of the border. They would be the ideal choice for such a clandestine operation. They could be paid cheaply, but well by Mexican standards, and were not likely to ask a lot of questions for fear of being deported.

The workers moved quickly, efficiently, deploying their heavy equipment with the precision of an army conducting military maneuvers. It was obvious that they had performed this kind of work many times before. As much as Higheagle hated to admit it, Prescott's operation showed a flair for diabolical genius. Here he was using a crack team of imported laborers to dump huge volumes of waste on his properties at night, then throwing up developments on top and making a bundle of money in the process.

Out of sight, out of mind.

All sense of time became lost as they gazed mesmerically at the operation below. The active disposal zone was moving downstream and encroaching upon them, but they didn't notice. Nor did they see the silver Range Rover until it was almost upon them.

CHAPTER 54

HIGHEAGLE PULLED his grandfather down as the headlights swept across the sandstone outcrop. Should they make a run for it? No, they wouldn't stand a chance. His grandfather may have been unusually spry for his age, but he was still seventy-five and they wouldn't get very far before being caught. With that in mind, Higheagle searched the night skyline for outcrops, thick brush, boulders—anything that might serve as protective cover during a careful retreat to the War Wagon—but he saw nothing.

A car door slammed shut, then another. He peered around the edge of the piñon pine and saw two men walking unhurriedly towards the other sandstone outcrop twenty feet away. Probably the field foreman and his top hand. There was a glowing red spot in front of the face of one of the men, and in the next instant Higheagle smelled cigar smoke. The two interlopers sat down on the outcrop and stared out at the workers, their upper bodies silhouetted against the night sky. Even in the dark, something about them seemed familiar.

And then he heard one of the voices.

"I got the go-ahead from the Health Department for Silverado. They're finished with their review."

Prescott, the bastard!

Now the second man spoke.

"Conditional approval?" It was fucking Hwong.

"No, full approval. I can build now at any time."

"So next week will still be the last shipment?"

"Nine thousand drums and eighty vac trucks."

"The three-foot cap's a good precaution, but you don't need to worry this time. This stuff is Bambi to Dakota's Four Horseman of the Apocalypse."

"Dakota was a mistake and there will always be regrets. But it's done."

"Is it? With Higheagle snooping around like a bloodhound?"

"He's being...dealt with."

"Doesn't seem like it to me. He's still alive."

"You're dissatisfied with the way I've chosen to handle matters?"

"I think he's a moray eel that won't let go. He needs to be put out of action."

The moon poked through the clouds. Higheagle ducked behind the rock, pulling his grandfather down with him, his heart clicking wildly as he waited for what Prescott and Hwong would say next. He had never overheard people plotting to kill him before. It was a strange feeling, surreal.

"And how would you suggest I go about it?"

"The same way you handled McTavish."

"He died of a heart attack. Don't you read the newspapers?"

"I know you did it. Come on, just come clean. You poisoned him, didn't you?"

"Asking questions like that could you into serious trouble. You do understand that, don't you, Doug?"

"It doesn't matter. I know you did it."

So that was it then, thought Higheagle. Prescott had killed Gus McTavish after all, or at least had him killed. Sally had said her uncle owned a heavy construction outfit that did work at Dakota Ranch and was now leasing equipment to Prescott for work on Silverado Knolls. Which meant the trackhoes, dumps, and loaders here tonight were on loan from McTavish's company. McTavish must have been involved in the operation at some point before his death—either here at Silverado, years ago at Dakota, or at both places. Or maybe he had stumbled upon the operation and threatened to expose Prescott. Whatever the exact circumstances, he must have known what was going on and been murdered for it.

Hwong turned his head in their direction, forcing them to duck down again. "It doesn't look like the whole ravine will be filled in by the end of next week."

"It'll be close enough."

"You're still going to need to bench it so it looks like a natural cut downstream. You'll need some scraping around the margins to make it look right. We should take a closer look around the bend."

Shit, they'll find the War Wagon! We have to get out of here!

Higheagle tugged gently on his grandfather's shirt and motioned for him to follow. Crouching down low, they started off towards the coulee. After a few feet, the moon flashed through the cloud cover once again, more brilliantly than before, bringing them to a halt.

Higheagle risked a glance over his shoulder. The red glow was moving towards them again.

"Wait until you see the tee box of the fourteenth hole," Prescott was saying. "It's going to be one hell of a dog leg right."

"Too bad I don't play golf. Hold on, I need to take a piss."

"Me too."

The moon slipped behind the clouds again. This was their chance to make a dash for it. And then Higheagle heard a familiar sound.

You've got to be kidding me—a fucking rattlesnake?

He held up his hand, bringing his grandfather to a halt, and listened closely. He heard the hollow jingle sound again. The rattler was not far off, a few feet at most. He knew he shouldn't be surprised: the area between South Denver and Castle Rock was a breeding ground for rattlesnakes, and they were especially prevalent in the late spring and early summer.

He whispered to his grandfather to remain motionless and scanned the grass for glowing reptilian eyes. He couldn't see anything. Slowly, a beam of yellowish light played across their heads as the moon once again penetrated the clouds. The moon's glow seemed to startle the hidden snake too because it rattled again, like a maraca.

Higheagle felt his grandfather nudge him; turning, he saw the old man tip his head at something.

The coiled creature was off to the right, staring straight at them within spitting distance. With its head up and cocked forward, it looked poised to strike.

"There are two things you can't afford this time around," Hwong was saying to Prescott. "The first is you can't have any kids get cancer."

"And the second?"

"That damned Indian—he has to go."

Higheagle shuddered at the chilling words. Now he could hear the sound of piss streaming onto the ground and he knew it was now or never for them to make their escape.

"We're going to have to make a run for it, Grandfather," he whispered. "Do you think you can make it to the truck?"

"I can sure as hell try. But what about the rattler?"

As if on cue, the snake rattled again. Higheagle stared into the softly glowing eyes, careful not to move a muscle. "As long as we pull back slowly, we should be all right. Then I need you to get to your feet and run as fast as you can. I'll be right behind you. Let's go on the count of three."

He looked one last time at the menacing snake before glancing over his shoulder at the two figures silhouetted against the night sky, pissing.

He took a deep breath.

Then he whispered the magic words. "One, two..."

ψψψ

Vic Shard watched Higheagle and his grandfather jump to their feet and start to run. He was viewing them through his latest toy: a pair of night-vision goggles purchased from a local law enforcement supply warehouse. The NV images came across in shades of fluorescent green, as if he was viewing a video game. The bright-green patterns corresponded to short-wavelength thermal images, which in this case denoted warm human bodies running for their lives.

For two hours now, he had been surreptitiously spying on Higheagle and his grandfather from his perch three hundred feet downstream. He knew they had collected soil samples at eleven locations. But now the game was up and they had been discovered. Prescott and Hwong had recovered quickly following their initial shock at the sight of the two men materializing from the sagebrush and dashing across the prairie. And now the situation was quickly developing into a chase.

Shard knew he had to get his ass down there.

He didn't want Higheagle or the old chief to be harmed. He wanted them to get away, and if they needed his help, he would give it to them. Nor did he want the soil samples to be seized from them, for he wanted desperately to know what types of toxic chemicals the samples likely contained.

But this created a problem: How could he aid their escape without looking as though he was helping them?

He knew Prescott would already be angry with him. After all, Shard was supposed to keep Higheagle under surveillance and promptly inform his client of everything he found out. As things stood now, he had failed miserably on both counts. But if he made his presence known, maybe he could rectify the situation.

He could say he had been tailing Higheagle and his grandfather all night and wanted to be one-hundred-percent certain of their intentions before waking up his client in the middle of the night with a phone call.

But how could he protect them and still appear loyal to his client?

He was still working on the answer to that one as he scrambled for his Grand Cherokee. Heart thumping wildly, he yanked open the door and hopped inside. Fifteen seconds had passed since the chase had begun. As the sixteenth ticked off, he popped the Jeep into drive and bolted towards Higheagle's truck with his headlights off, guiding himself through the darkness with his NV goggles.

You can't let anything happen to them, he told himself. *You just can't!*

CHAPTER 55

THE RATTLER had leapt at them, but, luckily, it struck nothing but a clump of long-stemmed prairie grass, and they now bounded across the high plains making their escape. Higheagle was pleasantly surprised by his grandfather's performance thus far. The old chief was moving at a decent clip, more or less a fast-paced jog, swifter than he had thought possible. It was amazing how fast an old fart could move when he was running for his life. But Higheagle also knew that the septuagenarian would be unable to maintain his current pace for very long.

They descended quickly into the dry channel, downstream from where the crews were working. The workmen hadn't yet noticed the two fleeing figures over the cacophony of heavy equipment. They were preoccupied.

But there was no such luck with Prescott and Hwong.

After making a half-hearted attempt to run down their quarry, they had scrambled back to Prescott's Range Rover, a vehicle as fleet over rough terrain as it was rugged. Now they were churning up dust along the high ground on the east side of the coulee, three hundred feet upstream of their footloose prey.

Higheagle heard the engine racing behind him, but fought back the temptation to glance over his shoulder. Like his grandfather, his eyes were fixed on the bend up ahead, beyond which lay the trusty War Wagon. They spurred down the gently sloped gulch, gobbling up ground. But to Higheagle's dismay, the Range Rover quickly caught up to them on their left and began plunging obliquely down the sidewall of the gully to cut them off.

"Come on, Grandfather! Just a little further!" Higheagle exhorted him, realizing that the old man probably wasn't going to make it.

"I'm running as fast as I fucking can!"

"Well, you're going to have to pick up your pace or we're both going to die!"

They ran on, kicking up the sweet smell of sagebrush. After a dozen paces, Higheagle pulled up alongside his grandfather, holding a key ring with one key sticking out from the others.

"Here, take this and run for the truck! I'm going to take care of Prescott and Hwong and then catch up!"

Gasping for air, John Higheagle reached for the keys like a relay sprinter taking a baton.

The Range Rover came to a dust-spewing halt just before the bend fifty feet in front of them.

"Hurry, Grandfather! We've got to get past them!"

The old chief was wheezing now, on his last legs, but he sucked it up and forced himself into another gear. Higheagle sped past him like a lead-blocking fullback. Up ahead, Hwong leapt from the passenger side without closing the door. Higheagle zeroed in on him, ramming him with his shoulder. Hwong's scream was strangely high-pitched, almost womanly, as he was driven violently into the sharp edge of the open door. The metal did not give as the world-renowned scientist took the full force of the impact, collapsing to the ground in a crippled heap.

John Higheagle ran on.

But he quickly came face to face with Hayden Prescott. In the Range Rover's taillights, the developer looked trim and athletic in his dark green jogging suit. Higheagle saw his grandfather dart left to avoid him, trying to slide past the rear fender, but he didn't quite make it as Prescott reached out and grabbed his arm.

The keys went flying.

The Contrary squirmed free and dove to the ground to snatch them. Higheagle sprinted forward and tackled Prescott, the two going down in a cloud of dust.

John Higheagle snatched the keys, deftly side-stepped the tangled bodies, and made his way for the War Wagon further down the drainage.

"Run, Grandfather, run!" cried Higheagle, and then it was just him and Hayden Prescott.

ψψψ

The two adversaries quickly scrambled to their feet and began moving in a revolving circle, sizing each other up like wild animals.

"Do you always bring old men out to do your dirty work?" Prescott spat, his glowering countenance half-black, half-white in the waxing moon.

"What old man are you talking about? He got by you, didn't he?" Higheagle fired back, assuming a wide fighting stance.

"Perhaps you didn't know that trespassing is illegal."

"I'll take my chances with the EPA."

Prescott scowled. The moon tucked behind the clouds, throwing a dark mask over his entire face.

Higheagle lunged at him.

He was dealt a jarring blow to his jaw that sent him reeling to the ground. He shook it off and started to his feet, taking a vicious kick to the ribs. Falling back down, he felt another punch hammer the side of his face, then ducked another before leaping to his feet.

They exchanged a series of violent blows, and then, with the silver moonlight on their shoulders and a small cloud of dust swirling around, they backed off again and stared each other down like sumo wrestlers before the monstrous collision that inevitably takes place in the center of the ring. Higheagle licked the blood from his split lip; it tasted metallic, iron-like. He looked at his adversary in a new light, with a mixture of hatred and grudging respect.

You may be silver spoon, but you can fight—I'll give you that.

Again, he charged, feet pounding across the stubby grass, and went airborne as he attempted a diving tackle. He brought Prescott down with a loud thud and swiped an elbow across his face, drawing blood from his left nostril. As he raised his arm again, he was kneed in the balls and suddenly found himself on top of nothing but ground. He groaned and felt the deep, sickening, burning sensation hit him like a sledgehammer. He staggered to his feet, catching a glimpse of headlights flicking on further down the drainage.

Grandfather—you made it!

Suddenly rejuvenated, he drove his dominant fist—his left—into Prescott's stomach, but received two stunningly quick jabs in return. He dodged the third punch and managed to clutch Prescott by his jogging suit. He drove upwards with his right, catching him in the chin. Prescott responded with a hard fist to his gut, and then they hammered away at one another in a seesaw battle for more than a minute, until the bombardment of fists trailed off as both men succumbed to exhaustion.

They backed away to catch their breath, moving torpidly like reptiles in the cold. Higheagle heard a groan on the other side of the car—Hwong coming out of his stupor?—followed by the sound of a revving engine.

Good work Grandfather! Now just stay there. I'll come to you!

Recovering his breath, he drove forward with a right-handed jab, missed, and delivered another feint before landing a left uppercut that grazed Prescott's chin. He then connected with two more jabs and a roundhouse left, drawing not just audible grunts, but a cascade of blood. Prescott wobbled dizzily and fell to one knee before collapsing to the ground on his stomach.

Higheagle dragged himself forward to deliver the knockout punch.

Summoning his last reserve of energy, he flipped Prescott onto his back and raised his fist to strike the final blow, unaware of the grapefruit-sized block of sandstone in Prescott's right hand.

A sudden blur of movement.

The rock smashed against the side of his head and he crumpled to the ground. The positions were swiftly reversed as Prescott, given new life by the sudden change of fortune, climbed on top of him and raised the big, angular rock high above his head. Through the pinpoint stars, Higheagle could just make out Prescott's gritted teeth, the gleam of animal rage in his eyes. With the implement of death poised to swing down in a cruel arc, Higheagle was certain his head was about to be crushed to a bloody, brainy pulp.

And then a strange thing happened.

A shot rang out, seemingly out of nowhere.

Higheagle heard a bullet whiz past his ear and crash into the earth. Then there was another shot and suddenly the ground around them came alive with bullets.

He looked at Prescott. His face registered incomprehension and the rock above his head hovered in suspended motion.

The unexpected barrage was just what Higheagle needed to reclaim the initiative. He drove his fist into Prescott's balls, raised himself up from the ground, and battered the developer with his shoulder. Prescott grunted in pain and rocked back on his knees.

Higheagle delivered two more blows to his face and ran for the oncoming headlights of the War Wagon, the bullets whizzing past him like swarming hornets, thudding into the loamy walls of the coulee.

CHAPTER 56

GRINNING, VIC SHARD holstered his silver Colt Mustang semiautomatic. He had always been one of the top pistol marksmen when with the DPD, and he was pleased to still have the gift. He had placed all the shots within inches of both men, but the last burst of gunfire at the retreating Higheagle was purely a show for the benefit of his employer.

He ran back to the Jeep and hopped inside, tossing his night-vision goggles onto the passenger seat. Throwing the jeep into reverse, he backed away slowly from the drainage to give Higheagle and his grandfather an open avenue of escape.

But as he pulled backed, he heard the sound of a honking horn coming from the coulee. Looking down, he saw Prescott and Hwong waving at him frantically from the Range Rover. They had spotted him and were signaling him to join the chase.

Shit! I just got myself out of one fix. Now I've got to get out of another?

The Rover lurched forward in pursuit, kicking up a plume of dust. Furiously working his chew, Shard had no choice but to at least pretend to stop Higheagle and his grandfather from getting away. If he didn't, he would be taken off what was proving to be, far and away, the most important case of his career. And if he was removed from the case, he would have no way to influence its outcome.

What the hell should I do? I can't just sit here and do nothing! Come on, think! What can I do to fool Prescott? There's got to be something!

Suddenly it struck him.

Flicking on his headlights, he stomped his foot on the accelerator, swung the Jeep around, and tore off across the bumpy prairie in the direction of the two racing vehicles.

ψψψ

Higheagle flicked a nervous glance in his rearview mirror. Prescott's Range Rover—a chariot among dog carts on the bumpy prairie—was hot on their tail. Its high beams were infuriatingly bright, making him feel like an escaped convict hounded by searchlights. He pressed the gas pedal to the floor, yelling at his grandfather to hold on tight.

There was no identifiable road and they were hurtling across uneven ground, tearing through sagebrush, bobbing up and down. This was supposed to be the Great Plains—flat as a billiard table, featureless, and desolate—but there was enough topographic variation and gnarly vegetation to vibrate the War Wagon like a rocket simulator.

They were rammed violently from behind.

Their necks snapped forward and the equipment and sample-filled coolers smashed against the wall of the pickup. Higheagle's foot slid off the accelerator and the Range Rover began to flank them on the driver's side.

With the sound of revving engines hammering his ears, Higheagle glanced down at his speedometer. Eighty-seven mph—death speed. Gravel, sod, and brush were being churned up and devoured by the War Wagon like a combine.

The Rover swung towards them like a rodeo bull. Higheagle swerved left to avoid the impact, but was too late as he heard the heavy scraping sound of metal on metal. He hit the brakes just as they dropped into another swale.

Now he saw a Jeep coming up on their right. Whoever had fired the gunshots had to be behind the wheel. The strange thing was, the first shot had probably saved his life by distracting Prescott, and those that followed seem to have been deliberately off mark. Whoever it was, he could have easily taken Higheagle or Prescott down, but chose neither.

The whole thing smelled of Shard.

Bringing his speed back up to eighty miles an hour, Higheagle heard the rumble of the other two engines above the roar of the War Wagon. He and his grandfather were now trapped between a pair of speedy tanks masquerading as SUVs.

The front left tire hit a cluster of anthills. The War Wagon bounded in the air, coming down hard and swerving to the left as Higheagle struggled to keep the vehicle under control. A moment later they were jolted by the Rover, which pitched them in their seats like a roller coaster on a tight curve.

The Jeep jerked right to avoid being hit. Higheagle looked over at the driver and saw that it was indeed Shard behind the wheel. His face was taut and professional, his concentration nursed to the highest level. He was obviously keeping his distance and deliberately holding back from ramming them, unlike Prescott.

He's not even after us. He's just putting on a show for his client, the clever bastard.

The engines groaned, the vehicles sending up individual jet streams of dust that coalesced into one large ribbon that appeared iridescent in the moonlight.

The main road loomed ahead. Higheagle quickly surveyed the terrain he had to cross to reach it: a swale, a short narrow embankment, a barbed-wire fence, and finally a drainage ditch. He had mere seconds to make a decision. If he slammed on his breaks, the other two vehicles would most likely race past him and collide with the embankment. If he tried to drive through to the road, he risked a violent crash.

He decided to gamble.

"Hold on tight, Grandfather! I'm going to have to pull an Evel Knievel!"

He jerked the steering wheel to the left, ramming Prescott and knocking him off course, and jammed his foot down on the accelerator.

The War Wagon dipped into the swale and flew out of the embankment on the other side like an Olympic ski jumper. The rear wheels of the truck barely nicked the top strand of barbed wire and struck the far side of the drainage ditch, while the front tires bounced off the paved road. All four tires quickly found traction as the War Wagon skidded safely across the asphalt like a fighter jet landing on an aircraft carrier. With an effort, Higheagle managed to bring the screeching truck under control before tumbling into the drainage ditch on the far side of the road.

After coming to a halt, they turned back to see what had happened to their pursuers. The Range Rover had careened into the fence, entangling itself in a jumble of wire, while the Jeep had come to a dust-driving halt in the swale. Now the trailing dust cloud of the three combined vehicles washed over the War Wagon, like the ash front that had swept down Vesuvius and enveloped Pompeii.

For an anxious moment, Higheagle and his grandfather were speechless, gazing at the wreckage through a haze of dust.

And then, swept away with relief, Higheagle popped open his seat belt and leaned over to hug the old chief. "We did it, Grandfather! We goddamn did it!"

"Like I told you, Grandson, it was a good night for a fight."

CHAPTER 57

HOOKING his front-end winch line to the rear of Prescott's Range Rover, Shard began reeling the massive hulk out of the tangle of barbed wire and uprooted fence posts. Prescott and Hwong were trapped inside the vehicle, waiting sulkily to be pulled free. The dust still hadn't settled and the moon was once again camouflaged by the clouds, shrouding the prairie in darkness. The electric winch made a low, metallic-groaning sound.

When Shard had pulled away most of the wire, Prescott swung open the driver's side door, coughed, and stumbled into the headlights of the Jeep. Shard braced himself for the verbal whipping he knew he had coming and went over for the tenth time what he was going to say.

"What the fuck just happened? How did they get away?"

Shard tugged at the slack cable, without acknowledging the presence of Prescott or Hwong, who was crawling out the passenger door. He spit some chew juice at the ground, the syrupy stream hitting a tuft of grass, and stepped to the rear of the Range Rover.

Prescott hovered above him as he knelt down to unhitch the metal cable. A moment later Hwong staggered up, looking as dazed and confused as a stoned teenager.

"Why the hell did you shoot at me?"

"I didn't shoot at you. I shot at Higheagle."

"Well, you didn't hit him. And you're too good a shot to have missed."

Shard didn't respond, pretending to be preoccupied with hooking the cable.

"There was equipment in the back of that truck. They took soil samples, didn't they?"

Shard saw an opportunity to turn things around. "Eleven to be exact. That's what was in the coolers." He pulled the cable tight and walked back to the Jeep. "The workmen surprised them. They hid the truck and crept back to take a look."

"Why the hell didn't you stop them?"

Why do you think? Because I wanted them to get away, goddamnit! "Without finding out what they were doing out here? I don't reckon that would have been too smart."

"So you just watched them?"

"Look, I'll get the goddamned samples back." He flicked a red button and the electric winch began slowly pulling in the cable.

"How can you be so sure?"

Looking up from the spool, Shard saw a once handsome face that was now darkly bloodied, curiously lidded, and ominously shadowed. "I said I'd take care of it, didn't I?"

Hwong stirred from his semi-catatonic state. "He could go to a laboratory night drop."

"No, he'll deliver them in person tomorrow. He went through a lot of effort to get them, and he's going to make damned sure they get to the lab intact."

Prescott raked the PI with cold dark eyes that carried the pallor of death. "I want those fucking samples in my hands by noon tomorrow. Do you hear me!"

The order ping-ponged Shard's eardrums, making him twitch involuntarily. He was certain in that instant that Prescott had not hired others to poison Gus McTavish, but had done the grisly job himself.

"I told you, I'll take care of it," he snapped back, wondering how he was going to pull off this newest challenge without compromising Higheagle.

"I can't believe this guy," Hwong groused in a wheedling voice. "He's making fucking fools of us. We need to terminate him." He arched his back and let out a groan, obviously still in tremendous pain from being driven into the open door of the Rover.

Shard finished reeling in the line and locked it in place. "What Higheagle knows is less important than what he has in his possession."

"Are you telling me I should just let this guy trespass on my property and collect samples without doing anything about it?"

"No, I'm saying that assault, kidnapping, and murder are serious offenses and I don't want any part of anything like that. Most times, dumping waste is nothing more than an out-of-court settlement without an admission of wrongdoing. As best I can tell, you can afford to cough up a half million or so to lay this thing to rest."

"Could it be that you're throwing your lot in with the other side, Vic?"

"No, sir, I'm doing exactly what you're paying me for. I signed a confidentiality agreement and I intend to honor it. I also told you I'd get the samples back and that's just what I aim to do. So if you'll excuse me, I best get started."

"What makes you so sure you can pull this off?"

Shard was about to slide inside his jeep, but the cool challenge in his client's voice brought him up short. "I've been following this man for a week. I know the kind of man he is—and more importantly, I know how he thinks."

CHAPTER 58

WHEN DAWN BROKE next day, the brooding gray clouds had dispersed and the sun's orange ball was poised to bear down on the Front Range with vengeance.

Vic Shard sat in his wife Hattie's cream-colored Dodge Caliber station wagon, his gaze fixed on the small ranch-style house with the Conestoga wagon wheels out front. As he had predicted, Higheagle didn't take the samples to a laboratory night drop. Instead, he and his grandfather went straight home. Twenty-two minutes after they lugged the two coolers and field equipment inside, the lights went out. Shard watched the house for another hour to make sure they weren't going anywhere before hurrying home to exchange his Jeep Cherokee for his wife's Dodge Caliber, so Higheagle wouldn't be able to spot him tailing him in the morning when he went to drop off the samples.

Shard knew Hattie wouldn't be pleased about the exchange—she never was—but such inconveniences, he believed, were to be expected from someone who shadowed people for a living. Careful to avoid waking her, he left a note he hoped would explain everything, but which, he knew, would be woefully inadequate. At 6:23 a.m., he returned to his stakeout with a bagful of Krispy Kreme donuts and two large cups of steaming black coffee. Vic Shard wasn't one to go for double mocha lattés, or for that matter, anything that had an accent over the *e*.

It wasn't until half past eight that Higheagle emerged, alone, from the house. After loading the two coolers, he backed slowly out of the driveway. Shard ducked down and waited until he drove to the end of the block before following in pursuit. He already had a fair idea of Higheagle's favorite routes to the major arteries linking the city.

Single-car surveillance—without being discovered or losing a mark—was a tall order, but Shard had found certain clever ways to overcome the inherent difficulties. Whenever possible, he used parallel tracking routes to avoid being spotted. He also placed magnetic company logos on the sides of his vehicle, and switched them out for others, during a given surveillance. He had accumulated a dozen logos over the years, from courier services to wholesale distributors, heavy equipment outfits, engineering firms, and all of the city's professional sports teams. He often disguised himself too. He had company caps and uniforms to match each of the logos on his car, in addition to a diverse assemblage of wigs, hats, glasses, and fake mustaches and beards.

Shard followed his mark north on University and then west on Quincy, keeping a pair of cars between himself and Higheagle. A pair of Pete's Wholesale Pet Foods logos clung to each side of his wife's car. He wore a cap and matching jacket with the company logo, a fake mustache, a long brown hair wig, and a pair of Ray-Ban sunglasses.

Higheagle took a right onto South Broadway and, a few blocks later, turned left onto Mansfield. Hanging back a hundred feet or so, Shard followed him in the direction of the Rio Grande-Santa Fe Railroad line. On Kalamath, Higheagle took another left and turned into the parking lot of Environmental Testing Services. Shard continued down Kalamath, parked the car, and, leaving the engine running, peered through his Leupold 5x binoculars.

He watched Higheagle carry a large red cooler to a door marked Sample Drop-Off and shoulder his way inside the swinging glass door. He waited a minute, expecting the Cheyenne to come back outside to collect the second cooler and submit it to the laboratory along with the first cooler. But Higheagle didn't return to the truck. Another minute ticked off and Shard waited. Still no sign of Higheagle.

That was strange. Why would he not submit the second cooler? Or had he just forgotten? And what was taking him so long?

I can't worry about that! I've got to get into position to snatch that cooler.

He swung into the ETS parking lot and tucked the Dodge Caliber into a space facing the door. He tossed aside his cap and wig and reached into the rear seat, grabbing a navy blue windbreaker and another cap, both brandishing a three-lettered acronym in bold gold print meant to command instant respect, and at the appropriate moment, fear in those who saw it. He quickly slipped on the cap, but in the confined space of the front seat, the windbreaker proved more daunting.

He glanced nervously at the door. *You shouldn't have cut it this close! But why in the hell isn't he coming back out for the second cooler? What's he up to?*

He could feel his heart pounding, breath quickening at the prospect of danger. It had been a long time since he had done an impersonation as risky as the one he was about to do.

Once he had the cap, windbreaker, and his pair of dark sunglasses on, he rifled through the storage nook between the two front seats until he found the fake credentials that would round out his masquerade. He clasped them in the sweaty palm of his right hand; they should be enough to bamboozle an unsuspecting lab tech or receptionist.

Moments later, Higheagle walked out carrying a pink sheaf of paper, which Shard knew was the sampler's copy of the chain-of-custody form. He watched him closely, wondering if he was now going to grab the second cooler and bring it inside. But instead Higheagle got in his truck, closed the door, fired the engine, backed out of his spot, and pulled to the edge of the street to look for oncoming traffic. Obviously, he was submitting only the one cooler to ETS.

Shard quickly brought the Dodge Caliber around to the front of the building. Heart thundering, he leapt from the car, ran to the entrance, and yanked open the door.

"Dirk Hamblin, FBI!"

The white-jacketed technician behind the counter looked up with surprise from her paperwork. Shard flashed his false FBI creds—an official-looking picture ID card and gold shield correct to the last detail—then jammed them back in his pocket. They were meant to be intimidating, and judging by the stunned expression on the technician, the desired effect had been achieved. With his left hand, he pointed to the red cooler sitting on top of the counter.

"Are those the samples submitted by Mr. Joseph Higheagle?"

"Y-Yes," the technician stammered. "He was just here."

"Mr. Higheagle is part of a criminal investigation. I'm going to have to impound these samples and the chain-of-custody form."

The technician backed away, too astonished to relinquish the form.

Shard leaned across the log-in desk, snatched the form, and stuffed it in his pocket. "The field office will be in touch," he said, hoisting the heavy cooler.

By the time the technician peered fretfully over her shoulder for her supervisor, Shard was out the door. Shoving the cooler in the back seat, he tore out of the parking lot without fastening his seatbelt and took a right onto Mansfield, guessing Higheagle had headed east. He had already removed the rear license plate from his wife's car and replaced it with one of the many he had collected over the years from the police impoundment lot. Even if the technician had mustered the courage to run outside and take down the tag numbers, which she hadn't, there would be no way to track down the owner of the vehicle.

It took several minutes—and three ignored yellow lights—before Shard spotted Higheagle again. Reestablishing his tailing position about ten car lengths back, he packed in a huge wad of Copenhagen and worked it with his tongue, getting some juice going.

Whoa Nelly, that was close!

He followed Higheagle for nearly ten minutes to another Englewood business location. When he saw the four-by-five sign out front, he stared up in startlement.

Arapaho Technologies.

He eased the Dodge Caliber into the parking lot, taking one of the more distant spaces from the entrance, and watched Higheagle walk inside clutching the second red cooler. Now he realized what the geologist was up to, and the sheer audacity of the stratagem brought a smile to his lips.

Higheagle was delivering the samples to Hwong's very own lab and having them tested right under his damned nose!

It was the perfect set-up. If the results were ever validated by a regulatory agency or admissible as evidence in a court of law, they would be severely damaging to both Hwong and Prescott. How could Hwong refute his own analytical results? He would have to cast doubt on every analysis his lab had ever performed. And how could Prescott disavow the results of his own analytical expert?

God damn if that don't beat all!

Hwong would never know what hit him. All Higheagle had to do was write in a dummy project name, site location, and sample numbers. Hell, he would even have Hwong's signature on the laboratory QA/QC and analytical report!

But that left Shard with a problem. His job was to get the samples back, and last night he had promised his crooked client that he would do just that. If he failed in his assignment, Prescott would destroy him and Shard would never again practice as a PI in Denver. It was that simple.

Still, maybe there was a way out. He hadn't actually told Prescott there were twenty-two samples. He had only said there were eleven sample locations, never mentioning the fact that Higheagle had collected two samples at each location. If he was forced to lie, Shard could say he'd lost Higheagle when he'd snatched the samples at ETS. It was almost true. He had come dangerously close to losing his quarry when he had rushed inside to grab the cooler, and he knew the best lies were grounded in at least a modicum of truth.

But could he pull it off? If Hwong found out and told Prescott, Shard would be toast. Prescott would make it his mission in life to destroy him. Then there was the even grimmer prospect of being charged as an accessory to Prescott. After all, Shard had conducted the background check on Gus McTavish, digging up details on his heart condition and prescription for triflurodigitalis. If Prescott was arrested for murdering McTavish, he might seek retribution and take Shard down with him, or even have his goons take him out.

Yep, Vic Shard knew he was in a fix all right.

The drop-off door opened and Higheagle walked back out, his pink copy of the COC form in his hand as before. He strode briskly to his pickup, fired the engine, and pulled up to the street.

Okay, what should I do?

Shard glanced at the door again. He pictured himself running inside, flashing his fake FBI creds, and seizing the cooler from the stupefied lab tech. He could see the whole thing unfold like a scene from an action movie.

Fifteen seconds, that's all it would take…and Joe would still have the results for Dakota.

He looked back at the pickup. Its left turn signal was flashing, but a Lexus turned the corner and blocked Higheagle's path, keeping him from pulling into the traffic.

Shard's hands tensed around the steering wheel. *Should I or not?*

He looked at the door again, then back at the pickup. Still no movement from Higheagle as another car turned the corner and blocked his exit.

And then Shard had no choice but to make a decision as Higheagle pulled out into the street.

Willfully, the PI took a deep breath. Then he turned the key in the ignition and pulled out of the parking space, pressing slowly down on the accelerator. He drove around to the sample drop-off door, just as he had done at the other lab.

Only this time he drove on.

CHAPTER 59

WHEN THE TELEPHONE RANG, Prescott was briefing Bishop on last night's startling turn of events at Silverado Knolls. He bore a nasty shiner beneath his right eye and the left side of his face was bruised like a spoiled apple. His excuse to his senior managers, who, along with the proletariat, were giving him suspicious looks because of all the recent activity at the office, was that he had been mugged last night in LoDo.

In a quick motion, he swept up the handset. "Prescott here."

"I got 'em," the voice said without preamble.

He felt a wave of relief. "Where are you?"

"On my way. I'll be there in five minutes."

"Come straight to my office. I'll tell the receptionist."

Prescott couldn't help but smile as he hung up. Despite the heavy bruises on his face, he still looked roguishly handsome, like a swashbuckler. He looked across his desk at Bishop. "Shard's on his way over. He's got the samples."

"Good news."

Prescott quickly dialed Cynthia the receptionist and told her he was expecting the PI and to send him right along. Setting down the phone, he slid back into his high-backed chair, wondering how Shard had pulled it off. Bishop sipped his coffee and looked on with a languid air. While Prescott was clearly taking a toll from recent events, both physically and mentally, the attorney appeared relaxed and well-rested. His lawyer's time clock was ticking, and at five hundred per hour, he would be pleased to chatter all day about just about anything.

Five minutes later, a knock sounded at the door. Prescott adjusted his hunter-green suspenders and fiddled with the collar of his cotton shirt to make himself more presentable.

"Come in."

His executive secretary, the drippingly sexy Sophie, motioned Shard into the room and closed the door. The private investigator walked to the front of the desk and took the right hand extended by Bishop. "Greg." He tipped his white straw cowboy hat towards Prescott and sat down in the seat next to the attorney. He had worked on and off with Bishop for more than a decade now, and it was Bishop who had recommended him to Prescott six months ago.

"How'd you pull it off?" Prescott asked, bursting to know.

"Snatched them right after he dropped them off at ETS. I got the paperwork too." Shard pulled out a pink sheet of paper and handed it to Prescott. "He had them on a twenty-four hour rush for dioxins, pesticides, and metals. Oh, and VOCs and SVOCs, whatever those are."

"Volatile and semi-volatile organic compounds," Bishop said, scratching at his bulbous red nose.

Looking over the form, Prescott thought: *Higheagle doesn't know what he's looking for. If he did, he wouldn't have analyzed for all these chemicals.* "Where are the samples now?"

"In my car. There's eleven total—one for each sampling location."

Prescott handed the form to Bishop, picked up the translucent Steuben glass giraffe from his desk, and began gently caressing the figurine. "You've done a fine job, Vic. I think a sizable bonus is in order."

"You pay me enough as it is, Hayden. I wouldn't feel right taking any more from you."

"Suit yourself. But I think you've earned it."

"I'm good. If that's all then, I'll be going now." He started to rise from his chair.

Bishop curtly motioned for him to remain seated. "Before you go, Vic, I have a few questions for you. Hayden's told me about last night. But one thing still puzzles me."

"What's that?"

"Why would Higheagle bring his grandfather out there like that? The man's seventy-five fucking years old, for crying out loud."

"I've been following our boy for a week, and I still don't understand the rhyme or reason for some of the things he does. He's a risk-taker, that's for sure."

"Did he report anything to the police about last night?"

"Not according to my moles at DPD."

"Has he reported anything else, anything out of the ordinary?" Prescott asked, wondering whether Higheagle had reported the Paine and Morelli break-in from the night before last.

"Nope. He's been quiet as a broken fiddle."

Prescott felt relieved. It meant Higheagle was keeping quiet about his investigation, probably until he had gathered all his evidence. Or maybe he was afraid of being arrested for trespassing. Whatever the case, he hadn't yet come forward with what he knew. Which meant that now was the time to strike. The Cheyenne still had computer records, maps, and files in his possession. They had to be seized, and somehow he had to be kept quiet.

Again, Shard started to rise to his feet. "I ought to be getting back to Higheagle's."

"That won't be necessary," Prescott said. "After what you've done today, I think you deserve the day off. You can pick up again tomorrow."

"You sure? He could try to meet someone."

"I'm sure, and I want you to take the night off too. You look like you could use some sleep."

"All right. I do believe the missus will appreciate that."

"One last thing before you go, Vic," Bishop said. "Has our boy received any packages or letters of any kind?"

"Just the one on Friday I told Hayden about."

Prescott nodded. "A courier delivered a package Friday morning. Higheagle was out front watering his lawn. There was no way for Vic to get it before the delivery was made."

"So we don't know what was in the package."

"Could've been aerials," Prescott said. "At the U Club, Higheagle said he had reviewed some aerial photographs. Maybe he ordered more to get better coverage. Or maybe he had copies made."

"Possibly. But we've got a bigger problem on our hands: we still don't know who he's working for." The attorney looked at Shard. "Since you've been tailing Higheagle, how many times have you lost him?"

"Just once. Last Friday night near Bonnie Brae Shopping Center."

"That's not far from the CDPHE office."

He must have been visiting Markworth? thought Prescott. *Damnit, the senator and I warned him not to have any further contact with—*

"I'll talk to my little bird inside, see what he knows. In the meantime, what do you want me to do with those samples?"

"Put them in my 911," Prescott said, referring to his sleek, black, low-slung Porsche parked out front. His Range Rover was scheduled to spend the next two weeks in a body shop. "First row, right out front."

Prescott tossed Shard the keys and the PI headed for the door.

"Just lock the keys inside. I have a spare."

"I'll take care of it." Shard opened the door and was gone.

Leaving Prescott to wonder: *What the fuck am I going to do about Higheagle?*

CHAPTER 60

AS THE CHEYENNE flew up the stairs at Eisenhower Memorial, he was blasted with bright fluorescent ceiling lights. From the message Sally had left on his answering machine, Tommy had collapsed onto the floor at home after returning from his afternoon radiation therapy session. Sally had rushed him to the hospital and they were now in Room 234.

Higheagle darted anxiously up one hallway, then another, until he found the right room. He rapped on the door, not waiting for a response before opening it.

Right away, he saw Tommy, but for some trick in the lighting, the figure behind the mask appeared too small and fragile to be the boy. He was asleep, his chest rising and falling in a shallow rhythm. Plastic hoses dangled from his mask and shot off to the far side of the bed, closest to the window. A clear pouch containing electronically-regulated IV fluids was suspended from a metal stand beside the bed, and a clear tube trailed beneath the bedcovers to his left arm. In the hospital chair next to the bed sat Sally, the book on Crazy Horse in her lap.

"Sally, it's me," he said. "I came as soon as I found out."

Looking up, she raised a finger to her mouth. "Let's step over here so we don't wake him up." She motioned Higheagle to the far side of the room.

As they stepped away from the bed, he caught his reflection in the mirror above the washbasin. He looked awful. His cheekbones still had the tender, pinkish appearance of a medium rare steak and he had a noticeable shiner around his left eye.

In the fluted light, Sally saw the damage too. "My God, what happened to you?"

"It's a long story."

She reached out and gently touched his face. Suddenly, he longed to hold her close. He pulled her in an embrace and she fell easily into his arms. The warmth of her body was like a freshly lit fire, stirring him inside. She looked up and he gave her a soft kiss on the lips, which were warm and moist. She kissed him back a little harder. They held each other for a moment longer and kissed again before breaking away.

He looked back at the bed, his expression transforming to concern. "Tell me about Tommy."

"It started this morning. When I tried to wake him for school, he was completely out of it. So I stayed home and let him sleep in. He slept until noon. When he woke up, he seemed all right. But then after his therapy, he looked really peaked. Just before dinner he fainted."

"What did the doctors say?"

"That he's plain worn out. They said it usually happens the second week of radiation treatment."

"I'm sorry."

"At least he's going to be okay." She sighed. "So tell me what happened to you? You look like someone put you through a meat grinder."

"I told you it's a long story."

"Tommy's asleep. I have time."

He hesitated. "We drove out to Silverado Knolls and took samples."

"We?"

"My grandfather and I."

"You took your grandfather out there?"

"He wouldn't take no for an answer."

"So you got in a fight. It was Hayden Prescott, wasn't it?"

Again, he hesitated.

"So he is dangerous."

"I'm afraid that's an understatement."

"My father thinks that Hayden killed my uncle."

"Your father's right. I overheard Prescott talking to Hwong."

"You heard him say he killed my uncle?"

"No, but I heard enough to know he did it. I'm sorry, Sally."

A disembodied voice interrupted them. "Joe, is that you?"

They turned towards the bed. Tommy was looking at them through his translucent oxygen mask. He pushed aside the mask so he could talk.

"Hey, Little Big Man," said Joseph as he and Sally stepped towards the hospital bed.

"Joe, it is you. I just…I just had the coolest dream."

Sally knelt on the bed's edge and took his hand. "What was it about, honey?"

"The Wise One. I actually saw him." The boy's face carried an ethereal glow, a sense of unearthly wonderment.

Sally looked at Higheagle. "What's he talking about?"

"*Heammawihio*, the Wise One Above."

"You mean like God?"

Tommy smiled dreamily. "Except he's Cheyenne like Joe. He spoke to me…told me things."

"What did he look like?" asked Higheagle.

"Well, he was really big and he wore a huge feathered headdress, like a chief. But he wasn't human. He blended in with the clouds, like he was part of them. His face was big and round and puffy like Thomas the Tank Engine's."

"And his voice?"

"It was like the wind, a kind of soft whistling sound. I just looked up at the clouds and there he was…talking to me. He told me not to worry, that things would work out for me. I've talked to him before, Joe, since you told me about him. But this time it was so real. This time I was floating along with him, high up in the clouds. Do you think that's how you feel when you die—like a bird in the sky, looking down on the world you're leaving behind?"

Higheagle smiled. "I don't know. Maybe."

Tommy sighed. "The Wise One told me I'd live to be an old man if I keep on fighting the cancer. He said I had to fight like a warrior, and that if I won the battle I would be buried in the old Cheyenne way. Does that mean I would be put in a burial mound?"

"No, in the old days we used to place our dead on a burial scaffold or beneath a cairn of rocks."

"And from there where would my soul go?"

"Like every *Tsistsistas*, your spirit would seek the trail where all footprints point in the same direction. Once you found this path, you would follow it to the Milky Way and then to the Great Camp Among The Stars. It is a peaceful camp where all your friends, relatives, and loved ones who have passed to the other side would be gathered. It is at this place—the Sacred Camp of the Dead Souls—that you would begin your new life."

"So I would come together with the Wise One."

"In the end, yes."

A peaceful silence settled over the room. "I like that, Joe. I like that a lot."

CHAPTER 61

HAYDEN PRESCOTT leaned back in his chair. "You really think you can win if this thing goes to court?"

Bishop gave a wan smile. "Without question. But first, when I say 'court,' I don't mean a civil action filed by the parents of the cancer victims or the home owners, but rather an EPA, DOJ, or CDPHE enforcement action. My guess is Higheagle will bring whatever he has to the regulators and try to convince them to go out to Dakota and Silverado and sample for themselves. They would simply get a court order from a federal judge and collect confirmatory samples. If that happens, I still think I can put together a strong defense and cast enough doubt to get an acquittal. Of course, that's assuming I can't get the case dismissed, or at least reach a favorable settlement, up front."

Despite his lawyer's unabashed confidence, Prescott had his doubts. What the Mumsie side of him came back with was a simple question: *Why not just kill Higheagle and put an end to it all?* After all, he had done away with McTavish and there wasn't a damned thing the cops could do about it. Eliminating Higheagle would be easy enough.

Then again, maybe such an extreme measure wasn't necessary. Maybe putting him in a hospital would be enough to discourage him from pursuing the case further. But there was no guarantee. And Markworth, Sally, or Tommy might disclose what they knew to a reporter. Admittedly, it probably wasn't much, but it might be enough to spark the media or arouse the EPA or DOJ.

"All right, suppose this thing does go to court, how would you try the case?"

Bishop shifted his paunchy frame. "First off, my able associates and I would do everything in our considerable power to keep it from going to court. But barring that, we'd plead not guilty and destroy them on circumstantial."

"And if they manage to get their hands on a credible witness or two?"

"Then we'd push hard for a settlement. We'd argue that you had nothing to do with the dumping, only the cover up once you found out about it."

Prescott's brow wrinkled with surprise.

"Look, here's how it would work. You heard rumors that illegal dumping might have taken place on your properties. That's why you conducted the assessments at Dakota and Silverado, to find out if toxic chemicals were buried out there. It was from your proactive sampling that you discovered the waste on both properties. Then you admit to having Hwong falsify the lab reports once you realized what a huge contamination problem you had on your hands. You'd say the astronomical cost of the cleanup, decline in property values, and exorbitant lawsuits would have thrown you into bankruptcy."

"How much of a fine would I see?"

"I'd say a few hundred thousand, but it depends on who handles the case. The EPA and Health Department have different philosophies. Both regulatory agencies like to go after deep pockets, but the EPA, because it has more resources, tends to go hard after the waste generators, while the Health Department typically takes the path of least resistance and puts the hammer to the property owners. With Dahlquist and his Senate sandbaggers behind you, you already control the Health Department, so obviously we'd rather face those guys than the EPA even though they like to go after the property owners."

"What would happen to Hwong? What kind of fine would he get?"

"Hundred K range. He'd lose his EPA certification temporarily. He'd restructure the company as a separate entity and go in with someone else, preferably another minority so he can get fat government contracts. He'd have his certification back within a year or two."

"What if the whole thing went south? What would I be looking at then?"

"We'd have to try and cut a deal. If you handed them the generators on a silver platter, I can guarantee it would be a sweet one. Probably a million in fines, but no jail time and immunity from prosecution. But the chance of it coming to that is minuscule. Environmental enforcement cases are a bitch for the prosecution, like white-collar crime cases in general. Somewhere along the line, I'll find a way to beat them. I always do."

"What if the feds try to strike a deal with someone besides Hwong? Like the waste handlers or generators?"

Bishop pulled a sheet of paper from a manila folder and handed it to Prescott. "There's twenty-seven different people on our list, as you know. The waste generators, the waste broker Hoskins, and the Mexicans—the drivers, drum handlers, heavy equipment operators, and laborers. The bottom line is there's no link to any of these people except Hoskins or the generators. And whatever evidence they have would still be circumstantial."

"There's no chance the EPA could find out about the payments to me or those I made to Hoskins?"

"There's no wire or paper record of any contractual agreement or transaction. It's his word against yours, a lowly waste broker versus a gold-plated entrepreneur and community activist. Hoskins will never talk unless he's forced to cut a deal. We could set him up with a golden parachute and send him out of state early on to be safe. And the waste generators won't talk unless they want to spend millions, and in some cases tens of millions, on the cleanups. The bottom line is there's no record of your involvement. They only call it money laundering if you get caught."

Bishop was right. Prescott's money laundering operation was not merely clean, it was perfect. All transactions were untraceable wire transfers made through a little known check cashing service on South Broadway that reported only what their clients wanted them to report to the IRS. From there, the money was wired to dozens of banks and financial centers before being disbursed to Prescott's offshore accounts on Grand Cayman, to the Council for Front Range Competitiveness, and to a complex assemblage of offshore dummy shell corporations within The Newport Company. There simply was no trail of wire or paper—no wire traces, no contracts, no checks, no government forms, no income reports—that could link him to the vast income he had garnered from his secret waste operations, or to the much smaller sums he had paid Hoskins the waste broker. Without a wire or paper trail, it would be difficult for the prosecutors to obtain a conviction.

"The bigger problem is Hwong. He knows a lot, probably more than he should."

"You're forgetting about Higheagle, Sally, and Shard."

"What the mother and her son know is hearsay, and Shard will never talk. He signed a non-disclosure agreement and he's got a reputation to uphold. Higheagle's clearly a problem, but no more so than Hwong, Hoskins, or the generators. The most he can prove is that waste was dumped on your properties. None of what he and his grandfather may have seen or heard out at Silverado would be admissible because they trespassed. Besides, we'd say what they saw out there was only a capping operation."

"Still, it all starts with Higheagle. If he talks, I'll be named as a principal responsible party. Which means the feds could seize my company holdings and the environmental liability account to pay for the cleanup costs. And that could be just for starters."

"Okay, so the worst case is you do a little time in a minimum security country club."

Prescott felt a vise tighten around his chest. "I'm not going to fucking prison, Greg."

The attorney held up a hand. "Let me qualify what I said. There's only one way I see this worst-case scenario happening. First, the other side gets Hwong, Hoskins, and at least one of the generators to start singing. Second, they miraculously track down all of the wire transfer records. I don't think it's possible, but let's say for the sake of argument it happens. Third, the cancer thing gets brought into the mix. That would be the ball-breaker, because that's what the press and public would feed off of like sharks."

Prescott stood up and paced anxiously in front of the window.

"Our defense would be to attack all the field and lab protocols and put the whole question of cancer into doubt. Bottom line: Refute any relationships they try to establish between the cancer and chemicals, and shatter any doubt that you could have known of the carcinogenicity of the chemicals. If they can prove those things, then they can prove wrongful death based on a preponderance of evidence. Assuming it's a civil case."

"And murder beyond a reasonable doubt if it's criminal?"

"That's just not going to happen, Hayden. I'm only setting out the worst-case scenario. As far as I'm concerned, you're the innocent victim of illegal dumping."

Prescott stared out the window. Despite his attorney's attempt at reassurance, his face was a mask of uncertainty. He ran his fingers along the glass and studied the endless stream of cars muscling along the interstate. The Rockies loomed in the distance as a massive silhouette against the moonlit night sky. But Prescott didn't see the mountains. He was too busy pondering the real worst-case scenario—the one where Gus McTavish's death was somehow linked to all of this. That might prove to be murder beyond *any* doubt.

Suddenly, he felt all the tension inside him turn to anger. He clamped his jaw tight and clenched his fists.

Goddamn Higheagle! He's the cause of all this! I should have Paine and Morelli do it tonight!

As he played out the fantasy in his mind, he felt his mother's presence stirring inside him, sending pleasant tingles down his spine. He pictured her dark clever eyes, her succulent lips parting into a supremely confident grin. And then he felt her body and his become one and he heard her voice inside him, soft yet commanding, daring him on.

Just do it, Hay darling. The time's ripe for...murder.

CHAPTER 62

IT WAS DIFFERENT THIS TIME.

It wasn't a dream sound. This time it carried a bite of reality.

And this time the source was unmistakable: Harold—Mr. Greenberg's stodgy bulldog that lived next door—was barking frantically.

Someone was definitely out there.

After the other night, Higheagle wasn't taking any chances. He slid quietly from the bed, slipped on his moccasins and elkskin jacket, grabbed his loaded Ithaca 12-gauge slide-action shotgun and a box of spare magazines, and went to wake his grandfather.

They were expecting the goons to return tonight.

And this time, he and the old Contrary would have a nice surprise for them.

ψψψ

Zachary Paine and Alphonse Morelli crept forward in the still of the night.

With their night-vision goggles, they moved through a world that registered in different shades of fluorescent green. Above, the moon radiated an eerie brilliance like a freshly burnished candlestick in a dark mansion. Under cover of a copse of blue spruces, they tread swiftly towards the driveway of the small, ranch-style house where they had bound their prey to chairs and threatened them with steely weapons only two nights earlier.

Tonight, they would do a lot more than that.

Stopping, they carefully surveyed the house a final time, having already worked out their approach. They knew there were only two entrances: front and back. A dim outdoor light illuminated the steps in front, but there was no light on at the back. They saw Higheagle's truck parked alongside the house. The dog next door had stopped yapping; hopefully, they would still have the element of surprise on their side.

It had never failed them before.

During the decade long partnership of the two hoods, Paine and Morelli seldom said more than a few words to one another and went about their unorthodox business—threatening and killing people—with a certain cold-bloodedness and dogged persistence that had allowed their careers to blossom as much as a career could be said to blossom for hired guns. They were professionals, not particularly clever, but clever enough not to have done any time. Though they called the Mile High City home, they divided their special brand of expertise between Prescott and a handful of other businessmen from Wyoming, Colorado, New Mexico, and

Texas.

Paine withdrew a shiny Smith and Wesson .45 semiautomatic, while Morelli pulled out a black Sig Sauer, also chambered in .45 caliber, but carrying a seven- instead of an eight-round magazine. Then they each plucked a custom-designed Brügger & Thomet baffle-type sound suppressor from their pockets and threaded them into the nose of their specially adapted hand pieces. The suppressors would not eliminate all, or even most, of the noise when a shot was fired, but they would dampen the sound enough to approximate a BB gun.

After synchronizing their watches and commencing their standard two-minute countdown, Paine motioned for Morelli to take the front door while he covered the back. They walked briskly but silently to their respective positions and waited. Both doors were locked.

At 3:57 a.m., Zachary Paine and Alphonse Morelli burst into the house from opposite sides.

The neighbor's dog started hysterically barking again.

Paine bulled his way down the hallway towards the front of the house, turning left into Higheagle's bedroom. Spotting a bulging mass beneath the blanket on the bed, he took careful aim using a two-handed grip and unleashed three quick silenced rounds.

But something was wrong.

There was no movement, no sound, no reaction of any kind. Even a sleeping person would show some response when shot, an involuntary shriek or spasm.

He charged the bed, yanked savagely on the blanket, and fired again. The bullet ripped through a pair of pillows. He stared in mute shock as little down feathers puffed up in the air.

By this time, Morelli had made his way from the front door, past Higheagle's home office, into Higheagle's grandfather's bedroom, and now to Higheagle's bedroom.

"Where the fuck did Higheagle go?"

"Hell if I know. Where's Gramps?"

"He wasn't in his room. He must be gone too."

"You check anywhere else?"

Morelli hesitated, unable to comprehend that their simple plan was actually going terribly awry. Then they heard the sound of shuffling feet, coming from behind the house.

Paine bolted from the room, shouldered the back door, and raced from the house with Morelli thundering right behind him. A pair of bright headlights exploded from the darkness, lighting up the two NV-goggled assassins on the back porch like a stage light, disorienting and paralyzing them in their tracks.

Only then did it dawn on them: they were no longer the hunters, but the hunted.

CHAPTER 63

HIGHEAGLE SWUNG BEHIND the War Wagon, raising the Ithaca 12-gauge to his shoulder. The shotgun was equipped with a specially designed "duckbill" choke so the shot spread laterally rather than vertically, which enhanced the weapon's kill ratio. It also sported a five-round magazine, instead of the one- or two-shot capability of most shotguns, and the shells were ejected and loaded on the underside of the receiver, eliminating the problem of hot, smoking casings flying into the face of left-handed shooters like himself and his grandfather. One need not be an expert marksman to inflict considerable damage with the weapon; it was designed to drop anything weighing less than a buffalo bull at close range.

Recognizing the two intruders as the enforcers from the other night, Higheagle let loose with a blast of Number 4 shot. At the same time, the old chief unleashed his coveted "Yellow Boy"—his Model 1866 Winchester lever-action repeating rifle adorned, in the Plains Indian way, with brass tacks, vermillion, and eagle feathers.

The two assailants—feet still glued to the back porch in the bright headlights of the War Wagon that rendered the NV goggles useless—were struggling in vain to rip off their goggles as the shots exploded into them. At the last second, the lanky man, the one called Paine, dove left and the stumpy one, Morelli, to the right, but neither man could escape the storm of lead. Paine managed to squeeze off a single errant shot with his handgun as he dove behind a woodpile. Morelli dropped his pistol and tumbled off the edge of the porch, crying out like a squealing pig as he crashed into the bushes.

Higheagle moved to a new position behind the tailgate of the War Wagon as his grandfather levered the action of his Winchester and took cover behind the brick wall that ran along the back alley. Harold, the dog next door, was barking and running back and forth along the chain-link fence, sounding the alarm down the entire block.

Higheagle and his grandfather fired again simultaneously at the woodpile where Paine had taken refuge, sending splinters of pine in the air. But there was no return fire. Shifting the barrel to his right, Higheagle locked onto the fat man Morelli, who was struggling to crawl behind the bushes on the right side of the porch.

As he was about to squeeze the trigger, Paine sprung up from behind the woodpile, shooting out both headlights.

The field of fire turned to blackness.

Higheagle and his grandfather both unloaded another volley at the woodpile. Their shots were answered by a muzzle flash, then two more, like splashes of lightning. The bullets ricocheted off the fender of the truck with a metallic twang.

Jesus Christ! It's like he can see me!

And then he realized that Paine *could see* him and his grandfather both. With no more headlights and a return to darkness, he could fix in on their position with vivid clarity with his night-vision goggles.

Higheagle fired again into the woodpile and saw two more bursts of light. The bullets whizzed past his left ear like sparrows in flight.

This was no good: Paine had locked onto him and he had to move to a new position.

He took a deep breath, counted down from three to one, delivered a round of cover fire, and then tore down the walkway next to the garage. Bullets plucked at his feet, but he managed to scramble over the low brick wall near the corner of the garage.

The firing stopped momentarily. Tucked safely behind the wall, he felt around to see if he'd been hit, remembering the story his grandfather had told him about how he had once been shot during combat in Korea, but hadn't realized it until an hour after the fighting because of all the adrenaline. Higheagle made sure to check himself thoroughly. He couldn't feel any wetness, no sign of a tear in his elk skin jacket, and he felt no pain anywhere.

Must be okay.

He checked his shotgun and realized he was out of ammo. Pulling another magazine from his jacket pocket, he quickly reloaded the weapon. Then he made eye contact again with his grandfather further down the wall; the Korean War vet stood on an old wooden crate and was calmly sweeping his Winchester across the field of fire, searching for signs of the enemy. There was a hint of a smile on his face and Higheagle realized that he actually relished the chance at combat.

Rising to his feet, he low-crawled to his grandfather's position. "Where'd the skinny one go?"

"I think he's still behind the woodpile. But he may have moved."

"What do we do about the other one?"

"Leave him be. He's down for the count."

"Do you think he's dead?"

"No, I heard him moaning. Here, let's take a look."

They poked their heads over the wall. There was no sign of Paine.

They directed their guns towards the bushes, where they had last seen Morelli. No sign of the fat man either, but like Paine, he might be hidden from view.

The field of fire turned preternaturally calm, noiseless. Time seemed to come to a halt. Higheagle couldn't escape the feeling something wasn't right.

And then he saw a movement on the right side of the house, at the edge of the bushes.

His grandfather saw it too. They drew a bead and fired. The lead shot rattled against the side of the house like a handful of gravel.

Paine darted laterally, returning fire not once, but three times, forcing Higheagle and his grandfather to duck behind the wall.

By the time they again raised their guns to fire, their lanky adversary had scrambled forward and was pulling his partner in crime from the bushes. Morelli groaned as Paine helped him to his feet and half-carried, half-dragged him towards the protective cover of the house.

Higheagle took careful aim at Paine.

"Let 'em go," said the old Contrary, pushing away the nose of his scattergun. "They're done."

"You sure about that?"

"Yeah, I'm sure. On a *vehoe*, I can *smell* defeat."

They watched in silence as the pair of henchmen skulked around the corner and limped off into the night. He and his grandfather would give their descriptions to the police and let the cops track them down. When they heard an engine rev to life in the street beyond, he and the old chief walked through the back gate and started towards the house to call the police.

"Hold it right there!"

Stopping in his tracks, Higheagle looked across the fence at a craggy silhouette pointing a pistol at him. "Don't shoot, Mr. Greenberg! It's me, Joe, and my grandfather!"

"What the hell's going on?"

"Someone broke into our house and tried to rob us. I'm going inside to call 911."

Leaving his grandfather to finish explaining the situation to their neighbor, Higheagle dashed into the kitchen and reached for the phone.

It was then he noticed the light on in the living room.

CHAPTER 64

"I WOULD HOLD OFF on that call for a minute if I were you. We need to have a little pow-wow."

Shard was sitting casually in the black recliner in the living room with a book in his lap, a Fat Tire amber ale in his hand, and his feet propped up on the coffee table as if he owned the joint.

Higheagle stepped from the kitchen into the living room, keeping the barrel leveled on Shard's chest. "You break into people's houses to read often?"

Shard smiled as he turned the book's cover towards Higheagle. "*My Life on the Plains.* I wouldn't have taken you for a fan of Custer."

"One can always learn from one's enemies. Even a fool like Long Hair shed light on Cheyenne customs, as much time as he spent among my people. Problem is he distorted the facts to fit his agenda."

"And what was his...agenda?"

"To project the image of himself he wanted everyone else to see. Like your client."

"*My Lie on the Plains*. Back then and now."

"Ah, so you know Captain Benteen's unauthorized title for Custer's book. I am impressed."

Shard kept an eye on the barrel as Higheagle sat down in the blue corduroy couch across from him. He tried to look calm and composed, but with the gun trained on him, he couldn't help but tense up. He sat upright in his chair and set the book down on the table, slowly.

Higheagle's eyes narrowed fractionally. "Somehow I don't think you came here to discuss Long Hair Custer or the Seventh Cavalry."

"I wish that was the reason. By the way, that was some fine shooting back there. Sure as hell didn't need any help from me. I think you can put the gun away now though."

"No, I like watching you squirm too much. Besides, why should I listen to you? You're Prescott's bitch. I don't think he'll be too happy though when the police show up here and start asking you questions."

They looked up as John Higheagle came walking in the room. "Who's this asshole? Is he with Abbott and Costello?"

Higheagle rested the barrel of the 12-gauge on his leg, keeping it pointed directly at Shard's chest. "I don't know. Are you with those two psychopaths who just tried to kill us?"

"I reckon not."

"You sure about that?"

Shard didn't answer. Feeling uneasy with the shotgun trained on him, he glanced up at the moody Jacob van Ruisdael print on the wall, showing a gurgling brook shaded by tall windblown trees. He pushed up his straw cowboy hat a notch, his face taking on a vaguely appreciative air.

"Look Shard, you've got to pick a side. You can't help me and fuck me in the ass at the same time."

"Perception versus reality, Joe—think about it. The only person I'm really helping is you, even though it might not seem that way. I know what you've got on Prescott. And though I can't prove it, I suspect he had Sally McTavish's uncle killed. When the time's right, I plan on telling my former colleagues at the DPD about this little conspiracy theory of mine. But in the meantime, I've got to keep up my little charade. You follow?"

Higheagle said nothing; his eyes remained narrow with suspicion.

"With that in mind, I'm afraid I have some bad news for you. You're not gonna like it." He could see no way to blunt the impact of what he was going to say, so he just came right out with it. "I had to take some of the documents in your file, but I did leave you with copies."

"What the hell? When did you do this?"

"When you were at the hospital. I thought you might be keeping your records in that old pickup of yours. And these new portable copiers, well, they just beat all—"

"You son of a bitch! Did you take the aerials too?"

"Had to relieve you of one set, which still leaves you with a backup. I noticed you had two of everything."

Higheagle tensed and swung the shotgun up, pointing it directly at Shard's head. "You're right, Mr. Private Dickhead, this isn't the kind of news I wanted to hear."

Shard kept his eyes on the shotgun. "Just give me a chance to explain."

"Don't waste your breath. I'm calling the cops now." He reached for the phone on the side table, dialed 911, and calmly informed the dispatcher that two men had just broken into his house.

When he hung up, Shard said, "You best listen to what I've got to say. I've got more bad news."

"There's more?"

"Sorry, but I also took your samples from ETS this morning right after you dropped them off."

"You what?" The barrel swung up again. "I need those samples!"

Shard gulped hard as he saw Higheagle's finger tighten around the trigger. He raised his hands towards the ceiling in surrender. "Now just hear me out. I left the samples you submitted to Hwong's lab alone. If I could have done it any other way, I would have. But I couldn't."

"Let me get this straight. You stole the ETS samples, but not the ones I delivered to Arapaho?"

"I promise you Prescott doesn't know about those. He thinks the samples I stole from ETS were the only ones you collected."

"Pretty clever, even for a private dick," said John Higheagle. "Vic Shard—

what the fuck kind of name is that anyway?"

"Well, my mother always said—"

"Shut up, both of you," snapped Higheagle. "I don't know why I'm even talking to you, Shard. You've stolen my samples and my backup set of aerials, and you've pilfered my analytical results. And last night you chased me and my grandfather and shot at us."

"My aim's deader'n old Wild Bill, Kemosabe, so if I had truly wanted to kill you, let's just say you'd be one dead fucking Indian. As for the records, I didn't take all the originals and I left you with good copies of the ones I did. I needed something to satisfy Prescott. I knew he'd send those two gorillas here again after last night. That's why I'm here. Truth is I liked the way you boys handled it."

Higheagle wasn't amused. "Fuck you. It doesn't matter that you're playing double agent with Prescott. He'll still send another death squad after me. And what about Sally and Tommy?"

"He won't touch them. Seems…seems he has a soft spot for 'em."

"Oh, like that makes a difference? The guy's crazy!"

"Look, it's complicated. If you don't know already, Sally and Prescott used to have a thing. I think he loved her, maybe still does. He was also quite fond of Tommy. Fact is, there's lots of gray in this world, Joe. Only ones who don't understand that are religious fundamentalists and tax collectors. Bottom line: Prescott won't touch Sally or the kid. Even he has lines he won't cross."

Higheagle's face turned reflective as he sat down again, leaning the shotgun against the table. "Does Prescott know I sampled at Dakota?"

Shard felt a wave of relief now that the gun was not pointing at him. "Nope."

"But now he will."

"I didn't say I was going to tell him. But I've got to give him something to convince him that I'm looking out for his interests. He's beginning to have some doubts."

"What would you give him?"

"I was thinking of the aerials for one, along with the list of the flight numbers. That goes for both Dakota and Silverado. Plus the original data for Dakota from that California lab. That's no skin off your back. Prescott already knows you have it."

"He'd think I decided not to sample Dakota because I already had the lab results and aerials. I suppose I could live with that."

"There's one other piece of information he wants real bad: the name of your client."

The faintest twitch crossed Higheagle's face. He looked at his grandfather then back at Shard, eyes narrow. "No fucking way."

"Too late, Joe. I already have a copy of your contract, signed by one Vincenzo Minesali."

"Don't do it, Shard."

"I'm afraid I'm going to have—"

Suddenly, all three heads turned at the sound of a siren. Their time was up and the cops would be here any second. Shard felt his heart rate pick up like a drumbeat. He had to get the hell out of here, but he wanted to come to an arrangement with Higheagle first.

"You can't tell Prescott about Minesali yet, Shard. I need more time!"

"How much?"

"A week. That's how long it'll take for me to finish my reports. Hey, wait a second. If you've been tailing me all this time, how come you didn't know about Minesali before?"

"I'm afraid that's the one time you lost me. Exposition and University. That would make our friend Minesali a Polo Club man."

The sirens were shrilling now. They darted to the window. The cops hadn't pulled up out front yet, but Shard could tell they were getting damned close.

"Give me to Saturday then," Higheagle pleaded. "I have some things to work out."

Shard hesitated.

"Come on, you fuck—I need this!"

"All right, but why do you need the extra time?"

"Let's just say I have questions about my client, just as you do about yours."

A police cruiser screeched to a halt out front, roof lights flashing, sending strobes of red light at the house. As a pair of uniformed cops hopped out, an unmarked Crown Victoria screeched to a halt behind the cruiser. Shard gulped hard when he recognized the plainclothed detective who leapt from the unmarked car and began barking orders to the two uniforms.

"Oh, shit! It's Marshak!"

"What, you know him?"

"Unfortunately."

"Who the hell is he?"

"You'll find out soon enough. And when you talk to him, just remember one thing."

"What?"

"I was never goddamn here!"

And with that, he tipped his cowboy hat, rumbled down the hallway, and bulled his way out the back door.

CHAPTER 65

THE NEXT MORNING, Hayden Prescott strode past a lofty Ficus and stopped at his receptionist's desk. His inky-black hair was slicked back like a male model and his beige feather-light suit clung to him perfectly. Despite his elegance, his face was still badly bruised and the special actor's makeup he wore did little to conceal the damage. He clutched several documents to be copied and emailed to Links Unlimited, the company designing the two 18-hole championship golf courses at Silverado Knolls. Normally, he would have given such correspondence to his personal secretary Sophie, but she was away from her desk so he handed the documents to his receptionist for her to PDF and send out for him.

He watched her perfectly honed ass wiggle as she sashayed into the production room and began punching in numbers into the photocopier, her blood-red fingernails glinting in the bright light, bringing back torrid memories of Mumsie. For a brief moment, he imagined himself pulling down her tight panties and doing her right there. She would be a nice wet one like Sophie, he could tell, which was the primary reason he had hired her in the first place.

"Thank you, Cynthia. Just put it in my box when you're finished," he said pleasantly, keeping his little fantasy to himself.

As he turned to head back to his office, the elevator doors parted and he saw a sunburned, stubbly-faced man in dark blue coveralls step from the elevator. Something about the man seemed vaguely familiar.

"Can I help you with something?"

"Yeah, I'm here to—" He stopped right there as his mouth flew open in surprise. "I'm sorry, Mr. Prescott, I didn't know it was you. I couldn't tell with the..." He made a nervous gesture towards the developer's damaged face.

Prescott felt a wave of irritation. He was growing tired of people commenting on his bruises, and wished he had put on more makeup this morning to cover them up. "Do I know you?" he inquired curtly.

"Yes, sir, I'm Bob Watkins. I'm the Head of Maintenance and Groundskeeping at Dakota Ranch."

"Ah yes, Bob," he said, though he still couldn't remember where they'd met or how long the man had been working for him. It had been over a year since he'd been out to the property and spoken to the field staff. To him, they all had a kind of blue-collar Wonder Bread homogeneity and he had trouble telling them apart. "It's been awhile. What can I do for you?"

"Something happened at the rec center last week. I wanted to tell you about it in person."

Prescott felt a sinking feeling in his stomach. "What happened, Bob?"

"Well, there was this guy. He was taking samples, but I don't think he was supposed to be there."

"Samples? What kind of samples?"

"Soil samples."

Prescott felt the breath catch in his throat. He looked around to make sure no one was eavesdropping. "Why don't we go to my office? We'll be more comfortable there."

When they reached their destination, Prescott closed the door and waved Watkins to a chair in front of his desk. "So tell me what happened, Bob. Start from the beginning."

"Well, Mr. Prescott, it happened the Monday before last. I was coming out of the rec center when I saw this guy pushing a wheelbarrow towards the curb. He was dressed like a landscaper or gardener, but I'd never seen him before. I noticed that the wheelbarrow was filled with all kinds of equipment—a hand auger, trowel, brass tubes, and such—and I stopped and asked him what he was doing. He said he had taken a bunch of soil samples and was having them analyzed. Said the root systems weren't holding up as well as they should and that's why he was checking out the soil. When I asked him who he was working for, he said he had been contracted by The Newport Company directly. At the time, I thought that was a little odd since subs are usually approved through me once we receive the work order from you folks. Still, it all seemed legit and I didn't give it any further thought. It was only later that I got to thinking that maybe something wasn't right."

"Did the man give a name?"

"Quintero. I can't remember his first name."

Details, Bob, details. That's how you get to be successful like me, you moron, and why the other 99% like you never get anywhere in life. He picked up a black pen from the top of his desk and opened his daytimer. "What did he look like?"

"Well, he was tall and he had dark skin and long black hair done in a ponytail. On account of his last name, I thought he was Mexican. But he looked more like an Injun to me."

It was Higheagle all right, the bastard! "Did you actually see him collecting the samples?"

"No, sir. He just told me he had taken them."

Prescott began bending the pen in his hands, holding it below desk level so his visitor couldn't see him. "Did he happen to say what the samples were being analyzed for?"

"He said he was running 'em for moisture content and nutrient levels. Phosphorous, nitrogen, that sort of thing. But like I said, he wasn't approved through me and I'm the one who's supposed to sign off on all outside contractors. He said you had set it up personally and that's why I wasn't contacted."

Prescott feigned a look of innocent confusion. "Hmm, I don't recall that. It must have been handled by Dick Roberts or one of my other departmental heads. I'll just make a note to myself here to look into it." He scribbled down a few notes of indecipherable gibberish in his daytimer and looked up at Watkins again. "Did this Mr. Quintero mention anything else?"

"Said he'd send me the results. That's the reason I'm here. He said it would take around a week and I still haven't gotten anything from him."

That's because he was never planning on sending them to you, you moron! He pretended to ponder for a moment. "That's not surprising. Consultants are often late with their reports."

"Yeah, but he didn't offer a business card or anything. Like I said, the more I thought about it the more his story didn't make sense. That's why I thought I should talk to you."

"Well, you did the right thing in coming to me, Bob. I'll take it from here. Is there anything else?"

"Not that I can think of." His face suddenly lit up. "Oh, there is one other thing. I went out and counted the number of holes."

With an involuntarily spasm, Prescott snapped off the metal clip to the pen in his hand, letting it fall from his lap to the floor. *Fucking Higheagle! What's it going to take to stop this guy? Paine and Morelli couldn't even take care of him and they're pros!* "How many holes were there?"

"Around twenty. Seemed like a lot just to tell if the soil's okay or not. I wouldn't expect the nutrient levels and such to vary that much across the field."

"Were the holes around the rec center?"

"No, they were all on the east side."

He felt bile seeping into his throat. "I'm sure there's a simple explanation, but you did the right thing in coming to me. Don't hesitate to contact me in the future if the need arises. Here at The Newport Company, we're family, Bob, part of a team. You don't know how pleased I am to have someone like you looking out for the company's interests." He rose from his seat, cueing his guest that the meeting was finished.

Watkins beamed. "Thanks, Mr. Prescott."

"You bet, Bob." Prescott escorted him to the door and opened it for him. After stepping through the door, Watkins turned around and smiled at him as if they were old friends. "What happened to your face there? Looks like you ended up on the wrong side of Mike Tyson."

Prescott found the man's tactless presumption nettling, but managed an uneasy chuckle. "Racquetball accident. My opponent mistook my head for a little blue ball."

Watkins gave an irritatingly nasal laugh, and Prescott sent him on his way. When he closed the door, he felt a splitting headache coming on. He leaned against the door for support, rubbing his temples with his fingers, wondering what to do. The situation had taken a dramatic turn for the worse.

Not only was Higheagle alive, he had new sample results from goddamned Dakota!

CHAPTER 66

ONCE THE WORST OF THE PAIN had passed, he reeled his way to the phone, dialed Bishop, and commanded the attorney to hurry over. For the past hour now, they had been going over the ramifications of the latest unexpected setback. The situation with Higheagle was an unexpected blow to be sure, the portly legal eagle admitted, but there was no reason to panic. They would find a way to limit the damage and bring things under control.

And then the phone rang.

Prescott checked the caller ID and saw it was his receptionist.

"Yes, what is it, Cynthia?"

"Detective Marshak is here to see you."

Prescott's body froze. It had taken him a whole hour to recover from Watkins's disturbing revelation, and he was woefully unprepared to deal with another problem.

Bishop looked at him with puzzlement. "What is it?"

Prescott covered the phone. The blood had drained from his normally bronze face, leaving it ashen. "Marshak," was all he could manage to say.

"Here now?"

"I'll tell him I'm busy."

"No, wait a second. I think we should talk to him. He must have something new and we need to find out what it is. He's not expecting me to be here—it'll be an ambush."

"Are you sure? I may not be up to this right now."

"Don't worry, I have a plan. Just let me do the talking."

"Okay, if you think this is the way to go." Then into the phone: "Cynthia, call Sophie and have her bring the detective to my office."

Hanging up the phone, he felt a sense of dizziness like vertigo and his headache returning. He reached into his desk drawer, grabbed a bottle of Tylenol, and tossed back four tablets, washing them down with lukewarm coffee. Two minutes later, there was a knock on the door.

"I'll get it," Bishop said. With an air of aggression, he strode to the door and swung it open.

Both Sophie and Marshak took an involuntary step backwards.

Bishop smiled harshly. "Why, Inspector Javert, we were just talking about you. Please come in."

Marshak stepped into the room tentatively. Prescott could see him trying to resolve the sudden change in circumstances. Seeing the detective in a state of disequilibrium helped him steel his jangled nerves.

"Thank you, Sophie," he said to his executive secretary.

"My pleasure," she said, and she closed the door.

Prescott stepped around his desk. "This is becoming something of a bad habit, Detective—you dropping in again unannounced like this."

Marshak remained poker-faced. "I just have a few questions," he said mildly, and the three men took the same seats as their last meeting.

Watching the detective pull out his notepad and glance over his notes like an absentminded professor, Prescott went over in his mind how to handle the meeting. Part of him, the Father side, urged cautious diplomacy. This side had warned him against meeting with Marshak, but now that the man was here, it told him to stay in control and not say anything incriminating. In contrast, his more reckless and daring side, the Mumsie in him, screamed for bold initiative. With Bishop here to deflect the tough questions and keep Marshak off balance, he stood more to gain than to lose from the meeting, this second voice told him. Not only could he discover where the investigation was headed, there was the scintillating challenge of matching wits with an able adversary.

"There was an incident early this morning in Littleton," Marshak began. "Two armed men broke into a house and attacked two innocent people. I was wondering, Mr. Prescott, if you know anything about it."

"Have you lost your mind, Detective? My client's a reputable businessman, not a common street thug."

"The reason I ask is the two witnesses got a good look at both men and the computerized police artist's sketch of one of the intruders bears an uncanny likeness to our mysterious second waiter."

Prescott felt a faint twitch cross his features, but recovered quickly. From Paine's description of last night's encounter, he suspected Higheagle and his grandfather hadn't gotten a good look at Paine and Morelli at all, but were describing them from the first visit. But it didn't matter. What mattered to him most was that they had failed to eliminate Higheagle and the man still posed a serious threat.

Those incompetent fools! How could they have botched the job against two amateurs!

"I still don't understand what this has to do with my client," said Bishop. "He's already told you that he has no idea who this second waiter is."

Marshak ignored the attorney and looked hard at Prescott. "If that's the case, how do you explain your name on the paperwork at the house that was broken into?"

Prescott tried to look confused. "Paperwork?"

"Typed-written notes, lab sheet printouts, that sort of thing. There were also references to two of your properties: Dakota Ranch and Silverado Knolls."

Bishop threw up his hands. "Please dispense with the melodrama, Detective, and tell us whose house was broken into!"

"Did I forget to mention that? His name is Higheagle—Joe Higheagle."

"And who was the other witness?"

"John Higheagle—his grandfather."

"Higheagle? That name sounds familiar," said Prescott, scratching his chin thoughtfully. "Wasn't he that Native American geologist involved in that earthquake business last year? It was all over the news. He's something of a celebrity. Do you think the men who broke in were stalking him because he's a celebrity?"

Marshak knew he was being toyed with and flashed a look of annoyance. "No."

"Then what's your theory, Detective?" Bishop pressed him. "You must have a theory."

"We'll get into that in a minute." He looked back at Prescott. "For now, why don't you tell me how you got those bruises on your face?"

Prescott allowed himself a little smile. "That's none of your damned business."

Marshak raised an eyebrow in a pantomime of skepticism. "Funny, Mr. Higheagle's face was a mess too. I asked him about it and he told me to take a hike, just like you. If I were to guess, I'd say you two got into a little scrap recently. Why don't you tell me what happened?"

"You're on a fishing expedition, Detective. Next you'll be saying my client and this Higheagle character share the same barber, so they must be connected."

"They're already connected. The paperwork and bruises confirm it. What I want to know is who sent these two hit men to the house? It wouldn't have been you, would it, Mr. Prescott?"

Bishop's jaw dropped. "*Hit men*? Did you just say *hit men*?"

"Yeah, they were pros. They weren't there to steal some stereo equipment. They were trying to put Mr. Higheagle on ice. Maybe his grandfather too."

"And how do you know that, Detective?"

"We recovered one of the firearms and have complete ballistics at the crime scene. These guys were packing some serious heat. We're talking heavy-caliber, noise-suppressed semiautomatic sidearms. Not the kind of weapons your average cat burglar carries around."

Bishop rolled his eyes. "You can't possibly believe my client has an association with these common criminals. That's preposterous."

"There was also a 911 call two nights ago, something about a burglary in progress at the house next door to Mr. Higheagle. It turned out to be a false alarm, but I'm thinking maybe these two thugs were casing the place."

Prescott felt little beads of sweat gathering at his temples. He started to reach for the handkerchief in his pocket, but stopped himself at the last second. He didn't want Marshak to have the satisfaction of seeing him on edge.

"You're playing a dangerous game, Detective," warned Bishop. "I believe it's time for you to leave."

"I've got just one more thing." Again, he looked hard at Prescott. "When Mr. Higheagle saw me checking out the paperwork in his office, he got real touchy. He said it was something he was working on and he couldn't let me see it. When I asked him if he knew you, he said 'no' and got all defensive. Now the feeling I came away with was not only do you know each other, but the two of you have some issues. Some serious issues."

Prescott turned his gaze away and pretended to pick a thread from his suit jacket; he knew if he made direct eye contact, he would look guilty as sin.

"This is all pure conjecture," snorted Bishop. "What you should be trying to do is catch last night's intruders. They're the ones you should be interrogating, not my client."

"We'll pick them up soon enough. Mr. Higheagle and his grandfather winged both of 'em. We've already established two different blood types and we're having DNA tests run. If our John Does have a criminal record—which I'll bet they do— we'll get it from the FBI's CODIS database. Name, face, case details, last known address, the works."

Prescott considered this. He wasn't worried about any DNA match on either Paine or Morelli. Neither had ever been arrested, which meant that their fingerprints and DNA were not on record. What did concern him, however, was that they still might be tracked down and arrested, especially since Higheagle and his grandfather had given accurate descriptions to the cops and Morelli had required serious medical attention, though from an underground physician who knew to keep quiet. To maintain their loyalty and silence, he had paid them their fee in cash even though they had failed their assignment. He was also keeping them on the payroll until Morelli healed from his wounds, with the understanding that only the lightly wounded Paine would be on call. Any attempt on Higheagle's life would now raise an alarm, so Prescott didn't see an immediate need for Paine's assistance. But something might come up.

"For what it's worth, I'll tell you what I think happened that night at the Pepsi Center," Marshak said, again looking directly at Prescott. "Gus McTavish was poisoned and either you did it, or you know who did. And the reason he was killed has something to do with what Mr. Higheagle's working on. All I have to do to find out is subpoena him. Ten to one, that'll give me motive and enough for an indictment." His look narrowed. "Now, Mr. Prescott, is there something you want to tell me?"

Prescott hesitated, drawing out the moment. "Yes, Detective, there is."

Marshak looked at him expectantly.

"If I were you, I'd consider writing Hollywood screenplays. You have a very fanciful imagination."

Marshak's eyes narrowed.

Bishop pointed belligerently at the door. "We're done here, Detective. You know the way out."

"Don't think for a minute this is the end of it."

"For you it is. You want to know why? Because I'm going to call your boss, Chief Richards, and lodge a formal complaint against you. This makes three times you've barged in here like Wyatt Earp and threatened my client with a complete disregard for proper police procedure."

Prescott watched as Marshak seemed to blanch.

"You should have done your homework, Detective. If you had, you would have known that the police chief happens to be a close personal friend of mine. Two decades ago when I was a lowly Assistant D.A., I put away a certain gang-banger named Roscoe Jones. Surely you've heard that name. The son of a bitch killed two cops. Dedicated, decorated family men, one black, one white. Most people say that's how your boss got the top job. Beginning to get the picture?"

"That was a long time ago."

"True enough, but you're overlooking one crucial detail: Chief Richards is a political appointee. I believe if you were to get hold of Mr. Prescott's campaign donation records, you'll find he's contributed heavily to everyone of importance in this town, including the chief. Somehow, I don't think your boss or Internal Affairs are going to be too pleased about your bullying tactics these past two weeks when I file my complaint against you."

"Now why would you go and do a thing like that?"

Prescott smiled smartly. "I believe Greg here would do it just for the fun of it."

He then walked calmly to the door and opened it.

Now Marshak's expression turned to mild panic. Clearly, he hadn't counted on the possibility of getting in trouble with his boss or losing his job. "You'll never get away with this," he said, but the threat came across hollow.

The developer's challenging grin widened: the moment was pure Mumsie. "I think, boy-o, it's the other way around. You've badly overstepped your pay grade by being openly hostile to one of Denver's leading citizens. And this time it's going to cost you—big time."

CHAPTER 67

THE BUCKHORN EXCHANGE was the Mile High City's oldest drinking and dining establishment. It could have been mistaken for a local natural history museum if not for the pungent aroma of broiled buffalo, elk, and rattlesnake wafting out of the kitchen. From floor to ceiling, the place was packed with the heads of bear, moose, bighorn sheep, bison, and other wild animals to go along with fuzzy black and white daguerreotypes and colorful oil paintings of the Old West. Back near the kitchen, glass cases displayed an eclectic assemblage of antique guns and the rusty wares of trappers and miners. The original proprietor, German immigrant Henry Zietz, had converted the two-story brick commercial building into a restaurant in the late 1800s, and the historic establishment had lost little of its rustic charm over the years.

Stepping onto the creaky oak floorboards of the restaurant, Joe Higheagle informed the maître'd that he had a reservation. While she scanned her list, he glanced at the framed photographs along the staircase leading up to the second floor. Sprinkled among the recent winners of the annual Buffalo Bill look-alike contest were grainy close-ups of Plains Indians from the nineteenth and early part of the twentieth century, dressed in their finest ceremonial garb and brandishing repeating rifles and feathered battle lances.

The maître'd informed him that his guest had already been seated and led him to his table. Sitting before him was a bear of a man wearing a hand-crafted silver bolo tie, an elaborately fringed and beaded buckskin jacket, and a black wide-brimmed cowboy hat. The man lifted his considerable bulk and held out a big leathery hand with callused fingertips. Hank Johanson was half Ute, but somehow the Indian element had been entirely swamped out. He looked more like a crusty old fur trapper than a descendent of those hardy nomads that had crossed the Bering Straits during the last Ice Age.

"Well, if it ain't Katy's grandson."

"Thanks for meeting with me, Hank."

"Pleasures mine, son. By God, I do believe you have Katy's eyes."

Higheagle smiled bashfully and pulled up a chair. He tried to picture his grandmother, but drew a blank. She had been murdered under mysterious circumstances along with his mother and father when he was only six years old and he had barely known her. But obviously, she had meant a great deal to Hank Johanson.

"You know, Katy was one of the finest people I ever had the pleasure to know. It's a shame what happened. I was at the funeral. You were just a young buck back then, but I remember you. Everything was done in the old way, as it should have been..."

For several minutes, Higheagle listened as Hank Johanson talked on about the great Katy, the grandmother he had never known. Of course, it was common courtesy for people to heap mawkish accolades upon the dead unless there was massive contrary evidence, but Hank's laudatory remarks seemed genuine. Higheagle found himself wishing he had known her better.

Soon a waiter came and took their orders. Johanson selected an appetizer of rattlesnake marinated in red chile and lime and an entree of broiled elk medallions. Higheagle ordered the smoked buffalo sausage, cooked with a red chile polenta and spicy wild game mustard sauce.

When the waiter walked off, they talked some more. Actually, Johanson did most of the talking and Higheagle did most of the listening. Every so often Johanson roared with laughter, his titanic body jiggling like a grizzly shaking stream water off itself. It wasn't until their salads and Johanson's rattlesnake appetizer arrived that Higheagle directed the conversation towards the true purpose of the meeting: Minesali.

"So you think the old gentleman's up to his saddle skirts, eh?" Johanson said after Higheagle explained what he'd found at Dakota Ranch.

"I don't know. That's what I'm here to find out."

"And supposing I tell you what you need to know."

"It stays between me and my client. I signed a confidentiality agreement."

"What about your grandfather?"

"He's the only exception. He's like an advisor and I pretty much tell him everything. You should know though, he's the one who suggested that I talk to you alone."

Johanson mulled this over a moment as he cut into a strip of marinated rattlesnake. "Smart fellow, your grandfather. As a lawyer, he doesn't want to hear whatever it is I have to say from the horse's mouth. And now you're here, looking for some answers."

"It's important to me for a lot of reasons."

Johanson took a hefty bite of rattlesnake, chewing it slowly. "Sometimes it nettled your grandmother the way old John thought so damn much. Even as a young man, he was like that. Always pondering matters and plotting strategy. I suppose that's what made him such a damned good tribal lawyer." He glanced off thoughtfully in the direction of an engraved Winchester '73 repeating lever-action rifle on the wall. "So how can I help you with your little problem, Joe?"

"I want to know what happened out at Dakota, and, of course, why."

"Your grandfather was right. I do know a thing or two. But before we get into it, I want to make sure you understand something. Vince Minesali was the finest boss a man could have. I worked at his plant for over thirty years, my last twenty as operations manager, and the whole time I was there he treated his employees like family. Even though he was the head honcho, he was out in the processing area or in one of the shops every day to see how we were doing. Every goddamned day—for over thirty years."

He paused to damp his napkin against his mouth, as if to underscore what he would say next.

"When he came out to see us, he'd say, 'Hank, how are my boys today?' That's what he called us operations folks in the seventies and eighties before women took those kinds of jobs. The bottom line is he took care of us. I'm talking one-hundred-percent health and dental coverage with no co-payments, time off without pay to care for sick family members, a hell of a retirement plan, confidential drug and alcohol counseling, and real profit sharing. And this was before even the big corporations were offering these things. In all the time I worked there, not one person was laid off or fired."

Higheagle considered this a moment while staring at the head of a bull moose. It was almost if the fallen beast was eavesdropping, and Higheagle looked around the room warily for signs of Shard. "Hank, you're going to have to trust me on this. I've already told you, I have a professional obligation not to disclose anything to outside parties, my grandfather notwithstanding. Minesali's my client so whatever you tell me will remain confidential. I just want the truth."

The big man forked another chunk of rattlesnake and drew it to his mouth. He chewed it slowly, scrutinizing Higheagle long and hard, probing for more reassurance. "All right," he conceded, gently wagging his fork. "I suppose the grandson of old John and Katy can be trusted. I'll tell you what I know, but I'll offer no conjecture."

"Fair enough."

"All right, it all started with Vietnam."

"Vietnam?"

"Yes, sir. There was a herbicide used on a massive scale called Agent Orange. It was a defoliant used to destroy the thick jungle brush and deny the enemy cover."

"So Minesali produced Agent Orange at his plant?"

"A hell of a lot of it, especially during the middle part of the war. He had a big fat government contract with the U.S. Army Chemical Corps, which distributed it not only to the Army, but the Air Force and Navy. Minesali was one of their biggest suppliers and they sprayed that shit all over that godforsaken country. Might as well have been bathin' in the stuff."

"Where does the name come from?"

"It's the code name for the orange band used to mark the drums the crap was stored in. Agent Orange was actually only one of a half-dozen herbicides used during the war. It just happens to be the worst one. You also had your Agent White, Blue, Purple, Pink, and Green. At Minesali's plant, we only processed Agent Orange. Basically, it was a fifty-fifty mix of two chemicals: 2,4-D and 2,4,5-T. The TCDD and other dioxins you were telling me about are just impurities."

"When did the EPA realize this stuff was toxic?"

"Not until after the war in the late-seventies. Since then, there have been thousands of medical claims filed. There are a whole slew of diseases that are supposed to have resulted from exposure to the stuff, many fatal. But only a small number of the ingredients have been found to cause cancer in humans based on lab tests. That's what's so strange about Agent Orange. We don't really know how bad it really is, what triggers nasty health effects in some people but not others."

"How was it used exactly?"

"During the war, they used Hercules C-123 Providers equipped with spray booms, but they also used Hueys, trucks, and riverboats and even sometimes sprayed by hand. They diluted the Agent Orange with kerosene or diesel fuel before dispersing it over the jungles. The Air Force had primary responsibility, but all branches of service were in the mix. They sprayed the stuff like crazy during the height of the war from '67 to '69. After that, it wasn't used as much and was eventually discontinued in late '71 when the last spray mission was flown. Needless to say, spraying all that crap didn't help us win the goddamned war. We still got our butts kicked."

"So how does Minesali figure into all this?"

"When the spraying missions were halted in the early seventies, Uncle Sam plum left Minesali holding the bag. He had processed millions of pounds of this stuff following the schedule set by the Army Chemical Corps and they backed out on him. They refused to honor the contract. He must have been left with well over a hundred thousand drums. He kept it on a property near his plant that he leased to the Army. The Army kept it under guard round the clock. You know, national security and all.

"By the mid-eighties, all the medical claims filed by soldiers were making the Army jittery and one day they just up and voided the leasing arrangement. They told him they didn't want anything to do with Agent Orange. They didn't care what he did with it—they just didn't want to deal with it."

"So what happened to the drums?"

"Nothing for a long time. There were no material safety data sheets or chemical inventories required by the CDPHE, and the EPA was just a fledgling agency back then, without much enforcement power. No one knew about the waste except the Army, but they quickly cut all ties with Minesali."

"But things began to change, right? The regulatory agencies began to have routine inspections and audits and standardized storage and handling forms."

"Exactly. The old gentleman tiptoed around it as long as he could. He moved the drums around from one place to another and eventually had them handled through a waste broker. By that time, the Health Department and EPA were getting nosy."

"So Minesali had the drums dumped at Dakota Ranch."

Johanson's brow froze into a sea of wrinkles. He said nothing, but Higheagle knew the answer.

"What about the metals?"

"That's a different story. We used to sandblast the storage tanks and process the residues at the plant. In the process, we generated a hell of a lot of liquid metal waste, not just Agent Orange. With the public outcry against Agent Orange, our reg compliance manager came up with the clever idea that we mix the herbicides with the metal waste to cover up both of their origins."

Higheagle shook his head in dismay. He didn't want to believe what Johanson was telling him. What troubled him most was not so much that his client had withheld something—that wasn't unusual—but that Minesali, not Prescott, might ultimately be responsible for the deaths of the boys.

"Why couldn't Minesali just have properly disposed of the waste?"

"You know why—cost."

"But he must be a millionaire fifty times over. He could have paid for it out of his own pocket."

"He's made a bundle, but in recent years, he's poured most everything back into the company. You saw his house. It's coming apart at the seams. He has no real staff. That fella Forbes does just about everything."

Higheagle remembered the air of neglect about the place. "How do you know so much about him? You haven't worked for him in years."

"I make it my business to know what goes on in this dusty old cowtown. I'm sure your grandfather told you that."

"Yeah, he did."

"Fact of the matter is, no one wanted to deal with Agent Orange after 'Nam. Minesali couldn't very well unload it. Don't forget, there were more than a hundred thousand drums of the stuff, and several thousand more of the metal sludge. At five hundred dollars per drum or more for F-listed haz waste landfill disposal, how long you think he would have been in business? We're talking about more than fifty million dollars."

Higheagle realized that such an amount stripped from the bottom line of even a large corporation would be disastrous. Assuming the waste had been dumped at night, it could easily have been done for less than a million. But Prescott had probably demanded a significant cut for allowing his land to be used as a dumpsite.

"How much money would Prescott have gotten?"

"Something far less than fifty million or it wouldn't have been worth the trouble to Minesali."

"You do realize that the waste may have caused the deaths of those boys."

"Vince Minesali would never have allowed anything to be dumped out there if he'd known."

"He's still ultimately responsible. If the boys have died from this toxic soup, don't you think he should pay a price just like Prescott?"

"Look, I've told you too much already. And the only reason I'm talking to you at all is because you're Katy's grandson and I can see you're in a bit of a quandary. But I ain't gonna play judge and jury here, and neither are you. Remember, we have an arrangement. You gave me your word. So don't get all high and mighty on me. Vince Minesali's a good man. He's done right not only by me, but thousands of other working stiffs. There ain't a durn thing in this world any one of his employees or former employees wouldn't do for him. And you can sure as hell bet he's been carrying a heavy burden all these years. Don't you see? He hired you because he wants to come clean."

"Or, he could just be setting things up so Prescott takes the rap."

"Maybe he has a good reason for wanting to do that."

"What are you saying?"

"I've told you enough, Joe. You're going to have to figure the rest out for yourself."

CHAPTER 68

WITH SECRET SATISFACTION and more than a little awe, Prescott watched as Bishop laid into DPD Chief Richards over the speakerphone.

The attorney's story was simple: his client was cooperating fully with the police investigation, but Detective Marshak was way out of line, resorting to verbal harassment and accusing his client of murder without informing him of his Miranda rights as required during a police interrogation. If something wasn't done to rein in the detective, and quickly, there would be serious legal consequences. With icy calm, Bishop threatened to lodge a formal complaint with the District Attorney's office and Internal Affairs for Marshak's egregious breech of police procedure. He also threatened to contact the media about flagrant abuses of power by the DPD, which as it turned out, had received substantial news coverage in recent months. Like any public official, Richards wanted to avoid a public smear campaign and subsequent witch hunt at all costs. He said he would look into the matter personally and get back to Bishop by the end of the day.

"So that's it?" Prescott said when the lawyer clicked off the speakerphone.

"Piece of cake. We won't be hearing from Marshak any time soon, that's for sure."

Prescott had his doubts. "But he knows everything."

"He thinks he knows everything. He has no real proof, nothing that would stand up in court. If he did, he would have slapped the cuffs on you and hauled you in. In any case, you'd better not have any further contact with Higheagle."

Rising from his chair, Prescott went to the window. Thick thunderheads consumed the sky in the foreground, and in the far distance, a bluish-purple haze of shower threw a giant curtain above the massive Front Range. He couldn't escape the feeling of impending doom and wondered what his father would do if he was in his shoes.

"Forget about Marshak," Bishop said, as if reading his troubled thoughts. "Higheagle's the one we have to worry about. This new information Shard got his hands on makes it even more imperative that we take a different approach."

Prescott sighed heavily. "I just want it all to go away."

"Don't worry, I'm a magician. But it's time for a different plan of attack."

Prescott sat back down. "What do you have in mind?"

"Hwong must fall and fall hard. It's the only way you come out of this unscathed."

"You're telling me we have to set up Hwong to take the fall?"

"Yep, and the script will read something like this. Hwong arranged for the waste to be dumped at Dakota and Silverado without your knowledge. Then he convinced you to conduct soil investigations at both properties to obtain a clean bill of health from the Health Department. When the results came up dirty, he blackmailed you into having false reports prepared by his lab. He did this to benefit himself in three ways.

"First, you paid him a huge sum for falsifying the results. Second, Arapaho took in substantial laboratory fees for analyzing the samples. Third, he positioned himself favorably for future lab contracts by coercing you into recommending him to other developers. You did recommend him to McGranahan-Peterson, Fielding and Associates, and that other developer, you know that small outfit."

"Stockton Limited."

"They all gave work to Hwong based on your endorsement, right?"

Prescott gave a nod. *Could this actually work?*

"It's perfect. Hwong doesn't know anything about Hoskins or the generators. And we could pin McTavish's murder on him too. He set you up to take the rap because you refused to make any more blackmail payments to him. But the plan backfired when you tried to save McTavish's life in front of all those sterling VIP eyewitnesses."

"Do you think a judge or jury would actually believe that?"

"Of course. Like I told you, in a courtroom I'm a fucking magician. Hwong's the one who dumped the waste. He's the one who blackmailed you into having the lab results falsified. He's the one trying to score big contracts from you for future developments and who forced you to recommend him to other developers. And he's the one who had McTavish killed in your presence to set you up."

"But it could all blow up in my face if the regulators cut a deal with Hwong."

"That's why we need him to do something stupid, something that will focus the attention on him instead of you. In short, we need to hand deliver Marshak—and Higheagle, too, for that matter—a new prime suspect."

Prescott had never considered feeding Hwong to the lions. But the plan did seem to have potential. "How would we go about it?"

"First, we need to meet with him. Tell him about the samples Higheagle took at Dakota. See if we can convince him to have the results altered or make them disappear. He owns a lab, for Christ's sake. He ought to be able to figure something out."

"And if he gets caught?"

"Then we've handed every law enforcement and environmental regulatory agency in the state a new suspect."

"But what if Hwong talks or tries to cut a deal?"

"He's been nothing but a technical consultant. Granted, he knows a lot about the chemistry and volume of waste, but he doesn't know the name of the waste broker or any of the generators. What's he going to tell them? He has no real proof of your involvement. And you have records of the payments to Hwong and the work you sent his way. Bottom line, for you to come away from this completely unscathed, Hwong has to take the fall."

Slowly, Prescott nodded his head. "I guess he'll just have to fend for himself."

Bishop smiled harshly. "Good, we're in agreement. Now here's how it'll play out...."

CHAPTER 69

OPENING THE FRONT DOOR, Higheagle greeted his grandfather. "Good workout, Grandfather?"

"Yes, but I'm getting too old for this pilates shit. I don't know why the hell I do it. I don't really want to live to be a hundred fucking years old." He handed him his sports duffel bag like a quarterback handing off to a fullback, then swept passed him into the house with an air of nonchalance. "How was your meeting with Hank?"

"It was interesting."

"That's it, interesting?"

Higheagle didn't respond. Instead, he poked his head outside and looked around for Shard, but the only thing he saw were roiling black storm clouds gathering along the western horizon. He closed the door and followed his grandfather to the blue corduroy couch in the living room.

The old chief dropped into the couch, joints crackling like popcorn with the wear and tear of a lifetime. "You know that after your meeting with Hank, he called me."

"I figured he would. What did he have to say?"

"He's worried about you."

"Worried how?"

"Worried that you might go to the police or do something stupid. Would you?"

"Of course not."

"In hindsight, I probably should have gone with you."

"So what else did Hank say?"

"He seems to think things may not be as simple as you believe."

"Is that so?"

"Just put aside your feelings for a moment and listen to me. It takes a special kind of man to hire someone to find out things which may implicate him."

"That doesn't change what Minesali's done."

"Maybe not. But there's little doubt he hired you so the truth would come out. You should be asking yourself, why would he go to all that trouble?"

"That's easy. He's just trying to pawn it off on Prescott."

"Maybe. But as Hank told you, perhaps there's another reason. That's what you have to find out."

Higheagle conjured an image of Minesali and felt only a sense of betrayal. "Anything else, Big Chief?"

"Just one thing. You know why you're doing this, don't you? Because you have become too personally involved with Tommy and his mother. I warned you about that."

As much as he hated to admit it, he knew his grandfather was right. He was getting too close to Sally and Tommy, and it was affecting his judgment. But that didn't change the fact that Minesali had betrayed him and was the one ultimately responsible for the Dakota situation. And, for all he knew, Silverado too.

"Don't think for one second you're telling me something I don't already know, Grandfather. I wasn't going to run to the cops and rat out my client. I'll listen to Minesali's side of the story. But at the same time, there has to be justice. He shouldn't have done it in the first place. He should never have gotten into this position. He had other options, but he chose not to pursue them."

"You don't know that. His dilemma may have been much worse than you imagine. Until you know for certain what really happened, you should not pass judgment. You're a scientist, not a lawyer. You're supposed to be objective."

"He could have disposed of the waste legally. It might have been expensive, but he could have done it. Or he could have filed a lawsuit against the Army and forced them to share the disposal costs."

"I only know what you've told me about this man. I always had the feeling he wasn't telling you the whole truth. But withholding secrets does not make him evil."

"He has to pay for what he's done."

"Goddamnit, are you even listening to me? You still don't know the whole story. And getting it—and getting it right—must be your top priority."

CHAPTER 70

PRESCOTT SAW AT ONCE that Doug Hwong was dangerously close to the edge. With the dark circles ringing his eyes, he looked as though he hadn't slept in days. His back was stooped like a hunchback as he shambled brokenly across the carpet and took his seat in the black leather chair next to Bishop. He was obviously still in excruciating pain from being driven hard into the Range Rover two nights ago. All in all, thought Prescott, it looked as though he had caught Hwong at an opportune moment of vulnerability.

"I'm afraid we have some bad news, Doug. You already know Vic Shard's recovered the samples Higheagle took at Silverado. What you don't know is that our Indian friend has also collected samples at Dakota and has had or is having them analyzed."

Hwong was stunned. "But how?"

"He walked out there in broad daylight and did it. We wouldn't have even found out about it if not for this maintenance guy who saw him."

"I told you something like this would happen."

Prescott found the accusatory undertone in the geochemist's voice offensive, but held his tongue. "In light of the situation, we need to discuss other options. Do you have any suggestions?"

"The most important thing is to make his evidence disappear. If nothing else, that will buy us more time until we can come up with a more permanent solution."

That was exactly what Prescott wanted to hear. He felt a little surge of triumph knowing the trap was being set. *If we can just lead him along, he'll do the job for us. And if somewhere along the line he stumbles, he'll take the fall alone.* With every ounce of his will, he resisted the temptation to show his cards. "How would you go about...making the evidence disappear?" he asked, flipping up his eyebrows in a look of sudden interest.

"By deleting the computer records and destroying all hard copies."

"Unfortunately, we don't know which lab the samples were submitted to," Bishop pointed out.

"We know he sent the samples from Silverado to Environmental Testing Services," Hwong said, leaning forward eagerly in his chair, looking far more energized than when he had first set foot in the room. "It's almost certain he would have used the same lab."

"But even if we manage to destroy all the analytical evidence and the aerials, he'll just go out and sample again. I've already set up additional security at both places, but how long will it be until he sneaks in again or until he convinces the regulators to investigate?"

"So you're going to just let this guy destroy us?"

"Of course not. But at this point, I don't have anyone that can handle this. My two top associates are unavailable at this time and Shard doesn't want to have anything to do with it. Says he's already gone above and beyond the call of duty. That's why we were hoping you might have a solution. After all, you do own a lab and know exactly what to look for."

For several seconds the room was silent. As always, Hwong's dark, beady eyes and rumpled forehead testified that his brilliant mind was fiercely at work. "Environmental lab security is lax. I can take care of it myself. All I have to do is find a way to log on and erase the hard disk files. Then I'll steal the LAN backup tapes and actual lab reports, if they keep hard copy records."

He's taking the bait—now reel him in. "How do you plan on getting inside?"

"Leave that to me."

"What about Higheagle?" asked Bishop.

"I'll take care of what he has too."

Prescott gave an appreciative nod. "Of course, taking care of both problems would be most beneficial. However, I should let you know that Greg feels he can beat this thing outright. And with half of the Silverado subdivisions already sold to Raleigh Homes and the other builders, I'll soon make a modest fortune. I can afford to walk away and take my chances in court."

Hwong did an angry double-take.

Bishop was quick to take advantage of his loss for words. "Are you still with Phil Harding at Holland & Hart, Doug, because you may need to get someone with more—shall we say?—trial experience. This thing has the potential to turn into a lengthy legal battle. And tuck your money in a safe place. For God's sake, get it out of the company and some place offshore where it can't be touched."

Hwong remained speechless, but his growing fury was evident in his dark, pinched expression. He looked as though he had caught a strong whiff of one of the nasty chemicals analyzed by his laboratory. "I don't believe this. You're talking like women."

Prescott knew it was time now to put the final stamp on the meeting. "Of course, none of this would be necessary if the evidence were to disappear and Higheagle had a little—how to say it?—accident. You know, like you suggested before."

Hwong looked desperate now. "I'm not going to fucking jail."

"Who said anything about going to jail?"

"Before I came to this country, I spent three years in a roach-infested cell in Taiwan. Three fucking years! That's not going to happen again!"

Prescott held up his hands to mollify him and spoke in a sympathetic tone, as if consoling a small child. "We know what you went through, Doug. But no one's going to jail. Even if we did, we'd be out quickly and still have our multimillions."

"I don't have multimillions."

"Well then, perhaps that could be arranged."

A light seemed to go on in Hwong's head; he gave the slightest nod. "You mean if I found a way to solve our little problem."

Prescott smiled. "Yes, Doug, that's exactly what I mean."

CHAPTER 71

THE EARLY EVENING sunlight filtered lazily through the stand of mighty blue spruces on the east side of Polo Club Drive West. Vic Shard sat in his Jeep sporting a chambray shirt, khakis, and his trademark straw cowboy hat with the rattlesnake skin band, pair of eagle feathers, and several colorful dry flies. He felt a little warm, so he rolled down his window. The gentle breeze touched his face and reminded him of his first kiss in sixth grade. Marcie Appleton: brown eyes soft as a deer, dark curly hair, a smile that would warm the heart of a Puritan.

Lordy lord, such a sweet thing. Where has all the time gone?

He picked up the Leupold binoculars resting on the seat next to him. Raising them to eye level, he peered over the wrought-iron gate at the vast Tudor mansion of Vincenzo Minesali, king of the Centennial State's herbicide and pesticide industry since the ignominious McCarthy Era.

It took him less than a minute to realize that what had once been an aesthetic wonder now had an element of neglect about it. To be sure, the architecture was remarkable, with the steep-pitched slate roofs that fed one another like a series of waterfalls, the spectacular glazed tapestry brick walls, the elaborate dormers and gables, the grand chimneys. But Shard's razor-sharp eyes also noticed defects he hadn't picked up on his drive-by. The imperfections were trivial—like one eye slightly larger than the other on a gorgeous supermodel—but evident nonetheless. Missing slate tiles on the roof, cracked windows, woodwork in need of a fresh coat of paint, vines engulfing the mansion. He suspected that if his private eyes had the opportunity to scrutinize the entire house, they would find innumerable blemishes both interior and exterior.

He had driven past the historic Tudor mansion numerous times during his first Polo Club stakeout ten years earlier, though back then he was unaware it belonged to Minesali. The case involved a wealthy bank president who had made the mistake of marrying a much younger woman whose sexual appetites he could never hope to satiate. Shard solved the case in less than a week when her husband was away on a business trip. The wife rolled around in the sack with two different men during Shard's stakeout: a lean, sinewy Australian who tended to the vast estate gardens; and the buff assistant golf pro from the nearby Denver Country Club. When the husband returned, Shard handed him not only a folder full of intriguing photographs, but actual tape recordings of the liaisons. Shard later learned that his surveillance provided enough for a crafty attorney to annul the prenuptial agreement that had guaranteed the woman some five million dollars; she ended up with less than three hundred thousand, undoubtedly not enough to maintain her lavish lifestyle.

The case was a defining moment in Shard's career. After the divorce settlement, he received a twenty-thousand-dollar bonus from the husband and began to take on more highbrow clients, largely through Bishop. Most of the new work came from word of mouth. Soon he was representing clients from exclusive Castle Pines, Cherry Hills, Denver Country Club, and Polo Club on a regular basis. Most of his cases focused on corporate espionage—stealing ideas or preventing others from doing so—but he also slipped comfortably into those involving runaway trust-funders, teenage dope peddlers, and lustful husbands and wives. Over the years, his gold list of clients had built him a nice little nest egg. Oil men, financiers, real estate and computer titans, rich widows—anyone with more money than they knew what to do with.

Shard had made a successful living from such people, and at one time, he had been glad they were in ample supply. But not anymore. He hated his job, hated that he was working for Hayden Prescott. When this case was over, he kept telling himself, he would take some serious time off to take measure of himself. His marriage to Hattie was fine, as was his relationship with his kids; his sole source of disappointment was his career. Some part of him felt forever damaged for what he had done, not only on behalf of Prescott but other shady clients as well. He needed time away from it all to bring some meaning back into his life.

But before he could do that, he had to see this case through.

Setting his binoculars down on the passenger seat, he punched a number on his cell phone.

"Hayden Prescott."

"Shard here."

"I'm here with Greg. Hold on, let me put you on speaker." Shard heard fumbling on the other end of the line. "You there?" The voice was hollow.

"Yep. I know who your boy's working for. Looks like our mystery man is one Vincenzo Minesali of 497 Polo Club Drive West."

A stunned silence fell over the line. Either they hadn't anticipated this new development or had expected someone else.

"Are you sure? I mean, how do you know?"

"I'm sitting in front of the guy's house. Higheagle's been in there for at least ten minutes now. He parked his truck inside the gate and went in carrying a big old satchel, so I figure he and Minesali have some important business to discuss."

Another stunned silence.

Shard eased back in his seat with a wry smile. *Weren't prepared for this little bombshell, were you boys?* He already had a pretty good idea how Minesali fit into the puzzle, but he still had lingering questions. Foremost among them was why one of the waste generators—a man who had much to lose if discovered—would pay someone to investigate his own wrongdoings?

Breaking the tense silence, he spoke into his cell again: "Do you know this Minesali?"

"I've heard of him."

Not much of a liar, are we? "He's the herbicide/pesticide guy, right?"

No one answered. "What makes you so sure Minesali is Higheagle's client?" asked Bishop.

"I lost your boy just a few blocks away from here late last week. That would make twice he came to this neck of the woods and I don't believe in coincidences. I'd wager that Higheagle's phone records and bank statements for April will back me up."

"We can worry about that later," Prescott said impatiently.

"Do you want me to run some background on Minesali?"

Shard heard emphatic whispering on the other end, Prescott and Bishop debating some point. "No," Prescott said, a note of suppressed urgency in his voice. "Just keep following Higheagle. Call me when you have something more."

"You got it." Shard hung up, smiling.

Now this was getting goddamned interesting!

ψψψ

Prescott fizzed with indignation as he gazed at the jagged silver peaks in the distance. The news from Shard couldn't have been worse: Higheagle was working for Minesali.

He turned away from his office window and shot a look at Bishop. "Why would that old goat do something like this? I did him a favor by taking that damned waste off his hands."

"I'm not sure. But he obviously knows about the cancer," responded Bishop.

"How in the hell would he get that information?"

"Same way Shard did."

"But he must know I'll destroy him if he talks. What kind of man would do such a thing?" He sat down abruptly and pulled angrily at his Armani tie, a costly silk arrangement with soft swirls of vermillion, blue, and creamy white. "He must have cut some kind of deal."

Bishop looked across the desk at him through flickering brown eyes; he was already gaming out the scenarios. "Well, at least we know its Minesali. We need to bring him to the negotiating table pronto. He may be able to call off Higheagle."

"Do you actually believe he'll listen to reason at this stage?"

"We have to try. Once he realizes what's going to happen to him, he may be more willing to cooperate."

"And if he doesn't?"

"Then we'll have to get more creative." He tilted back in his leather chair, looking like a fat cat in a rocker. "Look, my plan—or backup plan if it comes to that—will work. The McTavish investigation is history. Chief Richards has neutralized Marshak. So now it comes down to Higheagle and Minesali. They have to be dealt with, no question about it. But don't forget, Hwong is already doing his part to solve one of our problems. We need to step up to the plate and take care of the other."

"But Minesali can testify I received the waste knowingly. Doesn't that pretty much destroy our case, regardless of which way we go?"

"There's still no transaction record. The feds are going to have to establish that, or they haven't got a case. Without phone, computer, wire, or bank records, they're going to have one hell of a time proving anything. Minesali followed all of our instructions so it's untraceable."

"But if he talks and has Higheagle's data at his disposal, and if the EPA gets a court order to sample at both Dakota and Silverado, I'll be ruined."

"No, the generators will be ruined, because if things ever get to that point, we're going to cut a deal. Of course, you'd take a heavy financial hit, but I'd make sure you wouldn't do any time, not when you handed them the whole operation on a silver platter. I'd say a reasonable estimate would be on the order of fifteen to twenty percent of the cleanup costs."

"Jesus, that's over ten million." He reached across a pile of paperwork and snatched up the Steuben glass giraffe from the edge of his desk. He was tempted to smash it against the wall, but remembered that he had paid five thousand dollars for it at a charity auction. "Are you sure that's the worst-case scenario?"

"Unless they track down our waste broker friend Hoskins. But that's unlikely. Look, Hayden, it doesn't do any good to run through hypotheticals until we know what Minesali's going to do."

"What about Hwong?"

"My feeling is he can only help you, or hurt himself. Either way the result's the same."

Prescott set down the giraffe on the desk and paced in front of the window, hands shoved into his pockets, eyes blinking rapidly.

"It's all going to work out, Hayden. We just have to get the old man to cooperate."

"And if he doesn't?"

"When I get through with him, he won't have a fucking choice."

CHAPTER 72

BENEATH THE SURFACE, Higheagle was simmering as he strolled with Minesali through his outdoor gardens. He couldn't believe he had been duped, couldn't believe he had been taken in by Minesali's charismatic charm, his Old World sophistication, his panache. He was angry at himself for being manipulated like a puppet. His investigation was a complete joke now. Vincenzo Minesali had never been a scrupulous businessman looking into a potential investment opportunity; instead he was a fraud, a dumper of toxic waste, possibly even a murderer of young boys—and he had been so all along.

Something had to be done about it.

But what?

Higheagle wanted to just get it over with and confront the old man directly. But then he thought of what his grandfather had told him, how he shouldn't reach a verdict until he'd heard Minesali's side of the story. In spite of his outrage, he felt trapped in a morass of indecision.

"Joseph, is there something you want to tell me?"

The Cheyenne was taken off guard. *Was I that obvious?* He looked away to collect his thoughts, fixing his gaze on a knotty maple tree next to the wall, and beyond, the storm clouds gathering force to the west. When he turned back towards Minesali, he was struck by how surreally innocent and harmless the old man looked in his khaki gardening outfit. He decided the best way to confront him was indirectly, by presenting his latest results and letting the old man's conscience steer him into a confession. He would start with his risk calculations, and see where that led.

"I ran the cancer risk numbers for the cancer-causing compounds at Dakota," he said, keeping his tone scientific. "I used the most recent EPA slope factors and estimated intake based on the concentration data I collected and an average body weight. All the boys have been between nine and thirteen so I used a body weight of one hundred pounds. What I found is a high percentage of the boys who played at the dirt lot would be expected to develop cancer over a two year, three-day-a-week exposure period."

He paused to gauge Minesali's reaction. The old man's gaze fell to the ground, and Higheagle knew he had struck an emotional nerve. He pressed on, continuing to keep things technical.

"The cancer risks of the individual compounds fell in the ten-to-the-minus-one to ten-to-the-minus-two range based on the inhalation and skin adsorption exposure pathways. That's one in ten to one in a hundred. When I added the risks together to get a cumulative risk, the number went down to one in four. That means that one boy in four would have a probability of developing cancer sometime in his lifetime as a result of exposure to the carcinogens. In short, it means that cancer out at Dakota is not just a statistical possibility, but expected."

There was a tense silence. Higheagle gave Minesali a hard, querying look, hoping by the sheer force of his expression to get him to come clean. Through the dappled early evening sunlight, what he saw was a man crestfallen and utterly wracked with guilt.

Minesali's lips trembled as he spoke. "You know the truth," he said simply, his mournful voice as soft as the swish of bare feet through grass.

"You shouldn't have deceived me."

For several seconds, the old man said nothing. "If there was any other way..." His voice trailed off disconsolately.

Minesali's naked anguish gave Higheagle a moment's pause. "You'd better just tell me what happened."

"I don't know where to begin."

"Start with why you decided to dump Agent Orange on the prairie of Douglas County. I'm sure the rest will fall into place."

Minesali sighed with weary resignation as he sat down on a sandstone bench. "The truth is I was faced with the dilemma of a lifetime. It was a choice between selling my company and seeing more than a thousand of my employees terminated—or disposing of the waste illegally. After painful deliberation, I chose the latter."

"So you brokered a deal with Prescott to dump the waste at Dakota Ranch."

A regretful nod. "Our estimates for legitimate disposal were around sixty-two million dollars. There was no way I could afford that kind of money without selling out and making my employees bear the burden of my folly."

"Did you put the company up for sale?"

"We never got beyond preliminary negotiations and nothing was ever done publically. Three companies tendered offers. I had concerns about what impact the buyout would have on my employees and, therefore, insisted on full disclosure on their restructuring plans before any sale would go through. One company balked and the other two put in offers and a business plan for the buyout. Both companies planned to eliminate the accounting, marketing, and distribution departments once they took over. All they really wanted were my two processing plants and my key operations personnel. Knowing how many people would lose their jobs, I refused to entertain further offers. Half of the people that would have lost their jobs had over twenty years with the company. I could not bring myself to cut loose the men and women who had served me faithfully for so many years."

Higheagle stared off, thinking about the Ludlow Massacre and that damned black-and-white picture of Minesali's grandfather and uncle lying dead in the coffins. He was struck by the sheer irony of it all: they had given their lives fighting against Rockefeller's profit-driven tyranny, and now Minesali had made the mistake of a lifetime because he had chosen to protect his employees rather than his own financial interests.

"I looked at the numbers a hundred different ways, Joseph. There was no way out except to stand by and watch more than a thousand people lose their jobs. I could not allow that to happen."

"So it's not really your fault at all—it's the Army's. Excuse me, but that sounds a little too convenient."

"So you know about the Army too."

Higheagle said nothing, letting the weight of the silence do his work for him. His look narrowed again on the old man. The bags around Minesali's eyes appeared to have grown heavier in only the last few minutes.

"Why didn't you take your case to court?"

"My attorneys fought with the Army in closed-door meetings for more than a decade. Their position was they were doing nothing more than canceling their order."

"And you were left with how much Agent Orange?"

"Over one hundred thousand drums, fifty-five gallon capacity. They were stored on a property near my plant I was leasing to the Army. They terminated the lease and told me flat out that they wanted nothing to do with the Agent Orange. It was all highly classified. I had to sign a dozen government waivers."

"So you moved the drums around to keep the EPA and CDPHE at bay." When Minesali nodded, he posed another question. "When did you hook up with Prescott?"

"I went to Stanford with his father and we kept in touch over the years. In the spring of '99, I was invited to a function hosted by Hayden and his father. Hayden told me about his real estate ventures. He was just getting his feet wet after working several years in California. He needed up-front capital and I needed to get rid of the drums. We stayed in touch, and over the next few years, one thing led to another and we put together an arrangement."

"So it was your idea originally to dump the waste."

"I saw a way out and Hayden saw a business opportunity. The decision was a mutual one for which we both bear responsibility."

"Then why do you have it out for him? It's your waste, not his. He just buried it on his property."

Minesali's expression hardened. "Because I found out that he covered the waste with only a one-foot cap, instead of the three feet we had agreed upon. If he had placed a three-foot cap over it, none of those boys would have been exposed. I want him to pay for his greed."

Higheagle realized that, despite his anger, he was sympathetic to the old man. But then he thought of the damage already done to Tommy and Sally, as well as the other boys and their families, and he felt revulsion. "I take it that it was Prescott who handled the waste disposal."

Minesali nodded, his expression wracked with guilt.

"You must have paid him a flat fee? How much?"

"Ten million dollars. He had some elaborate, supposedly untraceable wire setup. I followed his instructions and have heard nothing about it since. We agreed that we would never speak of it again."

"And you have nothing to do with the waste that's being dumped at Silverado Knolls."

Minesali looked up alertly. "So he is doing it there too. I knew he wouldn't stop with—"

"Just answer the damned question!"

Minesali flinched at the sharp tone. "I was only involved at Dakota Ranch," he said softly. "I give you my word."

"Your word doesn't mean anything to me anymore."

"I understand how you feel, Joseph, and am willing to face the consequences of my actions."

"As long as Prescott goes down with you, right?"

The old man's eyes glittered with something as ancient as man himself: raw vengeance. "That is as it should be," he said bitterly.

"And that's also the reason you hired me in the first place, isn't it?"

"I'm not sure why I did it. I only know I had to make some kind of atonement. Perhaps I subconsciously wanted the blame to fall on Prescott's shoulders. I do not know."

"So what do you think should happen to you?"

The words hung over Minesali like a suspended axe, and Higheagle felt a surprising satisfaction in his discomfort. Still, he wasn't certain he could condemn him. Minesali had tried to do what he thought was the right thing, and only later had his actions proved harmful to others.

"I don't know the answer. If I turn myself in, they'll seize my company and sell it off to pay for the cleanup. Many people would lose their jobs. If I do nothing, then...well, that's not an option. I can't do nothing."

"So you agree that you should be punished, just like Prescott?"

"Yes, but I am not going to hand over my employees to a bunch of government hatchet men. They are the ones that would pay the highest price for my folly, not me."

"Are you saying you're going to try to cut a deal? Turn yourself in and hand them Prescott in return for a guarantee that they won't destroy your company?"

"I don't cut deals, Joseph."

There it is—that damned honor. "Too proud to turn yourself in, is that it? You want me to do your dirty work for you. But I don't think it's fucking fair to put me in that position."

Minesali said nothing. His Roman nose and chiseled jaw projected like an iconic marble statue.

"Say something, goddamnit!"

"What can I possibly say that would satisfy you? Years ago, I made a decision that I enormously regret. Now you have your own decision to make—one that I shall accept as final." He looked towards the roiling thunderclouds building to the west, as if resigning himself to the storm's approaching fury. "Do what you have to do, Joseph. But tomorrow I am going to meet with Hayden Prescott and settle this matter once and for all."

CHAPTER 73

THE WORLD LITERALLY came to a halt when he passed through the hallway. All it took was one look and people stopped typing at their keyboards, put aside their files and blueprints, stopped speaking in mid-sentence, halted in their tracks. There was just something about him, the way he carried himself. Here was somebody, a man of impeccable taste, someone whose picture one would find in the dictionary next to the word "gentleman."

With Forbes trailing behind him like a foot servant, Vincenzo Minesali continued down the hallway, unfazed by all the eyes upon him, carrying his trademark cane bearing a handcrafted silver dog's head, a cream linen suit hanging gracefully on his narrow shoulders and a peach ascot with blue stars with white rims lending him an Old World charm. His wrinkled face glittered like sterling silver and he held his head high when he walked.

He looked as perfect as Richard Cory.

They were led by a buxom secretary down another hallway until they came to an open office. Hayden Prescott stood at the doorway as if prepared to greet a foreign head of state. His flashy crimson suspenders stood out prominently against his starched white shirt. Minesali didn't spurn the extended hand, but took it politely.

"Hello, Hayden," he said, with precise formality.

"Vincenzo. I appreciate your coming," Prescott replied, but Minesali could tell he was tense as brick.

Prescott waved them inside and closed the door. After shaking hands with Prescott's attorney and completing the introductions, they were ushered to a sleek black leather couch against the wall. Minesali was surprised that Prescott didn't seem to recognize Forbes, who had been present at the negotiations years earlier. A strained uneasiness filled the room as everyone settled into their seats. Minesali's eyes passed over the magazines on the glass table: *Forbes*, *Money*, and the three latest issues of *Rocky Mountain Developer*, the glossy publication produced by Prescott's pro-development lobby, the Council for Front Range Competitiveness.

"I know you're a busy man, Vincenzo, so I will get to the point. We have been closely monitoring Joseph Higheagle for the past two weeks. We know he is conducting investigations on your behalf into activities at Dakota Ranch and Silverado Knolls. What we don't understand is why you would take on this enterprise when it could prove extremely detrimental to your own interests?"

Minesali remained silent a moment before speaking. "I have lived with what we have done for far too long. I feel it is now time for a bit of reckoning."

Prescott started to reach for his tie, but seemed to think better of it. "If I'm not mistaken, we had an agreement."

"No formal contract was ever signed that I am aware of." Minesali raised his eyebrows and glanced at his right-hand lieutenant quizzically. "Right, Mr. Forbes?"

"No, sir, I'm afraid there isn't anything of that nature." His response, coolly terse, produced a slight twitch on Prescott's face, which didn't go unnoticed by Minesali.

"This is not going to accomplish anything except your own destruction. Tell him, Greg."

Bishop cleared his throat and looked down his bulbous red nose. "In cases like these, where the principal responsible party can be identified with absolute certainty, the PRP assumes virtually full liability. That includes fines levied by the EPA's enforcement branch and other applicable agencies, as well as the actual cleanup costs. Even with a no contest plea, a property owner such as my client would be on the hook for no more than ten percent of the total remedial cost. The question is can you afford to roll over like a cocker spaniel and give away tens of millions to Uncle Sam?"

The attorney's barb deflected off Minesali like an arrow striking plated armor. "You make it sound as if doing the right thing were heresy. Funny, but somehow this makes it easier for me."

Prescott stared at him in dumb amazement. "Have you lost your mind?" His eyes darted to Forbes. "Is he on medication?"

"I assure you his health is outstanding for even a man half his age."

Prescott sniffed dismissively and leveled his gaze on Minesali. "You do realize that you could go to jail. And it wouldn't be in any country club, either."

"I will find consolation in the fact that you will be right there with me. Perhaps we could play gin rummy on Saturday nights together. I would think your father would be quite pleased to know that I was keeping an eye on you. By the way, how is your father?"

"This isn't a fucking joke. At your age, you may be a palpable feast for worms, but I'm sure as hell not. I know we've made mistakes. If I had to do it all over again, I would do it differently. But it won't do either of us any good to have this brought out in the open. You should be thinking about a way to get Higheagle to bury the whole thing. Pay him, cajole him, do whatever you have to do, but get him to walk away quietly."

"It's too late for that, I'm afraid."

Prescott turned desperately to his attorney. "Reason with this man. I think he has Alzheimer's."

For the first time, even Bishop appeared flustered. "Mr. Minesali, we understand you are a man of principle and that you were in a sense compelled to do what you did by difficult circumstances. But make no mistake: you will suffer tremendous emotional and fiscal damage if this situation comes to light."

"Don't forget, the truth about Silverado Knolls will come out as well."

Prescott shook his head belligerently. "That's not going to happen."

"Are you sure about that? Mr. Higheagle has found out some interesting things about your operation out there." He tipped his head at the developer's bruised face. "Remember, the night the two of you were getting better acquainted."

Prescott touched his blackened cheek, his face a mixed study in fear and hostility.

"You see, I may bear the lion's share of the responsibility at Dakota Ranch, but Esquire Bishop here shall have to defend you with regard to both properties. I should imagine this will garner him some very handsome legal fees over the next five years. And just so you know, Hayden, I do believe your attorney's estimate of your overall cost burden too low. I should think you would fall more in the twenty-five to thirty million dollar range."

Prescott whirled in his chair and flashed Bishop a stinging look.

"Don't listen to him, Hayden. He's just trying to create a wedge between us."

"He'd better be or you'll be the oldest fucking paralegal in town!"

Minesali smiled like a fox. "Honestly, I was merely being forthright in my assessment of the situation."

Prescott faced Minesali again, his expression transforming from anger to puzzlement. "Why are you doing this? With the rec center completed, the waste is out of harm's way. And besides, there's no way to prove conclusively that it caused the cancer."

"That's where you're wrong."

Bishop held up a hand. "That's total speculation. Impossible to prove."

"I do not concern myself with the legality of the issue. I care about truth, not law. Did the chemicals contribute twenty percent to the cancer? Fifty percent? Seventy? I don't know, nor do I care. All I know is those boys were exposed. They would not have contracted cancer if they had not played in that soil. But I didn't need Mr. Higheagle to tell me this. I knew the answer when my late wife's oncologist informed me that four children had died from a rare brain cancer at Dakota Ranch. That, gentlemen, was the day I knew what a grievous error I had made."

"This is madness. None of us knew things would turn out this way."

"You must come clean, Hayden. It's the right thing to do."

Prescott jabbed his finger at him violently. "You're the one who's going to go down for this! All you're going to do is destroy yourself!"

"You and I have inadvertently killed children. There can be no alternative but that we pay the price for our folly. Resign yourself to that fate and you will not only have learned something from all this, but one day you will be a better man for it."

CHAPTER 74

POISED BETWEEN HIGHWIRE TENSION AND IMPATIENCE, Douglas Hwong, PhD, sat in his car watching the front entrance of Environmental Testing Services. He wore a knee-length laboratory jacket. A black leather briefcase lay on the passenger seat next to him. The parking lot was deserted and no movement was visible in the lobby through the glass doors, but he hoped there soon would be.

Edgy, he glanced at his watch: nearly eight o'clock. The office cleaners had been inside for over an hour now. He could only pray their routine was as predictable as the one at his office and they would be finished soon.

He had waited for nearly three hours. Before the cleaners had arrived, he had watched each and every employee leave the building and drive off. The only vehicles remaining were his Nissan Pathfinder and the rusty Oldsmobile that belonged to the cleaning staff.

Fidgeting with a pen, he recalled the last time he'd been here. It was a routine lab audit two or three years ago. The lab had an excellent reputation, which had been his motivation for stealing away two of its staff members to work for him right after the audit. It was for this reason that he was banking on Higheagle using Environmental Testing Services to analyze the samples collected at Dakota Ranch.

Five minutes later, Hwong saw a flicker of movement behind the glass door. His body tensed. He saw one of the office cleaners, a rotund Hispanic man, heading for the front door carrying a pair of bulky trash bags over each shoulder. Suddenly, the man stopped and turned around, as if someone was calling out to him.

Quick, this is your chance! Go—go now!

Snatching the leather briefcase on the passenger seat, Hwong jumped out of the truck. There was no time to lock the vehicle. He walked purposefully towards the door, concealing himself behind the row of trees next to the walkway.

His heart palpitated wildly.

He went straight to the scrambled number entry keypad on the wall outside the laboratory and pretended to punch in the code. With the cover of the trees and dim light in the parking lot, the man still hadn't seen him yet.

The office cleaner started to push open the door, carrying the two hefty trash bags.

Hwong waited until the man saw him, keeping his hand poised at the keypad, before feigning a look of surprise. "Oh, I didn't see you. Here let me help you."

He moved quickly to the door and held it open.

The man took one look at him in his white laboratory jacket and gave a smile of thanks. Hwong realized he probably spoke only fragmented English.

This was perfect.

Now the other cleaner—a chubby Hispanic woman who looked to be the man's wife—materialized from the south side of the lobby. She walked up carrying a plastic spray bottle and half-filled trash bag, smiling bashfully and hurrying along as she passed through the open door.

Hwong pointed to his briefcase officially and motioned towards the interior of the office. "A lot of work to catch up on. I'll make sure to lock up when I'm done."

The two nodded and shuffled off. Stepping inside, Hwong lingered a moment to watch them head for the heavy steel dumpster on the far side of the parking lot. They tossed their bags into the dumpster, climbed into their beat-up Olds, and drove off.

Smiling, Hwong withdrew a pair of thin latex gloves from his pocket and put them on. He turned and bolted past the illuminated reception area and down the dark hallway without turning on lights. He knew the layout; he had visited the lab several times before during audits. When he was deep inside the office building, far from the front door, he flicked on one set of overhead lights. Then he quickly located the file storage room.

Bland, institutional, and lined with fireproof metal cabinets, it was a large room, about the same size as the storage room at his lab. Each of the cabinets was labeled with a start date for that particular file set and an end date. That was one of the reasons ETS was such an outstanding lab; not only was its QA/QC program impeccable, but its CD-ROM filing system was well organized. He moved down the line until he located the words "APR-JUN 2009" on the sliding drawer of one of the cabinets. Each of the individual drawers was arranged by quarter spanning back to 1998. The previous years must have been in storage. He fingered his way through the clear plastic CD-ROM storage folders until he found the CD for the Dakota analytical data set. He already knew the sampling date from what the maintenance man had told Prescott. Stuffing the CD into his empty briefcase, he turned off the lights and walked out the room.

Stepping into one of the cubicles, he rummaged through the desk drawer. He quickly found a company phone list and perused it from the top down until he found what he was looking for. Don Beckett, Network Administrator. He walked down the main hallway among the offices until he found Beckett's. He didn't step inside the network administrator's office, but instead turned into the dark room across the hall with the red and green blinking lights.

Turning on the light, he quickly discovered that the room did indeed house the local area network, or LAN, as he had suspected. Computer hardware lined the walls of the room: consoles stacked in control panels, a modem and pair of phones, surge protection devices, and a labyrinth of multicolored wires. His eyes zeroed in on the bookcase filled with transparent plastic boxes labeled by year. He opened the one for 2009. It contained twenty or so 90-millimeter tapes, slightly smaller than an ordinary audiocassette. These were the backup tapes for the LAN, which compiled all of the chain-of-custody, raw analytical, and QA/QC data stored or generated by the lab. Scanning the labels, he could see that the backup tapes were compiled weekly.

He found the tape for the week beginning April 17 and set it on the floor. Searching the shelves, he located a case of blank tapes, pulled one out, and laid it on the floor next to the labeled tape. Picking up the labeled tape, he pulled off the adhesive label that read APR 17-23 and carefully affixed it to the blank tape, then placed the counterfeit tape back into the big box. The real tape he stuffed in his briefcase. Now there would be no network tape record of Higheagle's analytical data.

After turning off the lights, he walked down the hallway with his briefcase in hand. The first two tasks of his mission were accomplished. Now he had to purge the electronic project file stored on the LAN. This task he knew would be more difficult than the first two tasks.

He checked every workstation to see if anyone had left a computer not only turned on, but fully logged on with the password already coded in. Several were turned on, but none were past the password stage. He had suspected it wouldn't be that easy, but it was worth a try.

He walked to one of the cubicles and looked over an ETS employee telephone list. Somehow, he had to get hold of an employee's password. He picked one name, Nancy Riley, Assistant Secretary. If anyone would unwittingly leave behind a clue it would probably be a junior secretary. The turnover rate for such positions was high and a new secretary was more likely to leave around a loose scrap of paper with a computer access code than someone who had worked there a long time. His preliminary effort would concentrate on Nancy Riley.

For the next fifteen minutes, he went through her cubicle. He checked her computer, her daytimer, every scrap of paper in her desk to find any clue that might give him her password. But he couldn't find anything. At one point, he typed in NRILEY at the Login prompt to make sure he could gain initial entry. It worked, but he still needed the password to get beyond the simple Login step. He rummaged a second time through her desk and drawers, but still couldn't find anything in her daytimer or paperwork.

Almost absently, he picked up a framed photograph of the woman with several female friends. They were wearing backpacks, posing somewhere in the mountains. He pulled the picture from its frame and looked at the note on the back. Nancy, Joan, Susie, Karen, and Sparky, Elk Mountains, Fall 2007.

Sparky?

He flipped the picture over again and saw only four women. Shaking his head with puzzlement, he studied it more closely. Eventually he saw the head of what looked like a golden retriever in the bottom right hand corner. The glittering gold and maroon autumn foliage had obscured the mutt. He hopped into the secretary's chair, his frustration giving way to possibility. At the Password prompt he typed SPARKY.

It didn't work.

He typed in SPARKY2007.

He was stunned when the computer actually thrummed to life. He couldn't believe that he was in as he stared at the updating screen. Thank God people were often simplistic when it came to passwords.

He breezed into Windows and clicked his mouse several times until he was into the folders that contained the laboratory's analytical results. The folders were listed by year and month. He quickly pulled up APR 2009. Staring at the screen, he realized that he needed the laboratory identification number to actually access the file. That wouldn't be a problem.

He opened his briefcase and withdrew the chain-of-custody form that listed the lab ID number for the samples submitted on April 17 by Higheagle. He clicked the mouse on the appropriate file and moments later he heard the computer humming. The file was being deleted.

The file had never existed.

He smiled wickedly as the computer continued to gobble up the last record of the samples collected at Dakota Ranch.

And then he saw something on the chain-of-custody form.

Oh shit! No!

In the right hand corner, in the column below the Remarks heading, he saw the words Split-A, Split-B, Split-C, and Split-D next to four of the sample numbers. A large hand-drawn parenthesis enclosed the letters and read simply, "Splits sent to Lab #2, 4/17/09."

Higheagle had collected four duplicate samples and sent them to another lab!

An unknown lab!

Any one of more than a dozen Denver-based analytical laboratories that Hwong had little hope of tracking down!

The anger hit him like a sledgehammer. He pounded his fists into the secretary's flimsy desk like a toddler throwing a tantrum.

But still, he had to make sure. He checked the form once again, to make sure his eyes weren't betraying him, but the notation was still there. The blood boiled in his veins.

Crumpling the form in anger, he stuffed it in his briefcase and turned off the computer. He felt his heart racing uncontrollably, his mind reeling with desperation at the thought that he might go to prison once again for a very long time.

Douglas Hwong, PhD, was through with fucking computer games.

CHAPTER 75

STANDING IN FRONT OF THE CAMPUS LOUNGE, Higheagle scanned the street for Dan Markworth, who was supposed to be here by now, then looked around for the elusive Vic Shard. He didn't see either one of them, though he was certain the private investigator was lurking furtively somewhere in the shadows, like a hyena. Turning around, he stepped to the front door, his hair tightly wound with traditional plaits, a light buckskin shirt hanging down to his faded jeans.

The Campus—as the bar was affectionately known—wasn't within two miles of Denver University or any other college campus, but this geographical tidbit had apparently never been taken into consideration by the original proprietors of the establishment. It had once been more juke joint than upscale yuppie pub, but with the emergence of Denver as Mecca for the disenchanted from other states, the interior had undergone a major facelift to cater to the new tony clientele.

Higheagle opened the door and stepped inside. There was smoke and laughter and the Allman Brothers' *Nobody to Run With* thrummed from overhead speakers. He took one of the booths along the right side of the restaurant, setting down his overflowing business satchel on the gray vinyl seat.

Five minutes later, Markworth stepped into the bar and looked around. Higheagle could tell that he was agitated as he motioned him from the booth.

"Sorry I'm late," Markworth said as he sidled up.

"No problem. I just got here myself."

A plate of bubbling chili rellenos flew past. Markworth pushed his thick-framed glasses up his nose, looked around one last time to make sure he wasn't being followed, and slid into the booth.

"You okay, Dan?"

"Is it that obvious?"

"Yeah. You want to tell me what's going on?"

"They told me to back off, Joe."

"Who?"

"Dahlquist and Prescott. They said they'd destroy me if I so much as mention chemical exposure played a role in the cluster."

"So what you're saying is they got to you."

"Yeah," he said ruefully, "they fucking got to me."

The tense silence that followed was broken by the voice of a friendly young waitress in a checkered shirt and blue jean skirt. "Evening fellas. What can I get you to drink?" she said as she set down a pair of menus, a basket of oily tortilla chips, and a bowl of chunky red salsa.

"Fat Tire," Higheagle said.

"Coors Light for me."

The waitress walked off. Higheagle looked at Markworth. "Tell me what happened."

"They gave me three options: quit my job voluntarily, continue the cancer study as I see fit and be terminated involuntarily, or play along. I told them I'd play along."

"You can't just roll over like this. I told you over the phone, I know what's happened at Dakota and Silverado and I now have the proof to back it up."

"Silverado? You didn't say anything about Silverado. Prescott's dumped out there too?"

"If you want to hear more, you're going to have to help me out."

"Meaning what exactly?"

"Meaning I need you to go with me to the EPA. Or the Justice Department."

"No way. Dahlquist will crucify me. I've got a family to—"

"You won't even be able to face your family if you don't go through with this. How old is Dan Junior now? Ten, right? Roughly the same age as those boys. Tell me, would you stand by and do nothing if it was your own fucking son?"

The table turned suddenly very quiet. Markworth looked away and Higheagle knew he had struck a nerve.

"I can't do this without you, Dan. I trespassed on private property and you're respected in the regulatory community. You know people at the federal level from your work on Summitville, Rocky Flats, and the Arsenal. They'll listen to you."

"Oh yeah, the EPA just loves me after Summitville. Have you been listening to what I've been saying? A line's been drawn and I can't cross it. You can call me a coward—hell, you can call me anything you like—but I'm not going to let them take away my job. It's not just my family. I've worked too hard to get where I am now to throw it all away."

Higheagle could feel the anger building inside him and decided to try another angle. "I've seen Prescott's operation at Silverado first hand. It's even bigger than I thought."

As expected, Markworth's interest was piqued. "You went out there and sampled?"

"Seemed the thing to do."

"What did you find?"

They looked up as the waitress reappeared with their beers. She took one look at them and said, "What's going on here, boys? You plotting to overthrow the Gov'mint or something?"

Higheagle grinned. "Yeah, you wanna help us?"

"Love too, but unfortunately I've got to work tonight." She set the beers and frosty mugs down on the table with a clunk. "One Fat Tire and one Coors Light. Now what can I get y'all to eat?"

"We're sticking to liquid refreshment," Higheagle said.

"All right, just let me know when you need a refill." She smiled perfunctorily and walked off.

Higheagle watched her for a moment before turning back to Markworth. "I found enough metals to start a foundry. Chromium six, copper, arsenic, lead, iron, mercury. Here I brought you a copy of the results for both Dakota and Silverado."

He pulled out two manila envelopes and pushed them across the table. Then he withdrew a map showing the locations where he and his grandfather had collected soil samples at Silverado Knolls. He set the map in the middle of the table and spent the next few minutes explaining the analytical results shown on the map.

As Markworth began to grasp the enormity of the operation, he looked like a changed man. "Jesus, it looks like the same set-up as Dakota. They're filling in this drainage here, right?"

"Except they're placing three feet of backfill on top. Prescott knew he'd made a mistake at Dakota with only one foot of cover soil. He knows that's how the kids were exposed."

Markworth took a gulp of beer. "So you actually saw the operation?"

"Yeah, when I was sampling." He pointed to the map. "They're filling in the drainage by working downslope from the headwall, just like they did at Dakota."

"So the work is completed in stages?"

"First, they get their grading permit from the city and county and conditional approval to proceed with light blade work from you folks. This is prior to your approving the site assessment reports. Then they launch the preliminary field phase: clearing, grubbing, and road construction. This does two things. It allows them to have heavy equipment on the site continuously throughout the home construction phase, and it allows them to blend the waste dumping in with the general grading. The third and final phase is the actual waste dumping and capping. They scrape soil around the areas where they're dumping so it looks like a routine grading operation. Then they cap the waste with native soil and compact it, controlling dust emissions with water trucks. I'm telling you, it is one smooth-ass operation. The only place you can see the fill is along the downstream end, or if you look closely at the aerials."

"Unbelievable. And now Prescott's fully permitted to begin construction at Silverado. We approved the environmental impact and site investigation report yesterday."

"So there's no way to stop him without bringing charges against him. Meanwhile, here I am with all this great data, but it was collected while I was trespassing."

"Not all of it. You told me you saw fill patterns in the aerials at Dakota. Plus there's the results from the original Dakota investigation, the analyses handled by that California lab. I'm just wondering who the generators are. Prescott may be less important than those guys. And there's got to be more than one. At Dakota you've got dioxins and metals, but at Silverado it's just metals. Any idea of who the PRPs are besides Prescott?"

He wasn't about to tell Markworth about Minesali, not yet anyway. "Nope," he lied.

"You sure about that?"

"Yep."

"But you have suspicions?"

"We'll find out who the generators are soon enough, but for now I just want to know who you think we should talk to."

"Not we, you. Remember?" He leaned forward in his seat. "But your best bet is probably the EPA enforcement branch."

"Not the environmental crimes unit of the DOJ?"

"What, you know someone there?"

"Only this guy." He yanked out his wallet and pulled out a business card. He pushed it across the table towards Markworth.

"You laminated it? Jesus, you are paranoid." He read the name aloud. "Ben Carrington, Director, EPA Office of Enforcement, Criminal Investigations Division."

"Said to call him day or night."

"You made some friends in high places with that Quantrill business. This just proves you don't need me."

"I trespassed, Dan. I'm not going in there alone."

"I already told you that I have to stay out of this. The feds don't give a shit who gets stepped on to get what they want. And now...well, now things have gotten even more complicated."

"How's that?"

"There's two more cancer cases."

"You're shitting me! Who are they?"

"Twin brothers, Toby and Jeremy Franzen. Twelve years old. Actually, their cases are both several months old. The family moved to Castle Rock last fall and the boys were going to a clinic near there. Apparently, the doctor at the clinic is the kids' uncle. But this doctor, he couldn't figure out what was wrong, so he referred the boys to a cancer specialist. The specialist called our office this morning. It looks like both cases are medullablastoma."

Higheagle flushed with anger. "Goddamnit, Dan, you've got to come in with me—now more than ever!"

Markworth started to protest, but seemed to realize it was pointless. He looked torn between self-preservation and a deep inner need to do the right thing.

"All right, suit yourself. I'm going to finish my reports this weekend. And on Monday, I'm going to take my story to Carrington or some other regulator who gives a shit. I'll give you until then to change your mind."

Biting his lip, Markworth looked down guiltily. "Prescott is giving a speech Monday night in front of that developers' group of his, the Council for Front Range Competitiveness. I heard about it from a friend who works at Van Schaack."

Why didn't you tell me this before? "Where's he giving the speech?"

"Executive Suites in Littleton. Seven o'clock."

The waitress came by, startling them again. Higheagle asked for the bill, which she swiftly delivered and he promptly paid in cash. "Let's get out of here."

They slid from their seats and walked out the door to the sound of Nirvana's *Come As You Are.* When they reached the asphalt parking lot on the south side of the building, Higheagle stopped to make one last appeal.

But the words never had a chance to leave his mouth.

CHAPTER 76

WHEN SHARD HEARD THE ROARING ENGINE, he expected to see an overzealous reveler who had planted himself behind the wheel with a few too many suds in his belly.

In the next instant, he realized how wrong he had been.

From the narrow alley to the west, the Nissan Pathfinder screamed into the parking lot like a bat out of hell. A flash of light hit the truck just as it made the turn, and Shard recognized the face behind the wheel. It was the face of a man that he had not expected. The man's teeth were bared like a wolf and his eyes were swollen to the size of plums as they locked onto their target. The hands gripped the steering wheel tightly, like the tentacles of an octopus, and Shard was momentarily paralyzed.

What could he do to warn Higheagle and Markworth?

Mind racing, synapses firing, he did the only thing he could do. He slammed his palm into the horn of his Jeep Cherokee.

The warning did not go unheeded.

ψψψ

Higheagle turned to face the onrushing truck.

The screeching tires had alerted him that something wasn't right, but it wasn't until he heard the shrill blast of a horn that he made a voluntary reaction to turn. He locked onto the bulging, rage-filled eyes bearing down on him and knew instantly who they belonged to. At the last second, before what was sure to be a disastrous impact, he drove his shoulder into Markworth to knock him out of the way.

But it wasn't enough.

The right front end of the Nissan tore through him and gobbled him up like a giant snake, spitting out a severely crushed body as the right rear tire disengaged. The thumping sound had a grotesque aura of finality about it as Higheagle rolled safely out of the way.

The truck came to a skidding halt, sending a plume of smoking rubber into the air.

A woman turning the corner from the bar screamed. The man with her yanked her by the arm and the two disappeared behind the wall.

Higheagle scrambled to his feet.

The attacker hesitated, as if debating whether to throw the truck into reverse and make another pass to ensure the kill.

Higheagle looked at Markworth, sprawled on the asphalt. The body gave an involuntary spasm then went deathly still.

The attacker threw the truck into reverse.

Heart thumping madly, Higheagle ran to the suddenly motionless Markworth, hoisted him up, and began dragging him towards the gap between two parked cars.

The truck accelerated towards him as he pulled Markworth away.

Twenty feet.

The sound of the screeching tires pierced his ears.

Ten feet.

The synthetic smell of seared rubber shot into his nostrils.

Impact.

The truck smashed into the side of a Buick. In that desperate instant—right before the Cheyenne flung himself and Markworth onto the pavement—he heard the jarring sound of metal being crushed. Out of the corner of one eye, he saw sparks fly, and a strip of bumper was ripped from the Buick and thrown to the asphalt.

Then the truck lurched forward and Higheagle heard a loud blast ring out over the sound of the screaming rubber.

Was that a gunshot?

The rear windshield of the truck exploded, shards of glass cascading down on Higheagle as he shielded the immobile Markworth with his body. Frightened off by the gunshot, the driver of the truck sped away, turned right onto University Boulevard, and was gone.

Higheagle looked around to see who had fired the shot—was it his guardian angel Shard again or someone else?—but he saw no one. Kneeling down, he checked Markworth's pulse. The crushed body lay motionless, like a child's rag doll dropped carelessly to the floor.

But there was still a faint heartbeat.

CHAPTER 77

WHEN THE PHONE RANG, Sally was looking in on Tommy.

He had that transcendent glow that children have when they sleep, that perfect combination of uncontrived innocence and beauty that makes a parent temporarily forget the trials and tribulations of parenthood. Hearing the phone, Sally pulled Tommy's cowboy and Indian quilt to his chin, folded it over, kissed his forehead, and quietly left the room, leaving the door partly open. She walked quickly but quietly down the hallway to her bedroom, wondering who could be calling at this time of night.

She picked up the phone on the third ring and spoke in a low voice, not wanting to wake up Tommy or her parents. Bill and Gail McTavish had flown in this afternoon from Phoenix to help with Tommy, who had been released from the hospital. "Hello?"

"Sally, this is Joe! I need to talk to you!"

His urgent voice took her off guard. "What...what is it?"

"Doug Hwong just tried to run over me and Dan Markworth."

"Where?"

"Outside the Campus Lounge. Dan's badly hurt."

"Is he going to make it?"

"I don't know. It doesn't look good. But right now, I need you to do something for me. Are your parents there with you and Tommy?"

"Yes, they're sleeping."

"Okay, good. Now I don't think Hwong or Prescott would try to harm you, but I still think you should take some precautions. Make sure all the doors and windows are fastened tightly, and turn on your outside lights."

Her entire body froze as a tremor of fear lanced through her. Was it her imagination, or had she just heard a sound downstairs? She paused to listen, suddenly breathless, but there was nothing. Was her mind playing tricks on her?

"Shouldn't I just call the police?"

"They'll ask questions, Sally. Questions I don't think you—or I—are prepared to answer right now. So here's what I want you to do. Call 911 and say that you heard noises outside your house. Ask them to send a patrol car to check it out."

Her head swam with vexation. *I can't believe this is happening! Tommy was just released from the hospital and now someone may be trying to kill us!*

"Sally, are you there?"

There it was—the sound again—like a soft footfall. She was suddenly acute of every sense. "Yes, yes, I'm here," she answered, her apprehension growing. She wondered if she should tell Joseph that she really was hearing noises—inside, not outside, her house—but she told herself that it was just her imagination.

"When the cops get there, go ahead and talk to them, but don't say anything about the hit-and-run or my investigation. And don't say anything to Tommy or your parents."

"I don't understand why you don't just go to the police."

"Because I'm close to wrapping things up and if I bring the cops in it could ruin everything. I promise that I'll contact them tomorrow once I've gotten hold of the EPA criminal investigations people. Now I wouldn't be doing it this way if there was a chance that any harm could come to you."

There was a pause, and again Sally felt a curious presence in the house. "Then why are you calling me?"

"I'm just being cautious. Look, I know what I'm doing here. The EPA will understand why I did what I did. The cops won't."

"All right," she relented, and this time she heard a definite footfall at the stairs. It hadn't been her imagination at all. She felt a shiver; suddenly, the room seemed terribly dark and sinister and she felt like she was being stalked.

She covered the mouthpiece with her hand. "Dad, Mom, is that you?"

There was no answer, and then she heard Higheagle again on the other end. "Sally, I've got to go now. Check the house, call for a patrol car, and make sure the cops look around. Good luck."

"Wait, Joseph, I think I hear—"

But he was already gone. Punching off, she exhaled slowly, a taut knot of muscle squeezing her chest. Was it her mom or dad, or was someone really in the house? Struggling to remain calm, she set the phone down on the side table as quietly as possible.

Another footfall invaded the silence. It came from the top of the stairs.

Thinking quickly, she reached for the glittering geode on the table. The size of an orange, it was the only weapon close at hand. When she turned around, a shadow fell across the doorway.

Pressing herself against the wall, she gasped for breath, wondering what to do. She glanced down at the geode, felt the solid weight of it in her hand. Summoning all her courage, she edged closer to the door, the crystalline mass gripped tightly in her right hand.

Slowly, the door crept open.

She raised the rock to strike.

"Good Lord, what are you doing?"

It was her father, dressed in flannel pajamas and staring at her incredulously.

"Jesus, Dad, you scared the hell out of me!"

"I'm sorry, honey. What...what's happening?"

She didn't answer.

"Sally, I'm your father. You'd better tell me what's going on right now."

She went to the window, knowing that if she looked him in the eye, he would know she was lying. "I thought I heard a sound," she said. "I think someone might be out there."

CHAPTER 78

THE 1% ENTREPRENEUR and the lubricious art history major in the crimson fishnet stockings, four-inch fuck-me pumps, and lacy brassiere kissed savagely and fondled one another on the big brass bed. The man ran his fingers along the upper thigh of the woman, stroking delicately and pausing to feel the taut skin of her leg as it pressed through the diamond-shaped openings. The woman gently rubbed his penis and he could feel it throbbing like a garden hose. The smell of incipient sex permeated the bedroom like a mass of hot, wet tropical air. The man knew that in a matter of seconds the pressure would be too great and he would have no choice but to climb aboard for the evening's first full-fledged, from-behind mounting.

And then the phone rang.

Once, twice, and still neither body made any attempt to pull away to answer the call. They were far too along to be interrupted—or so the woman thought.

At the third ring, Hayden Prescott reluctantly pulled himself away from his playmate, cursed under his breath, and picked up the phone from the side table.

"What?"

"Shard here. You alone?" The voice was edgy.

Prescott covered the phone with his hand and looked at his panting partner's cat-green bedroom eyes. He desperately wanted to finish what he had begun, but Shard wouldn't be calling if it weren't important. "I need to take this in private," he said, and he cocked his head towards the door, dismissing his perfectly moist sex kitten.

Pouting like a child, she slid from the bed, put on the white monogrammed bathrobe sitting on the chaise lounge, grabbed her purse, and traipsed off obediently into the living room, where she pulled out a mentholated Virginia Slim and lit it with a monogrammed silver lighter.

Prescott put his mouth to the phone again. "What the hell's going on, Vic?"

"Your boy Hwong's lost control. He just tried to run over Higheagle and Markworth."

"Where?"

"Parking lot outside the Campus Lounge."

"That dive at University and Exposition?" He swung his legs over the edge of the master bed, planting his bare feet on the plush mauve carpet.

"He followed Higheagle there, just like me. I was keeping an eye on him, but then he disappeared and I thought he'd left. He must have driven around to the north side and waited until they came out. He raced in from the alley. I didn't spot him again until it was too late."

"You said, 'tried to run over.' Did he run them over or not?"

"Just Markworth. Higheagle dove out of the way after pushing Markworth to the side."

"Is Markworth dead?"

"I don't think so, but he's definitely in bad shape. I doubt he's going to make it."

"Any eyewitnesses besides yourself and Higheagle?"

"A man and a woman saw at least part of it. I don't think they got the tag number, though."

"Did either Markworth or Higheagle recognize Hwong?"

"I don't think Markworth did. He wasn't looking at the oncoming vehicle. But Higheagle saw him all right. The parking lot's well lit."

Prescott cursed under his breath. Hwong's bungled murder attempt would most likely prove to be another thorn in his side. True, the man had incriminated himself, as planned, but he had failed to eliminate Higheagle and had probably failed to secure the laboratory records as well. If Higheagle talked to the police, as seemed likely, Hwong would soon be a wanted man. If apprehended and interrogated, he might spill what he knew of the waste operation to the police. In that case, Hwong's rash act could lead the police back to Prescott, potentially reopening the door for Marshak, who had officially been taken off the case.

Hearing the wail of sirens in the background, Prescott asked, "Where are you?"

"Across the street. The ambulance just got here."

"Police?"

"Whole army of 'em."

"Are they talking to Higheagle?"

"Not yet. They just got here a minute ago. Shit, where did he go? He was just there."

"What about the other two eyewitnesses?"

"They got the hell out. They didn't want to get involved. But you can bet the cops will find 'em eventually."

Prescott ran a palm through his slick ebony hair, thinking through the situation. Hwong had become a severe liability. If the police got him to talk, Prescott would be in real trouble. There would be a thorough investigation and exhaustive press coverage, a veritable circus-like atmosphere surrounding the case, especially given the prominence of the players involved. Thus far, the police had been thwarted, there was still no public clamor about the childhood cancer cluster, and those pursuing the case were known. Now all that would change.

Unless, of course, something could be done about Hwong.

"Hold on a second," Shard said, interrupting his thoughts. "There he is—it's Higheagle!"

"Where?"

"At the light on Exposition. Jesus, he must have snuck to his car when the cops got here. Either he doesn't feel like talking to them or he's in a real hurry to get somewhere else."

"All right, here's what I want you to do. Follow Higheagle and don't let him out of your sight. Call me every hour. You'll know from the police band if they want him for questioning or if they try to pick up Hwong, right?"

"Yep."

"Good. And Vic, I want you to know I had nothing to do with this."

"The light's changing. Shit, he's moving. I gotta go!"

When he heard the click, Prescott quickly dialed another number. After three rings, a familiar Western drawl trickled forth from the other end.

"Mr. Prescott, what a pleasant surprise. I figured you'd call."

"Got a job for you, amigo—and it needs to be done right away."

CHAPTER 79

"OPEN THE FUCKING GATE, FORBES! I need to talk to him!" Higheagle shouted into the intercom.

"Mr. Minesali has retired for the evening. Come back tomorrow."

"If this gate's not open in the next ten seconds, I'm calling the fucking cops and the old bastard goes to jail! Now open up!"

Higheagle looked at the gate. It still wasn't moving.

"Open it goddamnit!"

After several tense seconds, he heard something unlatch, followed by the sound of grinding metal.

The gate was opening.

Higheagle ran to the War Wagon, jumped in, and drove through the opening, parking the truck in the gravel driveway in front of the sprawling mansion. Stepping from the truck, he looked up at the soaring structure, its elaborate dormers and gables silhouetted against the cloudless night sky almost like gargoyles. There was a certain broken-down-palace feel to the place, a flawed grandeur—like Minesali himself. A waxing moon and a spangle of stars glimmered overhead, throwing eerie silvery illumination over the dark mansion.

Forbes opened the front door. Higheagle dashed towards it, his body language nakedly aggressive.

"I will not let you destroy him," warned the loyal servant.

"I don't think you're in a position to make that call."

"He's suffered enough for what's happened. Nothing can be gained by making him the scapegoat."

"You've known about this all along, haven't you? You've been involved since day one."

"I will not let you destroy him," Forbes repeated, and he stepped grudgingly to the side to allow Higheagle to pass. "He will see you now. But I'm warning you, don't do anything foolish or you will pay dearly for it."

"Don't you threaten me, Forbes. I'm in no fucking mood for it."

Forbes closed the door and led him through the marble-floored hallway, past the two Chippendale chests, and up the crimson-carpeted staircase with the ornate mahogany railing. The silence between them was rife with suppressed anger.

Minesali met them at the top of the stairs. He was dressed in the maroon smoking jacket and black-and-white ascot that Higheagle remembered him wearing at their first meeting. He extended his hand and smiled courteously, but it was clear that he was deeply concerned.

Refusing the hand, Higheagle snapped at Forbes, "Find something else to do."

The servant's eyes narrowed and his hands balled up into fists. It suddenly dawned on Higheagle just how tough the scrappy Welshman truly was. He probably came from twenty generations of coal heavers and bare-fisted brawlers. Clearly, he had been a very strong man in his younger years, and even now, the lingering vestiges of his great upper body strength were still visible through his white button-down shirt and black vest.

"Go ahead—I'll be fine," Minesali said.

"Are you certain, sir?"

"Yes."

For a long moment, Forbes didn't budge. Then, with what Higheagle could tell was enormous self-control, he said, "I'll be in my quarters if you need me."

"Thank you, my old friend," Minesali said, and Forbes moved off reluctantly, his face still flush with protective fury.

There was a moment of awkwardness. Higheagle swallowed against the knot in his throat as his impressions of his first visit to the house stampeded through his mind.

"Would you like to sit down?" Minesali said to break the tense silence.

"No."

"Well then, I hope you don't mind if I do." He sat down in a faded Napoleon chair.

Higheagle was so angry he didn't know where to begin, but he quickly found his voice and told Minesali what had happened to Dan Markworth, leaving no doubt as to whom he believed was ultimately responsible for the tragedy. Throughout, Minesali remained quiet, staring down at the unraveling Portuguese rug beneath his slippered feet. The lines on his face looked like farmer's furrows; the easy expression he had exhibited during past meetings was nowhere to be found.

"I am truly sorry about this," the old man said softly when Higheagle was finished.

"Of course you are. You're always sorry—but people still keep getting hurt anyway."

"I've already told you, as well as Hayden Prescott, that I am willing to accept whatever decision you make."

"You probably just tried to cut a deal with him to save your own skin."

"It's easier to think the worst of me, isn't it? It doesn't matter anyway. My business cannot last. I'm filing for bankruptcy."

"Is this your new ploy? Feed me a pitiful sob story so I'll show clemency? I can't believe I fell for your act from the beginning."

"Joseph, you are mistaken if you think I am a rich man. My company has been losing money for years. Millions and millions of dollars. Ever since I changed over my chemical processing and distribution operations to what I thought would be a new market—organic pesticides and herbicides. I have tried hard to go green, but the strategy has been a financial disaster."

"You just don't stop, do you?"

Now Minesali looked genuinely wounded, as if some line had been crossed. He stared off at one of his Impressionist-style paintings of a young ballerina with skin the color of a pale, fluted moon. Higheagle wondered how much the painting was worth. It had to be a fortune.

"You know in forty-eight years I have not laid off a single employee. In the end, that will no doubt be my ruin. I have saved jobs, but that's all I have accomplished. Nearly everything I have made the last few years has been pumped back into the company to keep it afloat."

"So I'm supposed to feel sorry for you? You're still worth tens of millions."

"That's not true. When all accounts are settled, I have only this house. And as you can see, even it is falling into serious disrepair."

Surveying the room, Higheagle took in the antique furnishings: the Steinway in the corner, the chintz valances and sashed drapes, the Italian giftwood sconces, the remarkable paintings. But as in his first visit to the house, his eyes were drawn to the imperfections. The air of neglect was everywhere—from the sunlight-faded walls to the dust on the wood furniture to the frayed rug to the peeling finish on the side tables. The outside of the house was even worse, with all the missing roof tiles and broken cobblestones in the driveway and the occasional cracked window and faded brown paint on the timber. Only Minesali's prized gardens looked to be well tended; everything else was falling apart as gracelessly as an aging film star.

"The only reason I stay is because Marguerite loved this old house. And those paintings on the walls are not the works of Impressionist masters. They are copies by nameless artists, each one worth less than a used car."

Despite himself, Higheagle felt an unmistakable tug of sympathy.

"I did my best to make my business prosper for everyone involved. But those days are gone. And Marguerite's house is dying too. I do not say these things to garner your pity. I simply want you to know the truth."

"What the hell am I going to do about you? How can I make sure that you've paid a price for what you've done and at the same time acknowledge your good intentions towards your workers? You've put me between a rock and a hard place. And you know what, I don't fucking like it!"

"You must follow your heart."

"That's just what my damned grandfather would say. Don't you see that tells me nothing? Nothing!"

Minesali appeared drowned in sadness. "I cannot tell you what to do, Joseph. I can only tell you that I am willing to accept whatever you decide. I have done enough damage for one lifetime."

"Why the hell don't you just turn yourself in?"

"Once you have completed your reports with all the supporting documentation, that's precisely what I intend to do. But until that time, my fate is in your hands."

There it was again—that damned code of honor. Why couldn't he have been a greedy murderer like Prescott? Then it would be easy to throw him to the wolves.

"Before the accident, I told Dan Markworth about what I'd found out at Dakota and Silverado. The soil sampling results, everything. Then we talked about what we should do about it, who we should contact to bring this thing to closure. But I never brought up your name. Now why in the hell would I do that?"

Minesali stared emptily at the polished marble fireplace. "I do not know the answer."

"Then what do you suggest I tell Sally and Tommy, the DOJ, the cops? That Hayden Prescott and Doug Hwong are the ones they want. Do I pretend that you have nothing to do with this? And what do I say to Dan Markworth if he lives? And to his wife?"

"You should tell them the truth."

"If I did, you'd spend the rest of your life in prison."

"You and I both know that's probably where I belong."

"You're damn right!" He brought his voice down a decibel, but maintained the biting hostility. "You have a twisted sense of honor, Vincenzo. You'll get your reports from me as planned, but what happens after that will be up to me, not you. I've changed my mind. I don't want you to turn yourself in." His look narrowed as hard and straight as a trunk of pine. "I want that honor for myself."

CHAPTER 80

AS HE STUFFED THE GARDEN HOSE in the exhaust pipe of his Nissan Pathfinder, Hwong dejectedly noted, for the third time, the severe damage to the rear of the vehicle. The evidence that would be collected by the traffic accident investigation unit would undoubtedly be linked to the punctured fender, scratched body paint, and broken taillight. The investigators would have all the physical evidence they would need to link his company car to the crime scene, and the chances of him being able to hide the vehicle were nil. He had failed in his efforts to kill Higheagle and seize the records, and now a look of profound resignation was embedded in the creases of his face.

He picked up the roll of sticky duct tape at his feet and wrapped a long strip around the exhaust pipe and garden hose, effectively sealing the hose inside the larger pipe. He carried the remaining hose a few feet and stuck it in the driver's side window, which he had left cracked open. Closing the window until the hose was held in tightly, he then covered the remaining crack with duct tape. When finished, he climbed into the driver's seat, fired the engine, and put on his favorite Yanni CD.

As recently as a half hour ago, while speeding away from the Campus Lounge, he had harbored the delusion that he could somehow survive his dire predicament. He was a brilliant scientist and leader in his field, and no two-bit crime-scene cop or prosecutor was going to put him behind bars. When he had tried to run down Higheagle and Markworth, he had been in a violent rage, but once he calmed down and put his flawless analytical mind to work, he would be able to finesse the perfect cover-up. If anyone could do it, Douglas Hwong, PhD, could raise reasonable doubt in the minds of simpleminded jurors.

By the time he reached his house, however, the fantasy was replaced by a feeling of imminent doom. Higheagle had identified him and would testify against him. There was also the person who had shot out his rear window. That person was sure to testify too, for it had almost certainly been an off-duty cop or armed law-abiding citizen. Hwong knew he would rot in prison for a decade regardless of whether Markworth died or not.

In hindsight, it seemed like Prescott had planned all along for things to turn out this way. He had wanted the scientist to become irrational and do something stupid, to deflect suspicion from himself. Only minutes ago, Hwong had pleaded for his help, but Prescott had told him he was on his own and there was nothing he could do. The bastard. Obviously Prescott had been scheming all along, waiting to throw him to the wolves. Hwong couldn't believe how foolish he'd been. While Prescott had accounted for every twist and turn, Hwong realized that he had wrongly focused only upon the scientific implications of the evidence, how he could refute the sample results to a jury, how he could destroy the credibility of the opposing expert witnesses. Instead, he should have been establishing a clear record of his relatively insignificant involvement and making sure that Prescott could not double-cross him. After all, he had done nothing more than falsify laboratory data, not that uncommon a practice and one for which the penalties were minor compared to those Prescott should be facing.

But now he had attempted murder. Regrettably, there would be no more speaking engagements, no more accolades from his peers, no more expert witness triumphs in a court of law, no more sterling papers in esteemed scientific journals, no more remarkable presentations before awestruck clients and regulators, no more short courses or webinars delivered to wide-eyed neophytes. The idea that he would be held culpable for a capital crime and would no longer be on top was simply too much to bear.

Suicide seemed the only honorable out.

As the odorless carbon monoxide gas seeped into his lungs, he began to feel drowsy. Little flashes of his childhood and early adult years ran through his mind. He tried to convince himself that he had led a mostly good life, albeit a short one since he was not yet forty. As a young university student vocally supporting democracy, he had escaped the persecution of a dangerous Taiwanese government and immigrated to America, where he had captured two master's degrees and a doctorate at MIT before the age of thirty. He had patiently worked his way up the ladder, eventually started his own lab outfit, and quickly transformed it into a large firm overnight by falsifying a few reports. In his own way, he was a perfect example of the American Dream.

Or at least that's what he was trying to convince himself as he heard a tap on the window and looked into the nose of the suppressor mounted on Zachary Paine's Smith and Wesson .45 semiautomatic.

Paine jerked open the car door with his left hand, keeping the gun steady on Hwong with his right. He wore a pair of black leather gloves and spoke in a twangy Texas drawl.

"I reckon you got two choices, Jackie Chan. A slow and painful death after I shoot off your dick and kneecaps—or a nice quiet suicide just the way you were doing it before I showed up. The first is on my terms, with a lot of blood and needless suffering. The second is on your terms, without any pain. And all you gotta do for the second is come inside and perform one last little service for Mr. Prescott."

Lightheaded from the carbon monoxide and unsure whether this was really happening, Hwong hesitated.

Paine squinted like an old time gunfighter. "Which is it gonna be?"

Scared witless, unable to summon the will to resist, Hwong decided that it would be best to take the second option. "I-Inside," he stammered. "I'll go inside."

Paine reached across his lap, turned off the engine, and yanked him out of the seat by his collar. "A wise choice, Jackie Boy—a very wise choice. Why subject yourself to torture when you can go peacefully? Do things on your own terms, that's what Momma used to say." He jabbed him in the back with the nose of the gun, pointing him towards the door.

When they stepped inside the kitchen, Paine shut the door behind them with the heel of his cowboy boot. "Now fetch a piece of paper and something to write with. Slowly now—so's I can see every single hair on your knuckles."

With trembling hands, Hwong opened one of the drawers and pulled out a blue ballpoint pen and a pad of paper. He was so scared he thought he would wet himself. "What am I supposed to d-do with this?"

Paine smiled crookedly, the jagged edges of his face seeming to sharpen. "Well Jackie Boy, this is what's called a suicide note." He pointed the gun at his head. "Now listen up 'cause I'm only going to go through this once. Then, if you do right by Mr. Prescott, you can go back in the garage and finish your business."

CHAPTER 81

LEAVING MINESALI, Higheagle drove to the hospital, where he had told Dan Markworth's wife, Sylvia, that he would meet her and the police. Keeping to the left lane of University southbound, he flew past the towering oak and elm trees planted at regular intervals along the boulevard, rehearsing in his mind what he would say to the cops. It was obvious that he, and not Markworth, was the true target of the hit-and-run, but he couldn't tell that to the police. Nor could he tell them about what he and Markworth had talked about, that the driver of the vehicle was Hwong, or about his little side trip to Minesali's. If he did, it would only be a matter of time before they started asking a lot of tough questions about his investigation.

He felt badly for Markworth, but whatever he said or chose not to say to the cops would be of little consequence to him. Of course, he would describe the full details of the hit-and-run and eventually he would hand over Hwong, but he couldn't possibly tell them about his escapades at Dakota and Silverado or his dealings with Prescott and his henchmen, not until he completed his reports and struck a deal with the EPA.

He swung the War Wagon into the parking lot of Park View Hospital, cut the engine, and got out. Walking briskly through the automatic doors into the emergency wing, he spotted a pair of uniformed policeman armed with semiautomatics, batons, and pepper spray. The older one, who was obviously in charge, had a thick black mustache and hooked nose that made him resemble Groucho Marx, except that he looked like he had no sense of humor whatsoever. The younger one was short and square, with a buzz cut and powerful muscles that stretched his immaculate uniform to the bursting point. Overall, they looked like the kind of men law-abiding civilians would want protecting their streets from murderers, rapists, crack dealers, and the like; however, they didn't look as though they would be open-minded to his unique situation. He felt suddenly self-conscious with his braided hair and buckskin shirt.

The older officer stepped forward aggressively. "You Higheagle?"

"Yeah."

"We need to talk to you."

"I figured you would. That's why I instructed Sylvia Markworth to inform you that I would meet the police here at the hospital. Is Dan going to pull through?"

"He's listed as critical."

Higheagle looked down the hallway. "Where is Sylvia Markworth?"

"She's outside the ER. We've already spoken to her. But right now, we need to ask you some questions. First off, why did you leave the scene?"

"I didn't leave the scene. I got in my car and chased after the assailant. But unfortunately, I didn't catch him."

"So the driver was male."

He pictured Hwong's bulging eyes and gritted teeth. "Yeah. He headed south on University. I went after him once two people came over to take care of Dan."

"And that's when you called 911 and Sylvia Markworth?"

"That's right."

"You know it's a criminal offense to leave the scene of a hit-and-run," the younger one said, sounding as though he was reading straight from a police procedural manual.

"Look, I just wanted to catch the bastard. I drove all the way to I-25."

The older cop continued to eye him suspiciously. "Have you been drinking?"

"I had one beer with Dan before the incident. Is that relevant?"

Neither of them responded. Instead, the older one asked him to describe what had happened during the hit-and-run. It took five minutes, and Higheagle told them only what he thought they needed to know. By the end, the older cop still looked skeptical.

"So let me get this straight. You and Markworth had a beer at the Campus Lounge, and when you left, he was run over by a car and you got away without a scratch. Is that what you're telling us?"

Higheagle didn't like what the cop was insinuating, that he was somehow responsible for what had happened, or had even played a part in it. "You conveniently left out the part where I tried to push him out of the way. And where I pulled him to safety when the driver came back to finish the job."

The two officers looked at one another, chafing at his impertinence. The younger one cleared his throat. "Do you think the driver was targeting you and Markworth both, or just Markworth?"

"I assumed he was after Dan."

"Are you sure you've never seen the person behind the wheel before?"

"I don't think so. But it happened so fast, I can't be sure."

The older cop took over the line of questioning. "What is your relationship to the victim?"

"I've worked with Dan on environmental cleanup projects over the years. Like I told you, I'm a geologist with my own firm, Higheagle Environmental."

"So you two are friends and you were just meeting to have a beer? It wasn't a work-related meeting that someone else might have known about?"

Higheagle ignored the first part of the question so that he didn't have to lie outright. "I don't think so."

The older cop squinted in the direction of his plaits. Higheagle could tell he didn't much care for them—probably thought it was some kind of hippie thing. "You said that the car used by the assailant was a dark Japanese model SUV. Can you give us something more? Anything special you remember about it?"

"All I know is it was a Toyota, Honda, Nissan, something like that. It all happened so fast."

"What color would be your best guess? Blue, green, black?"

"Dark blue, but I'm not positive. It turned the corner really fast and was right on top of us."

The younger one said, "You told us that you moved the victim. Why did you do that again?"

"Because he was hurt and the guy was coming back after us in reverse. I was just trying to get Dan out of there."

"The assailant, was he white, black, Hispanic?" asked the older one.

He decided to give up something more. "Asian, I think."

"Tall, short, thin, stocky?"

"Medium built, I guess."

Both cops frowned. Higheagle could read what they were thinking: Why hadn't he recalled these details during the first run-through?

"Look, the only thing I can remember is that it was an Asian man in a dark blue Japanese SUV."

"You're sure you didn't catch any tag numbers?"

"Positive." Looking down the hallway, Higheagle saw Sylvia Markworth with her young son and daughter. She was carrying a striped bag over her shoulder. She stopped a short distance away, pulled some toys from the bag, and set them up for the kids to play with before coming over to join the group.

Higheagle stepped towards her. "I'm really sorry about this, Sylvia. Have you heard anything?"

"It's still too early to tell. You weren't able to catch the guy, were you?"

"I'm sorry, I lost him." He felt a stab of guilt for not being up front with her about the driver being Hwong. He reminded himself that he had no other choice. He could not afford to tell the police what had really happened until he could cut a deal with the EPA. All he needed was a day or two.

"I don't understand why you two had to meet so late. I mean, couldn't it have waited until Monday?"

This was what he had feared, that in coming to grips with what had happened to her husband, Sylvia Markworth would somehow blame him or say something that would make him look suspicious in the eyes of the cops. "Unfortunately, it couldn't wait."

"Did the attack have something to do with what you and Dan were working on at Dakota Ranch?"

As the last two words rolled off her tongue, Higheagle felt the blood leave his face all at once. This was exactly what the cops were looking for—a motive, and the simpler the better—and his only chance was to squash the speculation quickly. "I don't see how. Our work isn't top secret or anything. Just routine environmental stuff."

"Dan's mentioned the project to me, briefly. He said there were some potential environmental impacts out there that you both were looking into."

Higheagle's heart sank. Sylvia Markworth probably knew very little about what was going on, but she knew enough to open the door for the cops. His fears were confirmed when he looked at them.

"You're doing an environmental study at Dakota Ranch?" the older cop asked gruffly. "That's what the meeting was about?"

"Partly," he equivocated.

"I thought you said the meeting wasn't work-related?"

"We talked about a lot of things."

Sylvia Markworth glanced worriedly at her children, who had stopped playing with their toys to watch the exchange.

"What does your study involve exactly?"

"That's confidential."

The older officer gave the younger one *The Look* and Higheagle cringed. He knew that if there was one thing cops hated, it was being told something was confidential. They wanted a world without secrets, which was somewhat understandable since they were supposed to solve crimes.

"Look, pal. Mrs. Markworth's husband has been seriously injured in a hit-and-run. If you have information about who might be responsible, you need to tell us."

He knew he was trapped. If he refused to answer, it would appear as though he was withholding something or had played a part in what had happened. On the other hand, if he came clean, the cops would probably detain him indefinitely, pestering him with endless questions about things that had nothing to do with the hit-and-run, and his investigation might be compromised.

"I'm sorry, but I can't talk about what Dan and I discussed." He looked at Sylvia Markworth for support, but she was clearly siding with the cops. In her view, anything that might help reveal the identity of the maniac who had run over her husband needed to be brought out into the open.

The younger cop pulled the older one to the side, out of earshot of Higheagle and Sylvia Markworth, and whispered something. Then the older one stepped forward with an exaggerated air of authority. "We're going to need to continue this at the station."

"No, I'm staying here until I know Dan's going to be all right."

"There are inconsistencies in your story that need to be cleared up. You need to come with us."

"Look, I've told you everything I know. If you want me to go back to the parking lot and show you what happened, I'll do it. But I'm not talking about what Dan and I discussed. Period."

The older cop turned to face Sylvia Markworth. "I think you'd better return to your kids, ma'am. We appreciate your cooperation."

She looked at Higheagle, unsure of what to do.

"I said that will be all, Mrs. Markworth."

Visibly torn, she went to her children, quickly gathered up their toys, and herded them down the hallway to the waiting area, looking over her shoulder nervously.

The older cop turned back to him. "Let's step outside."

Higheagle's mind worked frantically. *Should I make a run for it?*

The older cop looked down the hallway to the waiting area, his face a study in concentration, like a chess player planning his next move. Sylvia Markworth was busily attending to her children. The two elderly people near the coat rack appeared half-asleep, while the bearded man sitting near the sliding doors was buried in his newspaper. The two nurses behind the emergency counter were quietly chatting.

The moment seemed to unfold in slow motion and Higheagle had the horrible feeling something bad was about to happen.

"We need you to come to the station and make a statement," the older cop repeated. "If you refuse, we'll be forced to handcuff you."

"Under what authority. You haven't made an arrest."

"How about this?" In a crisp motion, he yanked his heavy black baton free and jabbed Higheagle in the stomach. He delivered the blow quickly, precisely, like a featherweight prizefighter throwing a well-timed jab. In the next instant, the younger officer yanked out his handcuffs, jerked Higheagle's arms back savagely, and clicked the cuffs into the locked position.

Higheagle gasped for air, but it would not come.

"What's the charge, Lieutenant?"

The veteran smiled truculently. "Resisting arrest and striking a uniformed police officer. Now let's get his redskinned ass out of here before he assaults us again."

They each grabbed an arm and, with brutal efficiency, escorted Higheagle to the emergency wing exit, the younger officer reciting a Miranda warning. As the trio passed the waiting area, Higheagle looked at Sylvia Markworth, but she turned away, choosing not to get involved. He then made brief eye contact with the man sitting near the exit. The man's paper slid down a couple of inches, exposing a heavy brown beard and the jet-black jacket and stiff white collar of a clergyman.

The man winked.

Recognizing the familiar face beneath the disguise, Higheagle smiled with secret satisfaction as he was shoved unceremoniously through the automatic doors.

CHAPTER 82

AFTER BEING FINGERPRINTED AND PHOTOGRAPHED, the Cheyenne found himself sitting on a cold steel bench in the holding cell of the District 7 police station. The cell was cavernous and institutional, covered floor to ceiling in cold gray concrete that echoed with the low, angry voices of a dozen petty criminals of varied dress and skin color. The pungent stench of vomit emanated from the detox room to Higheagle's right. He sat next to a young college kid, a junior at nearby Denver University, working on his third DUI and cradling his head in his hands as if he had just been found guilty of first-degree murder.

The main detention cell served as the temporary housing for all manner of low-level felons: drunk drivers, dope peddlers, spousal abusers, bar room brawlers. Those arrested for more serious crimes wore orange jail suits and were kept in the small Plexiglas-enclosed rooms that lined the main holding cell, each six-by-six pen holding one individual. A huge black man in one of the cells had his pants down to his ankles and was masturbating wildly while babbling something from Psalms.

Higheagle wanted to throw up.

He knew he didn't belong here with the dregs of the Mile High City. But here he was, against his will, arrested and booked like a common fucking criminal.

He had been in the putrid holding cell for nearly two hours when a Germanic-looking female cop with close-cropped hair and glacial-blue eyes appeared behind the vertical bars and barked his name like an SS guard. Higheagle followed her through the now quiet booking room, past the desk sergeant and the property, evidence, and report writing rooms, and into something resembling a cheap business office. Dirty gray linoleum spread underfoot and a brown pressboard table occupied the center. The table held a tape recorder and was surrounded by six plastic chairs. A few insipid framed pictures of airplanes and sports cars hung from the walls. He was clearly in the interrogation room, and though it was less sterile than the historical cinder-block variety with hot lights, rubber hoses, and an army of brass-knuckle-bearing detectives, Higheagle found the attempts to conceal its true identity superficial at best.

Seated at the table were the two men he was counting on to bail him out of the mess he was in: his grandfather, who hadn't worked a criminal case in a decade; and Ben Carrington, Director of the EPA Region 8 Office of Enforcement, Criminal Investigations Division, whom he knew, barely, from the Quantrill case and hadn't seen in a year.

"They're only giving us ten minutes, so let's get to it," John Higheagle said.

Higheagle's eyes carried a gentle glow. "Thanks, Grandfather, for being here for me."

"You can thank me when it's over. You know Mr. Carrington here. By the way, it wasn't easy rousting him out of bed at one o'clock in the morning."

The auburn-haired, hawk-faced Carrington reached across the table with a bony hand. "I had a feeling one day you'd call me again."

Higheagle's hand settled into Carrington's. "I'd hoped it would be under better circumstances. I appreciate your coming here during off hours and everything."

Carrington sat back down, pulled off his wire-framed spectacles, and rubbed his eyes. "Well, your timing was good. I was due for some criminal intrigue."

John Higheagle checked to make sure that the tape machine in the center of the table was off. Then he pulled the tape from the recorder and set it on the table.

Carrington glanced over at his notepad. "So, Joe, your grandfather's told me the basic facts of the case. But I still have a few questions. From what I've learned so far, I may not have enough pages here to take the full story. Seems you've been busy the last couple of weeks."

"Been running around like a fire ant that's had its hill stomped. Where do you want me to start?"

"How about the beginning?"

John Higheagle cleared his throat, giving a deliberate signal. "Be sure not to leave anything out. I wouldn't want any discovery down the road to sully your reputation—or mine."

Higheagle gave a nod—signal received. "All right, here we go. The whole truth and nothing but the truth, so help me God..."

ψψψ

Ten minutes later, when he had finished his briefing, a squatty bulldog of a man swaggered into the room with an imperious air. Higheagle's jaw dropped and he felt himself wanting to coil up in a fetal position.

Just my luck—fucking Marshak!

He thought back to his first run-in with the man after the break-in at his house. Marshak had grilled him mercilessly. Throughout it all, he had the uncanny feeling that the veteran detective could actually read his goddamned mind!

And now, he was going to have to lie to the son of a bitch again.

There were no introductions as Marshak plopped his stodgy frame into one of the cheap plastic chairs around the table and began fiddling with his ballpoint pen. The detective's face was excruciatingly unreadable and a feeling of dread began working its way through Higheagle's capillaries. He glanced to his left at Carrington, then to his right at his grandfather, and silently hoped that they were up to the task of protecting him from this man. A nondescript uniformed officer sat at a small desk in the corner as an official eyewitness and recorder.

Marshak stopped fidgeting with his pen and pulled out a Marlboro, sparked it, and inhaled deeply, holding the cigarette away from his body with obvious satisfaction.

"This a no-smoking building," said his grandfather. "You can't smoke in here."

Marshak scowled with a look that said, "Who the fuck is going to stop me?"

Higheagle knew that the detective was deliberately trying to provoke him and his grandfather and to demonstrate his authority. A manila folder and soft-covered book rested on the table in front of the detective; Higheagle was dying to know what they contained.

"All right, if you're going to insist on being an asshole and accelerating your own demise through lung disease, Detective," added the old chief, "I'm going to, as Mr. Higheagle's attorney, start out by laying down a few legal ground rules regarding this interview. First, everything we discuss is off the record until we reach an agreement. Second, your department must agree to withdraw the ridiculous charges against my client. The official record must clearly show that he is here voluntarily as a material witness on last night's hit-and-run, and nothing else."

Already Marshak was shaking his head. "You're in no position to––"

"Third, the hit-and-run is related to the environmental investigation my client is working on, an investigation that Mr. Carrington here agrees falls under the authority of the Justice Department's environmental division and EPA. Consequently, my client will not comment on any aspect of this investigation since it could compromise future legal proceedings. Now, if you can agree to these three terms, then Mr. Higheagle will give a full account of the hit-and-run, including naming the driver of the vehicle. And, as a bonus, I'll let you have your precious smoke without filing an official public complaint."

"If Markworth dies, this could turn into a homicide. That would change the scope of the investigation dramatically."

"It doesn't change a damn thing from where I sit. Look, Detective, the last thing you want is to be up to your elbows in Internal Affairs geeks." He quickly flipped through the pages of his notepad. "As I understand it, Lieutenant Lieber— what's his first name?"

Marshak hesitated. "Frank."

"Lieutenant Frank Lieber, it seems, used unreasonable nondeadly force on my client—who happens to be a public hero for his role in solving the Quantrill case—with a baton at approximately midnight at Park View Hospital." He looked at his grandson. "Pull up your shirt and show him the mark."

Higheagle did as instructed. In the powerful overhead lights, the residue of violence was unmistakable. A deep purple welt stained his lower ribcage and the skin was torn where the baton had driven upward. It was obvious that once the wound was photographed and described by a competent medical examiner, the police would have a lot of explaining to do.

Marshak examined the mark impassively. But something in his eyes betrayed an inner worry.

"You can pull down your shirt now," John Higheagle said, and he took a moment to look over his notes. "After my client was struck violently, he was forced to the police station against his will. It was just before they left the hospital that Lieutenant Lieber said, 'Now let's get his redskinned ass out of here.' I would venture that Lieutenant Lieber has something of a history in the use of excessive force and racist language and that, if this incident were to become public knowledge, it would prove embarrassing for the department."

For the first time, Marshak looked genuinely irritated. He exhaled a tiny cloud through his nose. "All right, enough of the Johnnie Cochran routine. We can make a deal."

Now Carrington spoke up in a mollifying tone. "You'll be fully briefed on our investigation. The environmental case itself will be handled in federal court. The hit-and-run will probably be handled by the D.A.'s office in a criminal trial, although there will be some overlap in testimony and witnesses. We're basically only asking that you let us handle the investigation into the environmental misconduct without interference from your office."

"If Mr. Higheagle signs a written statement about tonight's incident and gives us his story on tape, you've got a deal. But we'll need to follow up with him later on other aspects of the case."

John Higheagle frowned. "No written statement. He'll give you his version of what happened tonight on tape and you can ask questions. If you need to follow up later, that's fine. But he won't speculate on motive. If you want the driver of the hit-and-run vehicle, you'll have him in less than five minutes. Otherwise, your department gets blanketed in paperwork and pestered with endless questions from the ACLU and media. Which is it going to be?"

Marshak stamped out his cigarette in the ashtray. "Tape it is then. Let's get on with it."

"My client doesn't need a Miranda warning. He's not a suspect and he's not confessing to anything. He's an eyewitness to attempted murder."

"For your sake—and his—you'd better hope so." Marshak reached across the table and flicked on the record button on the tape machine. For the record, he stated the date and the full names of all those present. Then he had Higheagle give his name, a brief synopsis of his background and occupation, and an account of his meeting with Markworth and the hit-and-run.

Five minutes in, after lighting his second smoke, Marshak asked, "During the meeting, how much did you have to drink?"

"Dan and I both had one beer."

"And where did the car involved in the hit-and-run approach from again?"

"It turned the corner from the alley behind the restaurant."

"Southbound or northbound?"

"The driver came from the north and must have been watching us, because he caught us right as we reached the center of the lot."

"And did you recognize the driver of the vehicle?"

He looked at his grandfather. "Yes. It was Doug Hwong."

"And who is this Hwong?"

"He's director of Arapaho Technologies, an environmental consulting firm and lab in Littleton."

Marshak made eye contact with the cop in the corner of the room to make sure he was taking this down. Turning back to Higheagle, he said, "You're sure the driver was Doug Hwong?"

"One-hundred-percent certain."

Marshak motioned to the uniformed cop. "Get Peterson on this. I want to know this guy's address and the name of his fricking kindergarten teacher in the next ten minutes."

The officer jumped from his seat and was out the door.

Marshak leaned across the table and turned the tape machine off, then took a moment to flip through his notes. "So the reason you didn't tell Lieutenant Lieber about this Hwong was because of the sensitive nature of your study at Dakota Ranch?"

"Don't answer that," John Higheagle warned his grandson.

Marshak frowned. "Look, you're going to have to give me more. It says 'Dakota Ranch' right in my file here. Sylvia Markworth asked you if the hit-and-run might have something to do with what you and her husband were working on. It also says that you became argumentative at that point. And let's not forget I saw some interesting paperwork on this very subject—and on a certain planned development called Silverado Knolls—the other night at your house. Remember, the night you and Gramps here shot two men and withheld the fact that you actually knew Hayden Prescott and this Hwong character. You were trying to keep all this a secret, weren't you, Joe?"

"I think it's fair for Detective Marshak to know a few details," interjected Carrington. "For instance, that Mr. Higheagle's investigation is related to illegal hazardous waste dumping at Dakota Ranch and Silverado Knolls. The detective also has a right to know that Doug Hwong's lab may have falsified analytical reports on behalf of Prescott so these activities could go undetected."

Marshak grinned at John Higheagle, as if he had just scored a point. "Now was that so bad?"

"No, but you'd better not leak any of this to the press."

"Fair enough," Marshak said, but Higheagle sensed he was holding some trick up his sleeve and only pretending to be accommodating. "Why don't you continue, Joe, with how you knew that the man behind the wheel was Hwong." He pressed the record button again.

"I had met Dr. Hwong before. I'd seen him speaking at technical conferences. That's why, last night, I recognized his face even though he came upon us quickly. I locked onto him only for a second or two, but it was enough. The parking lot's well lit, and when he made the turn, his headlights weren't right on us yet. That's when I saw him."

"So this Hwong came at you both?"

"Calls for speculation. Don't answer that."

Marshak glared at the wily tribal lawyer. "All right, what happened next?"

"Just before the impact, when I saw it was Hwong behind the wheel, I dove and knocked Dan out of the way. But I didn't get all of him. What I remember next was looking back and catching a glimpse of Dan being rolled over by the right rear tire."

"What happened next?"

"Hwong came to a stop, maybe thirty feet away. He waited there for a few seconds, like he was deciding whether to finish Dan off and whether he should kill me too. That's when I ran to Dan, picked him up, and began dragging him to where the parked cars were. I threw him down between two cars and dove on top of him. Hwong rushed at us in reverse and crashed into the car next to us. His left rear bumper sustained most of the damage."

"What was the make of the vehicle?"

"It was a Japanese SUV. Not sure what specific make."

"Here, take a look at these." He pushed a soft-covered book across the table to Higheagle. Three of the pages were marked with a yellow adhesive note. Higheagle opened the book and took a minute to look over the pictures of three sports utility wagons shown on the marked pages: a Honda Passport, Toyota 4Runner, and Nissan Pathfinder.

"Pathfinder—I'm sure that's the one."

"Our crime scene crew will have their report done in a couple of hours. And just so you know I'm being up front with you, we've already collected plaster impressions and taken photographs and bag samples of the car paint, rear fender, glass, and broken tail lights." He took a big, lazy drag from his cigarette, as if he relished what was to follow. "Still, one thing still puzzles me."

Higheagle braced himself for the worst.

"You didn't say anything about the gunshot that was fired."

"Gunshot?"

"Yeah, the rear windshield was blown out from a gunshot. No one interviewed so far actually saw who fired the weapon, but several witnesses heard it. We found broken glass everywhere and a slug from a .38 was found embedded in the headrest of one of the parked cars."

"I don't remember hearing a gunshot. But I do remember the rear window blowing out when Hwong hit the parked car. I thought it was because of the impact."

"Somehow, Joe, I don't think you're telling me everything. Whoever fired that shot was trying to protect you. I think you know who it was."

"Yeah, it was his guardian angel the tooth fairy," John Higheagle said. "You have your man, Detective: it's Doug Hwong. We're through here. My client's not going to answer any more of your questions."

Marshak turned off the tape deck. "You've said your piece, Chief. Now it's my turn." He paused to blow smoke out of his nose like some sort of fuming dragon. "Come Monday, my boss and I are going to be up to our elbows in pesky reporters and lawyers from the D.A.'s office before I've taken my morning dump. Because this case isn't just about some petty environmental misconduct, and Hayden Prescott isn't just some two-bit corporate polluter." His gaze shifted to Joseph, who felt his pulse quicken. "You and I both know he was behind that break-in at your house the other night. And he's also responsible for the murder of a certain guy named Gus McTavish. That name ring a bell?"

"I don't know anything about that."

John Higheagle held up his hand. "Don't say another word."

Marshak looked hard at Carrington. "You'd better get things wrapped up on your end quickly. Because frankly, I don't give a shit about environmental misconduct. But I can promise you I will begin taking a strong interest in such things by Monday at noon. Capiche?"

No one said a word. They were all rendered speechless.

But Marshak wasn't finished with his tirade. "We've already searched your

Ford pickup, Joe, and we found no concealed weapons. We did, however, find a computer, some maps, and several reports carefully hidden behind the seat."

Higheagle leapt to his feet. "I've got to have those back! That's the entire case against Prescott!" He looked desperately at Carrington. "You've got to stop him!"

"Um, Detective, do you think that's really—"

"I'll see that the originals are returned to you after we're finished copying them." Marshak looked at his watch. "Should be finished about now anyway."

"You can't do this. You've exceeded your powers," John Higheagle protested.

Marshak smiled. "Is that so?"

The door swung open. The uniformed officer walked back in the room and handed a note to Marshak, who glanced at it and smiled.

"Well, gentleman, if you'll excuse me, I'm going to pay a visit to our friend Dr. Hwong." He turned towards the uniformed officer. "Sergeant, see that Mr. Higheagle here is promptly released."

"Yes, sir."

Marshak stood up from his chair. "You have until Monday afternoon to give me the complete story, gentlemen. In the meantime, I'll be working on my own version. If I were you, I'd get to work as fast as possible. Before the D.A. takes a strong interest in this case and you're hauled before a grand jury."

CHAPTER 83

HE FELT DOOMED. It gripped him like a vise as he stared out his office window at the Rockies, craggy and inky blue in the morning shadows. The hue was like the abyssal depths of the ocean—dark, mysterious, foreboding. Even the white snow capping the tallest peaks seemed bleak and ominous, a sign of just how cold things could be at the top. The world outside his window seemed to mirror his own fears, his own vulnerability. Or was it all in his mind?

Slowly, he turned away from that world and stared gloomily at Bishop.

"How could I have let this happen? They've got me by the fucking balls."

Bishop looked at him sourly. "Like hell they do. You should be celebrating."

"Celebrating? How's that exactly?"

"For starters, there's no way the cops can pin McTavish's death on you, not with Hwong's death and suicide note. And as far as Dakota and Silverado go, you're in great shape. Minesali and the other generators are the ones who will take the fall. You're going to come through this almost completely unscathed—that is, with Anderson, Milton on board."

Prescott looked at him dubiously, saying nothing.

"Now that doesn't mean that we still don't have a few roadblocks. But I promise I'm going to get you off with less than a million dollar fine, no jail time, and no more than ten percent of the total cleanup costs at both developments. I think we could be looking at no more than six to eight million dollars over the next five years in fines, legal expenses, and cleanup costs. All without any admission of wrongdoing, of course. How about that? Are you with me, Hayden? You don't look so good. Are you with me?"

"I don't see how I can just walk away from—"

"Hayden, you've got to stop this. This isn't doing you any good. Listen to me. You've got to trust me on this. You will see no jail time at all and you're going to be left with a net profit of well over ten million dollars—and that's the bottom line. Now I might be able to do better than that, but I think we have to take a conservative approach with the numbers. You could be in a lot worse shape, boy-o, as you like to say. Minesali and the others will be completely bankrupt. Meanwhile, you'll build spectacular developments for years to come. How's that for dodging a bullet?"

Prescott nodded understanding, but he was still skeptical. True, Bishop was a miracle worker, but could it really be that easy?

"Like I said, Hayden, I've got you covered. That's why, just for shits and grins, I took a look at some of the recent settlements not only in the Denver area, but statewide. I'm talking the U.S. Army, Petroco, Allied Chemicals, Toxi-Clean, and

Solvent Recovery Services. Now in the last five years all of these guys have broken some serious environmental laws and been dealt meager fines in the quarter- to half-million-dollar range. Why should you pay a stiffer penalty than any of those assholes when the waste didn't even belong to you? The answer is you shouldn't and you won't, and you want to know why? Because you, my friend, are in the hands of a true big-time…"

As his five-hundred-dollar-an-hour attorney blathered on like William Jennings Bryan, Prescott realized that he didn't really give a crap about the details. After all, he was entitled to do whatever the fuck he wanted. That was his birthright and that's what his mother and father had hammered into his brain since the day he could walk. The Prescott's were the chosen, the elite. They weren't like the other 99%—the blue-collar scabs and white-collar zombies scrabbling out an existence, barely scraping by. No sir, he and his family were the 1% that played by a whole different set of rules. They had special rights that were guaranteed to the wealthy and powerful. They did as they pleased, and if the little people got hurt in the process, well, it was their own goddamned fault.

"Hayden, you look like you've drifted away. Have you heard a word I've just said?"

"I was busy thinking."

"Well, did you hear what I just said?"

"Yeah, loud and clear. I can do whatever the fuck I want."

"I don't think…that's not what I was saying, Hayden. You've got to listen to me."

"Okay, okay, I'm listening."

"You can't tune out like this. You've got to be sharp at all times from here on out. You especially have to keep up your normal routine, your appearances. You're speaking in front of the Council on Monday night, right?"

"The Council?"

"You have to be there, Hayden."

"Yes, yes, the Council…I'm giving the keynote speech. Look, I just don't have time for this right now. Why don't you keep working on the case...you know, my defense and all that...while I take a break. I need some time to get my head together."

"My God, I think you need a shrink."

"A shrink?"

"You're not acting like yourself. You need to talk to a shrink."

"Okay, that's enough. Look, you've done a terrific job for me and I appreciate it. But my brain is fried right now. I can't think straight and need a break from all this legal strategizing."

"All right, but I don't think you should be left alone."

"I'm fine. Seriously, I just need a break. Go home and spend some time with your kids. Then we'll get back at it tomorrow."

"My kids? I can't stand my fucking kids. They're teenagers." He closed his folder and stuffed it in his fold-over leather briefcase. "Are you sure you're okay?"

"I think I just need a good workout. You know, to clear my head."

Bishop started for the door. "You'll call if you need me?"

"Yes, of course."

"You won't miss a step with any of this, Hayden, not a single step. Because Anderson, Milton is looking out for you."

"You don't know how relieved I am, Clarence Darrow. Now get the hell out of here. Go on now, I'm fine."

When his attorney was gone, Prescott leaned back in his sleek executive's chair and wondered: *Am I really going to get away with this?*

And then he realized the answer to his own question.

CHAPTER 84

AT THREE O'CLOCK THAT AFTERNOON, Higheagle and his grandfather slipped into their seats in the conference room at EPA Region 8 headquarters in downtown Denver. Across the table sat the thin, bespectacled Ben Carrington of the EPA's Criminal Investigations Division; and next to him, Ellen Widmark, Managing Attorney with the Justice Department's Environment and Natural Resources Division.

Widmark composed herself with what seemed to be either excessive governmental rigidity or perfect posture, Higheagle couldn't tell which. She looked to be around the same age as Carrington, early fifties or somewhere thereabouts, and had a sharply faceted, aristocratic nose that carried more than a whiff of arrogance. Her ash-blonde hair, obviously dyed, was cut precisely shoulder-length and her neatly pressed azure-blue business suit, complete with the obligatory power-executive shoulder pads, looked like it had been tailored for a middle-aged rather than a youthful Hillary Clinton.

Everyone had notepads in front of them, and although there were no tape recorders present, the atmosphere around the conference table was thick with tense formality. Following the introductions, Higheagle was instructed to proceed immediately with a summary of his investigation. He handed each attendee a copy of the report he had prepared on his Dakota Ranch investigation and informed them he was still preparing his report on Silverado Knolls. He then told the same story he had told Carrington at the police station. As before, he left out everything he had learned about or heard from Minesali, Vic Shard, and Hank Johanson. It was as if these individuals never existed. This time, however, he did describe the two break-ins at his house.

"Well, Mr. Higheagle," Widmark said with exaggerated raised eyebrows when he was finished, her well-bred voice giving off a touch of New England. "You seem to have been very busy these past few weeks."

Higheagle looked at his grandfather, but the veteran lawyer didn't seem to know what to make of the senior government official any more than he did.

"My client knows he should have handled things differently," responded the old chief in his defense. "Running around on private property and collecting samples is not standard operating procedure in his profession. But he feels that what he did was necessary to ensure that Prescott and Hwong are prosecuted to the full extent of the law."

Widmark gave a noncommittal nod. "If memory serves me correctly," she said, looking Higheagle right in the eye, "I believe you'd be looking at criminal trespassing and unlawful entry at Dakota Ranch and breaking and entering at

Silverado Knolls."

"My client may have used poor judgment, but he's no criminal," interjected his grandfather before Higheagle could respond. "He's done a fine piece of detective work and what's needed now is a thorough investigation of both developments."

Easy, Grandfather, you don't want to piss her off. "What's the news on Dan Markworth?" he asked, trying to change the subject so there wouldn't be an argument.

"It looks like he's going to pull through," replied Carrington. "It will be a long and painful recovery though."

"And what about Dr. Hwong? Has he been taken into custody yet?"

Carrington glanced at Widmark as if to say, "Should we tell them?" To which Hillary Jr. gave a nod of approval. "Yes, he's been located," answered Carrington, "along with the vehicle used in the hit-and-run."

"Has he talked?" asked John Higheagle.

"I'm afraid not. You see, Dr. Hwong is dead."

"Dead? Was he murdered?"

"According to Detective Marshak, it appears to have been a suicide. But the police are conducting a full investigation to find out for certain."

"Well, what do they know so far?"

"They found him in his car in his garage. It had been running for several hours and he appears to have died from carbon monoxide poisoning. It looks like a suicide, but they haven't ruled out homicide."

"Did he leave a note?"

Carrington removed his wire-framed glasses and began rubbing the upper bridge of his nose. "There was a note, yes."

"What did it say?"

"He admitted to the dumping of the waste at Dakota Ranch and Silverado Knolls, falsifying the lab data, and the hit-and-run."

"As well as the murder of Gus McTavish," added Widmark.

The old chief nodded skeptically. "Hell, while he was at it did he admit to assassinating JFK from the grassy knoll? A suicide note sure ties up a lot of loose ends."

"It most certainly does." She looked at Joseph. "Which leads me to my main question: what in the world, Mr. Higheagle, are we going to do with you?"

He felt a flutter in his stomach.

"That's a no-brainer," answered his grandfather. "Do what the Justice Department always does."

"And what is that?"

"Cut a deal and go after the bad guys."

"You really believe it's that simple?" Widmark shifted her steely gaze back to Higheagle, and he felt the breath catch in his throat. "We get informants like you every day, Mr. Higheagle. Yet only one in ten gives us anything resembling the truth, let alone enough to bring forward an indictment to the U.S. Attorney. Are you one of those people?"

"I've given you the facts of the case. I wouldn't have risked my career over this if I didn't think it was important enough to bend a few rules."

"You have done a bit more than bend a few rules. I still don't understand what prompted you to charge out to the prairie and start digging around like you did. Like all consultants, you must have a client. We'd appreciate it if you told us who it is."

Higheagle felt her gaze pierce right through him. "You know I can't tell you that."

She gave an ironic smile. "Client confidentiality, I suppose?"

"That's right."

"Why do I picture this so-called client of yours as some sort of Wizard of Oz pulling the strings behind the curtain?"

"I don't know," said his grandfather. "Maybe because when you were a kid, you wanted to be Judy Garland?"

"I see you have a sense of humor, Chief Higheagle. Let's just hope you feel the same way when the judge throws out your grandson's evidence on a technicality and tosses him in the slammer instead of Hayden Prescott. I don't know Mr. Prescott personally, but from what I gather he will mount a massive legal defense. Considering his limitless financial resources and many friends in high places, he may very well get off scot-free."

Higheagle looked at his grandfather. The cocky smile had evaporated.

Widmark rubbed her chin thoughtfully, as if to underscore her triumph.

"Regardless of how it all plays out," Higheagle said, "Prescott's your man. He's the mastermind behind the operation and the one who killed McTavish and tried to have me killed."

"And let's not forget about Hwong," John Higheagle reminded everyone.

"Nor should we forget about the army of waste generators, haulers, and laborers that would have been part of the operation," countered Widmark. "Look, the murder and attempted murder charges are in the hands of the DPD, not us. Our primary concern is the environmental crimes. And as far as they go, Mr. Prescott may very well be the tip of the iceberg. We may need to use him to catch the others."

Higheagle didn't like what he was hearing. "But the waste is on his properties. He's the one who arranged to have it put there."

"That's true," said Carrington. "But we feel that Mr. Prescott may have more value to us as a material witness. He may be willing to cooperate fully with both our departments in exchange for...some sort of clemency."

Higheagle looked at his grandfather; the old chief was not pleased. "Tell me you're not going to just let Prescott walk away with a slap on the wrist in exchange for being a snitch."

"The waste is on Prescott's property and in all likelihood was placed there by him, but the state handles things differently than we do," explained Carrington blandly. "Because identifying the property owner is often the easiest task, the state typically goes after them. But the EPA's thinking is different. We place as much emphasis—perhaps even more if records are available—on the generators. And if the property owner can come forward with information on just who those persons or entities are, we generally find ways to cooperate."

"I admit it's not the best situation," added Widmark. "But the bottom line is the generators typically have the deepest pockets. That's why yours truly—Uncle Sam—tends to go after them."

Higheagle had known coming in that things might not swing in his direction, but he was still disappointed. "So what you're saying is that you're going to strike a deal with Prescott in order to catch the generators."

"No, we're telling you there's a possibility that's how things might play out," responded Carrington. "Colorado doesn't set aside public money for state Superfund sites and we need some way to pay for the cleanups."

Higheagle felt Widmark's eyes heavily upon him. "Why Mr. Higheagle, if I'm not mistaken, it almost sounds as if you're concerned for the welfare of the waste generators."

"No, the problem I have is that you might be cutting a deal with the one guy who profited most from all this. And he's a murderer to boot."

"If that could be proved in a court of law, Detective Marshak would have already made the arrest. The fact that he hasn't isn't a good sign. Perhaps Prescott did kill Gus McTavish, but he may have simply been an accessory. Dr. Hwong's suicide note, I'm afraid, makes it a moot point."

"But there's a clear motive. McTavish had to have been blackmailing him."

"Perhaps. But the suicide note isn't the only problem. There's no evidence of any payments, not yet anyway, and no physical evidence linking Prescott to the murder. Add to that the fact that Prescott sent a lot of work McTavish's way and paid all of his bills in full. Plus there's the testimony of the five individuals who saw Prescott trying to save McTavish's life. The case has reasonable doubt written all over it, and right now, the D.A.'s office isn't going to touch it. Detective Marshak is furious, of course, but that's the way it stands. I'm afraid the only thing we can do is pursue the illegal dumping angle."

Higheagle couldn't believe what he was hearing. *Is Prescott really going to fucking get away with this?*

"We may be able to track down the generators without Prescott's help," Carrington said. "Of course, that's how we'll handle it if he doesn't tell us anything voluntarily."

"In any case, we're going to need some time to review your report before we decide how to proceed," Widmark said. "Why don't we meet again tomorrow once we've had a chance to go through all of this? You can bring us the Silverado Knolls report then."

Higheagle glanced at his grandfather to see if there was anything else, but there wasn't. "Oh, I almost forgot," he said, turning back towards them. "Prescott's giving a speech tomorrow night for his developer group, the Council for Front Range Competitiveness. Maybe some of the PRPs will be there."

"Are you going to attend?" asked Carrington.

"I was thinking about it."

"I'm not sure that's a good idea. You're a government witness now."

"You make it sound like I have a bull's-eye on my chest."

"Oh, I think we can allow Mr. Higheagle to attend," Widmark said, giving a dry smile. "With the proper chaperones, of course."

Higheagle looked at his grandfather. "What does that mean?"

"It means we'll be under the protection of government agents with dark sunglasses and concealed weapons under their suits. You're right, we might as well have bull's-eyes painted on our chests. We'd probably be safer."

Widmark gave a little chuckle and stood up from her chair, signaling the meeting was over. "I'm afraid that's all the time we have now, gentlemen." Her eyes, softer now, reached out to Higheagle almost apologetically. "And just so you know, we never considered your trespassing to be an issue. We want the people responsible for the dumping at both sites. And we're going to do everything in our power to nail them to the proverbial wall."

"Somehow, I don't think you'll quit until you do."

"The attorney general and directors of the EPA and FBI will never admit it publically, Mr. Higheagle, but they are extremely pleased with your efforts. You've not only done a great deal of the legwork for us, you've saved the taxpayers a prodigious sum of money, just as you did with the Quantrill affair. I'd like to thank you personally."

She gave an ironic smile. Funny, but he was beginning to like her.

"Now before you go, gentlemen, I need you to guarantee me one thing."

"What's that?"

"That you'll stay out of trouble."

Higheagle looked at his grandfather and they laughed. "We'll try, but unfortunately we can't make any promises. After all, we're Cheyenne."

CHAPTER 85

THE FLOWERS BROUGHT WARMTH to the whole dining room. There were crimson, salmon-pink, and yellow roses, wonderfully scented and glistening with water droplets. Sally pushed the vase towards the center of the table and stepped back to look at the arrangement again. She decided to trim a couple more of the taller flowers. With a small pair of pruning shears, she began snipping the base of each stem, setting the discarded greenery on a sheet of newspaper.

As she worked, she glanced through the kitchen at Tommy sitting on the family room couch. He was engrossed in his new book *Little Big Man* by Thomas Berger that Joseph had given him. A smile worked its way across her face. She was glad that he was out of the hospital and starting to feel better.

She thought of how much she loved him.

Her musings were interrupted by a light rap at the front door. It must be her parents, who had gone shopping and were due back any time now. Carrying the pruning shears in her right hand, she walked to the door, unfastened the lock, and swung the door open.

The happy expression on her face evaporated instantaneously when she saw who it was.

"I had to see you."

She clasped the shears tightly in her hand. "You and I have nothing to talk about."

"Who is it, Mom?" Tommy called out from the other room.

"It's nobody," she said coolly.

Her eyes narrowed on the man again. He shoved his hands deep into his pockets.

"Why don't you just get on with whatever it is you came here to say? The only reason I'm still standing here is on the off chance you'll say something incriminating."

Tommy came up behind her. "Oh, it's you," he said when he recognized the man in the doorway.

Hayden Prescott retracted a half-step. He no longer looked like a man of great wealth and power, more like someone wiped out in a stock market crash. "I came here to tell you that you've gotten me all wrong, the both of you."

Sally just stared at him, stunned. How dare he come here like this and pretend that he had done nothing wrong!

"I'm sorry for what's happened to Tommy and the other boys, but I promise I had nothing to do with it."

Sally squeezed her hand together so that the two metal blades of the gardening shears slid past one another, making a scraping metallic sound. A discernible twitch passed across Prescott's face. For a split second, she wondered what it would feel like to run him through with the shears. Would killing him make up for all the pain and suffering he had caused?

"I don't expect either of you to forgive me, or to feel anything but anger towards me. But you should know that I'm innocent in all this. You simply have to believe me."

She watched as he looked pleadingly to Tommy. Looking at her son's reaction, she saw that he was torn between hatred and sympathy, which, she realized, was the same way she felt deep down. She looked back at Prescott. Despite his bravado and apparent lack of guilt, beneath the surface she saw a haunted, withered figure, like a great statesman whose time has passed. It was hard to believe that she had once loved this man—a man who in all likelihood had murdered her uncle, tried to kill Joseph, and was responsible for her son's cancer.

She pointed the gardening shears at him, now feeling a little surge of anger. "You make me sick. You destroy people's lives in the name of profit and then you have the gall to come here and proclaim your innocence. Do you really believe we're that gullible? Did you really think you could come here and get away with this?"

"You're just confused right now, Sally. If you and I were back together, this would all go away. You, Tommy, and I could be together. I would take very good care of you both. I would spare no expense for your happiness."

"Spare no expense?"

"Yes, you wouldn't want for anything, I promise you."

"Are you crazy? I would kill myself before I would ever let you come near me or my son again." She raised the shears. "Now get the hell out of here before I run you through!"

He stared at her with shock, which quickly morphed into abject fear. In that moment, she realized that he had never had anything more than a facade of strength, a veneer of wealth and prestige not earned through hard work and sacrifice, but through clever deception. The revelation of his weakness infuriated and disgusted her.

He started backing down the steps, keeping a wary eye on her.

"They're going to put you away," she said with quiet anger, and somehow the words emboldened her. "Maybe not today or tomorrow, you bastard, but soon, very soon. Your life as you know it is finished."

He looked at her a final time—his face a mask of fury, outrage, and despair— then turned and walked dejectedly to his car. She closed the door firmly and turned the lock, without ambivalence or regret. Then she looked at Tommy, and in her reflection in the mirror behind him, she saw something new.

She saw a great strength.

CHAPTER 86

TWO HOURS LATER, Higheagle and his grandfather sat with Sally and her parents in the family room. They had shared a delicious dinner of green corn tamales, black bean tacos, and gorditas during which everyone had followed Sally's request and dutifully refrained from talking about the case. But now, with Tommy upstairs in his room asleep, Sally's father demanded to know what was going on. Higheagle told them about the latest developments: the hit-and-run, Hwong's apparent suicide, and the meeting with the EPA and DOJ. Sally followed by describing her encounter this afternoon with Hayden Prescott.

As Sally spoke, Higheagle noted the trace of anger in her voice as she described their confrontation, but there was something else in her manner: grit, clarity of purpose, mental toughness. There was no sense that she had been afraid. Overall, she seemed much stronger than when he had first met her, a far cry from the vulnerable, emotionally distraught woman he had first met at Eisenhower Memorial Hospital nearly three weeks ago.

She seemed in charge of her own destiny.

"Well, I'm glad he's gone," said Gail McTavish when Sally was finished describing the encounter. "Thank heavens he didn't try to hurt you or Tommy."

"That's the most important thing," agreed Bill McTavish. "I just wish we could have been here for you. That man...he's a monster."

Sally calmly picked up her glass of red wine from the marble coffee table. "Thanks, Dad, but I had it under control."

"I'm sure you did," her mother said. "But you have to be more careful. If he ever comes here again, I want you to not answer the door and to call the police right away. Okay, honey?"

"All right, Mom."

"If he comes back again, I'll shoot him myself," snarled Bill McTavish.

"Bill, you can't mean that," his wife scolded him.

"The hell I don't." He looked at Higheagle. "How strong is the case against this man?"

"You'll have to ask my grandfather. He's the lawyer."

All eyes turned to the old chief. "I don't want to paint an overly bleak picture here, but the people we spoke with said the D.A.'s office probably won't touch the murder and accessory part of the case. With Hwong's suicide note and a lack of physical evidence, they don't have enough to make it stick. And as far as the waste issue goes, the Justice Department and EPA said they might even cut a deal with Prescott to catch the generators. Truth is, unless they can get him on the murder charge, he probably won't see any jail time. And even that's assuming the feds can prove that he knowingly received the waste and profited by dumping it on his property."

Bill McTavish clenched his teeth. "But that bastard killed my brother. And whatever it is he dumped out here has harmed my grandson."

"Bill, let's not get upset," said his wife. "The police, EPA, and Justice Department are all working on this now. They'll take care of it."

Higheagle wondered what he should do about Minesali, having not yet reached a decision on a course of action. On the one hand, he knew that Minesali was ultimately just as guilty as Prescott. It seemed only fair that he pay for what he'd done. On the other hand, he realized that the old man had been put in a difficult position from forces beyond his control and it was hard to condemn him. If Minesali turned himself in voluntarily or if Prescott took him down with him, that was one thing, but Higheagle didn't want to be the one to seal his fate. Or at least not yet.

Sally asked, "So are you telling us that Hayden Prescott could get immunity from all of this?"

"Unfortunately, yes," replied the old chief. "If he told them exactly what the waste consisted of, where it was dumped, and who the generators were, they would certainly reduce his punishment."

Bill McTavish was incredulous. "So he might not even go to jail?"

"Unfortunately, that's a possibility. But he'd still pay a stiff fine. In the millions, I would think."

"But he's worth tens of millions. With his fat bank account, it would be nothing more than a traffic ticket to him."

Higheagle could feel the tension in the room building. He looked at his grandfather and Sally. Their anger was more restrained than Bill McTavish's, but they were no less disappointed. It defied all logic that Prescott might get away with a mere slap on the wrist, but that's the way the situation was trending.

"It's important to remember that we're only talking about the government's case on the dumping issue," John Higheagle pointed out, his tone cautiously optimistic. "You and the other families could bring civil suits against Prescott."

"Plus all the homeowners could bring a case against him for wrongful trespass and destroying property values," Joseph said. "When the extent of the problem comes out in the open, that's probably what will happen. Lawyers will flock here to sign you up. But they'll have to establish that the waste actually lowered the value of your property."

Sally shook her head dejectedly. "He'll just take it from the environmental impact fund he's set up. I heard about it from Mary Wilkins. He has a special fund paid for by the homeowners that covers litigation for geotechnical and environmental problems."

Higheagle felt as though the blood had frozen in his veins. He leaned forward in his chair. It seemed unthinkable that Prescott could have such an easy out. "How much is in the fund?"

"I don't know exactly. The contributions are based on the original home purchase price. A half-percent of the value of each home, something like that."

John Higheagle went through the calculations out loud. "Ten thousand homes, at an average price of three hundred and fifty thousand dollars each, times a half percent. That would be 17.5 million dollars."

Bill McTavish's face was crimson now, flush with anger. "So not only will the homeowners have to foot the bill for the cleanup, they'll have to spend a fortune on attorneys to settle the case. I can't believe this crap!"

Again, his wife looked at him worriedly, but this time she held her tongue. It suddenly dawned on Higheagle that Sally's father might very well take the law into his own hands. He was a big man, with broad shoulders and long arms, and despite his age, he looked like he could do some serious damage to those who crossed him. Higheagle remembered Sally telling him about her father coming inches away from ripping Prescott's head off when he had previously showed up at the house.

"I know all this comes as a disappointment, but it might be the best that can be done," said Higheagle, attempting to mollify the situation. "At a minimum, I think Prescott's career in Colorado is finished. Nothing can stop the avalanche of negative publicity that will fall out from this."

With sudden fury, Bill McTavish was up and on his feet. Sally and her mother looked at him with astonishment.

"Well, that's just not good enough, goddamnit! That's just not good enough for me!" And he stormed out the room.

CHAPTER 87

HAYDEN WINTHROP PRESCOTT III GAZED OUT AT THE ADORING CROWD.

His guests sat at their exquisitely arranged dining tables while an army of pampering waiters darted to and fro serving café bombón and desserts of crème brûlée, tiramisu, and chocolate profiteroles. There were high-ranking developers, homebuilders, lobbyists, golf course designers, attorneys, bankers, heavy equipment executives, and window and lumber manufacturers. As card-carrying members of the Council for Front Range Competitiveness, they had gathered here to celebrate themselves and their profession. Lavish two-thousand-dollar suits and evening gowns clung to their bodies like silk sheets over priceless paintings, and the jewelry at their throats, ears, and hands glittered in the pools of brilliance thrown down from the huge overhead chandelier. These were the beautiful people, the elite, the 1%. And here Prescott stood ready to address them in all their dazzling finery.

For the past four years, the annual meeting of the Council for Front Range Competitiveness had been held here, in the Tabor Room of the Executive Suites Hotel. Each year these people—and others just like them—came to hear keynote speakers expound on the intricacies of "smart growth" and "managed infrastructure" before kicking up their heels and reeling and rocking to the sounds of Huey Lewis and the News or Stevie Wonder. Of course, many of those present were vicious competitors, but they were willing to put aside their differences for their common goal. After all, the real enemy was not one another, but the radical environmental groups and meddlesome government bureaucrats who were stymying their efforts to bring sparkling new housing tracts, business parks, shopping malls, and cineplexes to the fine people of Colorado.

The Council was Prescott's brainchild; he had forged the muscular coalition and made it blossom. He felt a deep pride in that fact as he stared out at the luminous, admiring crowd from behind the mahogany lectern.

The lights dimmed and his first slide appeared on the large overhead screen behind him. He proceeded to show dream homes in dream settings bounded by dream golf courses, and the crowd gasped in awed delight. He showed them elaborate computer-generated images of what Silverado Knolls would look like when it was finished. He showed them spectacular floor plans and breathtaking landscaping arrangements and perfect neighborhoods. He demonstrated how a meager $1,000,000 investment in one of his developments would generate a twenty percent return on the investment within three short years. And the more he spoke, the more he felt his own perfection.

He felt just like his hero Hank Rearden, the steel magnate from *Atlas Shrugged*.

They were both job creators, visionaries, entrepreneurs fighting off a proletariat army of social and regulatory parasites. Sure, he was a little shadier than good-old, spit-polished Hank, but how could you get ahead in today's world without pushing the envelope? It was true he had buried haz waste in the ground to jump start his career and generate some much-needed capital, but what was so bad about that? In his view, he was no different than any other successful businessman. The average person simply didn't understand the heavy risks and responsibilities involved when you were a big-time *job creator*. True, he had broken a few laws, actually probably dozens of laws, but wasn't starting your own business and making a handsome profit by bending the rules the very definition of the American way? Hadn't Joe Kennedy been a bootlegger? Didn't Henry Ford cozy up to the Nazis to make a buck? If guys like Steve Jobs, Bill Gates, and Donald Trump hadn't stolen the ideas of their competition and been utterly ruthless in their business dealings, how could they possibly have attained the business prestige for which all three were renowned?

So then, like his hero Hank Rearden, was he not a shining example, a living metaphor, for America's entrepreneurial spirit? Even though he wasn't a self-made man per se, like Ayn Rand's heroic steel titan, wasn't he just as remarkable for his achievements?

The answer that came to him, as he stared out at the adoring crowd, was a resounding *Yes*! He was a truly great man. He was one of the sparkling 1%, a job creator, an entrepreneur, a risk-taker, a visionary. He was perfectly, exquisitely, one-hundred-percent All-American. Jesus Christ, he almost wanted to salute himself right here in front of all of these fucking people, he was such a perfect embodiment of the American dream! Goddamned Ayn Rand would have been proud as hell!

He finished his talk. The lights came back on and the crowd showered him with hearty applause, amplifying his feelings of self-adulation.

Like dear Mumsie, he felt like a God among mortals.

He smiled ebulliently as he introduced the next speaker, a developer from Colorado Springs. After saying a few complimentary words about the man's professional background, he waved him up to the stage. Handing off, he managed a final radiant smile for his audience, which was enough to bring a quarter of the well-heeled women present close to swooning. Then he started down the steps to his VIP table in front of the stage.

It was then he saw the group at the back of the room.

He felt a lightning bolt of anger followed swiftly by insane panic.

There were ten of them: Higheagle, his grandfather, a middle-aged man and woman in stiff suits that screamed U.S. Government, and to the right of them, two more suits, Marshak, a uniformed cop, and two men in casual dress, most likely a newspaper reporter and photographer since one of them was holding a camera. Prescott struggled mightily not to come unraveled as he took his seat at his table with Bishop and his other special guests. By the time the lights had dimmed and the next speaker had launched into his talk, his heart rate had clicked up over a hundred beats per minute.

What should I do?

They obviously weren't here just to ask him a few questions—this was a goddamned perp walk! They wanted to make a big, showy arrest in front of hundreds of people. They wanted to cuff him and drag him from the room kicking and screaming. They wanted to humiliate him and splatter his frightened face across the Internet and newspapers.

That would be so perfect for them!

Well, I won't give them the fucking satisfaction!

He could hear his own heart pounding now.

There had to be a way out of this.

And then it struck him. He would quietly walk out the room, make his way to his car, and drive off. Somewhere. Anywhere. Away from here, away from these people hounding him. And then he would summon Bishop. His attorney would know what to do! He would make these lowly parasites pay for their brazenness!

Wasting no time, he informed his guests that he would be back in a minute and strode calmly yet briskly for the door on the far side of the speakers' platform. As he reached for the knob, he glanced back over his shoulder.

Higheagle was pointing at him.

You're not going to arrest me, you bastards! I'll not give you the satisfaction! I'm out of here!

There was a moment of confusion—Higheagle, Marshak, and two of the suits were mouthing something and gesturing frantically—and then they started after him.

Prescott threw open the door and bolted out the Tabor Room.

The chase was on.

ψψψ

Watching him fly through the door, Sally couldn't believe her eyes. Hayden Prescott might actually get away!

Since this afternoon, when she had learned that he would be arrested at the conference, she had felt some degree of justice. He might not get the punishment he deserved, but at least he would be taken into custody and stand trial. At a minimum, he would be forced to cough up millions in fines for the waste, and despite the long odds, there was still a chance that he could be found guilty for the murder of her uncle.

But then she saw him stealing away.

As the door snapped shut and he disappeared into thin air, she felt violated, her chance at vindication stolen from her. She would not be able to see his terrified expression as the cuffs were slapped on him and he was unceremoniously hauled off to jail.

I don't believe this! He's going to get away!

It was bad enough that he might only have to pay a fine for what he'd done, but the possibility that he might avert justice altogether and actually escape—perhaps never to be caught, never to be punished—was too mind-boggling to imagine. And with all the money he probably had tucked away in offshore accounts and dummy shell corporations, he would be able to live out the rest of his life in secluded luxury.

Panic seized her as that unthinkable prospect raced through her mind, jarring her like a typhoon.

She could not let this happen. Prescott could not be allowed to get away.

I have to stop him!

Without drawing attention to herself, she quietly stepped out the back of the Tabor Room. When she reached the hallway, she darted in the direction she thought Prescott had gone.

Turning a corner, she spotted him running down a hallway on the other side of the atrium.

Suddenly, she saw the door he had just jumped through bust open.

It was Joseph!

He scanned the hallway, spotted Prescott, and started running after him.

And then, to her surprise, the door flew open again.

She saw a man in a white straw cowboy hat barrel through the opening, look around, grab a filled dining cart, and jam it into the doorknob, blocking the door.

Now why would he do that? Unless he was trying to—

She started off again, punching into overdrive, her sneakers burning across the carpet.

Her face was resolute. From her last two legal seminars, she knew this hotel.

More importantly, she knew where Hayden Prescott was headed.

CHAPTER 88

HIGHEAGLE WASN'T SURE HE COULD CATCH HIM.

His legs were already growing heavy and Prescott—damn him!—was as swift as an antelope and showed no signs of slowing down as he darted down one hallway, then another, gaining separation.

The guy could flat out run.

Up ahead, around the corner, he heard alarmed voices. Taking the corner in an all-out sprint, he saw two hotel guests that had been knocked to the floor scramble to their feet.

"Jesus Christ! What kind of hotel is this!"

Higheagle darted past them and drove his shoulder into the steel exit door, suddenly finding himself on Level 3 of a huge covered parking garage. The floor was concrete and sloped away from the hotel at a steep angle, leading to a lower level.

He quickly scanned the area. But there was no sign of Prescott.

And then, he caught a blur of movement on the other side of a parked car to his right. He tore off in that direction.

He saw Prescott leap to the ramp leading to Level 4, which sloped towards the hotel. Barely missing the red-painted steel bars on the other side, the developer crash-landed in a tucked position and then disappeared from sight.

Higheagle ran to the steel railing and hastily climbed to the top rung. Just as he was about to jump, he heard the door crash open behind him.

He turned back to see who it was.

Shard! What the hell?

Wheeling back around, he jumped, just missing the top rung on the opposite side in midair. He dove to the floor of the garage like a parachutist, cushioning his fall.

There was Prescott, running up the ramp.

Higheagle ran after him.

When he reached the fourth level, he turned a corner and saw Prescott pull something from his pocket and point it at a sleek, black Porsche. The car made a chirping noise as the doors unlocked.

"Stop!" Higheagle yelled, and he turned on the afterburners.

A look of panic appeared on Prescott's face as he fumbled for the right key.

Higheagle closed in fast.

Prescott found the key and quickly threw open the door.

Shit! No! No!

But as he placed a foot into the sports car, his hand brushed against the door and he dropped the keys. With trembling fingers, he reached down from inside the car to pick them off the pavement.

That was all Higheagle would need.

He exploded into the driver's side door with his left shoulder, smashing the door against Prescott's arm with violent force.

The keys dropped to the pavement.

Prescott cried out in agony as Higheagle yanked the door open and jerked him from the car by the collar, throwing him to the ground like a gunnysack.

"It's over! Stay down and you won't get hurt!"

Prescott lay there, puffing loudly, nostrils flaring like a racehorse. "I think you broke my fucking arm!" he spat, clutching the crippled appendage.

"You shouldn't have run away!" He kept him pinned to the concrete.

Again, Prescott groaned out in pain.

Suddenly, tires screeched into the night. A car was racing up from the lower level, the sound of the revving engine loud as thunder as it echoed off the concrete walls.

Higheagle looked down the ramp, but the car hadn't turned the corner yet.

The moment of distraction proved costly as he felt a sharp force strike his balls. Prescott had punched him with his good arm, and the fierce blow forced him to loosen his grip, enabling Prescott to break free and leap to his feet.

Shaking off the pain, Higheagle tried to tackle him, but was shoved back to the pavement, his left shoulder hitting hard on the concrete. Prescott sprinted up the ramp, turned a corner, and was gone.

Looking over his shoulder, Higheagle saw a dark car take the corner hard and speed in his direction.

Who the hell is it?

His mind racing, he reached down to grab the car keys and tore off on foot after Prescott. When he had reached the top level, Level 5, he was suddenly hit with the brilliant light of the moon and stars. The entire night sky opened up like a planetarium.

He saw Prescott running for the covered stairs leading to the ground level. His left shoulder throbbed with pain, but he forced himself to suck it up and bolted after him.

Behind him, the engine screamed.

He looked back to see a midnight blue Pontiac carom around the corner and roar past him without stopping. He didn't recognize the car, and with the sun visor pulled down low and the driver wearing some sort of strange mask, he couldn't make out the person behind the wheel. Yet, there was something vaguely familiar about the driver.

He ran after the car, his nostrils blasted by the smell of seared rubber.

Like a guided missile, the Pontiac locked menacingly on Prescott. Suddenly, he was cut off from the stairs leading to the hotel. He faked left and right, trying to get the driver to commit one way or the other, but the driver wasn't fooled and accelerated straight for him.

Darting to his left, Prescott ran alongside the four-foot high concrete wall that ran along the perimeter of the parking structure.

The driver threw the Pontiac into reverse and spun around, the tires blazing across the concrete.

Prescott ran around a line of parked cars, keeping to the edge of the wall.

Higheagle could tell he was making for the vehicle exit ramp on the west side of the parking structure. It wound down like a corkscrew from the top level to ground level.

He could hear the engine ahead of him revving, reverberating off the walls. Prescott had only twenty yards to the exit ramp, but the Pontiac was closing fast at an oblique angle.

It was going to hit him.

Backed against the waist-high concrete wall, Prescott turned in openmouthed panic towards the oncoming car.

In the glare of the headlights, Higheagle saw his last earthly expression: astonishment, followed by pure animal fear.

The Pontiac raced towards him.

He turned and jumped up onto the wall.

At the last second, the car broke hard right, deliberately veering away from the wall, but Higheagle could tell it was too late. Prescott lost his footing on the rough concrete, his body teetering helplessly, arms waving wildly, in a vain effort to regain his balance.

Slowly, like the unfolding of a dream, Prescott disappeared over the edge. The car shot through the opening between the concrete pillar and the wall without a scrape. Over the sound of the ebbing engine, a chilling scream shot up into the night followed by a heavy thud.

It had an unmistakable note of finality about it.

Higheagle ran to the wall.

There, five stories below on the pavement, lay Hayden Prescott's lifeless body. The area was well illuminated and he could see blood pooling around Prescott's head like ink on cotton. The arms kicked out at an awkward angle, like the backswept wings of a bird of prey, and the eyes stared up at him blankly.

Behind him, he heard the Pontiac rattle to a halt.

Turning, he felt his gut clench as he stared through the windshield at the driver behind the steering wheel. The headgear the driver was wearing consisted of an intricately beaded browband from which issued a single buffalo horn and below it a molded, red-painted parfleche mask with yellow vertical stripes, white hailstones, and a tuft of horsehair and strand of porcupine quills projecting from the jaw and chin.

It was a Cheyenne Contrary medicine mask.

Slowly, the driver pulled away the mask and Higheagle watched in stunned silence as his grandfather's face was exposed. The old man chanted a prayer in their native Cheyenne tongue and motioned with his hand, paying tribute to the four sacred directions and *Heammawihio*, the Wise One Above, in the traditional way.

What in the hell had the crazy bastard just done? And where had he gotten the damned Pontiac? Had he actually planned this all out?

To his right, Higheagle heard a shuffling sound. Turning, he saw Vic Shard puffing his way up the concrete ramp, maybe fifty feet away.

He looked back at his grandfather, his eyes transfixed by the flinty resolution on the other side of the windshield. In the old Contrary's eyes, this wasn't murder at all—this was a goddamned purification ritual!

And then, like a ghost, the old chief pulled the mask down over his face and the car moved off, nosed down the exit ramp, and was out of sight.

Higheagle went to the wall again and looked down at the body as Shard came trotting up, coughing and wheezing like a winded draft horse. Without uttering a word, the private eye peered over the edge, his expression one of focused concentration.

"You saw it, didn't you? You saw what happened?" said Higheagle.

The PI didn't answer. He turned away from the wall and looked down at the worn concrete. "No tracks," was all he said.

Higheagle stared at him with puzzlement. "No tracks?"

"No tire tracks."

Higheagle looked down at the pavement. Shard was right: there were no tire tracks. His grandfather had miraculously steered clear of the wall without leaving a trace.

"But you saw who it was, right?"

Shard pulled out his tin of Copenhagen and packed a monster-sized wad of longcut into his mouth. "The only thing I saw was a man losing his balance and falling off the edge there. It's a damn shame—he should have been more careful."

CHAPTER 89

THREE MINUTES LATER, the others began arriving on the scene. They came in waves: first Sally McTavish and the fleet FBI agents, then the reporter and photographer, next Detective Marshak, Ben Carrington, and the uniformed cop, and finally Ellen Widmark and a puffing, red-faced Gregory Bishop. Each newcomer went immediately to the edge and peered down at the lifeless form some fifty feet below. No one—not even Marshak—said a word as the photographer clicked off picture after picture, the camera flashes strobing eerily through the night like some sort of horror movie.

Vic Shard was busy trying to figure out what the hell he was going to say.

Finally, Marshak pulled out his cell phone and called 911. Finishing the call, he stepped away from the crime scene, stoked a Marlboro, and walked over to Shard and Higheagle. "Nice of you to drop by, Vic. You wanna tell me what the fuck you're doing here?"

In his mind's eye, Shard went back to all the cases he'd worked with Marshak and couldn't pluck out a single pleasant recollection. "Prescott was my client. Unfortunately, it looks like I won't be collecting my last paycheck."

"Uh-huh." Marshak took a deep puff from his cigarette. "So why don't you tell me what happened?"

"As near as I can tell, I'd say my former client fell about five stories."

Marshak blew a perfect smoke ring at Shard's face. "No shit, Vic. And just how do you think that happened? He thought he could fly, is that it?"

Shard felt Marshak's fierce gaze burning through him, but he wasn't worried. In some strange way, with Prescott's death, a huge burden had been lifted from his shoulders. "This Indian fella here was chasing after him," he said, looking at Higheagle as if he didn't know him. "As far as I could tell, Prescott got scared, climbed up on the wall, and then lost his balance and fell. He wasn't pushed—he just plum fell. I saw it all."

Marshak scrutinized Higheagle closely. Sally, Widmark, Carrington, and some of the others had turned away from the wall and now began to press closer, ears directed towards the conversation, faces tight with anticipation.

"It's the God's honest truth," Shard said, and he sent a stream of chocolate-colored spittle to the pavement. "This Indian fella was at least twenty feet from Prescott when the man fell to his death. Beats me why he climbed up on that wall, but he did. Somehow he lost his balance." He pointed to the edge of the ramp where it met the top floor. "I came from over there and saw it all."

"It's obvious he's lying, Detective," snorted Bishop, pointing an accusing finger at Higheagle. "That man killed him! He pushed him over the edge!"

Marshak wheeled on him angrily. "This is my crime scene, asshole! So unless I ask you a direct question, shut the fuck up!" He motioned to the plainclothed officer standing to the side. "Get him to the station! And get those damned reporters out of here too!" He flung out his hand in a gesture of good riddance.

Shard couldn't help a little smile.

Marshak turned around and the PI's smile dropped instantly. The detective stared at Higheagle for several seconds, looking him up and down. "Is that really the way it happened?"

Shard felt a stab of anxiety. *Now don't go and put our necks in a noose, Joe.*

For several seconds, the Cheyenne looked at Sally. Shard could see the conflict warring inside him; he didn't want to lie, but for obvious reasons he didn't want to tell the truth either. Gradually, he seemed to reach a decision and the uncertainty faded, his lips settled into a firm line, and he turned back to Marshak and looked him squarely in the eye.

"That's exactly the way it happened, Detective. The guy panicked and fell right over the edge. He really should have been more careful."

EPILOGUE

TWO MONTHS LATER

SUMMER CAME BLISSFULLY to the Front Range. In place of the spring flora sprouted pink pionese, bearded irises, columbines, lupines, and peach day lilies. The city parks, neighborhood lawns, and rural pastureland outside the Mile High City spilled over in luxurious green. It was after the Fourth of July and the sun shone torrid by day, but the nights were still somewhat cool.

Higheagle was walking with Sally and Tommy in Minesali's garden, the old man instructively describing his precious flowers. Sunlight sparkled off the freshly watered petals. A pleasant fragrance permeated the air, augmented by the scent of crabapple blossoms. The lawn and labyrinthine hedges were meticulously trimmed, and birds chattered contentedly amid the lush foliage. A great tranquility had settled over the vast estate. Higheagle could understand why the old man loved this quiet pocket of earth more than any other.

They came to a halt in front of one of the gardens. Holding his trademark cane, Minesali leaned down and plucked a violet flower. "Here's one you might like." He rose to his feet and handed the flower to Higheagle. "It's a Native American wildflower: *Aquilegia caerulea*. Perhaps you know it by its common name?"

"Columbine. Even I know what the state flower looks like."

Higheagle felt Sally brush up against him. "It's beautiful," she said, leaning forward to smell the fragrant flower.

"Not as beautiful as you," rejoindered Minesali, making her blush just a little.

The color brought a gentle glow to her face, and Higheagle thought of how much she meant to him now. He had been spending quite a bit of time with her and Tommy lately, going out to dinner, hanging out after his Outlaws games, sleeping over often, and—

"This is a special day for me, finally getting to meet the two of you," Minesali said. He put his hand on Tommy's shoulder. "Thank you so much for coming. After the struggles you have endured, it gives me great pleasure to have you both here as my guest."

"We're the ones who should be thanking you," Sally said. "For the Dakota Ranch cancer fund."

"Yeah, we owe you a lot," agreed Tommy. "Not just my mom and I, but our whole neighborhood."

The old man adjusted his silver ascot. "It's nice to feel appreciated." He touched Tommy on the shoulder. "Joseph tells me you are strong as a bull these days."

"Yeah, it looks like I'm going to beat this thing after all. Most of the tumor was destroyed by the radiation treatment, and they got the last little bit with a gamma knife." His expression turned thoughtful. "You know, we couldn't have done the gamma ray stuff without the fund you set up."

"And thanks to the special blood tests," Sally was quick to add, "we know there are no more cancer victims. The tests came up negative for all the other kids who played at the rec center play fields. So it's just the original seven cases."

"That is very good news," said Minesali, and he and Joseph exchanged a glance.

Higheagle was glad that he had talked the old man out of turning himself in and that he seemed to have worked out his demons. But what made him happiest of all was that Sally and Tommy seemed to have a new lease on life and could look forward to good times ahead. He hadn't told Minesali or Sally about what his grandfather had done, or about Shard's involvement in the case, and no one except Higheagle and Shard knew the whole story. In his view, nothing positive could be gained from the truth coming out.

The bottom line was that his grandfather was no killer. True, the old Contrary had chased Prescott down with the intent to run him over, but in the final moment, he had pulled away from the wall and Prescott had slipped and fallen to his death on his own. Higheagle looked at Minesali in similarly charitable terms. True, the old man had knowingly dumped toxic waste at Dakota Ranch, which, Higheagle believed, had ultimately led to the seven boys getting cancer and four of them dying. But on another level, he preferred to see Minesali as a man of deep principle: a businessman who had stubbornly fought to ensure that his cherished employees retained their jobs; a man who, once he had proof of the tragic consequences of his actions, had been prepared to turn himself in; and finally, a man who, in the end, had reached out to help those he had hurt. Ultimately, the waste would be cleaned up, Higheagle knew, because Minesali had hired him to investigate the problem.

"I see your name in the paper quite often," Minesali said to Sally. "You have been busy."

"Yeah, she's a celebrity now, just like Joe," said Tommy. "We're just glad it hasn't gone to her head."

"Thanks to Sally's efforts," said Higheagle, "the feds have seized fifty million from Prescott's and Hwong's accounts. The money's going to be applied towards the cleanups at both Dakota and Silverado. The irony is that it will also be used to pay my salary for the next several years."

One of Minesali's silvery brows went up. "What's this?"

"I've been awarded the contract to be the lead consultant on both cleanup projects. Looks like my fledgling company is going to be growing quite a bit."

Minesali sat down on a slabbed sandstone bench and leaned forward, shifting his weight onto his cane. "That is great news. When did you learn this, Joseph?"

"Yesterday. Bill Yellowtail, the head at EPA Region 8, told me. Privately, he said that only a Plains Indian could be counted on to properly clean up a mess this huge."

Tommy winked at him.

"So our arrangement for covering your legal expenses was moot," Minesali said.

"I guess Uncle Sam doesn't care about trespassing if you give them what they want," Sally said with a grin.

Higheagle looked at her as she took a seat on the sandstone bench next to Minesali. He was proud of her. Immediately after news of Prescott's death had broken, it was Sally who ensured that the illegal waste dumping operation, the childhood cancer cluster, and the suspicious death of her uncle were not lost in the sensationalist media coverage. Overnight, she became the most outspoken critic of how the Health Department was handling the cancer study. Her story galvanized the entire Front Range, forcing the EPA, Justice Department, and CDPHE to move swiftly in their joint investigation. Over the past two months no one—not Widmark, Carrington, Marshak, or the fully recuperated Markworth—had injected a sense of urgency into the investigation more than Sally.

"Is there any doubt in your mind that the waste caused the cancer?" she asked.

Higheagle tilted his head contemplatively. "With cancer clusters, there's always doubt."

"I know the party line, Mr. Scientist. What I want to know is your gut feeling."

"I think the waste killed four of the boys and that it came damn close to killing Tommy and the others. But the world's leading epidemiologists would probably disagree with me." He squeezed her hand and gave her a knowing look. "In the end, I think everyone has paid their debts."

Minesali nodded somberly and stared off at a cluster of golden flowers.

Something about the old man's expression stirred something within Higheagle, and once again, he realized that they had all earned a measure of peace with the way things had turned out. Having agreed not to turn himself in, Minesali was moving on with his life: he had tendered an offer to sell his company back to his employees at a bargain-basement price and they had accepted. Presumably, an advance on the payment was how Minesali had managed to secure the million dollars for the cancer fund.

"Now that you've sold your company," Higheagle asked him, "what are you going to do in your spare time?"

"You needn't worry about me. In the winter I shall have my books, and in the summer I shall have my gardens."

"Maybe you should get a lucky lady for the fall and spring," Sally needled him.

Another round of laughter. The sound reached up to the pastel blue sky, and then they shook hands and said their goodbyes. Higheagle felt powerful emotions sweeping through him as he thought of all that had been lost—and gained.

"Goodbye, Vincenzo," he said, knowing he was unlikely to ever see the old man again.

"Goodbye, Joseph," Minesali said, clasping both of his hands around the Cheyenne's, the old man's brown eyes showing a wet trace of tears.

Higheagle walked off with Sally and Tommy. When they reached the side gate that led to the front drive, he felt a tug inside and turned to catch a final glimpse of Minesali. He was reminded again of the first time they'd met. The old man had stood above him on the landing like some ancient noble sending off an armada into uncharted waters. Now he had that same proud, dignified look. He stood as tall and erect as the mast of a great ship, hands to his sides, chin lifted unflinchingly towards the sky.

In that instant he would remember for the rest of his life, Higheagle knew he had done the right thing in keeping quiet about Minesali and his grandfather.

When they reached the War Wagon, he fired the engine and pulled up to the electric gate, which slowly opened before them. Before driving off, he took a final look at Minesali's vast Tudor mansion. In one of the upstairs windows, he could see Forbes peering down at him. It seemed like an entire lifetime had passed beneath his moccasins since he had first laid eyes on the tough, devoted Welshman three months ago.

He waved up at him. To his surprise, Forbes gave a little nod of acknowledgement right back.

Higheagle smiled. Then, with a sense of reconciliation—perhaps even harmony—he pulled onto the street and drove off with Sally and Tommy into the afternoon sunlight.

AUTHOR'S NOTE AND ACKNOWLEDGEMENTS

Cluster of Lies, Book #2 of the Joe Higheagle Environmental Sleuth Series, was conceived and written by the author as a work of fiction. The novel is ultimately a work of the imagination and entertainment and should be read as nothing more. Names, characters, places, government entities, religious and political groups, corporations, and incidents are products of the author's imagination, or are used fictitiously, and are not to be construed as real. Any resemblance to actual events, locales, companies, organizations, or persons, living or dead, is entirely coincidental.

The original inspiration for *Cluster of Lies* was drawn from my professional experience working on the Rosamond cancer cluster case in Southern California. Visiting the town, reviewing the documents on file in the local library, and interviewing the residents who had experienced the cancer cluster firsthand had a profound impact on me, and I would not have written the novel without having worked on Rosamond. Like most environmental cancer clusters, the Rosamond cluster remains a mystery to this day. When one investigates such phenomena, one cannot help but feel the disheartening sense of sadness, frustration, powerlessness, and anger of the families and townspeople who have been impacted by these tragic events, for which the causal mechanism(s) have now eluded two generations of environmental scientists. The bottom line is that people just want the truth, but unfortunately, truth in such cases is an exceedingly elusive thing. There are not many mysteries left in our modern world, but the origin of non-occupational-exposure-related cancer clusters remains one of them, and will so for the foreseeable future.

I have also packed the novel with professional anecdotes from my nearly thirty years as a professional hydrogeologist involved in environmental health risk assessments, groundwater flow and transport modeling investigations, and serving as a groundwater expert witness in class action litigation cases. In addition to my work experience in the environmental arena, I consulted hundreds of non-fiction books, magazine and newspaper articles, blogs, Web sites, and numerous individuals to develop the story line, characters, and scenes for *Cluster of Lies*. I have also visited every real-world location in the novel in person as the story takes place entirely in and around my hometown of Denver, Colorado.

I would like to give credit to the critical individuals who dramatically improved the quality of the manuscript from its initial to its final stage. Any technical mistakes in the facts underpinning the novel, typographical errors, or examples of overreach due to artistic license, however, are the fault of me and me alone. First and foremost, I would like to thank my wife Christine, an exceptional and highly professional book editor, who painstakingly reviewed and copy-edited the novel.

Second, I would like to thank my former literary agent, Cherry Weiner of the Cherry Weiner Literary Agency, for thoroughly reviewing, vetting, and copy-editing the manuscript, and for making countless improvements to the finished novel before I chose to publish the novel independently.

Third, I would like to thank Stephen King's former editor, Patrick LoBrutto, and Quinn Fitzpatrick, former book critic for the Rocky Mountain News, for thoroughly copy-editing the various drafts of the novel and providing detailed reviews.

I would also like to thank Austin and Anne Marquis, Governor Roy Romer, Ambassador Marc Grossman, Rik Hall, George Foster, Betsy and Steve Hall, Fred Taylor, Peter and Lorrie Frautschi, Mo Shafroth and Barr Hogan, Tim and Carey Romer, Toni Conte Augusta Francis, Brigid Donnelly Hughes, Peter Brooke, John Welch, Link Nicoll, John and Ellen Aisenbrey, Margot Patterson, Cathy and Jon Jenkins, Kay and Charlie Fial, Vincent Bilello, Elizabeth Gardner, Danny Bilello and Elena Diaz-Bilello, and the other book reviewers and professional contributors large and small who have given generously of their time over the years, as well as to those who have given me loyal support as I have ventured on this incredible odyssey of suspense novel writing.

Lastly, I want to thank anyone and everyone who bought this book and my loyal fans and supporters who helped promote this work. You know who you are and I salute you.

ABOUT THE AUTHOR AND FORTHCOMING TITLES

Samuel Marquis is a bestselling, award-winning suspense author. He works by day as a VP–Hydrogeologist with an environmental firm in Boulder, Colorado, and by night as a spinner of historical and modern suspense yarns. He holds a Master of Science degree in Geology, is a Registered Professional Geologist in eleven states, and is a recognized expert in groundwater contaminant hydrogeology, having served as a hydrogeologic expert witness in several class action litigation cases. He also has a deep and abiding interest in military history and intelligence, specifically related to the Golden Age of Piracy, Plains Indian Wars, World War II, and the current War on Terror.

His first two thrillers, *The Slush Pile Brigade* and *Blind Thrust*, were both #1 *Denver Post* bestsellers for fiction, and his first three novels received national book award recognition. *The Slush Pile Brigade* was an award-winning finalist in the mystery category of the Beverly Hills Book Awards. *Blind Thrust* was the winner of the Foreword Reviews' Book of the Year (HM) and the Next Generation Indie Book Awards and an award-winning finalist of the USA Best Book Awards and Beverly Hills Book Awards (thriller and suspense). His third novel, *The Coalition*, was the winner of the Beverly Hills Book Awards for a political thriller.

Ambassador Marc Grossman, former U.S. Under Secretary of State, proclaimed, "In his novels *Blind Thrust* and *Cluster of Lies*, Samuel Marquis vividly combines the excitement of the best modern techno-thrillers, an education in geology, and a clarifying reminder that the choices each of us make have a profound impact on our precious planet." Former Colorado Governor Roy Romer said, "*Blind Thrust* kept me up until 1 a.m. two nights in a row. I could not put it down. An intriguing mystery that intertwined geology, fracking, and places in Colorado that I know well. Great fun." Kirkus Reviews proclaimed *The Coalition* an "entertaining thriller" and declared that "Marquis has written a tight plot with genuine suspense." James Patterson compared *The Coalition* to *The Day After Tomorrow*, the classic thriller by Allan Folsom. Other book reviewers have compared Book #1 of Marquis's World War Two Trilogy, *Bodyguard of Deception*, to the spy novels of John le Carré, Daniel Silva, Ken Follett, and Alan Furst.

Below is the list of suspense novels that Samuel Marquis has published or will be publishing in the near future, along with the release dates of both previously published and forthcoming titles.

The Nick Lassiter Series
The Slush Pile Brigade – September 2015 – The #1 Denver Post Bestseller and Award-Winning Finalist Beverly Hills Book Awards
The Fourth Pularchek – 2017-2018

The Joe Higheagle Series
Blind Thrust – October 2015 – The #1 Denver Post Bestseller; Winner Foreword Reviews' Book of the Year (HM) and Next Generation Indie Book Awards; Award-Winning Finalist USA Best Book Awards, Beverly Hills Book Awards, and Next Generation Indie Book Awards
Cluster of Lies – September 2016

The World War Two Trilogy
Bodyguard of Deception – March 2016
Altar of Resistance – January 2017

Standalone Espionage Thriller Novels
The Coalition – January 2016 – Winner Beverly Hills Book Awards

Thank You for Your Support!

To Order Samuel Marquis Books and Contact Samuel:

Visit Samuel Marquis's website, join his mailing list, learn about his forthcoming suspense novels and book events, and order his books at www.samuelmarquisbooks.com. Please send all fan mail (including criticism) to samuelmarquisbooks@gmail.com.